WITHDRAWN FROM STOCK

KT-429-542

Venetian
Gothic

Philip Gwynne Jones

CONSTABLE

CONSTABLE

First published in Great Britain in 2020 by Constable

Copyright © Philip Gwynne Jones, 2020

1 3 5 7 9 10 8 6 4 2

The moral right of the author has been asserted.

*All characters and events in this publication, other than those clearly in the
public domain, are fictitious and any resemblance to real persons, living or dead,
is purely coincidental.*

All rights reserved.

No part of this publication may be reproduced, stored in a retrieval system, or
transmitted, in any form, or by any means, without the prior permission in writing of
the publisher, nor be otherwise circulated in any form of binding or cover other than
that in which it is published and without a similar condition including this condition
being imposed on the subsequent purchaser.

A CIP catalogue record for this book is available from the British Library.

ISBN: 978-1-47212-974-1

Typeset in Adobe Garamond by Initial Typesetting Services, Edinburgh
Printed and bound in Great Britain by Clays Ltd, Elcograf S.p.A.

Papers used by Constable are from well-managed forests
and other responsible sources.

MIX
Paper from
responsible sources
FSC® C104740

Constable
An imprint of
Little, Brown Book Group
Carmelite House
50 Victoria Embankment
London EC4Y 0DZ

An Hachette UK Company
www.hachette.co.uk

www.littlebrown.co.uk

For Peter and Lou. Venice is always better with you.

'There are some secrets which do not permit themselves to be told'

Edgar Allan Poe

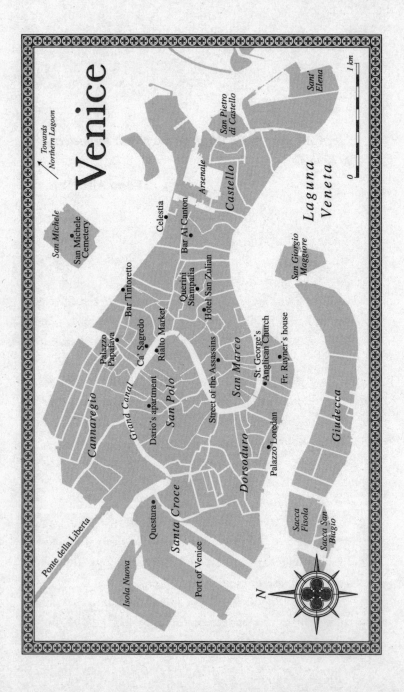

Prologue

The dream is always the same.

Mother and Father are arguing. They say nothing to me, but I know it is my fault. Again.

I am in the kitchen. I am standing at the refrigerator, something in my hand. It may be a glass of milk, a fizzy drink. I don't remember. But I do know that I have lived this scene a hundred times.

They are shouting at each other, their words tripping over each other in their anger. Grown-up words that are too difficult for me to understand. My father swears, and Mother hisses at him. Not in front of the boy.

They stop hurling their spite at each other, and turn to look at me.

There is silence. Just for a moment.

I look back at them, standing in the hallway. I am trying to be brave, to be a big boy, but all I want is for them to stop fighting. I want to run to them. I want Mother to hold me, to cuddle me, but there is something in her eyes that stops me.

I start to cry. I try to hold them in but the tears come, slowly at first, and then in great shaking sobs. Surely, I think, surely now they'll come. They'll stop fighting and run to me and pick me up and hug me. And then there will be warm milk, and more hugs and then bed. And everything will be all right, and normal again.

My father looks at me and then turns away. He looks at my mother and shakes his head. 'I give up,' he says, 'I give up.' He doesn't sound angry any more. Just tired.

I never cried very much after that. For I had learned that it didn't do any good.

Chapter 1

Sergio Cardazzo bowed his head and muttered a few words under his breath, as he bent over Paolo Magri's grave. To his left, Lorenzo Bonzio, taller and thinner, leaned on his cane for support and reached out with his other hand to pat his friend on the shoulder.

Sergio spoke again, audibly this time. '*Ciao, compagno.*' Then he bent to adjust the wreath, in the shape of the hammer and sickle, that was leaning against the headstone. I wondered if, somewhere in Venice, there was a left-wing florist that specialised in revolutionary funeral wreaths. If there were such a place, I thought, Sergio would be sure to know of it.

The three of us stood in silence for a moment. I gazed at the inscription. *Paolo Magri. Journalist. 1950–2014.*

The wind was chilly, and whipped at my coat, as a fine rain blew across the cemetery. Again, Sergio's lips moved silently; then he dabbed at his eyes, blew his nose and clapped Lorenzo on the back, as much for his own comfort, I thought, as for his friend's.

'I think he'd have liked this,' I said. 'All of us being here.'

'Maybe so,' said Sergio. 'But he'd have liked it even more if he was standing here with us.'

We turned and made our way back through the cemetery, our feet crunching on the gravel. Two little girls in bright red coats half ran, half skipped towards us, chattering excitedly and clutching flowers in their hands. I jumped to one side to let them pass, but one of them bumped into Lorenzo, who stumbled before Sergio's hand reached out to grab his elbow.

'Arianna! Lucia! Be careful! And show some respect!' The speaker was a young man, arm in arm with a woman of similar age. He shook his head as they made their way along the path towards us. 'I'm sorry.'

Lorenzo smiled, and doffed his hat. 'No problem.'

The young woman smiled, although her eyes were red. 'It's their first time here. To see *Nonno* and *Nonna*. We told them they could carry the flowers, and so they feel very grown-up. But they don't understand. Not really.'

Lorenzo smiled again. 'I think perhaps we should envy them. How lovely to hear the sound of laughter here. I think that would make *Nonno* and *Nonna* very happy.' She laughed. 'See, now you're doing it. And that would make them happy as well.'

'That's kind of you. Thank you.'

We stepped aside to let them pass, and then walked further along the path into the saddest part of the cemetery island of San Michele. The space reserved for children. An old couple stood, heads bowed, in front of a tombstone. *Marco Vianello. June 1st 1968–April 23rd 1975. Requiescat in Pace Ultima.* Rest in final peace. There was something terrible about that *final*. I looked at the fading, sepia-coloured photograph on the headstone. A young boy, painfully thin, stared back at me with a beaming, gap-toothed smile. The old woman's shoulders shook, as her husband hugged her. Over forty years ago, and the pain still as fresh as yesterday.

'God.' I whispered under my breath, and shuddered. Sergio caught my eye, and shook his head, before crossing himself.

'Come on, Nathan, let's go.' He rarely used my first name, preferring the jokey *investigatore*, his little pet name for me from the time when we'd first met. From when Paolo Magri had been murdered.

The cemetery was becoming busy now, as young and old made their way through the paths to the monuments where their loved ones lay. Lorenzo wasn't quite as light on his feet as he once had been, and so we took our time meandering back against the flow of the crowd.

November 2nd, 2017. The feast of *i morti*. All Souls' Day. The Day of the Dead, when Venetians made their way to the island of San Michele to lay flowers and pay their respects at the graves of their ancestors.

I cleared my throat. 'Back there, Sergio. By the grave of that little boy. Did I see you crossing yourself?'

'Maybe I did,' he grumbled, 'it's just good to show respect, you know?'

'And back at Paolo's monument,' I continued, trying to keep my voice light. 'Were you praying there?'

'Praying? Nonsense.' He mumbled under his breath. 'Anyway, what if I was?'

'Oh, nothing. I was just surprised. You being a Marxist, and all.'

Lorenzo chuckled. 'Sergio's always had a certain amount of time for Liberation Theology. You know about Liberation Theology?'

'Not really.'

'Well, it's a fascinating movement in Latin American Roman Catholicism which—'

'Which we're not going to talk about now,' said Sergio. His voice was gruff, as always, but I could see he was trying not to smile. Conversation between the three of us frequently worked this way, when we were trying to cheer each other up. 'Come on. Back to Giudecca. Back to the bar. And we'll have a jug of bad red wine and play a few hands of *scopa* for Paolo.'

I sighed. 'Great. So we celebrate Paolo's life by you stealing money off me?'

'Not stealing, *investigatore*, winning.'

'If that's what we're calling it.'

'It is.' He checked his watch. 'Come on, there's a boat in five minutes.' We stepped it out as best we could, Sergio slipping a hand under Lorenzo's elbow to support him.

The area around the *vaporetto* pontoon was crowded with *carabinieri*, all immaculate in striped red trousers, with boots and the peaks of their caps polished to a mirror finish. Amongst them stood a group of Catholic priests, and a couple of journalists that I vaguely knew from *La Nuova* and *Il Gazzettino*. In the middle of the clergy stood a tall, thin man robed completely in red, a heavy gold crucifix about his neck. His face was lean and ascetic, yet not without kindness. The Patriarch of Venice. He smiled as best he could as the photographers snapped away, whilst simultaneously giving the impression that he found this sort of thing just a little bit awkward. I caught his gaze and he nodded and smiled at me, his expression quizzical as if he was trying to recall when and where – not to mention if – we'd met.

Sergio elbowed me in the ribs. 'Friends in high places?'

'Not exactly a friend. But we've met a few times.'

'Still. Useful person to know, I imagine. Somebody to put in a good word when the time comes.'

'Exactly.'

'Never had much time for priests myself. But this one I like. He's on the side of the workers. He stood on a picket line at a factory once.'

I looked back at the thin figure in red, and found it hard to imagine. Still, Sergio was usually right about these things.

The next *vaporetto* was pulling up to the pontoon. ACTV ran a free service to San Michele for the day of *i morti*, a 'DE' for *defunti* on the side of the boat marking out its special nature. I had taken to calling it the 'Death Line', something Federica had pleaded with me not to use in company.

We waited for the passengers to disembark and were about to step on, when I felt myself being grabbed by my collar and gently, but firmly, pulled backwards. I turned around as best I could, assuming I had accidentally jumped the queue and someone had taken exception to it.

Father Michael Rayner, the Tall Priest, Anglican Chaplain to St George's Church, Venice, glared down at me from under the bushiest eyebrows in Christendom.

'*Padre*?'

'Nathan. Good morning.'

'What's all this about?' I heard the clang of the gate on the *vaporetto* slamming shut, and the *marinaio* calling to the captain to cast off. 'Hey, wait a minute,' I shouted. Sergio and Lorenzo looked back at me in confusion. 'Get a round in, I'll see you there,' I called after them as the boat set off.

I turned back to Rayner and managed to shake his hand from my collar. 'What do you think you're doing? I'm supposed to be on that boat. I've got money to lose in a card game.'

'Time for that later, Nathan. Right now, I need you to help me.'

Chapter 2

Rayner paused to exchange a few words in his fractured Italian with the Patriarch, who smiled and nodded politely. Then, without even checking to see if I was following, he strode off in the direction of the *Reparto Evangelico*, the Protestant section of the cemetery.

'I don't suppose you could tell me what this is about?' I puffed, as I laboured to keep up with him.

He reached into his coat, without breaking his stride, and passed a sheet of paper back to me. 'Just be so good as to read this, would you?'

I took a quick glance at it. Revelation 21. *God shall wipe away all tears*.

'Read it now?' I said.

He stopped, and turned. 'Not now, you bloody fool. During the service.'

'Oh. Why?'

He sighed. 'Nathan, on All Souls' Day we get, shall we say, a small but exclusive group of attendees.' He looked up at the steadily falling rain, and shuddered. 'To be honest, who can blame them? Anyway, I'm fed up asking the same old faces to read every year. When I saw you on the pontoon, I thought you'd be ideal.'

'I see. Wouldn't you rather have somebody who believes in God?'

'Plenty of time for all that. Anyway, think how much it'll mean to the regulars. They come out here on a cold, wintry day. Most of them don't even have relatives here. And then they see the Honorary Consul himself contributing. It'll mean a lot to them.'

'I'm flattered.' Then a suspicion struck me, and I frowned. 'Hang on, this means they'll be expecting me to do this every year, doesn't it?'

Rayner grinned. 'That's about the shape of it.' His expression changed and became serious, concerned even. 'I'm sorry, I never asked you. What brings you here?'

We were approaching Magri's grave again, and I nodded at it. Rayner did a double-take as he saw the hammer-and-sickle wreath.

'Good God!'

'Paolo Magri moved in comradely circles. Sorry, there was no offence meant.'

'None taken.' He looked at me. 'Was he a friend of yours?'

I paused. 'I'm not sure. I think so. Or at least I hope that he might have become one.'

'I see. I'm sorry.' It was his turn to pause. 'Do you want to add him to the list?'

'The list?'

'Of the departed. We read their names as part of the act of remembrance.'

'Oh, I see. That's kind of you. Yes, thank you.'

'Good man.' He smiled again. 'You can read that out as well.'

***

We made our way through the cemetery until we reached the iron gate that separated the Catholic area from the Protestant. The difference between the two was immediately obvious. Unlike the regimented rows of tombs that marked the Roman section, this one was ramshackle, with the air of a long-neglected English churchyard. There were few grand funerary monuments here, just simple stone crosses and cracked headstones, many of which had collapsed. Cypress and bay trees, aided by the low-lying fog, conferred an appropriately funereal atmosphere. The graveyard was surrounded by walls on all four sides, with the exception of a gate at the far end that had once led directly on to the lagoon. The *Reparto*, I knew, had long been in need of funds for restoration. And every year, with an ever-declining number of people with family resting there, money became more difficult to find.

Rayner made his way over to a great stone slab in the middle of the grounds. Twelve red roses lay atop the monument, with its simple inscription 'Ezra Pound'. He picked up one of the blooms, and turned it in his hand before replacing it with the lightest of touches. 'Someone leaves these every year, you know,' he murmured. 'Pound must have meant a lot to them, whoever they are.'

I bit my tongue. The blooms, I knew, were left by a fascist group who, for various reasons, looked up to the long-dead poet as a source of inspiration. Rayner, evidently, had yet to learn this. It didn't seem like the right time to tell him.

He looked up at the rain once more. 'It's a short service, you know, but it's too wet for us all to stand around in the open. Some of my flock are not in the first flush of youth.

Wouldn't care for them to come to pay their respects and remain to share them.'

I looked around. 'Where? There's no shelter to speak of.'

'No. Never a nice cosy mausoleum when you could do with one, is there?' I assumed he was joking, but it was always a bit hard to tell with Father Rayner. He jerked his thumb in the direction of the Trentinaglia chapel, a three-arched Gothic structure supported by scaffolding on the southern wall, the property of a family of Italian Protestants. 'Come on, there'll at least be a bit of cover over there. Although I see we've been beaten to it.'

Two men in woolly hats stood with their backs against the cemetery wall, smoking away. A look of annoyance flashed across Rayner's face, but then his gaze softened. After all, everyone was welcome in the *Reparto Evangelico* on All Saints' Day, whether they were smokers or not.

I had thought they were wearing identical grey waterproofs, but, as we drew closer, I could see they were in uniform. The grey lapel badges with a green, orange and blue flash indicated they were from *Veritas*, the organisation responsible for refuse collection, plumbing and general city maintenance.

'What are they doing here?' said Rayner, under his breath.

'No idea. Strange though. I wouldn't expect anyone from *Veritas* to be working out here on a public holiday.'

I walked over to them. '*Signori.*'

One of them dropped his roll-up to the earth and ground it underfoot, before wiping his hand on his lapel and offering it to me to shake. '*Buongiorno.*'

'I don't suppose you could tell me what's going on here?' I said. 'I mean, no offence, but we have a service here in,' I checked my watch, 'twenty minutes' time.'

He looked me up and down. 'Are you the *padre*?'

'No. I just wear too many black clothes.' We both chuckled. 'He is,' I said, indicating Rayner.

'*Buongiorno padre.*'

'*Buongiorno.*'

The workman smiled and chattered away in Italian. Rayner gave me a pained look. 'I'm sorry, Nathan, could you—?'

'Translate?'

'Please.'

'Sure.' I paused. 'How long have you been here now?'

'Three years.'

'How's the Italian coming on?'

'Slowly. I have churchwardens and an army of well-meaning parishioners for that sort of thing.'

'I see. It would help, you know?'

'I know.' He looked embarrassed.

I turned back to the workmen. 'I don't think anyone was expecting to see you here today?'

'*Nossignore.* Nobody told us there'd be a service in this part. We didn't expect it.'

'It's the Day of the Dead.'

'*Sissignore.* But, you know . . .' He looked around, gesturing at the dilapidated monuments that surrounded us. 'We didn't think people came here so often.'

'There are going to be people here in twenty minutes.' I turned back to Rayner. 'How many?' I asked, in English.

'Perhaps ten.'

I turned back to the workmen. 'At least forty or fifty,' I said. Then a thought struck me. 'Hang on a minute, it's a public holiday. Why are you working?'

He grinned, and rubbed a thumb and two fingers together. 'More money today.'

'Fair enough. Erm, can I ask what you're doing? And can it wait? Maybe an hour?'

He shrugged. 'It's the gravestones, *signore*. Take a look. Nobody takes care of them and the ground—' He dug his heel into the earth, with a squelching sound. 'The ground here is like a sponge. Every year, some of the tombstones collapse. It can be dangerous for visitors. And so Enzo and myself are here to make it safe.' He patted his colleague on the back. 'Isn't that right, Enzo?'

Enzo nodded and lit another roll-up.

He gestured towards their work. A heavy gravestone tilted at an impossible angle. 'We need to move that.' Next to it, a white coffin had been disinterred and the tombstone laid flat upon the earth.

Rayner bristled. 'You're exhuming graves? Why wasn't I told?'

I translated, and the workmen shrugged as one. 'We don't know, *padre*. That's the business of the *comune*.'

Rayner turned to me, helplessly. 'Nathan?'

I sighed. 'They don't know. To be fair, it's not really their business.' I turned back to them. 'What needs to be done, then?'

'Today, all we do is lay this headstone flat.' He pointed at the heavier one, thick with moss, and the inscription almost illegible with age.

'Fine. And the other one?' I pointed at the more recent headstone and the coffin. 'Why did you have to exhume that one?'

He reached into his pocket, pulled out a map, and traced

around the edges with a nicotine-stained finger. 'All these in this area here. The ground floods easily. They all need to be moved over to the south wall.' He looked over at Rayner, who was taking shelter from the rain in the shade of the walls of the Trentinaglia chapel, and shook his head. '*Nossignore!* Very dangerous. Come away please.' Rayner muttered something under his breath and moved away, a look of disappointment on his face as he looked up at the ceaseless rain. 'The chapel is not safe. Especially in the rain, when the ground is wet. One slip and,' he swept his hands apart, '*wuuumph!*'

I looked down at the headstone. Gabriele Loredan. 26th May 1968–24th August 1980. Another Italian name. 'Okay, can you just move the coffin out of the way in the meantime? And maybe the headstone, if you can. At least cover them with something. People are coming, it might be upsetting for them, you understand?'

'Sure we understand, *signore*. It won't take long. Come on, Enzo.'

Enzo dropped his cigarette, and nodded. He moved to take the rounded end of the headstone, his friend the other. It must have been some weight, even for two of them, and they struggled to move it into position.

'Okay, Enzo. We've got it. Now just put it down slowly, okay?'

The two of them moved to lower the slab to the ground but, just as they were doing so, Enzo slipped on a patch of wet leaves. For a dreadful moment, I felt sure the slab was going to hit him square in the head, but he managed to roll aside, sending the headstone crashing through the lid of the adjacent white coffin, which splintered into pieces.

'Shit. Oh shit,' his companion swore.

I looked at Rayner. 'Oh bloody hell.'

The four of us stood in silence. Rayner looked back over his shoulder to the entrance. Nobody, as yet, had arrived, but it wouldn't be long now. 'Okay. There's nothing much we can do about it now. We'll move the coffin, and cover it up; and afterwards . . . Well, I'll have a think about what to do afterwards.'

The two workmen nodded, but gave no sign of moving. Rayner sighed. 'I'm in a cassock. My friend here is wearing his best coat—'

I coughed, gently. 'Actually it's my only coat, *padre*.'

'As I said, his best coat. So given you two are proofed up against the elements, would you be so good as to move it for us?' The two of them looked blankly at me, until I realised they were waiting for me to translate. Then they nodded as one and set to work.

Enzo looked down at the smashed lid of the coffin, and crossed himself. He looked over at Rayner as if seeking approval. The *padre* gave him an encouraging smile.

The two of them bent to lift the headstone and drag it into position but the coffin, following decades in the sodden earth, collapsed in on itself as soon as the weight was removed.

'Oh bloody hell,' I repeated. Then I looked closer. 'Hang on, something's not right.' I took a step forward. Rayner laid a hand upon my arm, but I shook it off. 'Something's wrong.'

I dropped to my knees, right next to the remains of the coffin. The lid had splintered into two pieces, and I could just about see inside. I reached my hand across to shift the upper part, the wood feeling spongy and rotten in my fingers. I slid it away, and let it fall on to the wet grass.

'*Padre*. Come and look. '

'Nathan, for the love of God come away and let's just cover this poor fellow up until we can get someone out here.'

'There's no one to cover up, *padre*. No one at all.'

I pushed the remaining piece of the lid away, and got to my feet. The four of us stared down at the splintered remains of a small, white coffin.

A small, white and empty coffin.

Chapter 3

It was late afternoon by the time I got back to the Street of the Assassins, the wet streets shining in the warm glow from the Magical Brazilian Café. It was tempting to go in for a drink but Federica, I knew, would be cross if she realised I'd been without her.

I went upstairs to the flat, aware that my right boot had started to leak. Never mind. Warm socks awaited.

Gramsci came to meet me, woken up by the sound of my keys rattling in the lock. He gave a little mewl of recognition, then yawned, stretched and made his way into the living room where Federica lay asleep on the sofa, the adjacent coffee table covered with books and papers from her latest project. He leapt on to the back of the couch and miaowed at me once more. Then he looked down at Federica, jumped on to her chest and rubbed his face against her cheek.

She opened one eye. 'Hello, friendly cat. Does this mean Nathan is back?'

'He most certainly is. *Ciao, cara.*'

'*Ciao, caro.*' She sat up, scratching Gramsci behind his ears. 'Why do you think he's started doing this?'

'Doing what?'

'Being nice.'

'Oh, that. He's just happy, that's all. Nathan's home again. He wants you to join in the excitement.'

We looked at the coffee table, where Gramsci was now sitting on top of Federica's papers, purring away. 'Happy' and 'excitement' were words that had never been linked with him before.

'I'll try to contain myself. So, how was it?'

'Okay, I guess. Nice to see the boys.' She smiled at my use of 'boys' to denote two men who probably had a hundred and fifty years between them.

She looked at her watch. 'I must have slept longer than I thought. You're back late.'

'Yes, sorry. I was helping out the *padre*. Father Michael, that is. And then . . . well, we had a bit of a thing . . .'

'A thing?'

'Yes. We exhumed a body.'

She sat up. 'You *what*?'

'We accidentally exhumed a body. Or rather we didn't. *Veritas* were doing a bit of work. Making safe some of the crumblier monuments. They dropped a headstone on a coffin and the thing smashed into pieces.'

She shuddered. 'God. How horrible. Are you all right?'

'Oh fine. This is the thing, though – it was empty.'

'What do you mean?'

'I mean actually empty. No body, no clothing, no shroud.' I paused. 'Do they still use shrouds? Anyway, there was nothing at all.'

'What, had the body just rotted away to nothing? Is that even possible?'

'I think that only happens in films. Anyway, the grave was less than forty years old.'

'So, what did you do?'

'What could we do? Father Michael had a memorial service coming up, so we covered it over with a tarpaulin as best we could, and herded his flock over to the opposite side of the cemetery.'

'And afterwards?'

'We called the police. We couldn't think what else to do.' I sat down on the edge of the sofa. 'It was a kid's grave. That seems to make it worse somehow. I don't know why, but it does.'

She nodded. 'I understand. What do you think had happened?'

'I don't know. Do people actually rob graves any more?'

She shrugged. 'It seems hard to imagine, but possibly. Think about it. The Protestant section is the least visited section. It would be quiet if you wanted to – do – something.'

I shook my head. 'I'm not so sure about that. People go there to see Ezra Pound and Joseph Brodsky.'

'Okay. After hours then. That section used to open out on to the lagoon, before they built the extension. It would be safe enough to moor a boat outside and then go and do whatever you wanted to do. Whoever did it must have thought there'd be something of worth buried there.'

'No, that doesn't make sense. If you were going to do that, you'd leave the body behind.'

'Okay. So, what then?'

'Maybe it's like the Charlie Chaplin case?'

'The what?'

'The Charlie Chaplin case. His body was stolen just after his death. The idea was to ransom it to his relatives.'

'Could be.' She wrinkled her forehead. 'When did all this happen?'

'Charlie Chaplin?'

She sighed. 'Not him. The empty grave.'

'1980.'

'What was the name?'

'Loredan. Gabriele Loredan.'

'God. I remember that. He was a little boy and he drowned. Fell from his boat into the lagoon. I sort of know his sister, Ludovica. I wouldn't call her a friend, or anything like that – I don't know even if she has any friends – but she's on the board of a number of fundraising organisations. Restoration projects, that sort of thing. We're supposed to have a presentation in a couple of days. I wonder if she'll still go through with it?'

'A presentation? Can I come?'

'I can ask if you like. Why?'

'Well, I might need to speak to her at some point. Just to express condolences, if nothing else. Might be easier in a social context?'

Fede shook her head. 'Nathan, we're talking about the disappearance of her little brother's body. I don't think a glass of cheap prosecco is going to make it any better.' She paused. 'I was a very little girl at the time. I remember *Mamma* and *Papà* told me I wasn't to read about it in case it gave me nightmares.' She shuddered. 'Actually, this is really horrible. Can we not talk about it?'

'Sorry. It's just been a strange kind of day that's all. Vanni wants me to go along to the *Questura* tomorrow and make a proper statement.' I glanced at my watch. 'Okay. Time for a spritz downstairs. And then I'll cook tea.'

'What have we got?'

'Mushrooms. *Porcini* to be precise.'

'Just mushrooms?'

'They're good enough on their own. But I could put them in an omelette if you think that's not a square meal. Or on toast.'

'Mushrooms on toast?' She sounded less than convinced.

'Porcini on toast. There's a difference.'

'I trust you.' She put on her coat. 'But just in case maybe I'll have some *cichèti* at the Brazilians.'

I laughed, and we made our way downstairs.

Chapter 4

Father Rayner gazed at Vanni through a thick fug of blue smoke, before casting a quick glance – more in hope than expectation – at the '*Vietato Fumare*' sign. Vanni, if he had noticed, pretended not to, and tapped his cigar on the ashtray in front of him.

'Gabriele Loredan. Died in August 1980. Drowned in the lagoon, *poverino*. Buried in the *Reparto Evangelico* on San Michele. Or so everyone thought.'

Rayner raised his hand. 'You're sure about this? Absolutely sure? There's no possibility that the body wasn't,' he paused, searching for the least horrible word, '*removed* at a later date?'

Vanni shook his head. 'It seems impossible. If the body was stolen, there was no ransom demand. And if it was grave robbery, then why remove the body as well?'

'Could it have been exhumed and moved elsewhere?'

'No, *padre*.' Vanni paused. 'We checked with the family, of course. As diplomatically as we could. Given that there isn't really a diplomatic way of breaking news like this.'

'How are they?'

Vanni raised his eyebrows, and shook his head.

'I'm sorry. Do you think it might help if I offered to talk to them?'

'Up to you, *padre*. But I think it might be best if you gave them a couple of days. I get the impression the Anglican Church might not be high on their Christmas card list this year.'

Rayner grumbled something under his breath and I took the opportunity to speak up. 'Out of interest, Vanni, why are you assuming it's got anything to do with the Anglicans? There are other denominations in that area of the cemetery.' I thought back to the number of Germanic-sounding names on gravestones. 'The Lutherans are there, for example.'

'The Loredan boy had British nationality.' He looked at Rayner. 'That's why we assumed he was one of yours. The father is a man called Hugo Channing. Still alive, married to Cosima Loredan.'

'Do you know them?' I asked.

Vanni shook his head. 'I know *of* them. Well-to-do. I suppose you could say that makes them important. And the Loredan name still carries a bit of weight in certain Venetian circles.'

'So is there anything you need us to do?'

'I'd like the *padre* here to go through any church records of the time. Just in case there's something of interest. You never know.'

Rayner nodded. 'Shouldn't take long. We started a record of baptisms back in 1890. We're still on the first book.'

'Thank you, *padre*.'

'Although I do like to think that if something slightly out of the ordinary had happened – such as not actually having a body to bury – my predecessor would have made note of it,' Rayner added, drily.

Vanni beamed and puffed on his cigar before turning to me. 'That just leaves you, Nathan.'

'Me? What's it got to do with me?'

'Death of a British citizen. Your predecessor would have been informed. Isn't it the Consul's responsibility to verify the deceased is actually in the casket and who they are supposed to be before they screw the lid down?'

'That's just for repatriation. Do you have any idea how many Brits there are in the Veneto? I'd be spending all my time scurrying from place to place verifying that every coffin has a corpse in it.' Rayner winced. 'Sorry, *padre*.'

He waved my apologies away. 'It's really nothing to joke about, Nathan.'

'Sorry.' I turned back to Vanni. 'So you want me to go back through records?'

'Just in case. You have them, of course?'

My predecessor, Victor Rutherford, had bequeathed me a shoebox full of miscellaneous documents, to which I had added over the years. It served now as a secondary, and increasingly snug, cat basket for Gramsci.

'I have – some – records,' I said.

'Good. Good. All we need to do then is be sure that all procedures were followed correctly. And if they were, well, we simply declare that some terrible incident has occurred at some point during the last thirty-seven years and open a file on it.'

'And then?'

'Well, then we have an open file.'

'Oh. Is that it?'

Vanni shrugged. 'Not much else that can be done. The alternative, of course, is that correct procedures were not followed. Which, in turn, could mean terrible embarrassment for the Anglican Church, the British Consular Service,' he lowered his voice, 'and, of course, the police. We'll be checking as well.'

'You have records going back that far?' I asked.

Vanni looked a little embarrassed. 'We have – some – records.' He smiled.

Rayner stood outside the entrance to the *Questura*, eyes closed, taking deep breaths of the cold, damp air.

'So, *padre . . .*' He waved his hand to shush me, as he continued drawing in air, running his hands over his coat as if he could physically brush away the stink of stale cigar smoke.

He opened his eyes. 'That's better.'

'Don't be fooled, you know. The air quality's probably even worse out here. Too much PM10, they're saying. From the cruise ships.'

'I don't care. Whatever PM10 may be, at least it doesn't make me smell as if I've been kippering myself.' Then he paused, and stared at me. 'You're not . . . ?'

'No, I'm not.'

'You haven't . . . ?'

'I have,' I muttered.

'Good Lord, wonders never cease! Nathan Sutherland has actually given up smoking!'

'Again,' I added.

'No matter. Well done. Thoughts and prayers and all that. Any reason in particular?'

'Federica gave up a while back, so I stopped smoking at home. And it seemed easier at this time of year. You can't smoke indoors anywhere, unless you're Vanni of course, and it's too cold and wet to want to stand outside.'

'Marvellous. Have you noticed any difference?'

'Well, Gramsci no longer smells of fags.'

'What about you, though?'

I sighed. 'Negronis taste better. Actually, everything tastes better. And, I suppose I have to say, I do feel better myself.'

'Do you miss it?'

I gave him a bitter look. 'Let's just say that a visit to Vanni's office might prove to be the highlight of my day.'

'Oh, don't say that. Think of all the positive things. You could try one of those e-cigarettes.'

'I am not now, nor have I ever been, a *vaper*. I am not walking around puffing away on a gigantic plastic chisel, smelling of watermelons and strawberries.'

'Quite right. After all, huddling in a shop doorway desperately trying to shield the last cigarette in the packet from the horizontal rain is so much more dignified. Come on, this calls for a celebration. I'll buy you lunch.'

'Church Pub?'

'If you like.'

'I'd have said Bar F30 but it seems to have closed. A shame. I used to go there with Vanni. It wasn't the best pub in the world but it was handy for the station. And you could sit outside and watch the traffic going by on the canal. There are rumours it's going to be a fast-food joint.'

Rayner shook his head. 'So, the first thing you'd see of the Most Serene Republic upon getting off the bus at Piazzale

Roma would be a fried chicken bar. They'd never allow that. Would they?' We both laughed, mirthlessly. 'Come on then. Church Pub it is. Do you mind if we walk? It'll help to shake off the smoke.' He tapped me on the chest. 'And it'll be good for those newly rediscovered lungs of yours.'

We walked through a busy Piazzale Roma, dodging through the traffic, and over into the *sestiere* of Dorsoduro. The streets were becoming quieter now, after the long summer that had slipped almost directly into winter without ever really bothering with any of that autumn nonsense. The last of the season's cruise ships would soon be departing for warmer climes. November, in many ways, was one of the best times of the year. It felt as if the city was ours again, if only for a little while.

'There's one thing about that headstone that seems a little strange,' I said, as we walked. 'I'm surprised Vanni didn't pick up on it.'

'Which is?'

'The name. Gabriele Loredan.'

He shook his head. 'I don't understand.'

Rayner, I sometimes had to remind myself, had been in Italy for rather less time than I had. 'Loredan. It's his mother's name. Not his father's. Women don't change their names when they get married here, but children inherit the father's.'

He shrugged. 'It's a noble name, as the *commissario* was telling us. Presumably the mother wanted her children to keep it.'

'Yes, but it wouldn't have been allowed. Not in 1980. The law's only just changed.'

'I suppose it's not the sort of thing people would have

made too much fuss over. Not under the circumstances. We'll probably find the death certificate has the father's name. And, as far as I know, you're allowed to chisel whatever you like on a headstone.'

There was no real need for me to assist the *padre* in his research, but it seemed only fair given that he'd bought me lunch. The rear door of St George's squeaked and shuddered as it scraped across the stone floor, and Rayner cursed as he pushed the unwilling portal open.

'Never got round to getting that fixed, then?' I asked.

He shook his head. 'More important things to worry about.' I noticed our breath was still steaming, despite being indoors. 'Happens every year. We switch the boiler back on in October, it breaks down immediately, takes a month to sort out and so the place remains at Arctic temperatures until Advent.'

'Couldn't you try switching it on a month earlier?'

'Too expensive. Sometimes I envy the happy-clappies. At least they're moving all the time. That must help to keep them warm. Coffee?'

I stamped my feet and blew on my fingers. 'That might help.'

He switched the kettle on. Immediately the lights went out.

'Bloody bloody bloody.' He opened the fuse box by the door, and flicked every switch upwards. The lights came back on.

'No coffee?' I said.

'No coffee.' He sighed. 'Come on. Let's get on with it.'

He led me up a tight, winding wooden staircase to the organ loft, and unlocked the door on the far side of the gallery. I wasn't quite sure what I'd been expecting. The repository of the small Anglican Church, I had imagined, would not be something to rival those of St Mark's or the State Archives at the Frari. I had, however, expected something rather grander than an IKEA bookcase with a few leather-bound books sitting forlornly on the shelves.

'Here we are.' He bent to switch on a tiny, two-bar electric heater. He rubbed his hands together. 'Soon feel the benefit of that.'

I looked at the sad little red glow. I wasn't completely convinced. 'Yes. Much better. So, er, is this it? This is your archive?'

'You were expecting something grander?'

'Well, just a bit.'

'We're a small chaplaincy. We might have been here for over four hundred years, but we're still a small chaplaincy.'

'It's always packed when I come here.'

'You only come twice a year. Remembrance Sunday and Christmas. Try a freezing Sunday in January and count the numbers then.'

'Sorry. I'm just surprised, that's all.'

He tutted, and ran his hand across a row of faded blue registers. He took one down, opened it up to check the date, shook his head and replaced it. '1980, wasn't it? This should do it.' He took down the next volume, and blew the dust off. 'Here we go.' He sat down at the adjacent desk, and patted the seat next to him. 'Come on. Sit down, and let's have a look.'

I read the first line in the journal. 'Here beginneth the

ministry of Father Malcolm Stafford, February 2nd 1980.'
I looked over at Rayner. '"Here beginneth". Do you have to
write like that?'

'We did in 1980. Punk rock and the New Wave had rather
passed us by.' He licked his finger and flicked through the
pages.

'So, what have we got here?'

'Each service held throughout the year.'

'Oh, I see. You record audience numbers?'

'We prefer the word "congregation".'

'Sorry. And the amount of takings?'

He half closed his eyes, and looked pained. 'Again, we
prefer the word "collection". But otherwise correct. Every service of the year is recorded. So, if we take a look at August
or September, just after the Loredan boy was drowned . . .
here we are.' He jabbed his finger at an entry for the 5th of
September. Nearly two weeks after Gabriele's death. 'Funeral
service, Loredan, Gabriele. No other notes, beyond the
receipt of the usual fee. Oh, and it seems there was a locum
that week, not Father Stafford.'

'Is that unusual?'

He shook his head. 'Not at that time of year. Everybody
tries to get out of Venice and away from the heat if they can.
Meanwhile every retired priest in the UK is after a short holiday looking after a chaplaincy somewhere warm and sunny.'
He looked more closely at the signature. 'Father Jonathan
Marchbank. Don't know the name, I'm afraid. Poor fellow's
probably long since departed anyway.' He drummed his fingers on the desk for a while, and then fell silent.

'I'm not quite sure what we were expecting to find,' I said.

'Me neither, if truth be told. I suppose it would have been too much to hope that there'd be an entry reading "Coffin unusually light."'

I chuckled, and then wondered if this was the sort of thing that one should be laughing at. 'There's a thought. I mean, wouldn't that have been noticed at the time?'

'Almost certainly. But think about it. If you were in that situation, in the middle of a throng of grieving relatives and friends, would you say anything?'

I shook my head. 'Fair point. Any other ideas?'

'Not really. But hand me down the register of baptisms, would you? The one with the brown leather cover. Just out of interest.'

I passed it over to him. The book, I could see, was notice-ably less dusty than the blue registers of services, although the pages were yellowed with age.

'We still get a few of these, every year, you know. Some of them even come back.' He leafed through the pages. 'Every service of baptism held at St George's since 1890. And we're still nowhere near needing a second book. Now then, what were young Mr Loredan's dates again?'

'Hmm, I can't remember exactly. But definitely 1968 to 1980.'

'Okay. Let's have a look.' He ran his finger down the page. 'No. Nothing at all.'

'Are you sure? Not even the following year?'

'As I said, we only get two or three a year. No, if he was baptised he wasn't one of ours.'

'They're quite a well-to-do family. Might they not have had the service at home?'

He shook his head. 'You're not really supposed to do that. Only *in extremis*. None of this, of course, means that the little fellow wasn't baptised in another church.'

'That wouldn't have stopped him being buried in the *Reparto Evangelico* though?'

'Not in those days. It's difficult now, but I understand there was more space back then. We'd take anyone.'

We sat in silence for a while. My right ankle, in contrast to the rest of me, was blissfully warm from the two-bar fire. I rubbed my hands together and blew on them. 'Can we go now?'

'It seems we can. I'll double check the years between 1969 and 1980. It could be he was a little bit older when he was baptised. And I can check with the diocese, just in case there's any correspondence from around that time, but it seems a long shot. Sorry Nathan, there wasn't much need for you to be here after all.'

'No worries. Thanks for lunch anyway. I'm not sure what we've proved.'

Rayner got to his feet and stretched. 'Well, we've proved that everything was carried out in full accordance with Church of England Law.'

'Which means?'

He grinned, and poked me in the ribs. 'Which means, Nathan, that the responsibility now passes to you.'

Chapter 5

I sat outside Toni's bar in Mestre, and wondered if I'd ever be warm again, as Dario returned from inside with a pair of icy cold pints.

We clinked glasses. 'Cheers, *vecio*.'

I sipped at my beer, cautiously, as if afraid the temperature would be low enough to crack my teeth.

He noticed me shivering. 'Are you cold?'

'Dario, I spent half of yesterday in a cold, wet graveyard. I spent this afternoon in a freezing cold church. Now I'm sitting outside a bar, in Mestre, in November, drinking a cold pint. Yes, I'm cold.'

'Sorry.' He looked hurt. 'I just thought it would be nice to sit outside. Just like old times, you know? You could have said. I'd have got you a hot chocolate or something.'

'Nah, it's okay. It wouldn't be quite the same, would it?' I looked around us. A few hardy souls walked or cycled past, and I waved away a guy who was approaching us with the idea of trying to sell us some knock-off handbags. Cars whizzed up and down Corso del Popolo, belching out exhaust smoke. 'I'll miss this place, you know?'

'Me too.' Dario tapped his pint glass. 'Toni says he got

these in especially for us. We're the only people that ever use them.'

'I bet we're the only people who sit outside in November as well. You'd have hoped that after all these years he might have got us a patio heater.'

'Too expensive, he says. Even for us.' He smiled. 'I'll miss it too. You and me, beers after work. Getting back home too late and having to tell Vally that it was all your fault.'

'You did that?'

'Yeah, sure. Best excuse I could think of.'

'Well thanks for that. That explains a lot.' The chill from my glass was making me lose all sensation in my hand. A cigarette would have warmed me up but that, I reminded myself, was something I didn't do any more.

I looked over the road towards the Teatro Corso. 'Who's on tonight?'

'No idea. Hey, remember that time Joe Jackson was on—'

' —and those two guys came over to us thinking we were in the band?' We both laughed. 'Closest we ever got to being rock stars,' I said.

'Yeah. Mind you, it was probably because we were the only guys who looked old enough.' He paused. 'I'll miss Mestre as well, you know? I know nobody really loves it. But it's been a good home to us. We've made friends here.'

'You're not having second thoughts, are you?'

'Bit late even if I was.' He shook his head. 'No, it'll be great.' A lorry sped past, setting our table vibrating. The fumes that blew into our faces did at least add a welcome touch of warmth. Dario flapped his hands in front of his face. 'And I won't miss that. You can talk all you like about cruise ships and PM10, but it doesn't feel the same. And Emily will be able to play outside when she's older.' Another truck rumbled past and he shuddered. 'Imagine that here?'

'What are you going to do about the Moto Guzzi?'

He shook his head and sighed. 'I decided I had to let it go.'

I put my glass down more heavily than I intended, and it clattered against the tabletop. 'Seriously? You could have kept it garaged at Tronchetto or somewhere like that.'

'Ah, it wouldn't be the same. Besides, since Emily came along it's never felt quite right going out on the bike. I've started to worry about, well, what about if something went wrong? What if Vally and Emily were left waiting at home and – you know? All that sort of bad stuff.'

'I understand. Shame though.'

He shrugged. 'In some ways. Or maybe it's just about getting older. You gave up cigarettes, I gave up the bike.'

I sipped at my icy beer, and wondered if Dario's offer of a hot chocolate might actually have been a good one. 'You'll let me know if I can help with the move, right?'

'Sure I will. Maybe in a couple of days. I've got some friends in Venice who'll give me a good deal on moving all our stuff, but we could do with a hand with packing.'

'No worries. Just let me know.'

'You're not too busy?' He paused. 'There is one job in particular that I kind of need you for.'

I raised my eyebrows. 'Intriguing.'

I waited for him to continue, but he shook his head. 'Wait and see, *vecio*.'

'Doubly intriguing. Anyway, it shouldn't be a problem. It's kind of a quiet time now. The Biennale's over, so translation work is a bit thin on the ground. Although I gave a quote for a film script the other day. That'd be a bit different at least.'

'That'd be cool. Hey, maybe you'll be on the red carpet at the film festival with the beautiful people?'

'I think you mean, the *other* beautiful people.'

He put his head to one side. 'No, I think I was right the first time.'

'Bastard,' I laughed. 'Anyway, I've read it through. Trust me, this is a film that has absolutely no chance of being made.'

'What, too violent?'

'No. It's just not very good. But it'd still be a fun thing to do.'

'And is the Consulate keeping you busy?'

I grinned. 'It should be, but I think I've managed to body swerve something difficult. Did you read about that empty coffin on San Michele?'

'The Loredan boy?' He shook his head, and looked serious.

'Do you remember that? At the time, I mean.'

'Not really. I'd have been, maybe, in my teens. I remember the stories in the papers. And my mum and dad telling me that's what happened to bad boys.' He shuddered, again, but it was nothing to do with the cold this time.

'Wow. Tough parents.'

'Yeah.'

There was an awkward pause, and so I moved the conversation on. 'Anyway, Vanni's asked me to investigate. The kid had British nationality, so he wants the consular records from the time.'

'You have them?' He sounded surprised.

I laughed. 'Of course not. I've just booted it upstairs to Rome. If there are any records, they'll be there.'

'Smart move.' He drained his glass. 'Are we having another?'

I was losing sensation in my hands by now. 'I think I'll die.' I paused. 'Yeah, go on then.'

He picked up the empties, and walked inside. The interior looked warm and inviting. I wished I'd offered to get them. I drummed my fingers on the table, partly to try and restore warmth to them, and partly to take my mind off not having a cigarette. I looked over the road to the Teatro Corso. The lights were still on in the tobacconist's next door. I checked my watch. Two minutes to nine. I could just about make it over there in time. I could see the figure of the proprietor pottering about inside.

Two minutes to closing time. Come on, nobody's going to be coming in now. Close early. Maybe you'll be able to get an earlier bus home. Come on. Close up. Close up and save me from running across the road in a desperate last-minute attempt to buy fags.

The lights clicked off.

Thank you.

Dario returned and set the beers down. 'Everything okay?'

'Absolutely. Just one thing though.' I reached into my jacket, took out my wallet, and passed him my health card.

'What's this?'

'It's my *tessera sanitaria*.'

'I know what it is. What I don't understand is why you're giving it to me.'

'Dario, given the time, every tobacconist I know of will be closed. But on my route home there are at least five shops with cigarette machines outside. Now, I think I can summon up the willpower to walk past one. Two even. But five is asking too much, especially after a few beers. So if you look after my *tessera sanitaria* for me, there'll be no way for me to buy fags.'

'That's clever. That's very clever. When do you want it back?'

'Don't know. Next time we meet?'

'What if you get sick in the meantime?'

'It's a risk I'm prepared to take.'

He clapped me on the shoulder, the sudden movement sending our glasses rocking. 'Well done, Nat. You really are taking this seriously, aren't you?'

'I am.'

'Are you feeling any better?'

'People keep asking that. I wish I was.' I paused. 'Actually, that's not true. I am feeling better.'

He smiled, but then his face clouded. 'Mind you, this doesn't stop you from asking other people if they'll give you a cigarette.'

He was right. The begging of cigarettes from complete strangers and, indeed, the giving of cigarettes to complete strangers was one of those little quirks of Italian behaviour that nobody ever tells you about.

'I hadn't thought about that,' I said.

'Oh.'

'Now I'm thinking about it.'

'Well don't. Come on, let's talk about something else. Tell me about the case.'

I shrugged. 'It's not really a case. And, like I said, I've just passed it on to Rome. They'll make a better job of it.' Then a thought crossed my mind. 'I've never asked you, Dario, but do you have anyone on San Michele?'

'I did. Mum and Dad.'

'Not any more?'

'No. I had them cremated after the ten years were up. We don't have a family tomb or anything. I think they're up in the loft now.' He paused to take a drink. 'I've never been to the Protestant bit. What's it like?'

'Kind of graveyard-ey, I suppose. Not as well organised as the other bits. It's a bit run-down.'

'Hmm. So why do you think they wanted little Gabriele buried there?'

'I wondered that. You see, I don't think they were actual, practising, Church of Englanders. But the thing about that section of the cemetery is this – you don't get moved.'

'You don't?'

'No. Once you're in, you're in forever. Or until judgement day, I suppose.'

He stroked his chin. 'Makes sense, then. Maybe it was a comfort to them. Knowing he'd always be there, to visit.' Then he shook his head. 'This is pretty dark stuff. It doesn't feel right, talking like this.'

'I know what you mean.' I drained my glass. 'Okay, one for the road?'

'I'm not sure there's time.' He checked his watch. 'Ah, go on then, what the hell.'

I shivered. 'Can we stand at the bar though?'

He laughed. 'Okay.' He took out his *cellulare* and started texting away. 'I'll just tell Vally that it's your fault.'

'Git.' He laughed again, and clapped me on the back as we made our way into the blessed warmth of the bar.

Chapter 6

I stepped through the door on the Street of the Assassins feeling pleased with myself. I had not sought out late-night *tabacchi*, I had not stopped total strangers and asked them for a smoke, nor had I begged to borrow anyone's *tessera sanitaria*. I had even resisted the temptation to stop for a late night *Negroni* at the Brazilians.

Yes, I thought to myself, I was getting pretty good at this 'being a grown-up' lark.

'*Ciao, caro.*'

'*Ciao, cara.*'

'Have you had a nice time?'

'I certainly have.'

'Slightly pissed?'

'Not remotely.'

'Cigarettes?'

'Not a one.'

'Well done, *tesoro*. You get a bonus boyfriend point.'

'Fantastic! What can I cash it in for?'

'It means you get to sit down whilst I bring you a modestly sized prosecco.' She returned from the kitchen with a bottle, and held it up to her eye, squinting slightly, the better to see how much remained. 'Very modest, I'm afraid. Still, I've got some good news for you. I've managed to get you added as my plus one for tomorrow night. Nathan shall go to the ball after all.'

'Excellent. Thanks. Where is it?'

'Ca' Sagredo. Very smart, have you been there?'

'Have I been there? I've conducted a wedding there.'

'You *what*?'

'I conducted a wedding there. A few years ago. Before we met.'

'You can do things like that?'

'Well, not exactly. Not officially. But if somebody wants a civil wedding in Venice, they need to go to the Palazzo Cavalli, right? Which is fine, but it's basically just the town hall.'

'Hmm. True enough. If you've come to Venice for the fairytale, you might be a bit disappointed by the Palazzo Cavalli.'

'And you can't have your big glitzy reception there either. So people do the official bit there, and then have a kind of symbolic wedding somewhere a bit more special. Like the Ca' Sagredo.'

'I understand that. But why you?'

'Well, now. I imagine you might think there was a certain gravitas to having your pretend wedding conducted by the British Honorary Consul in Venice.'

'Perhaps so.' She paused. 'George Clooney had the ex-Mayor of Rome, didn't he?'

'I know. Somehow he forgot about me.' I sighed. 'He never calls. So anyway, yes, I did symbolic weddings a couple of times a year for a bit. Then the work just seemed to dry up. I worry that they might have found someone more dashing.'

'That seems hard to believe.'

'I know.'

'So, what, does this mean you're like a priest or something?'

'God, no. I've never told the Tall Priest about it. I imagine he'd be angry. Sort of stealing business off him, I suppose. Anyway, remind me what this event's all about.'

She sighed. 'I did tell you this.'

'Yes, but that was when I thought I wasn't going. So I didn't think I needed to remember it.'

Gramsci chose that moment to leap on to her lap. The two of them stared at me. They'd never ganged up on me before. I'd always hoped that he would, one day, establish a non-aggression pact with Federica. I just hadn't assumed that it would result in them making an alliance against me.

'I'm hearing the words "Useless Boyfriend" here, aren't I?'

She nodded. 'You are.' Gramsci looked on in silent disappointment.

'So this thing tomorrow?'

'This presentation, yes?'

'Yes. The thing.'

'Could we call it a symposium or presentation, perhaps? I think that's better than "the thing".'

'We could. So, erm, could you just remind me what it's all about?'

'The effect of *acqua alta* on the mosaic floors of the Basilica of San Marco.' A low, rumbling sound came from Gramsci that might, just possibly, have been a purr.

'Is it – now don't take this the wrong way – really your area though? I didn't think you ever did much with mosaics.'

'I don't. But I did write a paper on the effect of saline mould on cements. So that's my bit.'

'And who else?'

'Two people from the university. Nobody I really know. And Ludovica.'

'She's still going ahead with it, then? After the news?'

'So it seems.'

'Do you think she'd talk to me?'

'Well, I could introduce you at least.'

'Thanks. What's she like, by the way?'

She paused. 'Difficult to think of the best word. Distant, perhaps. I think she's the most precisely controlled person I've ever met in my life.'

'You don't like her?'

'It's not a question of liking her. It's just that I don't know her. Not at all. She seems completely impermeable.'

'Hmm.' I sipped at my prosecco, and wished I'd made myself a proper drink. 'Perhaps I don't want to speak to her after all.'

'Perhaps not, *caro*, but given what's just happened, there's every chance she might want to speak to you.'

Chapter 7

I never held surgeries on Saturday mornings. People with long-term problems always had better things to do. People with short-term emergencies could always telephone me directly on the consulate number. It never used to ring at all but, recently, there'd been a spate of distressed tourists arriving in town to find that their rental apartment did not, in fact, exist and so I'd taken to always having the consulate phone on me. I'd also taken to keeping a stack of business cards for bed and breakfasts in my pocket.

Fede had gone to the Querini for work, and so Gramsci and I had the flat to ourselves. I did an hour's work on the film script that would never be produced, and then got up to have a stretch and make a coffee. I went through to the kitchen, unscrewed the jar and looked inside. There was, at best, half a spoonful. An unwashed cup, dregs clinging to the sides, lay in the sink. Federica had used the last of the coffee.

I poured what remained in the Moka. A sad little trickle of lukewarm brown liquid dribbled out.

I tried to put a brave face on it. 'Best drink of the day eh, Grams?' I said, and knocked it back in one. I grimaced.

'Okay. This isn't really hitting the spot.' I made to grab my coat, in order to head downstairs for breakfast, but his piteous mewlings called me back to the kitchen.

'What's up, Fat Cat?'

He jumped down from the counter and landed heavily next to his bowl, which he jabbed at, miaowing all the while.

'You've already had your breakfast,' I said. I looked down at his bowl. It was empty. 'Haven't you?'

I scratched my head. Had I fed him that morning? I honestly couldn't remember. It was the sort of thing I was used to carrying out in a semi-conscious state in the early hours of the day. And yet, when I looked down, it was unarguable. Gramsci had not been fed. He was, I thought, taking it remarkably well.

I poured out his daily ration of kitty biscuits, whipping my hand away just in time, and he munched away happily. He'd started to become distinctly rotund recently, and so I'd cut back on his daily allowance. It didn't seem to be having much effect. Still, his attention was fixed elsewhere now and so I put my coat on and made my way out of the flat, pulling the door behind me as gently as I could. All I could hear from inside were happy crunching sounds.

I went downstairs, and into the Magical Brazilians; warm, amber and toasty in contrast to the grey, wet streets outside.

'Morning, Ed.'

'Morning, Nathan. The usual?'

'I forget. What's the usual at this time?'

'One moment.' He took out a pad of paper, licked his finger, and flicked through it. Then he looked up at the clock on the wall. 'Just about ten-thirty. Oh, and it's a Saturday of course. So that should be,' he ran his finger down the page, 'a *caffè corretto con grappa.*'

I stared at him.

'You have a dossier on me?'

He shrugged. 'I wouldn't call it that. Just essential notes. In case I'm not here.'

'Do you have "essential notes" on any other regulars?'

'No. Just you.'

'Right. Right. Well, variety is the spice of life and all that. So today I think I'll have a *macchiatone.*'

'With grappa?'

'Not with grappa, no. And, I tell you what, I think I'll have something to eat as well.' I looked in the glass cabinets. 'I'll have a brioche *integrale* with *frutti di bosco.*'

I leaned on the counter and ate my brioche as Eduardo fixed my coffee. I brushed flakes of pastry from my coat. There was no way to eat these elegantly. It didn't matter. From *grandi signore* in expensive fur coats, to *ragazzi* and *ragazze* on their way to school, this was pretty much the perfect breakfast. Ed slid my coffee across the bar. I breathed in its warmth, before stirring in sugar and sipping at it, the bittersweet flavours of the coffee blending with the buttery flavours of the brioche and the sweetness of the jam. I closed my eyes for a second. The King of Breakfasts. I looked out at the wintry streets, and smiled. Christmas would soon be on its way. And then January, when the wave of visitors would momentarily decrease even further and the city would become as normal as it ever did. Winter. The best months of the year.

I finished my coffee and gave a contented little sigh.

'Are you happy, Nat?'

'I think I am, Ed. All's right with the world.' I felt my phone buzzing in my pocket, and took it out. My heart sank when I saw the number. Rome. It didn't, I told myself, necessarily mean anything bad. 'Sorry, Ed, I'd better take this.' I put the phone to my ear. 'Ambassador Maxwell?'

'Nathan,' he drawled the word out in his rich, brown voice as if trying to add an extra syllable to my name. 'How are you?'

'I'm very well, Excellency.' 'Excellency.' Why on earth had I called him that? 'Very well indeed. All well in Rome, I trust?'

There was the briefest of pauses followed by the driest of laughs. 'Not very well at all, I think you'd have to say.'

'I'm sorry to hear that, Ambassador.'

'That's partly why I'm calling. That incident you contacted the embassy about? The empty grave?'

'Yes. I was just wondering if the embassy might have records on this sort of thing, what with the child having British nationality and an English father and . . .'

'Stop. Please stop.' A note of tiredness had crept into his voice. 'Nathan. It's the middle of November. People keep telling me we're supposed to be leaving the EU in a few months' time. Had you heard about that?'

'Erm, I had, yes. It's keeping me busy, you could say.'

'Good. Good. It's keeping me rather busy as well. All of us, in fact.' He paused again. 'Do you know how many British citizens there are in Italy, Nathan?'

'Not exactly. Fifty-thousand odd?'

'A bit north of that. About sixty-four thousand. Each of whom, it seems, wants to talk to me personally about what's going to happen to them next year.'

'It's a bit like that here.'

'And what do you tell them?'

'Not to panic. And if they're really concerned, well, they should go directly to the embassy.' There was silence on the line. 'Ah.'

'Ah, indeed, Sutherland.' The use of my surname was never a good sign. 'I'm just looking at my diary. It seems I have a reception tonight with an expat group, who will all be taking it in turns to shout at me. Then tomorrow, I'm in Milan where, again, disgruntled British citizens are going to take it in turns to shout at me. The day after that I'm in Turin. Can you guess what's going to happen there?'

'Would I be right in thinking that angry Brits are—'

'—going to take it in turns to shout at me. Well done, Sutherland. And it's not just me. Pretty much everybody here is having to do the same thing. So it's fair to say nobody has any spare time with which to look at your little local problem.'

'I understand, Excellency.' It seemed safer to move back to his honorific. 'I'm sorry, I shouldn't have bothered you with it. We can probably assume it'll go away of its own accord. I think it would be safe enough if I just let it drop.'

'No, you bloody won't.' I jerked upwards in surprise as his voice rang out. 'Sutherland, every expat in the country wants to know that the diplomatic service is doing its job properly and that they can feel confident that they'll be looked after whether in life or in death.'

'I understand, Excellency, but the case is nearly forty years old.'

'I don't care how bloody old it is. It's in the papers today. It's another big stick to beat us with. How can we protect our living citizens when we can't even look after the dead ones?'

'I'm sorry, Excellency. I'll look into it.'

'Don't look into it. Sort it out, quickly and quietly and, ideally, prove that it wasn't our fault. Do you understand?'

'Perfectly, Excellency.'

'Good man. I'm sure I can count on you, Nathan.'

'Oh you can, Excellency. You can.'

He hung up.

I looked through the window to the street outside, where the skies had darkened to match my mood. I turned back to Eduardo.

'You know, Ed, I think perhaps I need a *caffè corretto* after all.'

He gave a stiff little bow. 'Of course,' he paused, '*Excellency.*' Then he ducked behind the bar as I looked for something to throw at him.

Chapter 8

I hadn't spoken with my predecessor in over three years, and the last conversation – in which I had practically accused him of receiving stolen property – had been a difficult one. Nevertheless, Victor Rutherford had once been a friend of mine. It would be good to rebuild bridges. Moreover, I needed his help.

I dialled his number, and let my thumb hover above the 'Call' button for a couple of seconds, before taking a deep breath and tapping it. I let it ring ten times and was about to hang up, grateful for having been spared a potentially awkward conversation, when Victor answered.

'Hello?'

'Victor. It's Nathan Sutherland.'

'Nathan?' He paused. 'How are you?' I thought I could hear a touch of suspicion in his voice but couldn't be sure, and at least he hadn't hung up immediately.

'I'm fine, Victor. How are you?'

'A few more creaks and groans but generally well. I miss Italy of course but I think perhaps the English weather suits me better. Most of the time, anyway.' There was silence again. 'It's been a long time, Nathan. I take it this isn't just to enquire about my health?'

'It's not. But I'm glad you're well. Look, something's come up that I need to deal with. Or at least both the police and the embassy want me to deal with it.'

'Yes.' He drew the word out, and the suspicion was audible now.

'It's nothing to do with you.' Hell, that sounded as if I was making an accusation. 'Or me,' I added in haste. 'I was just wondering if you happened to know who the Consul was back in 1980?'

He laughed and, for the first time, there was genuine warmth in his voice. 'My goodness, Nathan, how old do you think I am? I'm sorry, but I really have no idea. That was long before my time.'

'Sorry. I thought it was a long shot. Okay, do you remember any stories about a child drowning in the lagoon around then?'

'Possibly. That, sadly, was not an infrequent occurrence.'

'The name was Loredan. Gabriele Loredan. Does that help?'

'Ah yes. Now that name I do know. I used to see his father quite a bit. Hugo Channing. Delightful man. We haven't been in touch in quite some time.'

'Did he – did he ever talk about what happened?'

'Good heavens, no. Everybody knew about it of course. But it certainly wasn't something that one could introduce into conversation, and he never spoke of it to me.' He paused for a moment, and when he spoke again the note of suspicion was back. 'Why are you asking me this, Nathan?'

I decided to be honest with him. I owed him that. 'Victor, I was in the *Reparto Evangelico* the other day. For the Day of the Dead. Gabriele Loredan's coffin had been disturbed. More than that, it was empty. And it's just possible there was never a body in there in the first place.'

'Good God!'

'So Vanni from the *Questura* would like me to go through our records. Just to see that everything was done properly at our end. And the Ambassador himself would like me to do the same.'

'I can see. Bit embarrassing if the correct procedures weren't followed. But I have to say, Nathan, it's unlikely you'll be able to find anything. I mean, I know records are supposed to be kept but this is nearly forty years ago.'

'I know. Thanks anyway. I knew it was a long shot.'

'Not a problem. I don't think I have any proper records left of my years there. And certainly not from my predecessors. But I will have a think. I'll be in touch.'

'Thank you, Victor.' I struggled to find something else to say, but he saved me the trouble by hanging up.

I closed my eyes and leaned back in my chair. Then I started as something brushed the top of my head. Federica. She'd come in without my hearing her.

'Everything okay, *caro*?'

I smiled. 'I think so. I think I've managed to put something right.'

'No *acqua alta* tonight?'

'Nothing predicted.'

'Just as well,' I said, pulling on my shoes. 'It's a drag carrying boots around.'

Fede checked her reflection in the mirror, and then took

out a mascara wand. She looked at it for a moment, and then tutted to herself before dropping it back, unused, into her handbag. We'd been together for nearly three years now and I'd seen her use makeup twice.

We made our way through the chilly streets to the *vaporetto* stop at Sant'Angelo.

'Will there be anything to eat?', I asked.

'Hopefully. Is there a plan B?'

'I picked up a few fillets of *San Pietro* at the market. I bought them for tomorrow, but they'd make for a quick dinner just in case. And they're good for drunk cooking.'

She gave me a gentle dig in the ribs. 'One does not do "drunk cooking" after an evening at the Ca' Sagredo, Nathan.'

'Slightly cheerful cooking, then?'

'That's more like it. Come on, this is our boat.' The *vaporetto* bumped into the pontoon, setting it rocking; then the *marinaio* pulled open the gate to let us on. 'Is it too cold to sit outside?'

I shook my head. 'I don't think so. Best time of the day, isn't it? Almost the best time of the year for that matter.'

We were making our way to the back when I heard the irate cry of '*La porta!*' from behind me. I turned to see an elderly lady jabbing her finger at me, before pointing to the cabin doors. I'd forgotten to close them and cold air was now flooding into the interior.

'I'm sorry,' I said, pulling them to. '*Chiedo scusa.*' She harrumphed, and turned back to her friend, muttering something about *ignoranti* just loud enough for me to hear. I made my way through the cabin, and outside to where Federica was waiting.

She smiled at me. 'Fearsome elderly Venetian lady?'

'Absolutely. Mind, it was my fault. I'd forgotten again.' We snuggled together as the canal slid past. 'So what's the plan for tonight?'

'Oh, there'll be the usual introduction. One of those very Venetian ones that go on for as long as the actual talk. And then we'll all say our bit, take questions, and then,' she smiled again, 'it's prosecco time.'

'Fantastic. Should I speak with Ludovica first?'

She shook her head. 'I wouldn't. Really a bad idea. You don't want to upset her beforehand. Not that I've ever seen her upset.'

'She hasn't said anything to you? About cancelling?'

'Nothing at all.' We passed under the Rialto Bridge, the lights of the *vaporetto* reflecting off the water and casting shifting patterns of light on the underside.

I shook my head. 'That's strange. In fact, that's downright weird. This is her little brother, after all.'

'As I said, she's a cold one. And,' she sighed, 'I suppose it was a long time ago.'

'Still. Something like this. Would you ever get over it?'

She got to her feet. 'I don't suppose we would. But other people . . . who knows,' she shrugged. 'Come on then.'

We were just passing Rialto Mercato, the bars quieter at this time of year, as the cold weather encouraged them to keep their doors closed. Up ahead, we could see the great Venetian Gothic palace of Ca' d'Oro and, beyond that, the palazzo Ca' Sagredo supported by Lorenzo Quinn's hands. Or, rather, by his sculpture of two giant hands, rising from the lagoon and pressing against the exterior of the building, as if holding it in place. The artist had installed them back in May and nobody knew exactly how long they'd be there, helping to shore up the crumbling city.

Next-eh stop-eh Ca' d'Orrrro, said the recorded announcement.

I smiled.

'What's so funny?' said Federica.

'Just listen.'

The announcement played again. *Next-eh stop-eh Ca' D'orrrro.*

Fede looked at me, blankly. 'I don't understand.'

'Don't you think she has a lovely voice? The way she just endlessly rolls the "r". *Ca' D'Orrrro,*' I repeated, doing my best to approximate her accent.

Her expression changed to one of pity. 'I'm starting to worry about you.'

I wondered if perhaps I shouldn't have started this particular line of conversation.

'I mean,' she continued, 'it's not every day that I think I need to start feeling jealous of a recorded announcement.'

'Oh.' I paused. 'Shall we just not talk about this again?'

'Probably best.'

The *vaporetto* bumped against the pontoon of Ca' d'Oro, and we made our way through to Campo Santo Sofia and the palazzo. It had been a while since my last visit, and I had always found the space slightly intimidating. Ca' Sagredo was an example of a hotel that would always be too expensive for me to stay in.

'*Dottoressa* Ravagnan. *Che piacere.*' The little receptionist bowed, and ticked her name off a list. He gestured towards the grand staircase, lined with thick red carpet. 'I'm told we will be starting shortly.' He checked the list again. 'We are still waiting for a few guests, but *Signora* Loredan is already with us.'

I made to follow Federica, but the receptionist raised his hand, just ever so slightly, and gave a gentle cough. He inclined his head towards the guest list. 'Sir?'

'Ah, of course. My name is Sutherland. Nathan Sutherland.'

He ran his finger down the list of names. Then he rubbed his chin. 'I'm sorry sir, could you just repeat your name for me?'

'Nathan Sutherland. But I won't be on the list. This is all a bit last-minute.'

He gave me the practised smile of someone who is going to give you bad news but wants to avoid making a scene. 'I'm very sorry sir, but—'

Federica took my arm. 'Mr Sutherland is with me. I was told I could have a plus one. I am sorry, I should have tele-phoned earlier.'

He bowed, even deeper this time. 'Of course, *Dottoressa*.' He swept his arm in the direction of the staircase. 'Please . . .'

We smiled at him, and made our way up. The stairs led to a mezzanine, the walls and ceiling heavily frescoed in a riot of pinks and blues and ochres, illustrating some kind of mytho-logical scene that I was unable to decipher. I craned my head back, but the colours swirled around me and refused to form themselves into a shape that I could interpret.

'Pietro Longhi,' said Federica. '*The Fall of the Giants.*'

'Longhi? You're kidding me.'

'Not his usual style, is it?' She smiled. 'It was a terrible failure. Venetians might like everything done to excess, but this was a step too far. Even for us. Nobody liked it. So, he went off to Bologna to study. And when he came back, he was not the same. No more great frescoes, but in their place all those perfect little interiors of Venetian life. Dancers, tailors, gamblers, drunks . . .'

'Rhinoceroses,' I added.

'Indeed. How could we forget the rhinoceroses?' She stared upwards at Longhi's gigantic figures. 'This is fun. It's not a great work, but it's fun. I think he made the right career choice though.'

Pink marble steps led up to the *piano nobile* and were guarded by a couple of disturbing cherubs bearing flowers. I tried to avoid their gaze as we made our way upstairs to where two great Murano glass chandeliers illuminated the *portego* with a warm, golden glow. Tables had been laid along the centre of the room, leading the eye to the great Gothic arched windows that overlooked the Grand Canal.

White-tuxedoed staff were already setting out ice buckets filled with bottles of prosecco whilst, in the corner, a string quartet was tuning up. Longhi would most definitely have felt at home. This, evidently, was going to be something rather more than a dry academic presentation. It was an event to see and be seen at. I wished I had worn a better jacket. Then I looked over at Fede, resplendent in what might have been her second-best dress, and decided that if she wasn't worried about it then neither should I be.

'They say Galileo once visited here, you know?' said Federica.

'Really?'

'He was a great friend of Giovanni Sagredo. Some of the greatest artists and thinkers in history would have met here.'

'And now there's you, of course?'

'Too much flattery. But thank you, *caro.*' She touched my cheek, and then checked her watch. 'I should probably go through. Is it safe to leave you on your own in the company of a table of prosecco?'

'Of course. I'll just mingle. *In bocca al lupo.*'

'*Crepi.*'

A glass appeared in my hand, as if by magic. I made a tour of the room, smiling and nodding at people, none of whom I knew, until I found myself at the far end. My prosecco, it appeared, had evaporated along the way. Another waiter – was it the same one? – discreetly plucked my glass from my fingers and replaced it with another in one smooth motion.

A silver-haired woman was standing alone, looking out through the windows. I looked around. We were the only ones in the room not in a group. On impulse, I took another glass from the waiter, and went over to her.

'Prosecco, *Signora?*'

She turned to me, and looked confused for a moment. Then she laughed. 'I'm sorry. I was expecting you to be a waiter. That's very gallant of you, thank you.'

Her hair was cut in a Louise Brooks bob, and her features were lined but still beautiful. I found it difficult to estimate her age. Her eyes were grey and, perhaps, the one part of her that seemed to have aged. There was a tiredness, a sadness there.

I raised my glass, and then turned to the window.

'Magnificent, isn't it?'

'It is,' I replied.

'Is it your first time here?' Then her hand flew to her mouth. 'I'm so sorry. That must have sounded terribly rude. It's just – your accent – I tend to assume everyone with an English accent must be a tourist. Or a visitor, I should say.'

I smiled. 'No, I'm not a tourist. Oh dear, is my Italian that bad?'

'No, it's very good. Apart from your accent.'

'Well, they say that's the most difficult thing to master. I don't know if I'll ever quite get it. I'll probably never sound like a Venetian.'

'Well, I don't think that matters so much. So what line of work are you in Mr . . .?'

'Sutherland. Nathan Sutherland. I'm a translator.'

'I see. I thought you were in the art world. Most people here tonight are.'

'My partner is. *Dottoressa* Federica Ravagnan.'

'Oh, I know of her. She's quite brilliant, so I'm told.'

'She is. Far too brilliant for me.'

She laughed. 'I'm sure that's not true. Well I'm pleased to meet you, Mr Sutherland. My name is Cosima Loredan.' She caught the expression on my face, and looked puzzled. 'Is something wrong?'

'I'm sorry.' I couldn't think of anything better to say. 'I'm so sorry about what's happened.'

She bent her head. 'Thank you. It was a great shock, as I'm sure you can imagine.'

'I'm not sure I can imagine it. I'll do all I can to help. I promise.' She looked confused. 'I'm also the British Honorary Consul,' I added.

She frowned. 'I'm not sure I understand.'

'It's possible that one of my predecessors might have been consulted or involved in some way when Gabriele was –' I hunted for a gentler word, but couldn't find one, '– buried.'

'Why would that be?' Her eyes were fixed on mine, but filling up.

'He was a British citizen. So is his father, I understand. Which means the consul of the time may well have been involved.'

'My husband isn't aware of the situation, Mr Sutherland. He's not aware of very much at all.' Her voice was shaking now.

'I'm so sorry. I didn't know. It must be very difficult for him. For you all.'

I couldn't think what else to say. I wondered if it might be best if I just made my apologies and left, but that would leave Federica in an awkward situation. I was trying to think of something suitably platitudinous when I was interrupted by a younger woman, perhaps in her early fifties, with long, flowing dark hair and impossibly high cheekbones.

'Mother?' She reached a hand out to Cosima's face, and touched it gently. 'Mother, you seem upset.' She moved closer to her, and turned to me with an expression that varied between curiosity and accusation.

'I am sorry,' I repeated, again. 'I didn't mean to upset anyone. I'm Nathan Sutherland. I was there when the coffin . . . I was there on San Michele the other day.'

She stared at me in silence, and then turned to Cosima. 'Come, Mother. We're about to begin. Don't let anyone upset you.' She put an arm around her shoulders and tried to steer her from the room.

Cosima put a hand on her arm. 'It's all right, darling. I'll take a breath of air for a few moments. I think it will do me good.'

Ludovica gave the briefest of nods, and continued to stare at me. I couldn't hold her gaze, and stared down at my shoes. 'I do apologise,' I muttered. They both turned and left the room in opposite directions, leaving me alone with my reflection in the great Gothic window. I raised the remains of my prosecco to myself. Not so well played, Nathan.

Chapter 9

'Ladies and Gentlemen, *Signore e Signori*.' The speaker was a young man, tanned and handsome, with an immaculately trimmed goatee beard. One would have expected nothing less from the Ca' Sagredo. 'The presentation will begin in five minutes. Please step this way.' He beamed out at us all, before languidly stretching out his arm in the direction of the Music Ballroom.

It had been a few years since I'd conducted one of my pretend weddings here. It was still capable of getting a *sotto voce* "wow!" out of me. The salon had been decorated by Gaspare Diziani, who had decided that nothing would succeed like excess. The ceiling fresco showed Apollo, in his golden chariot, casting down the vices from the heavens, which tumbled to earth in a similar manner to the *Fall of the Giants*. Around the room, in an effective piece of *trompe l'oeil*, stood the gigantic figures of Minerva, Neptune, Cybele, Venus, Mars, Mercury, Juno and Jupiter.

It must have been one hell of a place to get married. It was certainly one hell of a place to hold a series of lectures. Tables had been placed along the entire length of one side, in front of a series of frescoes that concealed the secret door that led to the *Casino Sagredo*, a series of hidden rooms where, in times gone by, the master of the house might have waited for his mistress with terrible acts of wickedness on his mind.

Federica saw me come in and flashed me a quick smile. Two professorial types chatted animatedly to each other and shuffled papers. Ludovica sat impassively in the centre, occasionally jotting down notes on a pad in front of her.

I thought it better not to sit myself right at the front. Federica, I knew, would only worry about me falling asleep and snoring. I sat three rows from the back, taking an end seat, the better to be able to stretch my legs. I exchanged smiles and nods with the man next to me, and then took my phone out and got to my feet in order to take a photo of the panel.

I should, perhaps, have remained in my seat and tried to do it more discreetly as they all noticed as one. Federica tried and failed to look cross, whilst the two *professori* grinned and posed; putting their arms around each other's shoulders. Ludovica smiled thinly, and then shook her head before returning to her notes.

Someone behind me nudged the back of my chair, and I felt a hand on my shoulder. 'Sorry, did I kick you?'

I turned around. 'No problem, don't worry.'

'We're a bit crammed in, aren't we?' The speaker was a man in, perhaps, his late forties, pink-faced with curly hair that needed a bit of a trim. He had the look of a cheerful hobbit about him, and was wearing a green waxed jacket which, whilst evidently practical given the weather, seemed out of place in such a grand space and made me feel that at least I was not the most underdressed man there. 'Sorry again. I should have got here a bit earlier.' He took his scarf from around his neck, and laid it under his chair, spraying me with a fine mist of cold water in the process. 'Oh God. Sorry, again.'

I raised my hand in a 'don't worry about it' gesture, and turned towards the front. He tapped me on the shoulder once more.

'Sorry, can I bother you for just a minute?'

'It depends. Are you going to keep apologising?' He looked worried for a moment and then laughed.

'Sorry. Oh God, I've done it again. I was just going to ask, do you know who everyone is? On the panel I mean?'

I smiled. 'Sort of. The very pretty one is *Dottoressa* Federica Ravagnan.' I paused.

'Your partner?' He smiled.

'I didn't say so.'

'You didn't have to.'

'Well you're quite right. It still surprises me. The two gentlemen to her left, I have to say, I don't know. From the university, as I understand. And the other one, the very serious-looking one, is Ludovica Loredan.'

I thought I'd kept my voice sufficiently low, but Ludovica suddenly looked up from her notes and straight into my eyes. I stiffened in my seat, sending it jolting back into the knees of my new companion, who couldn't suppress an 'Ow!'

Ludovica got to her feet and stood, staring at me, her fingertips resting on the table. Then she pushed her chair back, squeezing her way past Federica and the two *professori*. She stumbled slightly as she did so, before catching herself and making her way slowly, but deliberately, towards us.

Federica mouthed the words 'What the hell have you done?' at me.

I waved my phone at Ludovica. 'I'm sorry,' I said. 'I didn't realise. I'll get rid of it if you like.' I held the phone up to her so she could see me deleting the photo. Then I realised she was not looking at me, but at the man in the row behind. Her face was impassive, mask-like, at first glance, but as I looked more closely I could see the corner of her mouth twitching.

'You have an invitation?' she said.

'I do, yes. And lovely to see you too *Signora* Loredan.'

'Could I see it, please?'

'Of course.' He reached into his jacket and took out his passport and a folded sheet of paper.

She looked at both. 'I see. Clever of you.' Her voice was icy, but wavered. Then she drew in a deep breath, her body shivering. 'I would like you to leave, please.'

'And I would like not to.' There was the hint of a chuckle in his voice.

'My mother will be here soon. I will not allow her to be upset. You understand that?'

'Perfectly.'

'I will call security.' There was just a touch of desperation in her voice now.

'Please do.'

I wanted to turn around properly, to see what was going on, but I was afraid of throwing petrol on the fire. I looked towards the front. The two *professori* had stopped joking, and Federica was trying to engage them in conversation in an attempt to stop them from staring. I caught her eye and she gave a minute shake of her head.

Ludovica walked away, slowly, her heels clacking on the floor as if she was emphasising every step for effect. I counted to ten and then turned around.

'There seems to be some misunderstanding,' I said.

He gave a dry little laugh. 'There does, doesn't there?'

I rubbed my forehead. 'Look there's quite a crowd here tonight. And my partner is up there. And so I'm thinking . . .'

He cut me off. 'That it would be nice if I were to leave without making a scene?'

'Well yes. Exactly. I'm sorry, I don't mean to be rude.'

'And I do. Not to you, of course. I'm sorry about that.'

Ludovica swept back into the room, the little man from reception trailing in her wake and flapping his hands in alarm. She stopped next to my new companion, and glared at me as if to indicate that nothing was going to happen that could be of the slightest interest to me. I held her gaze for a moment and then broke, turning back towards the front. I could still feel her eyes on the back of my head, as if she were trying to tell me that it would be better for me not to listen either.

'*Signora,* I am so sorry. I am so, so sorry. But as you can see, his name is on the guest list.' I risked a glance. He held the sheet of A4 up to her, holding it just slightly out of her direct reach, as if afraid she would snatch it from him and tear it into pieces. He indicated a name – unreadable to me – with a trembling finger.

She gave it the most cursory of glances. 'I know that. Mr,' she paused, and lingered over the word, '*Flemyng* does indeed have an invitation. The question is, what are you going to do about it?'

I risked another glance behind me. He was perspiring, flexing his knees to make himself look shorter, and then bouncing on the tips of his toes to draw himself up to his maximum height. He turned to Flemyng. '*Caro Signore*, I do not wish to be rude but—'

Ludovica gave a sigh that might have been a hiss, or a hiss that might have been a sigh. 'You have people to deal with these things, I imagine. Call them. Now.' She closed her eyes for a few seconds, and then looked down at the little receptionist. 'You may go.'

'Yes, *Signora*. Of course, *Signora*.' He paced backwards a few steps, before turning and walking from the room as fast as he could without actually becoming airborne.

The guests in the surrounding seats were sitting with eyes fixed firmly towards the front, stiff with embarrassment, although a few were watching the scene unfold as discreetly as possible, secretly hoping that something disgraceful was about to happen that they could relate in the office on Monday morning.

He reappeared in the doorway, standing on tiptoe in order to whisper into the ear of another, bigger, man with cropped grey hair and a growth of salt-and-pepper stubble. He was wearing a black tuxedo with a dress shirt and a bow tie, possibly for the first time. A radio mic was clipped to his ear, and a name tag fixed to his lapel that might have read 'Security'. Or 'Thug'. He patted his little companion on the shoulder, and made his way over.

Ludovica smiled the most dazzling smile, with her eyes as well as her mouth, her face lighting up with genuine pleasure.

She looked at his name tag. 'Giorgio?' He gave a stiff little nod. 'This gentleman appears to be in the wrong seat.'

The corners of Giorgio's lips turned down, and sadness flickered across his deep brown eyes. 'I'm sorry to hear that, *Signora*.' He looked down at Flemyng, and spread his hands wide. 'Please sir, do come with me. I'll show you where to go.' He extended an arm.

Flemyng looked up at him. Giorgio was not a big man, nor a young man, but there was something about his presence that suggested he was not to be trifled with. He smiled. 'Of course. I'm sorry, I've been terribly stupid.' He got to his feet and smiled at Ludovica. 'Nevertheless, it's been lovely to see you again, *Signora* Loredan. Have a lovely evening. I'm sure we'll have the chance to talk further. Both ourselves and your mother, I hope. At some point.'

Ludovica stiffened, and glanced at Giorgio. He patted Flemyng on the back and waited for him to get to his feet. Then he threw an arm around his shoulders and guided him towards the exit.

I got to my feet, half expecting to hear the sound of breaking glass from the adjacent room. Ludovica turned to me and laid her right hand on my shoulder. Gently, but firmly, she pushed me back into my seat.

'Please, Mr Sutherland. Don't concern yourself.' Her smile was even broader than before. 'The evening is about to begin.'

Chapter 10

We were, as we often were, the last to leave the party. Empty bottles of prosecco had been whisked away, and the remaining plates of *cichèti* were being removed. I grabbed a small octopus from a passing dish, under the eyes of a reproachful-looking waiter who evidently couldn't wait to get home.

The lectures, I assumed, had been splendid. I hadn't heard much of them, my ears having been constantly straining towards the adjacent rooms, with my phone at the ready in case I needed to call the police, an ambulance or both. Ludovica, impassive and inscrutable beforehand, had seemed re-energised after her encounter with Flemyng. I could not, for the life of me, remember the substance of her talk, but only the way she delivered it. Every word had been just a little over-enunciated, every gesture consciously overstated for effect. When she sat down, allowing one of the jovial *professori* to hold forth, she seemed to shrink back into herself. Occasionally, she nodded, as if in agreement, but I had the disturbing thought that she, like me, was listening for Giorgio administering a punishment beating to Flemyng.

'So, what did you think?' said Federica.

'Um, I'm sure it was very good—'

'Except?'

'I'm afraid to say I couldn't really keep my mind on it.'

'I could tell.'

'Sorry. I spent the entire ninety minutes wondering if the man behind me was being measured for a pair of concrete boots, and if I should call the police. What was going on there?'

She shook her head. 'I have no idea. Ludovica is a bit strange – I imagine you can tell that – but tonight was something else.'

'You should have seen her face. The way she smiled. She was genuinely looking forward to that guy being hurt.'

'Who do you think he was?'

'No idea. A journalist maybe?'

'Mmm. British though, wasn't he?'

'Yes.'

'Why would a British journalist want to speak to her. It's kind of a local story, isn't it?'

'I guess so. I didn't see anybody from *La Nuova* or *Il Gazzettino* though.'

'Oh, there were. But they wouldn't go off-piste. They find her a little frightening.'

'I can imagine. I wonder if poor Mr Flemyng or whatever-his-name-really-is is wearing concrete shoes at this moment.'

'It depends where he is, *caro*. Most of the lagoon isn't that deep. Even if he was, he could just stand up.'

'I hope that's a comfort to him right now.'

She laughed and touched my arm. 'Home then?'

A waiter walked past with an open bottle of prosecco on

a silver tray. There was, I could see, a good half-inch in the bottom. My hand twitched for an instant, and then I caught the expression in his eyes. The expression of a man whose last bus was leaving in twenty minutes.

'Home,' I said.

We linked arms and walked down the stairs, under the gaze of the falling giants.

Sunday morning. Blessed Sunday morning. No surgeries to hold, no shopping to be done, and – to Michael Rayner's continuing disappointment – my bottom would not be gracing the pews of St George's.

I padded through to the kitchen and unscrewed the Moka, tipping yesterday's grinds into the bin. The pot was cool, and I could see a teabag amongst the rubbish. I'd forgotten to tell Federica that I'd replenished the coffee supply. She must have got up before me and decided an early-morning cup of tea would do just as well.

I looked at the packet of coffee that I'd picked up at a *torrefazione* in Cannaregio the previous day. A mixture of seventy per cent Arabica beans and thirty per cent Robusta that would, the label assured me, deliver a mixture of chocolate and spices with a hint of tropical fruit. I tore the packet open, closed my eyes, and smiled. It was a universal Law of Coffee that it could never, ever taste as good as a fresh packet smelled.

I rinsed the Moka out, and spooned fresh coffee into the filter. Then, as I always did, I made three indentations in the surface with a spoon. The theory, I had read, was that it helped the water to percolate through, and hence reduced the chance of the coffee burning. I had no idea if this was true or not, but I wasn't prepared to risk not doing it. Then I put the Moka on the smallest ring and on the lowest heat. It would take some time, I knew, but one couldn't be too careful.

Gramsci, fast asleep mere minutes ago, had materialised like the Cheshire Cat but minus the grin. He stared at me and gave a plaintive little *m'yow* as I measured out fifty grams of kitty biscuits. I started to tip them into his bowl.

Then I paused. I looked at him, sizing him up. He really was putting on weight, although he was still getting the same amount of food as ever. I supposed that, in middle age, he was becoming less active, yet he'd always been a sedentary fellow, content to sit and watch the world go by whilst being permanently disappointed by it.

I took a deep breath, and decided to risk it. I reached out my hand, gave him an experimental prod, and whipped it back before he could do any damage. There was no doubt about it. He was a well-padded cat and, if there were any ribs under all that fur, they were now very well covered indeed.

I tipped perhaps half of the biscuits into his bowl. He stared at me with a mixture of contempt and disappointment. Then his eyes widened, and he looked at me imploringly.

'Don't look at me like that.'

M'yow.

'This is for your own good, Fat Cat.'

M'yow.

'I'm primary caregiver, okay? I'm just trying to do what's best.'

M'yow m'yow.

He seemed ready to work himself up into a full-blown

howl. I risked darting out of the kitchen for a second in order to check on Federica. She was still asleep, with an untouched mug of tea on her bedside table. I wondered how pleased she'd be to be woken up again by a caterwauling Gramsci. Probably not very. I went back to the kitchen and poured the remaining biscuits into his bowl.

'I'm only doing this because it's Sunday morning, all right? Sooner or later we're going to have to find a solution to this.' Happy crunching sounds came from around my ankles.

The smell of fresh coffee filled the air, as the bubbling sounds from the Moka told me that it was nearly ready. I waited until they stopped, then moved the pot from the ring, and opened the top, the better to keep it from overheating. I had a pod machine in the office, but – convenient as it was for guests – it never seemed quite the same as the early-morning ritual for the first coffee of the day. I poured out a cup, stirred in one and a half spoonfuls of sugar, stirred it ten times clockwise and gave a contented little sigh. The best drink of the day. If it was to be a Negroni-free day, of course.

I went through to the living room and stared out of the window. It was still dark outside, the rain pattering on the windows. A day for spending indoors, snuggled up in bed. Could we even be bothered going downstairs for lunch at the Brazilians, or would we just snooze through the day? Then I'd fry up the fillets of *San Pietro* for dinner, with some butter and a handful of capers. A day for not doing very much at all.

I heard my phone buzzing on the bedside table. I ran through and snatched it up before the noise could wake Federica. She murmured something unintelligible before rolling over, and pulling the duvet over her head.

The call was from a UK mobile phone. I didn't recognise the number. Almost certainly from a British tourist who needed help. On a Sunday.

Oh hell.

I held the phone away from me and let it ring. It was, technically, my day off. I had no need to answer it at all. Nobody could blame me if I let it ring out. It was, almost certainly, nothing serious. And yet there was always the chance that it could be something very serious indeed.

Damn.

I tapped the 'Receive' button.

'*Pronto*. Erm, I mean, good morning.'

'Good morning. Am I speaking to Mr Nathan Sutherland?'

'That's me. How can I help?'

'My hotel gave me your number. You're the UK Consul, is that right?'

'Honorary Consul, that's correct.'

'I wonder if we could meet. I'd like to speak to you.'

'Of course. I'm not sure if the hotel gave you my hours, but I'll be holding a surgery tomorrow morning from 10 until 12.'

'If we could meet today I'd be grateful.'

I tried not to sigh. 'Can I just ask you if this is an emergency?'

There was a brief pause on the line, and then the caller laughed. 'No, I wouldn't call it that.'

'Well then, perhaps it would be best if you called—'

He interrupted me. 'I would like to see you today, if at all possible.'

I tried to keep the tiredness out of my voice. 'Okay. Tell me all about it.' I braced myself for the words 'Lost passport'.

'My name's Guy Flemyng. I'm staying at the Hotel—'

I dropped the phone, which went skittering across the floor, and snatched it up before Gramsci could start playing with it.

'I'm sorry. What did you say your name was?'

'Flemyng. Guy Flemyng.'

'Oh my God. Are you all right?'

There was a pause. 'I don't understand.'

'We met last night. At Ca' Sagredo. I was sitting in front of you when you,' I was about to use the words 'were asked to leave' but thought better of it, 'left with that gentleman.'

He chuckled. 'You're being very diplomatic, Mr Sutherland. I can see why you do the job you do. The phrase you're looking for is "when you were thrown out". And I'm quite all right, thank you. We had a vigorous discussion, nothing more.' He paused again. 'So, as I said, I was wondering if we could meet today?'

'It's important then?'

'I think so.'

I sighed. 'You have the address?'

'I do.'

'Then I'll see you at midday.'

'Wonderful. Thank you very much, Mr Sutherland.'

I hung up and cursed. Bloody Sunday.

The door phone buzzed promptly at midday. If I were being cynical, I might have assumed that Mr Flemyng had been waiting for the Marangona bell to chime before buzzing. He was damp from the drizzle, and rubbed his hands together from the cold. I hung his coat up, having first checked that there was nothing there likely to be of interest to Gramsci, and showed him into the office.

'Coffee?'

'No thanks.' He tapped his chest. 'I'm not supposed to.'

'I've got decaf.'

He waved his hand. 'No, that just reminds me of what I'm missing. Please don't worry.' There was, I thought, the faint whiff of stale cigarette smoke about him. High blood pressure, yet he continued to smoke? Well, he wouldn't be the first.

'Well now, Mr Flemyng.' I paused, and raised my eyebrows. 'Would I be right in thinking that you're not here in need of any consular services?'

He smiled, a cheeky grin that made him look younger. 'You would be right, Mr Sutherland.'

'And would I be right in thinking that it was something to do with the events of last night?'

'You would indeed.'

I looked at him. He didn't look as if he'd been in a fight last night. He didn't look like a man who'd ever been in a fight at all.

'So all the – unpleasantness – was sorted out?'

'Yes. A bit of a misunderstanding. Nothing more.'

I was starting to find him just a little bit irritating now. He seemed pleasant enough and hadn't said anything directly annoying but he was still a man seemingly intent on buggering up my Sunday for no good reason.

I decided to get to the point. I spread my hands. 'So. What's it all about then?'

'I think you know, Mr Sutherland.'

I sighed. 'No, I don't. Bored with this now. Get to the point, please, or I'm going to go for lunch.'

He laughed. 'I think that's the worst threat I've ever heard. But I'm sorry. Okay then, it's to do with an empty coffin on San Michele.' He pronounced the word as *Michelle*.

'You've heard about that?' I was surprised. Grim as it was, I hadn't expected it to make the international press.

'I have. The little Loredan boy. Lying somewhere, but not in his grave.' He shuddered theatrically which, given his halfling-like appearance, made him look a little silly. 'A terrible business.'

'It's very sad, yes.'

'A diplomat's answer.'

'If you like.' I tapped my index finger on the desk. 'You're a journalist, aren't you?'

'Is it so obvious?'

'I meet a lot of them. So yes, it is.' We sat and smiled at each other in silence. 'So,' I said, finally, 'what is it you want, Mr Flemyng?'

'I would *like*,' he stressed the word, 'to know if you have any information on what happened to the little Loredan boy.'

The repetition of 'the little Loredan boy' was starting to irritate me, its tweeness redolent of tabloid-speak and one step away from 'tragic tot'.

'Well, in that case, Mr Flemyng, I'm afraid I'm going to have to disappoint you. I imagine I have no more information than you have.'

'Really.' It wasn't a question.

'Really.'

'You've not been asked to investigate why a British citizen's body has gone missing?'

'Why would I have? I'm the Honorary Consul, not Philip Marlowe.'

'The death of a British citizen would involve the Consulate though. Wouldn't it?'

'This was nearly half a century ago. I know I'm not in the best of shape, but how old do you think I am? More to the point, you seem to know an awful lot about Gabriele Loredan.'

'Ah, well. That's just part of my job. Look,' he held his hands up, 'we've got off on the wrong foot. I'm sorry. It's just I think that there might be a story here, and you might be able to help me.'

'I don't see how.' The window pane rattled, as the wind blew rain across the glass. I shivered as a thin blade of cold air slid under the imperfectly sealed frame and brushed the back of my neck. Gramsci yowled and jumped down from the sill, scowling at me. Sunday, it seemed, was going to be a washout. 'I don't see how,' I repeated. 'But if I am, why don't you tell me what sort of story you're planning to write?'

Flemyng smiled at me. 'Okay, Mr Sutherland. But first of all, what do you know about the Loredan family?'

Chapter 11

They're fighting again.

I can hear their voices through the wall.

Fighting. Arguing. As always. But it's worse now. Of course it is. There is something different, as well, in the tone of my father's voice. Usually he rages and swears and threatens. He doesn't sound the same now. There's something else there. Desperation.

'Don't leave me.'

I slip out of bed. The floor is cold. I shiver in my pyjamas. I open my bedroom door, just a crack.

Mother has her coat on. It must be nearly midnight. She really is going to leave. Father is red-eyed and angry, but he sounds desperate.

'Don't leave me. Not after all this. If you leave me now, I will have lost everything.'

Mother is going to leave. And then I will be alone. I can't bear it any more. I open the door and cry, 'Mummy'. Immediately I feel ashamed, embarrassed at sounding like a little boy, but no other word will come.

Her face was red with anger, but now she looks at me and softens.

'Mummy, don't go.'

Father speaks. 'Oh, look at him. Just look at him.' The desperation has gone from his voice now, replaced by utter, absolute contempt.

I run to her, into her arms, and start sobbing. She hugs me to her, and strokes my hair.

'Don't go, Mummy.'

She pulls me tighter. I can feel her cheek against mine, wet with tears.

'Never.'

'Promise.'

'I promise.' She kneels down in front of me, pushes my damp hair back from my face and kisses the tears away. Then she takes my hands in hers. 'Gabi, go to your room now. Pack some things. Just for a couple of days. The two of us are going away together. Not for long, I promise.'

I smile, and my heart leaps. I run back to my room. Everything is going to be all right again. I pull my school bag from the wardrobe, and throw some clothes into it. How long are we going away for? I'll need something to read. I run my fingers across the bookshelf above my bed. 'Il mastino dei Baskerville.' Sherlock Holmes. Mother likes me to read in Italian. I drop it into the bag, then pull the drawstrings as tight as possible. Then I struggle into my clothes – I can't find a matching pair of socks, but that just makes me laugh – and then I run from my room, my bag swinging from my shoulder.

Immediately I realise that something has changed. The door to the staircase is open. Light is flooding into the hall. Father stands there, silhouetted in the entrance.

'Leave if you want', he says. 'Take him with you. Both of you.

Go.' Then he pauses. He wants the following words to have the maximum effect. 'But if you leave, as soon as that door closes, I promise that you will never see Ludovica again. I promise you that, my love.'

Silence, thick and heavy and dreadful, hangs in the air.

Father moves towards the two of us. I can see his face now. I cannot read his expression and yet I know – and the thought turns me cold – that he is enjoying this.

Mother drops to one knee, and puts her hand to my face.

'Gabi. I need you to be brave. Go back to bed now. Don't forget to say your prayers. And then go to sleep. Everything will be different in the morning.'

No words will come this time. I simply nod. As I turn to run back to my bedroom, I catch sight of my father's face. He is smiling now, properly smiling. A smile of triumph.

'What's good here?' asked Guy.

'Everything.'

The Bacaro da Fiore was busy, but not so busy that we had to stand. We grabbed a couple of stools by the window, and looked out into the street. A couple of smokers stood outside, pressing themselves backwards in the hope of sheltering from the rain. One of them, vaguely familiar to me, smiled and beckoned. I mouthed the words 'given up', and made a sad little face. He laughed, shook his head, and turned back to his companion.

Guy was looking at the *cichèti*. 'I'm afraid I don't know where to start.'

'Well, the soft-shelled crabs are something else, but they're just out of season. We could share a plate of fried fish?' He stood up to take a closer look, and then sat back down again, looking uncertain. 'Let me guess, you're not sure about little fish with the heads still attached?'

He gave an apologetic little smile. 'Does that sound pathetic?'

Yes, I thought. 'No,' I said. 'Shall we just get a few meatballs and a couple of spritzes then?'

'That'd be great.'

I went to the bar and ordered, returning with a plate of mixed *polpette* and two Campari spritzes.

Guy looked uncertain at first, but a broad smile spread across his face as he bit into his first meatball.

'Good?'

'Fantastic.'

'I'm glad. I sometimes think I could live an entirely meatball-and-spritz based existence.' We ate in silence for a few moments, as I tried to size him up. He was handsome for a hobbit, although his curly hair, shaggy and unkempt, looked as if it was trying to be bohemian and failing. He wore the same waxed green jacket as the previous night, practical yet ever so slightly geeky.

'Is it your first time in Venice?' I asked.

He nodded.

'And what do you think?'

He shrugged. 'It's nice.'

My hand paused in the act of raising my spritz. In all my years in Venice, I had never, ever heard anyone describe the city as merely 'nice'.

He read my expression and looked apologetic. 'It's just that I'm here for work, you know?'

'I understand,' I said, not understanding. 'So tell me about it.'

'I'm writing an article. Well, maybe more than that. I'm hoping it might be the basis for a book.'

'About the Loredan family?'

'Yes.'

'Do you think there's a market for that?'

'I think there might be. They were a glamorous couple, back in the day.'

'I didn't know that. I don't know much about the husband.'

'Hugo Channing. Made a fortune back in the 1960s from diamond mining in Rhodesia. Which sounds like the dodgiest thing on earth, I know.'

I shrugged. 'Different times, I suppose.'

'They were. Oh, and he was also a racing driver for a bit. Not a very good one. But I suppose there's something glamorous about even not-very-good racing drivers. And Cosima was very beautiful.'

'She still is,' I said. 'Great bone structure. Like her daughter.'

He looked momentarily annoyed. 'If you say so. As I was saying, they were a very chic couple in their time.' He paused, drawing his finger down the side of his glass. Then he looked at me with a sly expression in his eyes. 'There were – *stories* – you know?'

'I don't, no.'

'About Hugo.'

'Ah. The fatal charm of the unsuccessful racing driver?'

'That sort of thing.'

'And you're writing a book about this.'

'Researching a book about this.'

I sipped at my spritz. Suddenly, the Campari had an even more bitter taste. 'Cosima is still alive, as you know. And you're writing a book about her.'

He threw up his hands. 'It's not going to be like that, I promise.'

'Is there any public interest to a story like this?'

He ignored the question and took a drink. 'You were there, the other day. Weren't you? On San Michele.' Again, he pronounced it *Michelle*, which was starting to irritate me.

'I was, yes. How do you know that?'

'It was in the papers.'

'Really?'

'The Italian papers, I mean.'

'You read the Italian press?'

'Only when it's of interest. Like I said, it's for research.'

'I understand.' I took a deep breath. 'Look, Guy, I'll be honest with you. I don't like dealing with journalists. Or at least with those I don't know.' He made to protest, but I held my hand up. 'No, no. Hear me out. I've been burned by the press before and I didn't like it. Neither do I like the idea of your book. I don't like being called out on a Sunday to deal with something as sordid as this. And I like the idea of an elderly woman having to see her dirty laundry aired in public least of all. But I'll hear you out. So just tell me. What exactly do you want from me?'

If he was angry, he did a good job of concealing it. He drummed his fingers on the table for a moment, and then looked across at me with the same sly look as before. 'Well, thank you for your honesty, Mr Sutherland.' He paused, and took another drink. 'If I understand correctly, your job as Consul would have been to make sure a British citizen was correctly buried.'

'I would have been in short trousers at the time. I'm afraid I can't help you.'

'Of course. But the Consulate will have records, I imagine.'

'Yes.' Or sort of, I thought.

'And so . . . ?' He left the question dangling.

'And so you'd like me to reveal confidential information about the death of a British citizen nearly forty years ago?' I laughed. 'I can't possibly do that.'

'Not even if I . . . ?' He rubbed two fingers together, and grinned.

'Two things. One, it would be a grotesque betrayal of trust. I'd almost certainly lose my unpaid job which, bafflingly, I still quite enjoy. Secondly, this is a pretty small city and getting smaller every year. I know a lot of people here by now. I like to think they think well of me and not as someone who might be selling grubby little stories about them for a grubby little book.'

He showed no sign of being offended. 'Okay. I understand. No hard feelings.' He finished his spritz. 'Sorry if I've wasted your time. Let me get these.'

'There's no need,' I half protested, but I let him anyway

'I'll be in the city for a few days. Maybe I'll see you around. In the meantime, if you change your mind, you can always call me.' He took out a business card, scribbled on the back, and passed it to me.

I took it from him and stuck it inside my wallet. 'Thanks for lunch.'

'No worries.' He patted me on the back, squeezed his way to the door, and then made his way through the smokers. He stopped for a moment, as if acknowledging someone, and the broadest of smiles broke across his face. And, for a moment, there was something of the malevolent hobbit about him.

Paolo, the barman, gave me a quizzical look. I indicated my empty glass, and nodded. 'Same again, Paolo, I think.'

Chapter 12

'So how was lunch?'

'Interesting. Modestly boozy. But strictly work-related.'

'Really?'

'Sort of. It was the guy who got thrown out of Ludovica's presentation last night. He's a writer, or so he tells me. He wanted to know if I had any dirt on the grave.' I chuckled to myself. 'Dirt on the grave. I like that.'

Fede wrinkled her nose. 'English humour. So what did you say?'

'I told him that even if there was any dirt I wasn't going to help him shovel it around.'

'Right. Do you think you've done the metaphor to death now, *caro*?'

'Sorry. Well, basically I just told him that it would be unethical and I couldn't help him. He was all right about it. Even insisted on buying me lunch.'

'A two-spritz lunch. You must have made a good impression.'

'The second one was mine, to be honest. I thought I needed it. It just all seemed a bit odd. Would there really be a market for a book uncovering the secrets of the Loredan family?'

She shook her head. 'You'd be lucky to get it published in

Italy. I imagine they know some heavyweight lawyers. And in England? *Pffft* – who would want it?'

'Don't know. Guy told me that Cosima's husband was a not-very-good racing driver.'

'Hmm. That's a very niche market, isn't it?' She ruffled my hair. 'Okay, Mr Sutherland, what are you going to cook me for dinner?'

'I picked up some *moscardini* at the Rialto yesterday. I'll stew them with some tomatoes and garlic.'

'How much garlic?'

'Oh, an indecent amount I should think.'

'Wonderful.' She paused. 'Any time soon?'

I pointed at Gramsci, sprawled across my chest. 'Only when he moves. And when he's settled down he could be there for hours. Nothing will move him. I suppose you could bring me a glass of prosecco in the meantime.'

She gave me a hard stare and then quickly jabbed her finger out to poke Gramsci in his well-padded ribs. His eyes snapped open and blazed furiously at me, his little paws scrabbling away at my chest until he found sufficient purchase to push himself off.

Fede smiled down at me.

'I'll be in the kitchen,' I grumbled.

Moscardini, small octopuses from the Adriatic, were at the very end of their season; and I'd picked up a kilo from the market. That sounded like a lot of octopuses for two people but Marco and Luciano, from my regular fish stall, really were on the level this time when they assured me they'd reduce down in cooking.

I put some Pink Floyd on the stereo, realised Federica was attempting to do some work, and replaced it with Bach. Then I tipped the *moscardini* into the sink and set to work.

Nobody dies wishing they'd spent more time cleaning octopuses. The process of turning the head inside out and removing some of the gooier and more unidentifiable bits is not a lovely one. Still, once cleaned, the little chaps practically cook themselves.

I tipped them into a pan and covered it, then stuck them on the hob on the lowest heat possible. My usual recipe for *moscardini,* squid, octopuses or anything vaguely tentacley was to put them in a pan on a low heat, mix a Negroni, run a bath, have a bath whilst drinking the Negroni, and then return to see how things were getting on. This time I made a brace of Spritz Nathans for Fede and myself, before gently frying some chopped tomatoes and garlic and adding them to the *moscardini.*

Later, much later, Fede was showing signs of falling asleep, and so I decided they'd probably had enough. The little octopuses had reduced, their juices coating everything in an intense purple-pinky glaze. I tipped them into a bowl, while I whisked up some instant polenta.

A great big bowl of colourful tentacley goodness. Perfect for both a baking hot summer's day and a wintry November. We sat and ate, accompanied by Bach and a cheap-yet-almost-perfect white wine, whilst Gramsci stared at us.

'I don't understand it,' said Fede. 'He's supposed to be a cat, yet he doesn't like seafood.'

'I've never worked it out myself. He doesn't really like anything apart from tinned tuna and chicken. And not even chicken, really. Just chicken-flavoured things.'

As if to prove me wrong, Gramsci hauled himself up on to the table and sniffed around the edge of my plate.

Federica shook her head. 'You shouldn't let him do that.'

'I know, but what if it helps to get him interested in a more balanced diet?' I took a stray tentacle, and placed it on the edge of the table. He sniffed at it a couple of times, then sat back on his haunches, the better to gaze at it. Then he swatted it to the floor.

I sighed. Fede shook her head, again. Then she smiled. 'It was good though. Ignore Fat Cat, he's got no taste.'

'Shall I wash up?'

'Not now. Just come and have a lie-down on the sofa. I'll do it in the morning.'

She wouldn't, I knew. But it didn't matter.

I switched the CD in the player, and Fede pretended not to notice. We snuggled up on the couch, as a six-note bass riff rumbled out of the speakers, over a spacey mellotron wash. Two drummers kicked in, followed by a plaintive flute melody.

Fede rested her head on my chest, and looked up at me. She raised her eyebrows, but didn't say a word.

'Hawkwind,' I said.

'Oh.'

'"Assault and Battery". It's from *Warrior on the Edge of Time*.'

'Oh.' She closed her eyes. 'Were you single for a long time, Nathan?'

We listened to Dave Brock declaiming the words of Henry Wadsworth Longfellow, until the track segued into the psychedelic voyage of 'The Golden Void'. I knew what was coming next and braced myself. Michael Moorcock, his voice echoing under a battery of effects, started to thunder out 'The Wizard Blew His Horn'.

Fede opened her eyes again, and looked up at me. 'Do you think, *caro*, that perhaps it's delighted us enough?'

I tried not to look sad. 'Sorry.'

'It's okay. I know these things are important to you. It's just that—'

'Small doses?'

'Exactly.'

I reached for the remote control, and switched it off. 'Any requests?'

'Yes. No more music. Please.'

'Oh.' I sighed. 'You're no fun.'

She rolled her eyes. 'Early Sunday evening, snuggled up against the cold outside. My not-unattractive boyfriend has just cooked me a lovely meal. What could we do? I know, what could possibly be more fun than listening to Hawkwind?'

'Oh.' And then I realised what she'd just said. 'Oh!' I repeated.

She smiled. 'Well now. What are we going to do in the absence of that horrible music?'

'We could try some Jethro Tull?' I suggested, innocently.

She dug me in the ribs, and then pulled me towards her, kissing me and stifling my 'Ow!'

Inevitably, the phone chose that moment in which to ring. Fede sighed and stretched her hand across to the table to pick it up.

'Leave it,' I said, nuzzling at her neck in what I hoped was my best Christopher Lee manner.

She made to hang up, and then frowned. 'No. I think you need to take this.'

'I don't need to,' I murmured, but she had already picked up the call and pressed the phone against my ear. I suppressed a curse.

'*Pronto.*'

'Mr Sutherland.' I thought I recognised the voice. 'This is Ludovica Loredan. We met last night. Briefly.'

'*Signora* Loredan. How can I help you?'

'I need to talk to you, Mr Sutherland. About my brother. And other things.'

'I understand. I'll do – I am doing – everything I can, I promise you. If you like, we could meet tomorrow morning at my office.' I stole a look through the living-room door to where Gramsci was sitting on top of a pile of papers in what constituted my 'office'.

'I would prefer it if you were to come here.'

'As you like, *Signora.*'

'Good. Tomorrow evening, at six pm.'

'Are you sure, *Signora*? I'm free all day tomorrow. We could meet earlier if—'

She cut me off. 'I am unavailable during the day. Early evening would be best.'

'As you wish.'

'You have the address, of course.'

Of course? Of course not. 'I think Federica may have it.'

'Federica?' She paused. 'Ah. *Dottoressa* Ravagnan. She can give you directions.'

'Indeed.' I made to hang up. '*A domani. . .*'

'One moment please. I would like to say, Mr Sutherland,

how grateful my mother and I are for your work in trying to resolve the situation.'

'No problem, I just hope—'

'Please let me finish. I was about to say it would be appreciated if your investigation could be carried out in as unobtrusive a manner as possible.'

'Of course, I—'

'Again, please let me finish.' There was a note of irritation in her voice, the nearest she'd come to displaying any emotion at all. 'I would like this all to be resolved behind closed doors. Strictly behind closed doors.' I was about to speak but, again, she cut me off. 'This is something to be discussed between ourselves and the relevant authorities.' She paused. I didn't know if I was allowed to contribute to this part of the conversation, and so waited for her to continue. 'It is not a matter for idle chatter in *bacari* with strangers.'

I tried to keep the surprise out of my voice. 'I'm sorry?'

'We shall say no more about it. I shall expect you tomorrow evening. *Buona serata*, Mr Sutherland.'

She hung up before I could say anything more. Federica looked at me quizzically.

'A notable lack of pleases and thank-yous,' I said.

'They're not things one can easily expect from Ludovica Loredan,' she said. 'You have to know her for some time before you can even expect a smile.'

'Oh. How long have you known her?'

'We first met during the Biennale in – let me think – 2009. So, eight years.'

'And in all that time?'

'One smile. But I think she might have mistaken me for someone else.'

'Wow. Eight years, eh? You must have been very young.'

'Flattery unnecessary. But welcome.' She sighed, and looked at her watch, her elbow digging into my ribs as she did so. 'It's getting late. I suppose you've got a surgery in the morning.'

'I suppose I have.'

'I suppose you need an early night?'

'Oh, I don't think so. Unlikely to be anything too urgent at this time of the year.'

'That's nice.' She lay back down on my chest. 'So, what now then?'

'More Hawkwind?' I suggested.

She kissed me, but not before digging me in the ribs again. 'Maybe not.'

Chapter 13

I sat with my feet up on the desk for most of the morning, pausing occasionally to throw balls for a bored Gramsci. Federica was dividing her time between research at the Querini Stampalia and occasional work at the Church of the Frari, the great and the good having decided that Titian's *Assumption of the Virgin,* despite a series of recent interventions, was perhaps not quite as beautiful as it could be and so was deserving of yet another attempt to make it more perfect than it had ever been.

I checked my diary. I was due to go over to Mestre tomorrow, in order to help Dario finish packing. That evening I had my slightly unnerving appointment with Ludovica. I checked my watch. Just ten minutes to go. Nobody, but nobody, bothered the Honorary Consul in late November.

The door phone rang.

I sighed, and buzzed them up. Lost passport? I took out a 'Brexit Survival Guide' just in case.

My visitor was a young, beardy guy with an enormous backpack that made it hard for him to get through the door.

'You look cold,' I said.

He nodded.

'Would coffee help?'

He nodded again.

I showed him into the office and clunked a capsule into the machine. He took the cup from me and wrapped as many fingers as he could around it to try and restore some feeling to his hands. I looked him over. Woolly hat, Gore-Tex jacket, proper boots. His rucksack was expensive and properly water-proofed. It seemed, however, as if his savings hadn't stretched to a proper pair of gloves.

'So how can I help, Mr . . . ?'

'Whale. James Whale. Jimmy if you like.' I smiled and was about to speak but he gave a tired wave of his hand. 'Like the film director. Yes, I know.'

'Well anyway, what can I do for you?'

'Somebody's stolen my B&B.'

'I'm sorry?'

'It's not there.' He took out a damp sheet of paper from his jacket. 'I've got a reservation for this place,' he tapped a finger on the page, 'and it's not there.'

I strove to keep a neutral expression on my face. 'You can't find your B&B and so you came to the Honorary Consul?'

'The police thought you might be able to help.'

'The police? Jimmy, Mr Whale, I'll help if I can, but did you ever think perhaps a decent A-Z might be better?'

He shook his head, sending a fine cloud of cold water droplets through the air. 'Shall I start at the beginning?'

'That might be best. I'm obviously missing something.'

'I booked this place a couple of weeks ago. It was with that big online B&B company, you know?'

I nodded. The same one that was indirectly responsible

for depopulating the city, as landlords turned their properties into temporary homes for tourists instead of renting them out long-term to locals.

'So, I flew in this morning and took the bus into town. Going by the address it didn't seem to be that far away from the bus station. So I checked my phone—'

'Ah, well now,' I smiled as I interrupted. 'I wouldn't trust your phone for directions. The streets are so narrow here, you can't rely on GPS or Google Maps.'

'You're not listening to me.' He sighed and rubbed his face. 'The place doesn't exist at all. It's not on my phone.'

'Again, that can happen. The street numbering system is a bit strange here. It's not like any normal city. You need to—'

He interrupted me, and reached across the desk to thrust his phone under my nose. 'Look. It's not there, is it? Rio Terà del Ghetto Nuovo. It's not there.'

I took a look at it. 'May I?'

He jabbed it into the palm of my hand. 'Go ahead.'

I tapped away. He was quite right. It didn't seem to know about any such place as 'Rio Terà del Ghetto Nuovo'. And the more I thought about it, I realised that I'd never heard of such a place myself. I was starting to get a familiar, bad feeling about this.

'Do you have a map by any chance, Mr Whale?' I asked.

'Sure.' He rummaged through his backpack. 'Sorry, I'll be as quick as I can. It's in here somewhere.' He pulled out an orange and placed it on my desk. Gramsci leapt up, and I whipped it out of the way. Then a banana. Then a packet of cigarettes. A headcam. His rolled-up laundry. A book, *Abandoned Islands of the Venetian Lagoon*. I recognised the cover. And then a flat box covered in brown vinyl, with a stainless-steel clasp fixed to the top. Cigars, I wondered?

He saw me looking and smiled for the first time. 'My camera,' he said with a touch of pride.

'You're kidding?'

He smiled again, pulled on the attachment, and folded it out.

'A Polaroid? Wow. I didn't know they still made those.'

'They're difficult to get hold of. And this isn't just any Polaroid. This is an SX70.'

I scratched my head. 'I'm afraid you've lost me there.'

'Warhol used them. Ansel Adams, Helmut Newton. I was lucky to find it.'

'It's a lovely thing.' I took out my telephone. 'I'm afraid I'm only just getting to grips with this.'

This was evidently the wrong thing to say, as his smile froze and he folded away the precious Polaroid. He rummaged in his backpack again until he found his map. Then he spread it out on the table before replacing his belongings in precisely the right order.

The scale wasn't ideal for identifying individual streets. Indeed, the detail of the *centro storico* itself was small in comparison to the rest of the lagoon and its islands. I shook my head. 'We need something more detailed.' He made to fold the map away, but, before he could do so, I noticed that a number of the smaller, outlying islands had been circled. He'd packed it away before I could recognise them all, but I noticed that, amongst others, the island of Poveglia had been marked out.

'You've picked a wretched time of year to go island-hopping,' I said.

He glanced out of the window, to where the rain was still pattering down. 'So it seems.'

I paused. 'Just one thing. You might want to think twice if you're planning on visiting somewhere like Poveglia. You're really not supposed to go there. You could end up in trouble, even if you could find someone to take you out.' He shrugged, as if to indicate that was neither something that he'd thought about nor something that would bother him.

'Anyway, let's take a look for this apartment of yours.' I took down a copy of *Calli, Campielli e Canali*, the Venetian equivalent of the A-Z, and flicked through the index without success. Then I tried to google the address on the computer, with a similar lack of results.

It really didn't appear to exist. I tried to keep a smile on my face, whilst being aware that a difficult conversation was bearing down on me at high speed.

'Can I take a look at your booking?'

He slid it across the desk to me, a look of suspicion in his eyes. 'What's the matter?'

'Probably nothing,' I lied.

I read through his confirmation email. Everything looked legitimate. The map, admittedly, could have been more detailed. Rio Terà del Ghetto Nuovo was indicated by an arrow pointing to an area that could best be described as 'somewhere in the vicinity of the Ghetto'.

I took my glasses out and rubbed the bridge of my nose. 'Are you sure it's not there?'

'Yes, I'm sure. I've asked maybe a dozen people. I went to the police. Now I'm here. Nobody seems to know where this bloody place is.'

'Okay. I'm sure it's nothing to worry about.'

'Really?'

'Almost certainly.' I took another look at the email, with my glasses on this time.

'Oh.'

'Oh?'

I looked across the desk, to where hope was dying in his eyes.

'I think we may have a problem.' I took a pen and circled the email address. 'You booked this with,' I gave the name of the big online B&B company, 'am I right?'

'That's right. What's the problem?'

'How did you pay? Via the website?'

'No. Bank transfer. The details are in that email. What's the problem?' he repeated.

'The problem is this. The email address – dot net not dot com. It's a fake site.'

'Which means?'

'Which means,' I sighed, 'you've been scammed. I'm sorry.'

He shook his head. 'I don't get it?'

'This isn't the real company. This is a bogus one sending out a convincing-looking email for a non-existent property.' I paused. 'They wanted payment up front, you said?'

'Yes. What do you mean I've been scammed?'

'How much money?'

'It's on the booking, look.' He jabbed at the paper again. 'What do you mean I've been scammed?' he repeated.

'It means you've paid—' I looked at the paper. Oh God. 'It means you've paid this money to a fraudulent company for an apartment which doesn't exist.'

'It must exist. Look, there are photos.'

I paged through the images. One showed a view of the church of the Redentore. It was described as being the view from the front window. The front window of an apartment allegedly in the Ghetto, on the opposite side of the city. The interior shots showed an immaculately clean, modern apartment. So clean and modern I suspected they'd been lifted from an IKEA catalogue.

'Stock photos. I'm sorry.'

'But what about my money?' He was panicking now, half risen from his seat.

I shook my head. 'It's gone. You'll never see it again.'

'And what are you going to do about it?'

I was struggling to find alternative words to 'sorry' and settled on 'I really must apologise. There's nothing I can do.'

'Then I'll go back to the bloody police and maybe they'll bloody do something.'

I shook my head. 'They won't. This sort of thing is starting to happen more and more often. There's nothing they can do. Whoever's running this is probably not even in Italy. They might not even be in Europe. Look at these photos – no Venetian would ever make a mistake like this. It's like the nice gentleman in Nigeria who just needs some temporary help with a financial transaction. It's a trap to catch the—' I bit my tongue.

'You were going to say "stupid", weren't you?'

'I wasn't,' I blustered. 'I was going to say "unwary".'

'I've been here before, you know. I just didn't spend my time going around the usual tourist traps. Just because I didn't recognise the view doesn't make me stupid!'

Look,' I held my hands up in a placatory gesture, 'I've got a list of B&Bs here. You're welcome to stay here and use the phone to try and find somewhere else. I'll make you another coffee. A sandwich, if you like?'

He stared at me in disbelief and contempt. Then, without a word, he reached over and crumpled his reservation into a ball and dropped it into the wastepaper basket. He got to his feet, zipped up his coat, and stalked out, slamming the door.

I closed my eyes and gently thumped my head on the desk.

There was a knock at the door. I opened it. Mr Whale was standing there.

'I forgot my rucksack.'

'Oh yes. Right.' I dragged it out of the cupboard, and, between us, we manhandled him into it. He gave me a brief nod and muttered 'Thanks,' before squeezing himself through the door frame and making his way downstairs as best he could, tortoise-like within his Gore-Tex shell.

I went back into the office. The wastepaper basket was satisfyingly full. Gramsci hopped on to the desk to watch me as I mechanically scrunched up a pile of 'Brexit Survival Guides' into balls, and dropped them in.

I placed the basket in the middle of the floor and nodded at him. 'Okay, puss. I think you know how this goes by now?'

He miaowed and tensed his muscles to leap, as I took a long run-up and kicked the basket with all my strength across the room.

Chapter 14

I felt better once I'd picked everything up.

I stuck my head out of the window, and breathed in the smell of wet stone. Still raining, properly raining. A day to put off going outside for as long as possible. The Loredans, I understood, had a palazzo on the Zattere, looking over towards Giudecca. Perhaps twenty minutes' walk. Not too bad, even if it kept raining. I wasn't sure exactly what Ludovica was expecting from me but, whatever it was, I was sure I was unprepared for it.

Father Rayner had failed to turn up any documentation that might be of use. Victor might turn out to have a lead, but I didn't feel that I could call him back so soon. There were a few journalists for *Il Gazzettino* and *La Nuova* that I could call upon for help but, in the meantime, I decided I'd try and find whatever little I could manage by myself.

Mildly famous and terribly rich Hugo Channing seemed a good place to start. An online search brought back a number of articles scanned from 1960s celebrity gossip magazines.

He had been, I suppose you'd have to say, a handsome man. One photograph showed him behind the wheel of a classic Riva speedboat, a carefully placed cigarette dangling from his lips as his hair blew in the wind. Unfeasibly hairy-chested and every inch the picture of businessman as rock star. Another image showed him wet from swimming, posing in a doorway with his hands on his hips and naked except for, God help us all, a pair of Speedos.

Another image, from a Spanish celebrity magazine, was a family shot from the late seventies. Channing lay on the prow of his Riva, his elbow resting on the deck and chin propped on his hand. On the other side of him, mirroring his gesture, lay Cosima in a white swimsuit, beautiful and gamine as Hepburn. In front of them sat three young people, their legs dangling over the side. A girl, sunny and smiling, in, perhaps, her late teens. Ludovica? Difficult to say, given I'd never seen her smile in real life. Just behind her, with a hand resting lightly on her shoulder, sat a young man with thick, curly hair. And then to her right, a younger boy, scowling and sulking and staring at his feet. Gabriele? Possibly, given what I knew of the difference in age with his sister. I looked at their faces again; Ludovica poised and beautiful, Gabriele unhappy and out of place. There was another adult, behind the wheel of the boat, dressed in shorts and a white polo shirt, and throwing back his head as he laughed. The green dome of the votive temple on the Lido could be seen in the background.

I tried to make out the date of the article but it had been imperfectly scanned. I strained my eyes and could just about make out the words 'August 1980'. The caption was more legible. 'Hugo Channing and family relax with old friend and business partner Darko Kastellic and his son Andrea.' I looked again at Gabriele. August 1980. The poor lad had just weeks, perhaps only days, to live. The rest of the family smiled and posed for the camera, with Channing's grin the widest of all. *Look at me. Look at my beautiful family and my brilliant life.*

I shook my head. Okay, he'd obviously been a terrible narcissist and perhaps his business dealings had not been as ethical as one might wish, but that was no reason to dislike someone I'd never met. I had to admit that he'd been a good-looking guy. If you liked that sort of thing.

The final article was from a 2010 edition of *Hello!*. 'Celebrations and smiles for Hugo Channing on the occasion of his 80th birthday.' I recognised the location. The garden of the Palazzo Soranzo Cappello, up in Santa Croce. Henry James had set *The Aspern Papers* there, or so I'd been told. Tables had been placed in front of the classical loggia, its eight columns crowned with a triangular gable that, in turn, supported allegorical statues. Channing stood in the middle of the picture, his hands outstretched, whilst the great and the good of Venetian society gazed up at him from both sides. It resembled a grotesque reconstruction of The Last Supper. Hugo Channing, silver-haired, elegant and as handsome as he'd ever been; and no more troubled by humility than he had been in the seventies. Cosima, silver-haired now, sat at his right hand, her hands clasped together as she gazed at him in adoration, whilst Ludovica sat next to her, her arm protectively around her mother, and her head resting on her shoulder. She was smiling.

I searched for another photograph of Gabriele. Surely there had to be something more than the one of the sulky boy on the prow of his father's boat?

There was, indeed, just one more. It was not to be found

in the glossy pages of a celebrity magazine, but on the front of *Il Gazzettino, Il Corriere* and *La Stampa*. Gabriele, lying in the arms of his mother, her face bent over him as Hugo turned to the photographer with a look of white-hot fury. I read the headlines. 'Sad return home for Hugo and Cosima Channing' and 'Tragic death of little Gabriele'. There were further articles, in a similar vein, but I felt no inclination to read them.

Poor lad. Almost forty years in his grave, and the only two images of him that remained were of a sad, downcast little boy, out of place in the midst of his beautiful family; and a lifeless bundle in the arms of his mother.

Keys rattled in the door. Federica was home. It was time for a bracing spritz before my appointment with Ludovica.

Chapter 15

'You have everything?'

'I think so.'

'Umbrella?'

'No.'

'Take an umbrella. It's supposed to be wild tonight. Boots?'

'No.'

'There's *acqua alta* predicted.' As if on cue, the mournful wail of the high-water alarm sounded. Two plings. Not too high, but enough to flood the Street of the Assassins.

'I'll be back before then.'

'And what if you're not?'

'Hmmm. Yes, you're right.' I took my rubber boots from the cupboard under the sink and put them in a plastic bag. 'I wish I had something a bit smarter than this to carry them in.'

'It rains on the just and unjust alike, *caro*. And the same applies to *acqua alta*.'

I smiled. 'Okay. How do I look?'

'Presentable.' She put her head to one side and then adjusted my tie. 'I've not seen you dressed up like this for a long time.'

'Well, Ludovica seems a bit . . .'

'Scary?'

'I was going to say formal. But scary works as well. I thought I'd better try and look ambassadorial.'

'Good idea. Well, have a good time. Don't let her scare you.'

'I'll try.' I kissed her on the forehead. 'I'll see you later.'

She smiled, and kissed me back. 'Go on. On your way. You really don't want to be late.'

I made my way downstairs, where I could hear the front door rattling in the wind. Within thirty seconds, I knew, I would be looking less than ambassadorial.

Rain blew off the Giudecca canal and across the Zattere, soaking me despite the best efforts of my umbrella. In the half-light I saw a figure walking towards me, waterproofed up from head to toe and accompanied by nine excited, yappy little dogs, each on their own lead and each with their own day-glo protective jacket. The deacon of the church of the Gesuati. At least, I assumed it was him. I could think of few people in the city with as many dogs, and even fewer who would think of taking them for a walk on such a night as this. I prayed he wouldn't want to stop and chat, but he restricted himself to a brief wave and walked on.

Nico's bar was shut. In a few days' time, the weather would change and tourists would gather to sit outside on the terrace, looking over to the Giudecca in the cold winter sun, nursing mugs of hot chocolate in mittened hands or – for those hardier souls – eating ice creams through chattering teeth. Then Christmas would be upon us, following which the restaurants on this stretch would close for refurbishment in readiness for the onslaught of *Carnevale*.

Lightning flashed on the horizon, turning the smog from the oil refineries of Porto Marghera a burnt orange. The smokestacks, briefly illuminated against the horizon, looked strangely beautiful. Or, at least, as beautiful as they ever would. The *fondamenta* was wet with rain, but, even though the waves of the canal were lapping against the sides, the water level had yet to rise sufficiently to flood across the pavement. For another hour, perhaps ninety minutes at most, it would be possible to get by with shoes and not boots.

I walked across the bridge over the San Trovaso canal, feeling ever more exposed as the wind and rain lashed at me, then further along the *fondamenta* in the direction of San Basilio until I reached the address Federica had given me. A thin sliver of a Venetian Gothic palazzo, its walls the same burnt orange colour as the smog clouds over Porto Marghera. Six nameplates had once been affixed to the wall next to the door, but five of them had long since been removed, faint horseshoe-shaped imprints on the plaster being the only memory of previous occupants. Just one remained, a heavily tarnished brass plate with the name 'Loredan'. I rang the doorbell and waited.

The speakerphone crackled into life. '*Chi è?*' Who is it? When I first moved to Venice I had been surprised by the blunt, vaguely accusatory air to the question, especially as a thick Venetian accent could make it sound like a snarl. At first, I'd been far too embarrassed to do the same, settling for a terribly English 'Hello, can I help you?' But now, at least outside of surgery hours, I settled for a snarled '*Chi è?*' like everyone else.

'*Signora* Loredan, it's Nathan Sutherland.'

'Come up, please. The *piano nobile*.' But of course.

The rooms on the ground floor had been boarded up, long since abandoned to *acqua alta*, whilst a feebly illuminated stone staircase led up to the *piano nobile*. A heavy wooden door lay ahead of me, whilst to my right the staircase continued up into darkness.

The door opened, and Ludovica Loredan stood there, framed against the faint glow from within, a glass of wine in her hand.

'Mr Sutherland. Come in, please.'

The room was dimly lit, the only light coming from two heavy bronze candlesticks on the dining table, and a standard lamp in the corner. The lamp was of Murano glass with just a hint of green in it, which made the room look as if it had been lit by Mario Bava for a 1960s Italian *giallo*. An old man sat in a wheelchair at the end of the table, his head slumped to one side.

'Mr Channing. Good evening,' I said.

I saw his lips move in the half-light, but could not make out what – if anything – he had said. Ludovica looked at me with a touch of annoyance, and then went to her father. She adjusted the back of the wheelchair, and reclined it ever so slightly, before gently moving his head back to rest in a more comfortable position.

'I'm sorry about the lighting, Mr Sutherland. His eyesight is not good. That, together with . . . everything else . . . means he finds overhead lights disturbing. Even their reflection in a surface upsets him.' I looked around. Up until then I hadn't noticed the lack of mirrors. 'And so the curtains are drawn during the daytime, and the candles are lit at evening.'

My eye was drawn to the ceiling, which, despite the dim light, appeared to glow. I strained my eyes to make out the image. A bat-winged figure tumbling through clouds in a shaft of golden light, towards a fiery pit. An angelic figure in armour hovered in triumph above it, a blade flashing in one hand. The image, as far as I could see, was not frescoed but rather painted directly on to canvas, which had then been fixed to the ceiling.

I turned to look at Ludovica. There was a half-smile on her lips. *"From morn to noon he fell, from noon to dewy eve . . . and with the setting sun dropped from the zenith like a falling star".'*

'*Paradise Lost*', I said.

'You know it?' She sounded surprised.

'I studied it at university.' I craned my head back to look at the canvas again. 'But I'm afraid I can't identify the artist. Federica might know.'

'It's a copy. In the style of Francesco Fontebasso. From the nineteenth century, I believe. St Michael casting Lucifer out from Heaven. Slightly more apocalyptic than Fontebasso's original. His version has the three figures of the Trinity at the centre of the frame. No such comfort to be found in this one.'

'Marvellous work, nevertheless.'

'It was one of my father's favourite paintings. I remember when Gabriele was very little.' She smiled. 'I remember how it used to terrify him.'

'As much as I love *Paradise Lost* I'm not sure I'd care to have an image of it on the ceiling of my living room.'

'You are not my father. Or perhaps you have a smaller living room.' Her smile faded. 'I don't think he ever read *Paradise Lost* in his life. He just enjoyed what he'd read about it. He identified with Lucifer, of course.'

'Well, Milton was a very good devil's advocate.'

'The great anti-hero, raging against Heaven. The truth is, Father never had much to rage against. Everything always dropped into place for him.' She moved to the end of the table, and hunched down next to her father's wheelchair. He had shown no sign of awareness of our conversation, yet seemed to take comfort in her presence, and smiled a simple child's smile as he leaned his head against her shoulder. She kissed the top of his head, and then got to her feet.

'So, Mr Sutherland, we should talk.'

'Of course. Now, how can I help?'

'You must understand this: Father has no memory of Gabriele. He doesn't know that he ever had a son. He barely knows that he has a daughter.'

'And your mother?'

'Mother is well. She is old now, of course. But she is well.'

'And so?'

She placed her glass on the table. 'Both my parents are elderly now. Mother needs no further unhappiness in her life. Father – Father is in his second childhood.' She fixed her eyes on mine. 'Understand this, Mr Sutherland. I will let nothing – nothing – disturb their later years.'

'Of course. I understand completely. I—'

She waved her hand and interrupted me. 'With respect, you understand nothing. Can you imagine what it must be like to be their age, shut up in here,' she spread her hands wide, 'in this mausoleum? And then to have this dreadful thing from forty years ago dragged up?'

'I am sorry.' I said. 'I don't know if it helps at all, but the newspapers do seem to have been discreet.'

She smiled, again. Three times now, but there had never been a sense of happiness or good humour in them. 'Yes. They would have been.'

'I understand.'

'Good. Good.' The smile was turned off. 'You met with a journalist called Guy Flemyng at a bar off campo Santo Stefano yesterday.'

There seemed no point in denying it. 'I did.'

'He offered you money, of course?'

'He did.'

'How much?'

'No specific amount was mentioned.'

I was starting to find the machine-gun questioning difficult, and wondered – as Ludovica's eyes's remained fixed on mine – if I'd even be able to lie if I wanted to.

She paused. 'You declined. Of course.'

'Of course.'

'And so,' she lingered over the words to give them weight. 'I need to know what exactly you told him.'

I felt just a little bit affronted. '*Signora* Loredan, I told him exactly the same as I'm telling you now. Which is to say, I know absolutely nothing about this case and neither do I expect it to be resolved soon.'

She closed her eyes for a moment, and nodded, very slowly. 'Thank you, Mr Sutherland.' I couldn't be sure if she was showing genuine gratitude, or if I was being dismissed. 'Is that all?'

'No, I told him I could not possibly tell him anything more as it would be a grotesque abuse of my office.' I had no idea if my job could be described as an 'office', still less if it were possible for me to grotesquely abuse it, but it sounded like the sort of thing I thought she needed to hear.

'It would, of course. Thank you again.'

We sat in silence for a moment, listening to the rain patter against the windows. 'Might I ask a question?' She nodded. 'How did you know I met Mr Flemyng at a bar yesterday afternoon?'

She was unable to keep the anger out of her voice. 'Why, he telephoned me in order to let me know, of course.'

'I see.' I wondered why, and why the 'of course'. Then I thought back to the expression on Guy's face when he appeared to recognise someone outside *da Fiore*. 'Is there anything else I can help you with?'

'I think not. If you do manage to find anything of significance – and I imagine this is unlikely – it would be best if you were to contact me first. Mother is well, as I said, but she is old now. I want nothing to shock her. I do not want a repeat of the performance of two nights ago.' She closed her eyes momentarily and bowed her head as if to stress just quite how much pain this had caused her.

'Well, again I must apologise. I had no idea.'

'No, of course not.'

'There is just one thing that might be important. How exactly do you know Mr Flemyng? More to the point, what do you know about him?'

'Is that relevant?'

'Very.' She looked unconvinced. 'I'm not the only person in this city who he thinks might be able to help him. I don't imagine it will be long before he starts making enquiries of them.'

'Such as?'

'The Anglican priest. The police. Old friends and family.' I wondered if Ludovica would be calling in each and every one of them for a personal audience. 'He will be in touch with them, you understand, if he hasn't been already.'

She took a deep breath. 'And can you help me with this?'

'I can help with the priest. He's a friend of mine. And also the police, although I doubt they'd talk to him anyway.' I wasn't one hundred per cent sure of that. 'But I'll need to know exactly why they shouldn't.'

Again, she took a deep breath. 'What do you know of my family, Mr Sutherland?'

'Precious little, if truth be told.'

She looked more than a little affronted. 'How long have you been in Venice?'

'About a decade now.'

'Oh. I see. My father was quite a *charismatic* figure. You may have heard?'

'So I understand.'

'My mother was – still is – a very beautiful woman. We were, I suppose, a glamorous family in ourselves. And that brought a certain level of attention. From the press.'

She hesitated. I thought she wanted me to continue the conversation. 'And there were stories?' I suggested.

'There were. Unpleasant stories. The yellow press. The gutter press, if you prefer.'

It was my turn to pause, as I searched for the right words. 'May I ask what those stories were about?'

'The condition of my parents' marriage.'

'I see.' I had guessed as much.

'Nonsense, of course. Mother was very beautiful. Father was a handsome and successful man. They moved in fashionable circles. It was only natural that they would meet similarly beautiful and successful people.'

'I see,' I repeated. 'And Guy Flemyng is one of those "yellow press", would I be right?' She nodded, and I continued. 'And he contacted you?'

'A few years ago now. He has, or had, the intention of writing a book about us.'

I frowned, and hoped that she couldn't see my face clearly. Was there really a market for someone who, with the exception of a short feature in *Hello!* seven years ago, was surely long forgotten by the public? 'And so you told him . . . ?'

She cast her eyes upwards towards the ceiling, and the image of the fallen angel. 'I told him to go the devil.'

The old man mumbled, and shifted in his chair. Ludovica got up and moved over to him, settling down beside him and stroking his hair, speaking softly all the while. It was, perhaps, the first show of emotion I'd seen from her.

'Could I just ask . . . ?' I left the question hanging.

She looked at me as if knowing what it was going to be, but challenging me to ask it anyway. 'Yes?'

'How long has your father been ill like this?'

'Five years now. He suffered a massive stroke one evening. He was never the same again.'

'I'm sorry.'

'It's something that will come to us all. To ourselves, to those we love. One day.'

I became conscious of the fact that I had seen no one else around. 'It must be hard work for you?'

'It is.' That voice. Controlled, flat, neutral.

'But you have help, of course?'

She gently kissed the top of her father's head, and got to her feet. 'Why do you say, "of course", Mr Sutherland?'

'Well, I assumed in a place this size,' I stretched my arms wide, 'you would at least need *badanti*.'

'Carers? No. Mother and I can manage. He still recognises us. Just about. I will not have him given into the care of strangers. Not while I have any strength about me.'

'That's a fine thing for you to do,' I said. 'A kind thing.'

'It's nothing to do with being kind, Mr Sutherland.'

I shook my head. 'I don't believe you.'

Her eyes flashed, and for a moment I feared I'd angered her. But then she smiled. Really and properly, this time. 'It's just, well, "Daddy's little girl", you understand?'

I smiled back. 'I think so.'

Wind rattled the panes once again, and the candle flames flickered. She went to the central arched window and looked out, her body framed against the night sky. 'It's a foul evening. Thank you for coming out. May I offer you a brandy or a grappa before you leave?'

'That's also kind. A grappa would be lovely.'

She nodded. The warmth in her eyes had cooled now. 'One moment.' Hugo moaned and shifted in his chair again. 'Father needs his medicines. I will be just a few minutes.'

She left the room, leaving the two of us together.

I became aware of the chill in the air, and shivered. Granted, Ludovica looked as if she never felt the cold at all, but surely this couldn't be good for her father? As if on cue, the old man groaned again.

I got to my feet, unsure what to do. '*Signora* Loredan?'
I called, hesitantly, not wishing to disturb him further. The
words were lost in the space of the great room. I decided I
could risk being informal. 'Ludovica,' I called, louder this
time.

There was no answer, and still Hugo continued to shift
and moan.

To hell with it. I couldn't just leave him there in distress.
I stood up, my chair scraping on the *terrazzo* floor, and went
over to him. His eyes looked unblinkingly into mine, as I
crouched next to him.

His lips moved, and I made out the word 'Ludovica'.

'Ludovica's not here, Mr Channing. My name's Nathan
Sutherland. Maybe I can help?'

His eyes sharpened. 'I don't know you.'

'We don't know each other. My name's Nathan Sutherland.
I'm the Honorary Consul in Venice. Can I help?'

He moved his head slowly from side to side. 'No.'

'That's fine. Shall I just stay with you until Ludovica comes
back?'

'No. You must be someone else. Victor is the consul. We're
meeting tonight at the Circle.'

I was about to contradict him, then thought better of it.
'That's nice, Hugo.'

He grimaced. 'Mr Channing to you.'

I tried not to smile. 'I do apologise, Mr Channing.
Ludovica will be here soon.'

'She will. She always is. Always been Daddy's little girl.'
He took my arm, and patted my hand. 'Do you have children, Victor?'

Again, I thought it better not to correct him. 'I don't, I'm afraid.'

'A shame.' He leaned his head forward, the better to see me. 'You should do. There's still time.'

I laughed and patted his hand with my own. His skin was cold. Surely he needed to be wrapped up better than this? 'Maybe there is, Mr Channing.'

'Why do you call me Mr Channing? We've been friends for years. You must call me Hugo.'

'All right then, Hugo it is.'

'You should have children. I'm lucky with Ludovica. But,' he took his hand from mine, craned his head further forward and rubbed his forehead. 'I should have had a son.' He leaned his head back again, and closed his eyes. 'Would be good to have a son,' he whispered.

'Gabriele?' I said, and instantly wished I hadn't.

He shook his head, violently this time. 'Not Gabriele. Not him.' He started to shake.

Oh shit. You bloody fool, Nathan.

'Hugo. Mr Channing. I'm sorry. I didn't mean to upset you.'

'Gabriele!' He dragged himself as upright as he could manage with his palsied limbs. Then he reached out and grabbed my shoulder with surprising force. 'Victor, he shouldn't be here at the Circle.' I could feel the cold of his hand through my jacket as his fingers dug into me. 'He should be on the island. Cold on the island.'

I heard footsteps running along the corridor. Channing pulled me closer and closer to him. 'On the Isle of the Dead. Not here,' he keened. 'Not here!'

The footsteps stopped. I turned my head to see Ludovica in the doorway. She said nothing, but I could tell from her expression that had there been coals available, I would have been hauled over them slowly and painfully.

Channing was still trying to pull me closer to him as I endeavoured, as gently as I possibly could, to pry his fingers from my jacket. Ludovica knelt down beside me, and moved my hand away, her fingers icy cold against my own. She rubbed Channing's hands, as if attempting to get some warmth into them and then, slowly, the old man released his grip and slumped back in his chair.

I got to my feet and breathed deeply. 'I'm sorry,' I said. 'He seemed distressed, I thought perhaps I could help.'

She waved my apologies away. 'I understand. He can be unpredictable, with strangers. He needs me, or mother.'

'I do apologise.'

'There's no need to keep saying that. He will be fine now.' She got to her feet, placed the old man's hands in his lap, and pulled his blanket around him. 'There you are, Father. All safe now.'

'I notice you speak to him in English,' I said.

'His memory has gone. He's forgotten his Italian.'

I shook my head. 'That must be dreadful.'

'Why? He has nobody to speak it to. Sometimes I believe he thinks he's back in England.'

'I see.' I paused. 'Although just now he was talking about Victor – my predecessor as consul here. And he mentioned something called the "Circle".'

Her eyes narrowed. 'Did he? What did you say to him?'

'I just said I was the consul in Venice.'

She sighed in exasperation. 'That will be it. You've confused him.' I opened my mouth. 'No, don't apologise again. The harm is done but it will pass.'

'I think it brought back some memories. You said he didn't remember having a son. But he mentioned Gabriele.'

She shook her head. 'That's impossible. You must be mistaken.'

The old man's lips moved. 'Not here. Not in the Circle.' Ludovica looked down at him in alarm. 'Isle of the Dead.'

'Hush, darling. It's okay. I'm here now.' She stroked the thinning hairs on his head. 'I'm here now.' Then she turned to me. 'He's disturbed now. He needs his medicines, and then I'll put him to bed.' She looked at the clock on the wall. 'I think perhaps it's too late for that grappa.'

I could only agree. We said our goodbyes, and I made my way outside, into the night.

Chapter 16

The storm was yet to pass and the rain was still lashing down, so much so that I considered getting a boat home. I decided against it. It was, perhaps, a ten-minute walk. On other evenings a *vaporetto* journey might have been a pleasure, but it was no night for sitting outside and watching the city go by.

Water was spilling over the edge of the *fondamenta* but the areas closer to the buildings were just about dry and I decided I could make it home in my shoes and save the hassle of changing into boots. I supposed I could have done that at Ludovica's but that opportunity had well and truly passed.

I had the Accademia Bridge entirely to myself and did my best to shield myself from the horizontal rain. The view of the church of the *Salute* lit up by lightning would doubtless have been spectacular, but I was in no mood to dally.

I walked down into a deserted Campo San Vidal where Vivaldi's *Four Seasons* sounded forth from the church, as it did for much of the year. Then I scurried through Campo Santo Stefano, ignoring the welcoming, warming lights from the bars and restaurants. Ed would be putting chairs on tables at the Brazilians, but I might be able to fit in a drink before he closed up.

It had been an unusual evening and not in a good way. Perhaps I deserved a drink and a cigarette? Just the one. I ran my free hand through my hair, soaked through now despite the umbrella. Was I really going to stand outside in the pouring rain, smoking in the half-shelter of my own personal smoking gazebo?

Yes. Yes, I was.

Then I realised that Dario still had my *tessera sanitaria* and felt grateful for it.

I splashed my way through Campo Sant'Angelo and to the beginning of Calle de la Mandola. Then I stopped. The Street of the Assassins might still be more or less dry. Calle de la Mandola, however, was under a couple of feet of water.

Someone – man or woman, it was impossible to tell under the layers of waterproofs – was making their way in the opposite direction, each step carefully measured so as to disturb the water, lapping perhaps a centimetre below the level of their boots, as little as possible.

It was just ten metres to the Street of the Assassins. It might as well have been ten kilometres. I cursed, and took my rubber boots from my plastic bag, then stood on one leg to remove my shoe whilst I attempted to keep the umbrella steady, hopping all the while in order to maintain balance. Then I repeated the procedure with the other shoe. The well-wrapped pedestrian, having finally reached the shallow end of the *calle*, strode out with more confidence, pausing only to give me a pitying look.

Ed, of course, had closed the bar by the time I arrived.

'*Ciao, caro*, have you had a nice evening?'

I stood in the doorway, dripping steadily on to the floor, and said nothing.

'Oh dear, not so good?'

'I've had better.'

'She wasn't too scary, was she?'

'Scary? It was like being asked out for dinner by Barbara Steele.'

She shook her head. 'You're going to have to explain the reference.'

'Barbara Steele. British actress in 1960s Italian horrors.' She shook her head, again. 'Worked with Mario Bava, amongst others. You must know this? This is your heritage.'

'*Mamma* wouldn't let me watch those sorts of films. Do I need to know more?'

'Very beautiful in a terrifying way. Cat-like eyes, razor-sharp cheekbones. Made a film called *An Angel for Satan*. Ludovica reminds me of her. They even look alike.'

'Oh dear. That bad?'

'That bad? I spent an hour in semi-darkness talking about empty graves with a woman who Dario Argento would refuse to cast on the grounds of being too scary. Oh, and get this, in a room with a bloody great painting of Satan fixed to the ceiling.'

'I thought you liked that sort of stuff?'

'In the cinema, yes. Not in real life.'

'Oh well. Come and sit down. Actually, no. Go and dry off a bit first. Actually, no.' She held out an empty wine glass to me. 'Go and top me up first. Then go and dry off. And then come and sit down.'

'Is this my evening for being told off by scary women?'

'Only if you want it to be.' She shook the glass at me. 'Come on. Hurry up. And then tell me all about it.'

I kissed the back of her hand as I took the glass from her. She gave a start. 'My God, you're freezing.'

'It's cold outside. Not to mention wet.' I went through to the kitchen and opened the fridge. 'Prosecco or white?' I called out.

'Prosecco. It's a school night.'

I poured her a glass, then went through to the bathroom to towel myself dry as best I could. Then I fixed myself a glass of red, thinking I'd appreciate its warming properties, and went to sit down. Gramsci jumped into my lap, realised how cold I was, then leapt away and fixed me with a filthy look.

'Come on then,' said Fede, 'tell me all about your Angel for Satan.'

'So, what do you think?' I said.

She looked at my glass. 'I think you need another drink.'

'Good idea. But apart from that?'

'Apart from that . . .' She paused. 'Apart from that I think that if she'd put the overhead lights on and they had different tastes in ceiling furnishings, you wouldn't have thought anything of it.'

'It's not just that. There was that thing the old man said about Gabriele and the Isle of the Dead. And something called the Circle.'

'The Isle of the Dead is San Michele. Obviously. Which is where Gabriele is supposed to be. He's a confused old man. Someone has let it slip that the grave has been disturbed and his mind is imagining all sorts of terrible things.'

'Did you ever meet him?'

'Once or twice.'

'What did you think?'

'Creepy. But not in the sense that you mean. I mean creepy around women. A little bit over-friendly, shall we say? But still, I wouldn't have wished anything like this on him.'

'Hmm. What's this "Circle" then?'

She shrugged. 'Who knows? His mind's gone. It could mean anything. Why do you think it's important?'

'Circles are always bad. Circles and Rings. They're always bad.'

She rolled her eyes. 'Okay. Maybe you don't need another drink.'

'Look. There's an empty grave on San Michele. It belongs to a member of a family that can best be described as a little odd. And then there's a reference to a "Circle".'

'And so . . .'

'And so is it just possible that—,' I paused and drained the last dregs of my wine, '—there's something "witchy" going on?'

'"Witchy?"' She wrinkled her nose. It reminded me of Elizabeth Montgomery, but I thought it better not to mention that.

'Occult. Satanic. Am I crazy?'

'Crazy? You've gone beyond crazy and out the other side.'

'There's more. Channing thought I was Victor. He kept saying that Victor was with him at this "Circle".'

She closed her eyes. 'Okay. Let's think a bit. Victor was one of your best friends in Venice, wasn't he?'

'He was.'

'And then you found out that – on one occasion – he took

some money in order to look after stolen goods. When his wife was ill and he desperately needed the cash.'

'Yes.'

'And you've only just made it up with him?'

'Again, yes.'

'I've never met him. What sort of man is he?'

'Gentle, kind. Well-spoken. Stereotypical English gentleman abroad.'

'Right. Not the sort of person to be involved in grave robbery and diabolical cults then?'

'No, that's crazy . . .' I let the words tail off.

'Exactly. It's crazy. You've just been overcome by all the *messa in scena*, that's all. A confused old man talking nonsense in an old dark house on a stormy night.'

I ran my hands through my damp hair. 'You're probably right.'

'Of course I am. Anyway, why not just ring Victor and ask him about this "Circle" thing?'

'I should do. I'm just wondering how best to phrase it.'

'"Victor, don't take this the wrong way but were you in fact the leader of a coven when you were in Venice?"'

I smiled. 'Maybe not.'

'Call him though. Just to get things clear.'

'I will.'

'Good.' She yawned. 'And with that, *caro*, I'm going to bed.'

Gramsci pricked up his ears at the word 'bed', which, for him, had become synonymous with 'late-night feed'.

'I'll be right along. I'd better look after *him* first.' I nodded towards Gramsci.

Fede laughed. 'I love that. The way you won't speak his name when you don't want him to know you're talking about him. It makes him sound like "He Who Must Not Be Named" or something in one of your terrible films.'

I glared at her. 'First of all, they are not "terrible". Secondly, I don't think he's a particularly Satanic cat.'

She looked unconvinced. 'Are you sure?'

Gramsci looked from me to Fede and back again, his amber eyes narrowed to slits.

'No. Not Satanic. But I think he'd make a very good witch's familiar. Wouldn't you, Grams?'

He gave a long, rumbling grumble that might, just, have passed for a purr. I scratched him behind the ears and he snatched at my fingers.

Fede raised her eyebrows. 'You might be right, *tesoro*.'

Chapter 17

Federica was right. Things did look different in the morning. The *acqua alta* had receded and the streets were drying, aided by the sun that had decided to put in a half-arsed appearance. Thoughts of Satanic cults and circles seemed more than a little silly.

There wasn't much more that I could do. If Father Rayner was unable to find anything more in what passed for the archives of St George's, and Victor had nothing in his records, then I would just let it drop. I would go back to the Ambassador and tell him that there was honestly nothing more to be done, and he could get back to being shouted at by irate Britons.

Besides, I had more important things to do. For this was the day in which Dario Costa returned to Venice.

Eduardo, I knew, would already be up and starting the laborious process of getting the Magical Brazilians fit for opening again; rinsing the floors with fresh water, sweeping it out and putting furniture back in place. Like so many other businesses in Venice, this was something he'd become used to over the years. It never made the job any lovelier or less frustrating though. He could do without being bothered, even by his best customers. With that in mind, I made a pot of coffee and we called it breakfast.

'You could come along with me, you know?'

She shook her head. 'No thanks. Besides, I don't think Dario wants me there.'

'That's not true.'

'Yes, it is. He wants you all to himself. Look, the two of you are driving a van from Mestre to Tronchetto, right?' I nodded. 'There's no need for two of you to be there at all. He just wants his pal to be with him. You're not going to have to switch drivers for safety reasons, are you?'

'Probably not.' I smiled. 'I know what you mean though. It's kind of a big thing for him. Returning home after all these years.'

'It's not like Marco Polo spending twenty-four years in China. He's been in Mestre.'

'Maybe that's more foreign in some ways. Anyway, the idea is that I just go and help with the last of the packing, whatever that may be. Then Vally and Emily head off to stay with *Nonno* and *Nonna* for a couple of days whilst Dario gets the new place into shape. So the two of us are going in the van to Tronchetto to help the delivery guys unload everything on to a boat.'

Fede laughed. 'They're not going to let you do that. You've got no insurance, neither of you really know what you're doing and there's every chance of backs being put out or furniture ending up in the lagoon.'

'Do you think so?' I said, pretending to be hurt but secretly pleased at the idea that no proper physical activity was likely to be involved.

'I know so. As I said, he just wants his pal to be there, that's all.' She finished her coffee and got to her feet. 'And that's all right.' She slipped her arms around my neck and hugged me. 'It's quite sweet really. And now I've got to go.'

I gave her a peck on the cheek. 'Okay. I'll see you later. Not too late, I hope?'

'Hope not. What's for dinner?'

'Haven't decided yet. No idea what's in the fridge. I'll think of something.'

'Fabulous, though?'

'Is it ever anything else?' I pretended to huff.

She smiled. 'Never. Well, rarely. In the meantime, if I'm wrong and they do allow you to manhandle heavy furniture, you say no, understood?'

I grinned. 'Understood.'

'Bye-bye, diabolical cat,' I said, and made my way downstairs. I could see Ed inside the Brazilians, taking chairs off tables, and I tapped on the glass. He gave me a weary nod. I mouthed the words 'See you later' and he did his best to smile. Poor guy. If you never had to live or work on the ground floor, it was easy to forget how much hard work *acqua alta* could be.

I walked down to Rialto, and took a *vaporetto* up the Grand Canal. The boat was quiet at this time of day, busy with neither tourists nor commuter traffic. I sat outside for the first five minutes, marking myself out as a non-Venetian, and then moved inside when the cold started to reach my bones.

I got off at Piazzale Roma and checked my watch. Five minutes until the next bus. Ten minutes for a tram. Chances of getting a seat, approaching zero in both cases. Might as well take the bus, then. Venetians would consider five minutes sufficient to buy and drink a coffee, and still get to precisely the right place at the stop for the doors to open directly in front of them, allowing them the best possible chance of grabbing a seat on a service that never seemed anything other than crammed. I decided not to risk it, and restricted myself to buying a copy of *Il Gazzettino* from a news-stand. It might not have been my favourite newspaper but it had an advantage over *La Repubblica* in that its tabloid format made it feasible to read on crowded public transport.

I made my way to the stop and waited, casting my eyes left and right to see who was likely to be competing for position. I briefly checked the headlines in the *Gazzettino*, which, as expected, were about the likely cost to the city of the recent flooding.

I looked up to see the bus pulling in, rolled up my newspaper and stuck it inside my coat pocket. The doors hissed open and my fellow competitors waited as the passengers flooded out, shopping trolleys and wheelie bags snarling up in each other; shouting in frustration as some tried to force their way on whilst others were still getting off.

I looked to my left. Too late. The passengers alighting at that end must have been unusually nimble as the door had cleared before ours and all seats in that section were now taken. Then I looked to the right, and grinned. Two tourists at the front were trying to manhandle a giant suitcase out of the door, completely blocking it for those trying to get on. People were already running towards my position in the middle, but too late. I slid into my seat, and took out my newspaper. The luxury of sitting down.

And then I saw her. Ludovica Loredan, standing near the front, resplendent in grey fur coat and dark glasses. A young man, his nose buried in his mobile phone, studiedly ignored her until a passenger in the seat opposite gave him a gentle poke and pointed in her direction. He looked around in the hope of spotting someone younger and then, forcing a thin smile on to his face, got to his feet and offered her his place. She gave the briefest of nods, perhaps irritated at having been deemed old enough to be worthy of a seat, and sat down, her face turned to the window as if not wishing to be seen. As if, indeed, not wishing to be there at all.

Ludovica Loredan. On a bus to Mestre.

I tried to concentrate on my newspaper, and not on the back of her head. Why on earth should she be going to Mestre? I shook my head. Why shouldn't she be? There were any number of possible reasons. She could have friends or family on *terraferma*. Perhaps she visited them every week. Yet there was something so incongruous, so downright out-of-place about one of the *grandi signore* of Venetian society taking public transport – a bus, no less – to Mestre, that didn't sit right with me.

Her face was turned away from me, but I held my newspaper in front of my face nevertheless, trusting in its powers of conferring invisibility. Try as I might, however, my eyes kept sliding off the words.

We made our way over the Ponte della Libertà. I decided it might be safe to put the paper down, folded it away, and turned to look out of the window. For all I knew she was on her way to the posh shops. Were there posh shops in Mestre? Who knew? And wouldn't she have someone to go there on her behalf? Again, who knew?

Two young women were muttering *sotto voce* in the seats opposite me. I couldn't identify the language, but recognised them as two of the professional 'baroque' beggars who usually worked the area around Piazzale Roma. Why were they travelling back at this hour? One of them took out a smartphone and texted away. The other reached into her bag and took a swig from a half-empty bottle of vodka. The man sitting on my right looked at them with disgust, and swore under his breath.

The weather was chilly, but dry. Good. I didn't like the idea of Dario's gear being unloaded and floated across the lagoon in the pouring rain. We left the bridge and the lagoon behind, as we stopped by the great shipyard of Fincantieri where yet another monster cruise ship was taking shape, prior to hauling its enormous bulk down through the Giudecca canal and the fragile *bacino* of San Marco. We stopped, and the doors hissed open, allowing a dozen workers to cram themselves on board as best they could, every passenger shifting around to make themselves as comfortable as possible for the short remainder of the journey into central Mestre.

We pulled up outside the railway station, an area to be avoided after dark but considered safe enough during the day. The two beggars stood up and made their way to the door, smelling of cigarettes and cheap booze. My neighbour cursed again, this time loud enough for them to hear. They were met by a smartly dressed man, who ushered them into the back seat of an Alfa Romeo, patting one of them on the shoulder as he did so.

I shook my head. I didn't know exactly what was happening, but was sure that none of it was good. I thought of possible reasons as to why they'd chosen to start drinking spirits before midday, and felt guilty.

The bus continued past the Venice Plaza hotel, notable for neither being in a plaza nor in Venice, then past the mixture of grim-looking bars and shops that constituted Via Piave before stopping and disgorging grateful travellers onto the pavement. I looked up. Ludovica, shaking her head and looking slightly embarrassed, had made her way to the exit where a stranger, his hand on her elbow, was helping her to get off.

Alarm bells started ringing. I could imagine Ludovica having need to visit Mestre. I could not imagine her needing to go to Via Piave, a part of the city occasionally referred to as the *far west*. It was not a place to linger after dark, being a popular hang-out for drug dealers, prostitutes, and petty and – occasionally – violent criminals. Even in daylight, Ludovica – a middle-aged woman in her fur coat and designer glasses – would be seen as an easy target for a pickpocket or bag snatcher.

Had she got off at the wrong stop? She smiled and mouthed the word *grazie* to the young man helping her down. My suspicions hardened. I fought my way through the crowd to the nearest door, and jumped off, intending to make my way down to her exit, just to check that he hadn't dipped his hand into her bag under the guise of helping her.

I was too late. The doors had swung shut before I could reach her. I stared through the glass into the face of the young man. He was smiling and chatting with his friends. He didn't look like a thief. Then again, what were thieves supposed to look like? He caught me staring at him, but then the bus moved off and he disappeared from view. I felt embarrassed.

And given that I was now standing in Via Piave with perhaps twenty minutes until the next bus, I also felt pretty stupid.

Ludovica gave no sign of having seen me and looked around as if unsure of where she was. Then she walked off in the opposite direction and paused at the next turning. She looked up at the street name, and turned right.

She'd made a mistake, that seemed obvious. I could catch her up and offer to wait with her for the next bus, or at least set her on the right path towards the Mestre Centro terminus. I stepped it out, not wishing to lose sight of her, and followed her around the corner. I was wondering whether it would startle her less to jog the last few yards between us and tap her on the shoulder or simply to call out her name, when she stopped and rummaged in her handbag. She took out a scrap of paper, or possibly a business card, and looked up at the nearest building, a 1960s high-rise. It seemed a world away, in both space and time, from her palazzo on the Zattere.

She put the card back in her handbag, nodded as if to assure herself that all was well, and pressed a button on the speakerphone. There was a moment's pause, then the door clicked open and she stepped through.

My phone buzzed. Dario, wondering where I'd got to. I texted him back, *Running late, just be a few minutes.* I looked around. A couple of kids were smoking on the street corner, and kicking a football half-heartedly between them, but otherwise the street was quiet.

This had all been a bit silly. So what if Ludovica knew someone in one of the rougher parts of Mestre? A distant relative, an old schoolfriend; it could be anybody. I'd wasted my time. On the other hand, I told myself, I'd have felt guilty if she really had been lost and got into trouble. I checked my watch again. There'd be another bus from Via Piave in ten minutes. I'd be a bit late but then, chances were, so would the removal van. No real harm done. Stop being so British, Nathan.

And yet, and yet . . . I looked over to the high-rise, and walked over to the main entrance, running my fingers down the list of names on the entry phone. Nothing of any interest, except for one. *Lucarelli. Investigazioni Private.* I hadn't been near enough to see which one she'd pressed. No reason at all to think it should be this one. No reason at all.

I turned on my heels, and made my way back to Via Piave.

Chapter 18

'You took your time, *vecio*,' said Dario.

'Sorry. I got off at Via Piave by mistake.' He raised his eyebrows. 'I know. Bit of a long story.'

He looked puzzled, and then smiled, the corners of his eyes crinkling as they always did. 'No worries. Grab a seat.' We sat down on two packing cases in his almost-bare living room.

A young man in a blue boiler suit came in and looked around. Dario stood up again. 'You can take this one, I guess,' he said. Then he looked over at me. 'And that one.' I rolled my eyes, and got to my feet. The lad stacked the two cases on top of each other and – craning his head over the top in order to see – wobbled towards the door.

'Can I help?' I said.

He shuffled round in order to face me, and narrowed his eyes as if he was trying to take a better look. '*Nossignore*,' he said, before turning around and teetering off again.

Dario grinned at me.

'I have to say, I'm feeling a bit useless,' I said.

'*Be'*, don't worry about it. We're nearly done.'

'I mean, I'm beginning to wonder why I'm here at all.'

He grabbed me by the shoulders and shook me, a little more than I'd have liked. 'Because we've got the *proper* work to do, *vecio.*'

I looked around the almost-bare flat and shook my head. 'Nope. Still not getting it.'

'These guys – the young, fit guys—'

'Not helping!'

'Sorry. The professional guys take all the heavy things. But we – we take the important stuff. We take the treasure.' He got to his feet, opened a cupboard set into the wall, and took out a large cardboard box. It must have been heavy, even for him, as he looked around to put it on a table that wasn't there, before lowering it to the floor with a grunt. He opened the top. 'Take a look at these.'

He removed a sheet of tissue paper, and drew out a vinyl record. 'Emerson, Lake and Palmer. *Pictures at an Exhibition.* Keith Emerson signed it for me, look.'

'Wow!'

'Trieste, it was. 1988, I think. I hung around after the show. Nice guy.'

He reached into the box again. 'Goblin, soundtrack to *Profondo Rosso*. Signed by Claudio Simonetti. Never met the rest of the band, though. Shame. And here we've got Genesis, *Lamb lies down on Broadway*. Signed by Gabriel. Mind you, I got this one on eBay so maybe it doesn't count?'

'Oh, I think it does,' I said.

He ran his finger along the tops of the other sleeves. '*Le Orme*. Finest prog band ever to come out of Marghera.' He paused. 'Okay, maybe the only prog band ever to come out of

Marghera. But that doesn't matter. The complete works, all signed by Aldo Tagliapietra himself.'

I whistled. 'It must have taken him a while.'

'Friend of mine was painting his house, so he took me along there one day. Nice—'

'—guy?' I finished.

'He is.'

We sat there and stared at the albums in reverential silence for a few moments, until Valentina entered, Emily in her arms. She rolled her eyes when she saw what we were doing, but smiled at the same time. 'I see Dario's showing you his treasure, then?'

I got to my feet and gave her a hug and a kiss. 'He is. I'm very jealous.' Then a thought struck me. 'Oh, I think I understand now. This is why I'm here, isn't it?'

'You've got it. The removal boys are taking everything heavy. I'm taking the precious one here.' She kissed the top of Emily's head. 'And you and Dario take everything that he doesn't want anyone else to carry.'

'That's the shape of it, *vecio*. This we have to do ourselves. I don't trust anybody else.'

'Wow. I've got to say I feel incredibly honoured. So, what, do we just hop on the next bus with them?'

He shook his head. 'Too risky. What if we can't get a seat? I don't want to hold a fragile box of vinyl all the way to Venice.'

Vally coughed. 'Although, of course, it's perfectly all right for me and Emily to go by bus.'

'That's different, *cara mia*. You've got a little girl in your arms. People will give you a seat. Nobody's going to give their seat up for two middle-aged guys with a box of records. So we go to Tronchetto, and get on the boat with the delivery guys. Besides,' his eyes twinkled, 'it's kind of a cool way to arrive.'

Vally sighed, but smiled again as she bent to ruffle his hair. 'You do what you have to do. Just make sure everything is ready by the time we get back from *Nonno* and *Nonna*.' She kissed him on the cheek and turned to me. 'Just make sure he arrives in one piece, Nathan. And don't keep him out too late, he's got work to do.' I opened my mouth to protest, but she smiled. 'Joking. Now say goodbye to *Papà* and Nathan, Emily.'

Emily gave us both a sleepy wave. Dario waved them both out through the door, and then moved to the window so that he could wave once more when they reached the street. I thought it unlikely that Emily would choose that precise moment to look up, but didn't want to spoil the moment for him.

He turned away from the window, still smiling. Then his expression changed, and he looked serious. 'Okay, we're just about ready. There's just one more thing.'

He went back to the cupboard, and took out a black briefcase. He set it on the floor, sat down next to it and clicked it open. 'Take a look at this, Nat.'

I looked inside. A simple white folded paper tablecloth with three signatures.

Richard Wright.

Nick Mason.

David Gilmour.

The Pink Floyd tablecloth, signed outside Nico's over twenty years previously.

'Wow,' I breathed. I stretched my hand out, ever so gently. 'Could I . . . ?'

'Sure. But just be careful, okay?'

I trailed my fingertips gently, ever so gently, over the surface of the paper and closed my eyes, trying to imagine myself there. Hot sun on the *fondamenta* of the Zattere. Ice cubes chinking in spritz glasses. The chatter of excited tourists and the smell of petrol from Dario's motorcycle. Gilmour, Mason and Wright.

'It's beautiful,' I said.

'I don't take it out much. Not these days. Kind of worried about something happening to it. So it has to be a special occasion. Like today.'

'You make it sound like the Shroud of Turin.'

'Yes, but that's a fake. This is real.'

I withdrew my hand. 'Thanks, Dario.'

'No problem. I wanted you to see it.' He clicked the briefcase shut, and got to his feet. 'I think we're done here.' He put his hands on his hips, and breathed deeply. 'Okay, goodbye old flat. You were a good home to us.' He rubbed his eyes. 'Kind of dusty in here.' He patted the top of the box. 'I'll take these, you take the briefcase.'

'You what? Are you sure?'

'Absolutely. Firstly, this box is too heavy for you.' I bristled, but thought he was probably right. 'Secondly, if anything happens to the tablecloth, I don't want it to be my fault. I'll need someone to blame.' He was smiling, but only just.

'Wow. Thanks, Dario. I'm honoured.'

'I need someone I can trust for this. And, of course, I'll break your balls if anything happens to it.' There might still have been the ghost of a smile on his lips, but I couldn't be sure.

'Do you want me to, I don't know, chain it to my wrist or something?'

He looked concerned for a moment, then shook his head. 'I think we're okay. We've only got to get to the van. Once we're at Tronchetto we should be safe enough.' He hauled the box on to his shoulder, grunting with the effort.

I picked up the briefcase, feeling its precious weight in my hand, and nodded.

'Let's go to work.'

I'd always found Tronchetto just a little bit strange. Piazzale Roma – unlovely as it was – at least felt like the beginning or the end of a journey, being the point in the *centro storico* that was directly linked to the mainland via the Ponte della Libertà. Tronchetto, by contrast, felt like the city's alternative car park. A flat, featureless slab of identikit, anonymous buildings; its only features of note were Tronchetto Mercato, the wholesale fish and vegetable markets for the restaurant trade, and the 'People Mover', a monorail that carried people to the mainland along a track that resembled the spine of a dinosaur, emerging from a terminus that resembled an attempt to construct a 1930s science-fiction ray-gun in glass and steel. We waited as the removal men transferred Dario and Vally's worldly possessions from the back of the van on to the deck of a barge.

I stood and watched them load the boat – younger, fitter men – and felt awkward. Dario, by contrast, seemed lost in the moment. It might have been the unloveliest, grimmest part of Venice, but he didn't care. After many years away, Dario Costa was coming home.

I thought back to the events of the morning. Dario, I thought, could give me as good an answer as any.

'How long were you in Mestre?' I asked.

'As long as we've known each other, *vecio*. More than ten years now.'

'Okay. Tell me – this is going to sound a bit mad, I know – do you know any private investigators there?'

He looked puzzled for a moment, and then his face broke into a broad smile. 'Why? Do you need one?'

'No. I just need to know a bit more about them. How they work, that sort of thing.'

'Well, I could put you in touch with a friend of mine—'

'Lucarelli?' I interrupted.

He shook his head. 'No. Let me finish. Pal of mine, guy called Franco. Old army friend. He went into security after he left the forces, and then he became a private detective. He could tell you anything you need to know. So who's this Lucarelli guy?'

'It sounds silly, Dario. But on the way here I saw a woman I know – and this is a big, society woman – ringing the bell of a private investigator in Mestre. And I'm just wondering why.'

'Okay. That's kind of strange. Are you sure?'

'That's the thing. Not one hundred per cent. It's just that she was on the bus with me. It seemed strange, you know, her being on the bus to Mestre.'

'What's her name?'

'Ludovica Loredan. The sister of the young lad we were talking about the other day.'

'Uh-huh. I know who you mean. No reason why she shouldn't be in Mestre though.'

'I know. But in Via Piave?'

'Hmm. That's a little weird, I'll admit. So where does the private investigator come in?'

'I'm not sure. It's just that she went into an apartment block. In Via Piave, as I said. And one of the names listed on the intercom was a private investigator. A guy called Lucarelli.'

'And that was the one she rang?'

'No idea.' He shook his head, and chuckled. 'Am I making too much of this?'

He continued to laugh. 'Way too much. Come on, I think we're ready.' The three young men on the boat were looking up at us, and one of them checked his watch just a little too obviously. Dario jumped down, and I passed him the box of vinyl, followed by the briefcase, which he placed on top of a pile of packing cases.

I pulled my coat around me, shivering in the cold air, and sat down next to him, our backs resting against the boxes. We pulled away from the jetty, and out into the canal. I sat there, breathing in petrol and watched the sun shining over the refineries of Marghera.

'I've never asked you how we're going to get there?'

'It's quite easy really. We go under the People Mover. Then under the road bridge. And then we're in the Grand Canal.'

'Cool. Arriving in style.'

'You bet we are. Then we take one of the canals down through Santa Croce. There's a restaurant along there, *Il Refolo*, you know it?' I shook my head. 'I'm told it's good. We'll have to check it out. Anyway, that's where the guys are going to moor. The flat's round the back of the Co-op in the campo, so not too far for them to carry stuff.'

'You're on the top floor though, right?' He nodded. 'Would it be fair to assume there's no lift?'

He laughed. 'Not much chance of that in Venice.'

'Wow. These guys are really going to be earning their money.'

'Tell me about it.' He looked serious for a moment. 'This is costing us a packet. Still, it's got to be done.'

'*Signori.*' It was one of the removal guys who spoke. 'We're going under the bridge now. Heads down, okay?'

We ducked down as the barge slid under one of the shallow arches of the *Ponte della Libertà*, and then we were out the other side and passing by the *Questura*. I checked my watch. Vanni, I thought, would still be hard at work. I looked ahead to the *Ponte della Costituzione,* and shook my head when I saw the small red podule still fixed to its side. The mayor had been promising to remove the useless disability lift for years now, but nobody was holding their breath as to when it might happen. Then we passed underneath Calatrava's unloved bridge and into the Grand Canal proper.

Dario looked up at the sky. Grey and cloudy still, but as yet no sign of rain. 'I think we're going to get away with it,' he said.

'Fingers crossed. It's hellish cold but it could have been a lot worse.' I buried my hands in my coat pockets, and felt my fingers brush against something cold and metallic. I smiled. 'I'd better give this to you now before I forget,' I said. 'It's a moving-in present.'

I held it out to him. A horseshoe-shaped name plate with 'Costa–Visentin' engraved on it.

He took it from me. 'Thanks, man. That's really kind.' Then his expression changed.

'Something wrong?' I said.

'It's just – well, it's Vally's surname. It's not Visentin. It's Visintin. With two "i"s. That's the way they spell it up in Trieste.'

'Oh hell.'

'It must have been the guy in the shop just making a mistake. Force of habit, probably.' It had not been the guy in the shop. I knew it. Dario knew it. But he was giving me a way out, bless him. How had I never noticed before?

'I'll take it back. Get it changed.'

'Are you sure? Maybe he can just change the "e"?'

It seemed unlikely that the man in the key-cutting shop would be able to change an engraved 'e' into an 'i', but it was worth a go. I took the plate back from Dario, and dropped it into my pocket. I leaned back again as we turned off into the side canal that would lead us down to Campo San Giacomo dell'Orio.

'*Signori* . . . Mind your heads.' I looked over my shoulder. We were passing under a couple of low-hanging trees, their branches scraping along the tops of the packing cases. We crouched down a little lower.

And then I saw it.

The branches. Pushing the Pink Floyd briefcase inexorably towards the very edge.

I tried to cry out but the words stuck in my throat. I threw myself towards it, oblivious to the branches that were tearing at my clothes, and grabbed it with both hands. I overbalanced, but Dario was there to grab me and pull me back on board before I fell into the canal.

He looked at me, his eyes wide and his mouth open in

horror. And then he hugged me and spun me around as best he could in the space available.

The crew tied the boat up at the side of the canal, and Dario and I stumbled on to the *fondamenta*. I was still clutching the briefcase to my chest, my knuckles white with the pressure. And then the two of us half sat, half fell onto the canal side and laughed and laughed and laughed, to the bemusement of passers-by.

Chapter 19

Wednesday. No surgery to attend to. I could, I suppose, have turned my attention to the film script that was never going to be optioned, but I didn't think I needed to hurry too much on that. I'd go down to Rialto and buy some fish. But later. Much later. I turned over and buried my head in the pillow.

Fede jabbed me in the ribs. 'Time to get up then, lazy boyfriend?'

I yawned. 'Seriously? I thought I might lie in a bit. After all my hard work yesterday.'

'Hard work? You carried Dario's briefcase for him.'

'It was a responsible job with a great deal of mental stress involved. It's taken a bit of a toll on me. Anyway, is there anything I really need to get up for?'

Gramsci hopped onto the end of the bed. Fede nodded at him. 'You're primary caregiver, remember. Entertain him.' He yowled. I grumbled and hauled myself out of bed. 'So,' she continued, 'I have to go to the Querini today. There are a few books I need to look at in the library.'

'Lovely. Perhaps we could have lunch there afterwards?' I said.

'I'm not sure I'll have time today. Tomorrow though?'

'Absolutely. Don't worry about me, I'll grab a sandwich downstairs. Perhaps even a spritz.'

'Hmpph. Aren't you going to be busy with the San Michele case?'

I yawned. 'It's not really a case any more. If Vanni has found anything, he's not telling me about it. Nobody else has any records. So there's nothing to be done.'

'You've changed your tune from two nights ago. Black Magic Circles and strange satanic cults.'

'I think I let the occasion get the better of me.'

She smiled. 'Just possibly.'

'They're a bit of a weird family, that's all. A weird family that had something horrible happen to them, many years ago. And if I could help them, I would, but there's genuinely nothing to be done.'

'Are you going to tell Ambassador Maxwell that?'

'Not in so many words. I might add the word *Excellency* here and there. That usually helps. But I'm afraid he's just going to have to get used to being shouted at.' Gramsci yowled again. 'Just like me,' I sighed, and padded through to the kitchen to fetch his breakfast.

I put the phone down, and rubbed my ear. Ambassador Maxwell had indeed undergone several days of intensive shouting and, by way of compensation, had decided to take it out on me. Multiple uses of the word *Excellency* had failed to improve his mood. Sort it out, Sutherland, one way or the other.

I leaned back in my chair and closed my eyes.

Circles.

Ridiculous. Nonsense. Doesn't happen in real life. I drew one in the air with my finger, and then gave an *ow!* and snatched it back.

Gramsci sat on my desk, black-furred and sulphur-eyed.

I wagged my finger at him, taking care to keep it out of range. 'Now then, diabolical cat. Federica, or, as you call her, *secondary caregiver,* thinks this is all nonsense. And we agree, don't we?'

He didn't move, but continued to stare at me.

'This is twenty-first-century Venice. Things like this don't happen here. Just because a man has an image of the Devil on his ceiling, talks about the "Isle of the Dead" and mentions something called the Circle does not mean anything strange or occult is going on. Does it?'

He made no sound.

'So, as lovely secondary caregiver says, we should just let it all go, shouldn't we?'

We sat in silence, and stared at each other. Then I folded my arms on the table, and rested my head on them.

'Except, of course, we don't agree, do we?' I raised my head to look at him, his eyes narrowed to slits and boring into mine. 'We're going to have to do something, aren't we?'

He jabbed at my forehead. 'Ow,' I said.

I sat upright. 'Okay. I think we need to call in the experts on this. God help us both, I think we need a man of the cloth.' I picked up the phone and dialled Michael Rayner's number.

'Chaplaincy?'

'Michael. It's Nathan. I wondered if you had time for a bit of a chat?'

'Spiritual comfort?'

'God, you never stop, do you?' I sighed.

'Nope. Comes with the job. Seriously, what can I do for you?'

'It's about San Michele.'

He paused, just for a moment. 'I see.'

'Look. It's probably nonsense. And if I try to describe it over the phone I'll sound like an idiot. Can I come over?'

'Of course.'

'Church Pub?'

'No, that won't do today. I've got a wedding this afternoon. A couple of minor Norwegian royals, as I understand.'

I whistled. 'Classy.'

'Very. You should see the flowers. And I'm hoping the fees will pay for replastering the exterior. But that does mean I'd prefer to work at home this morning. I'd rather nobody saw me leaving the pub just before the wedding. Come to the chaplaincy house. Do you know where it is?'

'Next door to Ezra Pound?'

'Exactly.'

'Okay. What are you like at mixing Negronis?'

'At this hour? Coffee and biscuits. If you're lucky.'

'Fair enough, I suppose. As long as they're good biscuits. I'll be there in thirty minutes.'

'I'll see you then.' He paused for a moment. 'Oh, and Nathan?'

'Yes.'

'I don't know what you have to say but – for what it's worth – I suspect it isn't nonsense.'

He hung up, leaving me staring at the phone in frustration

as Gramsci, his work done, hopped off the table in search of something to eat.

The church of the *Salute* loomed out of the mist, its dome lost in the fog. Fine rain was starting to fall, as I pondered why the Italians had no translation that really did justice to the word 'drizzle'. *Pioggerella* was far too pretty a word to be wasted on something as mundane as a light rain.

In spite of the damp and the cold I stood for a moment to gaze up at Baldassare Longhena's masterwork. He'd been a young man when he first drew up the plans for a new church giving thanks for Venice's deliverance from yet another plague. He died, at a great age, a year before it was completed; when memories of the pestilence that had killed a third of the city were just grandparents' tales, to be told around the fireside to chill the blood of children.

The *Festa della Salute* was less than a fortnight away, when the basilica would swarm with worshippers and visitors. Masses would be said around the clock and every *vaporetto* would be packed with the faithful, the curious and small children with enormous balloons.

With the exception of St Mark's, there was no building that said 'this is Venice' as much as the *Salute*. Conspiracy theories had built up around the significance of its octagonal shape and Kabbalist symbols and measurements that Longhena had covertly introduced into its design. Theories that I was happy to dismiss as being manifest bollocks. I wiped the fine sheen of rain from my hair, and stepped out towards Rayner's house. Manifest bollocks. Probably.

In another time, Michael Rayner and Ezra Pound would

have been neighbours, the pitted brass nameplate reading 'Anglican Chaplaincy' being one door down from the one that read 'Rudge/Pound'.

I rang the bell and heard his feet thundering down the stairs from inside. He pulled the door open, his great frame filling the gap in an almost comical way.

'Nathan.'

'*Padre.*' He frowned. 'Sorry. Michael.'

'Better. Come in then. Sit yourself down.' We walked into the kitchen, and I dragged a chair back from the table.

'Not that one!'

'No?'

'It's broken.'

I gave it a shake. It did seem as though it might collapse were any serious weight to be applied to it.

'Erm, so isn't it a bit dangerous to keep it here, then?'

'I save it for chaplaincy council meetings. Good to keep people on their toes. Coffee?'

'Lovely. And you said something about a biscuit?'

'Proper English digestives. One of my flock brings them back for me every time she goes back to the UK. I don't suppose you like Marmite by any chance?'

'Not my thing. Sorry.'

'Pity. She always brings me a jar of that as well. And she's such a nice woman I don't feel able to tell her I can't bear the bloody stuff. I'm building up a bit of a backlog.'

He switched the kettle on and twisted the top off a jar of instant coffee. I winced, and tried not to show it, but he caught the expression on my face.

'Sorry, would you prefer a proper Italian one?'

'No, it's all right. Really.'

'It's just I've never quite found the knack of using one of those Moka things. One time I forgot to put water in. Only noticed when the handle dropped off. But I'll have a go if you like?'

I waved my hand. 'No. Really. Instant will be fine.'

He brought over two great, steaming mugs of disappointing black coffee, and a plate of biscuits. He snapped one in half, dunked an end into his mug and tapped it on the side. 'So then, Nathan, you want to talk about San Michele?'

'That's right.'

'Well, if you want to know if I've managed to find anything then I'm afraid I can't help you. We have no records. Neither does the diocesan office in London. No records at all of young Gabriele ever having been baptised. It does all rather suggest that his burial on San Michele was more a matter of convenience than a matter of faith.' He munched on his biscuit, and then sighed. 'But perhaps I'm not being very Christian. If it brought his parents some comfort then that, surely, is the important thing?'

I sipped at my coffee, and spooned some sugar in, hoping to take the edge off it. 'I suppose so. Well, it would have been nice if you'd found something. But that's not really why I'm here.'

'No?'

I took a little more coffee, still burning and bitter, and added yet more sugar. 'No. I'd like to ask you about . . . Well, I know this sounds mad, but what do you know about witchcraft? Satanism, if you like?'

I was expecting him to laugh. Instead he merely spread

his hands wide and said, 'What exactly do you want to know, Nathan?'

'It sounds ridiculous, but—'

He cut me off. 'You keep saying that. Tell me what you want to say and then I'll tell you if it's ridiculous or not.'

And so I sat there and drank bad coffee and ate digestive biscuits and told the Tall Priest about an elderly man with an image of Satan on his ceiling, who had told me about mysterious Circles and the Isle of the Dead.

Rayner sat there, and snapped another biscuit in half. 'Hmmm.'

'You don't think it's mad?'

He sighed. 'Nathan, for one thing, I think you watch too many horror films.'

'Oh.'

'For another, I also think you drink too much and live a terrible lifestyle.'

'Do all your flock have to put up with this?'

'Only the ones I like. Now tell me about Mr Channing and the painting on his ceiling.'

'As I said. It's St Michael expelling Lucifer from Heaven.'

'Not all that unusual as an image in art, of course.'

'No. But would you want it in your living room?'

'Well quite. That is, I suppose, a little off the wall. Do you know, Nathan, I used to come across this sort of thing quite a lot?'

'You did?'

'When I was back in the UK, as a young priest in the 80s. Lots of young people who were listening to too much "goth rock" or whatever they called it, wearing far too many black clothes and styling their hair in regrettable ways. All romancing the idea of death and darkness and the beyond. And I suppose at that age there's something attractive about it. Why shouldn't there be? Precious few of them had ever known loss at that age. Death didn't seem like forever to them.'

'I didn't think it seemed like forever to you, *padre*.'

He glared at me. 'Don't tell me what I do or do not believe, Nathan.'

'I'm sorry. Go on, please.'

'As I said, I saw a lot of this stuff. It's mostly harmless. Most of the time it's just too many black clothes and a record collection they'll come to regret. Oh, and Dennis Wheatley novels that they'll pick up again in middle age and wonder what they ever saw in them.'

I smiled, thinking back to my teenage years. 'Apart from the naughty covers?'

'Apart from, as you say, the naughty covers. But then there were the ones who'd read the *Inferno* and *Paradise Lost*. They were different.'

'You mean worse?'

'Much worse.' He grimaced. 'You know, Nathan, there aren't many things worse than a snotty-nosed teenager who's read the juicier parts of Dante and Milton telling you exactly why you're wrong and exactly why they're right. They've cherry-picked the famous bits – "better to reign in hell than serve in Heaven" – all that stuff, and the next thing you know they're telling me why my job is a load of nonsense.'

'Youth ministry was never your thing, then?'

'I don't miss it, let us say. But this Hugo Channing sounds

exactly like that. Viewing Satan as the great romantic outcast. It's ultimately an adolescent point of view. If he exists, if he ever existed, what would he be? The cheap crook, the abusive husband, the war criminal. That's all.' He paused. 'So what do you know about Mr Channing?'

'Successful businessman, albeit one with, shall we say, flexible ethical standards. Good-looking chap in his day – touch of the matinee idol about him when he was a young man. Tried his hand at being a racing driver. Beautiful wife and family, beloved of celebrity magazines.'

'Arrogant, would you say?'

'I don't know. I suppose he'd have every reason to be. There's something about him though, in all those glossy magazines – there's a touch of "look at me, look at my fabulous life" about them all.' I sipped at my coffee and tried to suppress a grimace. 'I don't think that's just me being jealous.'

'Hmm. Well, if being rich and successful were enough to make one a Satanist we really would be living through the End of Days.'

I smiled. 'Indeed. There's something more, though. He mentioned the "Isle of the Dead".'

'San Michele, of course.'

'Of course. And something called the Circle.' Rayner shook his head. 'You don't know anything about that?'

'I'm afraid not.'

'Nothing about – oh, I don't know – witchcraft in Venice? Satanism in Venice?'

'Well, I suppose there must have been. At one time.'

'What about today?'

'I'm not the best person to ask. I've only been here three years. But I doubt it very much.'

'Can you be sure though?'

'Nathan, the Ecumenical Council of Churches in this city comprises ourselves, the Roman Church, at least three varieties of Orthodoxy, the Copts, the Waldensians, the Lutherans and the Seventh-Day Adventists. Oh, and the Mormons were once invited by accident. If there was any sort of even minor Satanic activity going on in this city, then one of us – at least – would know about it.'

'I see. Okay. Okay, I'm kind of convinced.'

'Except—' Rayner was looking at me now, with a strange expression on his face.

'Except what?'

'Except perhaps it's not quite as clear-cut as all that. I was at church yesterday morning. I say Matins every Tuesday and Thursday. Just in case anybody needs it.'

'And do they?'

'Precious few. But a few is enough. Anyway, there weren't any regulars there. One family wandered in by accident and then wandered out again on purpose. But there was one fellow who came in and sat down and remained for the whole service. And he wanted to speak afterwards. About San Michele.'

'Ah. I wondered if this might happen. Name of Guy Flemyng, by any chance?'

'That's him. You've met him?' I nodded. 'Well, he wanted to chat. About San Michele and empty graves.'

'And did you?'

'He was very charming. Even managed to help me out

with translating a letter from the *soprintendenza* regarding the resurfacing of the exterior.'

'Hang on, he translated for you?'

'Yes. I usually ask my churchwardens for help with that sort of thing. Sorry, should I have come to you?'

'No, no, it's all right. Just something I've misunderstood. Anyway, I take it he then got down to the nitty gritty?'

'Yes. And I was polite. But told him I knew next to nothing, and – even if I did – it wasn't the sort of thing I felt comfortable discussing.'

'Pretty much what I did,' I said.

'The thing is there was something about the way he spoke to me. I got the impression he didn't particularly care if I was able to give him any information or not. More that he was wanting me to ask *him* questions. As if he knew rather more than he was letting on.'

'I have to say I didn't pick up on that.'

Rayner chuckled. 'Ah, well now, you're not a priest. But, as I said, it made me think that there's something strange going on. And it's to do with that empty grave.'

'Well now. Mr Flemyng really is a busy man, isn't he? Anything else?'

'One more thing. He thanked me for my time, and so I showed him out into the campo – I was going to close up – and you'll never guess who was standing outside, with a look like death upon her face?'

'Ludovica Loredan?'

'Oh.' His face fell. 'How on earth did you know that?'

'Just a hunch. Mr Flemyng seems to be making a habit of going around Venice asking questions of people. More than that, he seems to enjoy being seen asking questions of people. By *Signora* Loredan in particular.'

'Why on earth would he do that?'

'No idea. But I wonder if it explains why she went to visit a private detective in Mestre the other day?' Rayner made to speak, but I shook my head. 'Long story,' I checked my watch, 'and there are a few people I need to speak to. Ideally during the hours of daylight. So I'm afraid I'd better be going.'

'No problem. Always nice to have visitors.' He gestured at the empty plate of biscuits. 'I just hope I haven't ruined your appetite.'

I patted my stomach. 'Trust me, *padre*, it takes more than a few digestives to take the edge off my appetite.'

'I'm sure. Keep in touch, Nathan. Let me know if you find anything interesting. In the meantime I'll ask around the ecumenical council. Priests are terrible old gossips, you know. Trust me, if there is some sort of Satanic Circle in Venice, one of them will know about it.'

I smiled. 'Thanks, Michael.' Then I drained the last of my cold, horrible coffee, and set off for the *vaporetto*.

Chapter 20

I could, I suppose, have walked but it was good to get out of the wind and the rain. So I sat on the *vaporetto* pontoon at Spirito Santo, waiting for the next boat to the Zattere, and flicked through the cards in my wallet until I found the one that Flemyng had given me. There were just two words on it. 'Guy' and 'Flemyng'. I felt a flash of irritation. Why on earth have a business card with just your name on it? The implicit suggestion was that you were so well known there was no need to provide any further information. Hugo Channing, I imagined, had once had cards like this.

I turned it over. Flemyng had scribbled a mobile number on the back, and the name of a hotel over near San Zulian. I recognised its name, and knew nothing unpleasant about it. It was a modestly priced and decent enough hotel in the sestiere of San Marco. I dialled his phone and let it ring until the voicemail message kicked in. It hadn't been personalized in any way, but was just a standard, bland answerphone recording.

'Guy? It's Nathan Sutherland. I'm wondering if we could meet up sometime and talk. Just call me back when you get this, okay? Thanks.'

I hung up. There was still something productive that I could do, something I could at least report back to Ambassador Maxwell the next time we spoke. I tucked the card back inside my wallet, and got to my feet as I saw my boat approaching.

I stood outside the Loredans' palazzo, with my finger hovering above the doorbell. I hoped that Cosima would answer as I didn't relish the idea of another conversation with Ludovica. If she was there, well, I would just have to tell her how far my investigations had not got. I checked my watch. Mid-afternoon. Perhaps she'd be calling on her friends in Via Piave again?

I rang the bell. There was a long pause, and I began to think that no one was there at all. Then the speakerphone crackled. '*Chi è?*'

Ludovica or Cosima? I couldn't be sure. '*Signora* Loredan? It's Nathan Sutherland. The British Honorary Consul.'

There was a pause. 'Oh yes. We met a couple of nights ago.' Another pause. 'Come up, please.'

I smiled to myself as I walked through the *cortile* and up the stairs to the *piano nobile*. It seemed I was in luck.

Cosima was waiting for me at the top of the stairs, looking as elegant as she had three nights previously.

'Mr Sutherland?'

I gave a little bow. '*Signora* Loredan. I hope I'm not intruding.' She said nothing. 'I was just passing by, and thought I should call in.'

'Come in, please.' Her expression was guarded, yet not unfriendly.

Hugo Channing was fast asleep in his chair, snoring gently. I lowered my voice. 'Perhaps it would be better if we were to talk elsewhere?'

She shook her head. 'No. We won't disturb him. He sleeps for longer and longer these days, you understand?' I nodded. She beckoned me over to the window. 'I think we can open the curtains, don't you?' she said.

'If you're sure? I understood Mr Channing found too much light distressing.'

'As I said, I doubt we'll wake him. And I don't think too much light is going to be a problem on a day like this.' She flung the curtains open, with a surprisingly vigorous gesture, and we looked out on to a grey and drizzly Giudecca canal. She turned to me. 'Where do you live, Mr Sutherland?'

'San Marco. The Street of the Assassins.'

'Some way from here, then?'

'It is. But I happened to be in the area and—'

She interrupted me. 'You just happened to be passing.'

'Exactly.'

'One wonders what might bring the Honorary Consul out to the Zattere on a wet and windy day. The cruise ships have finished for the season. No hapless passengers will be needing your help.' The wind blew the rain against the windows, which rattled, and she shivered. 'Neither, I think, is it a day for a spritz or an ice cream outside Nico's. And surely the supermarket isn't that much of an attraction?'

'Well, Conad has its charms, but, no, that's not the reason. Would you believe I had an appointment with the Anglican chaplain?'

'I could. Although you're choosing a strange route to

return home.' There was a touch of humour in her eyes now. 'Do you know what I think, Mr Sutherland?'

I smiled at her. 'Please tell me.'

'I think you're feeling very grateful that my daughter isn't here.'

I laughed, glad that at least I could drop the pretence of what was, I had to admit, a pretty feeble cover story. 'Yes. I'm afraid I can't argue with that.'

'Ludovica can have that effect on people. She means well. She does rather try to wrap us both in cotton wool. Hugo and I, that is. And whilst poor Hugo needs proper care, I'm not quite ready yet to have to be sheltered from the manifold wickednesses of the world.'

I thought I could risk another gentle laugh. 'I can see that.'

'So why are you here, Mr Sutherland?'

'I thought I should apologise for the other night. I must have sounded terribly clumsy.'

She waved my apology away. 'It's not a problem. Please don't feel bad about it.'

'And then of course, there was some unpleasantness. With that journalist.'

She shook her head. 'Ludovica made sure to keep me well away from all that. As I said, she cares a little too much at times.'

'I see.' I tried to ask my next question as discreetly as possible. 'Nobody from the press has tried to contact you?'

'Oh, it's quite possible that they have. But Ludovica is very good at filtering such people out.'

'I understand. That's kind of her.'

'It's what she does.' We sat in silence for a moment. 'Is there anything else, Mr Sutherland?'

I took a deep breath. 'Perhaps there is. But I don't want to upset you.'

The sadness I had seen in her eyes at our first meeting returned. 'I don't upset easily, Mr Sutherland.'

'Gabriele was a British citizen. So naturally the Ambassador wants me to do whatever I can to make sure that all procedures were followed correctly. So – and you don't have to answer this – could you tell me what happened on the day of . . .' my voice trailed off, 'the event?'

'"The event" being the day my son drowned? Is that what you mean?'

I nodded.

'Then say what you mean, Mr Sutherland. And you're absolutely right, I don't have to talk to you about it. But I will.'

Chapter 21

Andrea and his father have come to stay. Mother says they will be with us for perhaps a few weeks. They are old friends, she tells us.

His father has a funny name. Not Italian, like mine, or English like Father's. Mother says he comes from the east. I am to be very polite, she tells me. We must be friends with Andrea, both Ludovica and I. It must be strange for him to be in a foreign city. It would be nice if we could all be friends. Father has work to do, and business to discuss. It would be good if we could play together outside, to leave them in peace.

Andrea is older than me. Perhaps older than Ludovica. I think he finds me annoying. He is nearly a man now. He does not want to waste his summer playing with a small boy.

Ludovica and I have not played together since I was very young. I thought she would want to be with Andrea, with someone of her own age. But now, as we explore the city together, running through the calli in search of adventures, she seems to like me being there.

Sometimes Andrea touches her on the shoulder, just for a moment. Once he flicks her hair back out of her eyes. Ludovica shakes his hand off. He catches me staring at them, and he looks cross.

I hope they will not stay long. Mother looks tired, and Father is angry all the time. He looks at me, always, as if I have done something wrong. I am afraid to speak to him.

Mother tells me everything will be all right. Father and his friend are very busy, she tells me, and so he does not have time for us. But soon Andrea and his father will go away, and things will be like they were before. We just need to be patient.

Andrea's father seems to be a kind man. He tells me that I am a fine boy. How, very soon now, I will be a grown-up. A strong and handsome man. Soon, all Ludovica's friends will come calling, wanting to be my friend. Ludovica tuts, and rolls her eyes when he says things like this. Then he smiles, and laughs, and ruffles my hair.

Things change after dark. When we have gone to bed, I can hear him arguing with Father and I do not know why. I cannot hear them clearly through the thick walls of my bedroom. Mother is cross with me when I tell her of this. It is not my business, she tells me. Father would be very angry if he thought I was spying on him.

And so every night I go to bed, and try not to listen to the angry voices beyond the door. And I pull the covers over my head, and hope that Andrea and his father will leave soon.

Chapter 22

'It was another hot Venetian summer. Like all of them. Hugo was so busy in those days. I always wanted him to work a little less hard, just to have more time to spend with us. It was left to me to look after Ludovica and Gabriele. She was older, of course. Even in those days, I could tell she was a little resentful. She didn't want to be with her mother and her baby brother – she always thought of him as her baby brother – all the time. It reminded her that she was, after all, still a child.'

'They were quite different, then?' I asked, trying to keep my voice as gentle as possible.

She gave the most delicate little laugh. 'Very. Ludovica was always Hugo's little girl. And Gabriele – well, Gabriele was what we might call a *mammone*. A mummy's boy. He was quiet. He never seemed to have many friends. That used to make me sad. Ludovica was just at that age of wanting to bring friends home, or to stay out late. Gabriele was happy just as long as he could stay in his room and read his books or his comics. He always had his head in a book. That's how I remember him.'

'Not so much like his father, perhaps,' I said, and instantly wished I could take the words back. But Cosima just smiled.

'No. Not like Hugo at all.' She sighed. 'Sometimes there'd be "why can't you be more like your sister?". That sort of thing. Sometimes worse things. It must have hurt him. I don't think I recognised that at the time.

'And so, it was late August. They'd have been counting down the days to the new school year, trying to reassure themselves that plenty of the holidays still remained. Gabriele was tense, nervy. More so than usual. I put that down to the fact that he'd be going to a new school. We'd just moved him from his previous one. He'd never been happy there.'

'I'm sorry. School isn't always easy at that age. Not for everyone.'

'No. I was worried about him, I'll admit. He was still young for his age. I was afraid that he was still going to find it difficult. Frightening, even.

'I was tired. Every day, all summer, back and forth in the baking heat to our cabin on the Lido. How wonderful it would be, I thought, to have a few days to myself. Just a little silence, a little peace. So I asked them if they could play by themselves. To give Mother one day off.

'And they did. They went off on a little adventure together. They took our boat out into the lagoon. I sometimes wonder if Gabriele was trying to prove something. To show he was a man. To do something his father would have to pretend to be angry about whilst thinking "that's my boy" at the same time.

'The police came round early evening. Ludovica was with them. Hysterical, of course. The boat had been spotted between Mazzorbo and Torcello. She was alone. Gabriele, she said, had fallen in. Standing on the prow of the boat, and showing off. He was a strong swimmer. He should have been all right.'

She paused. 'I'm sorry,' I said. 'You don't have to go on.'

She shook her head. 'It was getting dark by then. The police said there was no point in sending divers out at that hour. I asked them why they needed divers. And then I realised what that meant.

'Hugo wouldn't listen to them. He hugged us both. Told us it was all going to be fine. Gabriele could swim, he said. He'd be on one of the deserted islands, cold and hungry and wanting his dinner. So we went out to find him. To bring our son home.'

She fell silent for a moment as she took a long, deep breath. 'And we did. The coroner told us it would have been quick. That was some comfort, as you can imagine.'

I shuddered. 'I'm so sorry. I saw the photograph – the one that was in all the papers. It must have been dreadful.'

'Somebody had told the press. There was a photographer waiting outside our house, but I hardly noticed. Hugo, though, was ready to kill him.

'Now, you might wonder why we wanted Gabriele to rest in the Anglican cemetery? The reason is simply this. We knew he would lie there forever. We could always go and visit him, be with him, talk with him. I expect that sounds crazy to you?'

I shook my head. 'Not at all.'

'We did, at first. And then weekly visits became monthly. And then once or twice a year. And then perhaps occasionally, just to clear his grave. But one comes to realise quite quickly that these places – are just places. Nothing more.'

'I'm not sure I understand.'

'You will. One day.' She shook her head. 'And now, of course, it transpires that my son has not been lying in his grave for these past thirty-seven years. It's a nonsense of course to talk of people lying "cold in the ground". The dead are, simply, the dead. Nevertheless, the thought is not a pleasant one.' She fell silent.

I reached across the table to take her hands in mine. 'I'll do whatever I can to find out what's happened. I promise.'

She smiled. 'Thank you, Mr Sutherland.' She checked her watch. 'Ludovica will be back soon.'

I paused, but only for a second. 'From Mestre?'

She looked puzzled. 'Why on earth do you say that?'

'I'm sorry. It's probably nonsense, but I thought I saw her in Via Piave the other day.'

'Well now, I really think you must be mistaken. I can imagine my daughter, perhaps, having occasion to go to Mestre. Not, however, to Via Piave.'

'I'm sorry. A silly mistake.'

'Well, there are perhaps only so many faces in the world, Mr Sutherland.'

'Quite right. And now I really must be going.' I tried, and failed, to keep my voice neutral.

She laughed. 'My daughter really isn't quite so terrifying, you know? But she is, perhaps, just a little bit overprotective.'

'I suppose that's understandable. Given what happened.'

'I think so. She changed, you know. After Gabriele died. No more boys calling round. No more staying out late. She never left home. Everything she did seemed to be turned towards protecting us.'

'She must love you very much.'

Cosima smiled again, but there was a touch of bitterness to her voice as she gestured towards the old man in his chair. 'Daddy's little girl. Always.'

I got to my feet. 'Thank you for your time, *Signora* Loredan. As I said, I'll do the very best I can.'

I made to kiss her, changed it into an awkward handshake at the last moment, and made my way out into the rain.

Chapter 23

Guy Flemyng still hadn't returned my call by the following morning. I tried his number again and left my usual message. Then I telephoned his hotel, and left the same message there. I sat behind my desk, turning his card over and over in my hands and wondering what to do.

Guy Flemyng. Journalist. Slightly unusual name. It shouldn't be too hard to discover something more about him. A quick search on the internet revealed him to be a modestly prolific writer. He'd written a few pieces on responsible tourism for the *Telegraph* and the *Guardian*, had contributed to both the *Rough Guide* and *Lonely Planet Guide to Italy*, and had published some well-received books on travelling around Spain and Portugal by rail.

He didn't seem to have a Twitter handle or Facebook page, both of which I had a vague idea of how to use, and neither did he have anything on Instagram, which I didn't. It was, I supposed, possible that he used a pseudonym or that he was on some other form of social media usually restricted to young people. I checked his LinkedIn profile but found it to be even more out of date than mine.

I leaned back and crossed my hands behind my head. I'd

done him a disservice. He really did seem to be who he said he was. But just what had led him to investigate an empty grave on San Michele?

The telephone rang as I was musing away. The *Questura*. My heart gave a little leap. Vanni was going to tell me he'd found something. I could wash my hands of the whole affair and forget all my crackpot theories about Black Magic Circles and Satanic Rings. Or Satanic Circles and Black Magic Rings.

'Good morning, Nathan.'

'Vanni. How're you doing? It's good news, right?'

He said nothing.

'It's not good news, is it?' I sighed. 'Okay, tell me the worst.'

'I'm sorry, Nathan. I think you'd better come in.'

Vanni spread the photographs out on the table. A face, photographed from three angles, greyish-blue in colour, a wicked open wound across the forehead.

'How did you know to call me?'

'His wallet was on him. His driving licence was still legible. That's how we knew he was British. And once we had a name we could trace him back to his B&B.'

I nodded. Visitors, of course, were required to leave proof of their identity with their lodgings so that the information could be passed on to the police. I looked down at the face again. Eyes wide, and mouth lolling open. There was nothing to read from the expression. Not fear, not horror. Not even emptiness. Nothing. The absence of everything.

Jimmy Whale's eyes looked sightlessly into mine.

I shivered.

'Are you all right, Nathan?'

'Not really.'

'Can I . . . ?' he left the question hanging, as he reached for a cigar.

I waved it away. 'I'd bloody love one. But I'm not going to. A coffee would be good. Or should I say, a coffee will have to do?'

'Of course.' He picked up the telephone and muttered a few words into it. Shortly, the door opened and a young man in *divisa* came in with two mismatched little cups on a tray, together with a box of sugar sachets and two plastic spoons. He set them down in front of Vanni, nodded stiffly, then turned and left.

'That's Giancarlo,' said Vanni, pouring sugar into his cup. 'Nice lad. Bit too serious. He's only been with us six months and it's taken all that time to stop him saluting when he brings the drinks in.' He stirred his coffee, and licked the spoon. He looked over at me. 'I think this calls for something else.' He opened a drawer and took out a bottle of grappa. 'Let me just correct this.' He unscrewed the bottle and topped up my cup.

'Bit early in the day, isn't it?' I said. My voice was still a little unsteady.

He smiled. 'Oh, when is it ever too early in the day for Nathan Sutherland?'

I smiled back at him. I knew what he was doing. He knew I was shocked and was giving me a bit of time. It was one of the things that made him a good cop.

I sipped at the coffee, closing my eyes, feeling its warmth rush into me.

'Good?'

'Well, you can't beat the first one of the day, can you?'

'You certainly can't.'

We drank in silence for a while. Then I forced myself to look at the photographs again. I'd seen dead people before. Often close up. But the sheer emptiness of his gaze was unsettling.

'Vanni, I know this guy.'

He raised his eyebrows. 'You do?'

'He came by the office on Monday morning. He'd been scammed. Non-existent Bed and Breakfast.'

'Oh dear. Are people still falling for that one?'

'It seems they are.'

'What do you know about him?'

'Not much more than you do. He just wanted some help. There wasn't very much I could do, of course. Well, by "very much" I actually mean—'

'Nothing?'

'Exactly. He wasn't just a regular tourist, though. He had a book about abandoned islands of the lagoon, and he'd marked some of them up on a map. Poveglia was one, I don't know about the others. But I think he was planning on some illegal island-hopping.'

Vanni scribbled away. 'Okay. Might help. Thanks.'

'Where was he staying?'

'A cheap B&B in Castello.'

'So where did you find him?'

'We got a call about one o'clock this morning. One of the porters from the hospital. He'd been working late and was waiting for his mate to pick him up in his boat from Celestia. He noticed something floating in the lagoon. Couldn't see anything clearly of course, but then the lights from the boat picked it out. Picked *him* out, I should say.'

'So what happened?'

Vanni shrugged. 'Can't say for sure. The autopsy will tell us more. Maybe he'd been drinking, maybe he just slipped and fell in.'

'And the wound on his head?'

'Who knows? Again, the autopsy might help.'

'In your opinion, though?'

'He was a foreigner. No offence, Nathan, but how often do you see them on the pontoon, waiting for a boat to arrive, standing out on the edge taking photos? It's November, there's a bit of a swell, he's unsteady on his feet and he falls in, banging his head.' He lowered his voice. 'And the lagoon is so cold at this time of year. He wouldn't have lasted long.'

I shook my head. 'Horrible.'

'Indeed.'

I sighed. 'Okay, I'll get on to it. I'll see if there are relatives to inform. And then I'll arrange for the repatriation of the body as soon as you'll let me.'

'Thanks, Nathan.'

'So, have you got anything for me? Anything that might speed up identifying next of kin?'

'Nothing at all. As I said, all he had on him was a wallet. His driving licence and a stack of receipts. Oh, and this . . .' He slid a small plastic bag across the desk to me.

I picked it up. 'Can I take it out?'

He shook his head. 'Better not. It's still evidence.'

The bag contained a Polaroid photograph. Faded now, and water-stained, yet still clear enough.

A ruined chapel. An emaciated Christ looking down upon a simple altar, with a plain cross chiselled on to the front.

'Do you know where this is?' I asked.

'I'm afraid I don't. How about you?'

I brought it closer to my face, then reached into my jacket for my glasses. 'Sorry, Vanni. No idea. Can I photograph it at least?'

He shrugged. 'Sure. But why?'

'I know people who might know. Federica for one.'

'If you think it's important.'

'Might be. It might tell us why Mr Whale was out waiting for a boat from Celestia in the small hours of the morning. It's not a place many tourists hang around at that hour.' I took out my intelligent phone and snapped away; and then got to my feet. 'Thanks for the coffee, Vanni.'

He reached across the desk and we shook hands. 'Thanks, Nathan. I'll be in touch as soon as we're ready to release the body.'

I had some time to kill before meeting Fede at the Querini Stampalia for lunch, but didn't feel like going back to an empty flat and making conversation with Gramsci in the meantime. Instead, I took one of the smaller *vaporetti* from Piazzale Roma down the first stretch of the Grand Canal, before turning into the Cannaregio branch and out into the lagoon itself, passing by Sant'Alvise, Madonna dell'Orto and Fondamente Nove. I got off at Ospedale. The boat, I knew, would make its next stop at Celestia, but I wanted to take the last stretch on foot. The skies were dark and grey, with the ever-present threat of rain, and I turned my collar up against the biting wind that blew across the lagoon.

I walked to the edge of the *fondamenta*, sliding my shoes

against the stone. Slippery? Just a little. Might it even have been frozen late at night? I wasn't convinced. It had been cold but not that cold. I made my way to the end of the *fondamenta* where a bridge led to a metal gantry that clung to the great walls of the Arsenale, allowing one to walk along the very outside edge of the *centro storico*.

An elderly man was smoking a roll-up outside the Celestia stop. I walked past him, on to the pontoon, and looked out. It swayed in the swell from the lagoon, and I rested my hand on the side of the cabin, gripping the edge as I leaned outside to look across the surface of the water.

'*Signore.*' I gave a start as I felt a hand on my shoulder. I turned around. It was my elderly companion, his roll-up still clenched in his teeth. He smiled and addressed me in English. 'Sir. Please stand back. It's very dangerous. A boat comes past, very fast, the cabin moves like this,' he waved his hands like a marionette, 'and *pfffft* – in the water you go. Very dangerous.'

I smiled back at him. 'Thank you,' I said. 'I'll be careful.' He grinned, and patted me on the shoulder again, his eyes twinkling; pleased at having been able to help a visitor.

I stepped back into the cabin, and sat down on one of the benches. I took my phone from my jacket, and looked at the photograph. A grim-faced Christ. A simple altar. There wasn't much more to see. The ground was strewn with rocks and weeds. An abandoned church, then, but Venice wasn't short of those. Federica would know, if anyone did. The windows of the cabin were fogged, and I wiped the sleeve of my coat against one, the better to be able to peer out at the grey, choppy waters of the lagoon.

Why in God's name had Jimmy Whale chosen to come to a lonely *vaporetto* stop in the northern reaches of Castello in the early hours of a freezing cold November morning? I looked down at the turbid waters slapping against the sides of the pontoon. Cold now. How much colder would it have been at midnight? I closed my eyes, imagining the terrible moment when he realised he was falling. The freezing water knocking the air out of him. Fingers scrabbling in vain for purchase on the side of the *fondamenta*, slimy with algae. How long would you have before the cold and the water took you?

I shuddered, opened my eyes, and stared out across the lagoon. There was nothing to be seen beyond the bulk of the island of San Michele.

The Isle of the Dead.

Chapter 24

I was glad of the rain. It stopped me wanting to buy cigarettes. I made my way down through Castello until I reached Campo Santa Maria Formosa and the Palazzo Querini Stampalia.

The palazzo was by no means the most beautiful in Venice, but it had become one of my favourites. If I had a particularly difficult piece of translation to do, and Gramsci's demands for attention had become intolerable, I would come here to work in the library. Or, at least, I would listen to Pink Floyd on headphones, daydreaming away and occasionally tapping at my keyboard until it was time for lunch. Similarly, Fede would come here whenever she had research to do. Only without Pink Floyd.

The Marciana Library, of which I had recently become a member, was closer, much closer, to the Street of the Assassins, but the Querini Stampalia had one great advantage. It had a bar downstairs.

In days gone by I would have taken the lift up to the library, but the new Nathan – new, healthy-living Nathan – took the stairs. I considered taking them two at a time but that, perhaps, was something to be worked up to. I swiped my card through the reader and banged my shins on the turn-stile as I forgot, as ever, the momentary delay whilst it clicked open.

I ignored the modern reading rooms with rows of shared computer terminals, and went straight through to the original wood-panelled library with the familiar, comforting sound of the floors squeaking beneath my feet.

Fede was seated with her back to me, in a carved wooden chair, tapping away at her laptop and pausing occasionally to check the yellowing pages of the small, leather-bound book at her side. I took a quick look around the room. There were only two other people. I bent over behind her and kissed the back of her neck.

She sat bolt upright with a shriek, the back of her head banging into my nose and drawing an 'argh!' out of me. The heads of the other readers immediately snapped up, an irate 'hsssst!' issuing from both.

Fede turned round, and rolled her eyes upon seeing me.

'What do you think you're doing?' she hissed.

'Sorry.' I rubbed my nose. At least she hadn't drawn blood. 'I thought I was being romantic.'

'Well don't. It doesn't suit you.'

'Is everything all right, *Dottoressa?* It's just that I heard some noise.' The speaker was a middle-aged woman, evidently the chief librarian.

'Everything is fine.' She pointed at me. 'It's just my idiot boyfriend.'

'I understand, *Dottoressa.*'

There was silence, for a moment, as the other readers returned to their, well, reading, and the librarian returned to her post, the floors squeaking reproachfully beneath her feet.

'Well, that wasn't embarrassing at all,' I muttered.

'Your fault, *caro mio,* for making a scene.'

'I don't know,' I grumbled, 'a man tries to make a grand romantic gesture and the next thing that happens—'

'—is that he's banned from every library in Venice.'

I pulled up the chair next to her, and winced as it screeched across the floor.

'So. Read any good books recently?'

'This one.' She made to tap the open pages of the book then thought better of it. '*Miracoli della gloriosa Vergine Maria*. An *incunabulo* from 1475. Published by Leonardus Achates who, I'm told, is quite important.'

'I didn't think this was your sort of thing.'

'It isn't at all. But there might be some work in it, in the future. Come on, let's go.'

'Go?'

'Lunch. Lunch now. Come on,' she looked around the reading room. 'I don't think they'll miss us. Come on,' she repeated, closing up her laptop, linking her arm in mine, and half dragging me towards the exit.

Fede swirled the last of the ice cubes in her spritz. 'I don't know it,' she said, without even looking at it again.

'Are you sure?' I said.

'Definitely sure that I don't know it? Yes. I couldn't even guess.'

'Nothing? Nothing at all that might give us a clue?'

'What have we got? A bare altar. Nothing to go on

there. A figure of Christ. Perhaps fifteenth-century. From what I can see of the image, it's of the Venetian or, at least, Veneto school from that period. That's as much as I can do.'

'Hell. I was hoping for something more.'

'There is someone who would know.'

I felt my heart sink. 'Oh God. Your uncle.'

'Uncle Giacomo. We should have him round. Come on, you haven't cooked for him in ages.'

'I know. I know.'

'Come on, he likes you.'

'Okay. Tomorrow then. I'll do the best I can.'

'Well done, *tesoro*. Cook something brilliant, and I'm sure he'll be able to sort out all of your problems.'

I munched upon the last of my sandwich and grumbled, 'I hope so.'

She touched my cheek, briefly, and looked around. 'And now I need to be getting back to work. What are you going to do?'

I looked down at my empty glass, and then over towards the bar. 'You know, the spritzes here really are first class.' Federica narrowed her eyes. 'But I suppose I should get back to the office and start filling out the paperwork for poor Jimmy Whale.'

'What do you think he was doing out there late at night? There aren't any restaurants in that area. I don't think there's even anywhere to get a drink. Nothing to interest your average late-night tourist.'

'That's the thing. I don't think he was an average tourist. He seemed interested in trying to get to Poveglia, and some other places off the beaten track. Perhaps he wanted some late-night shots of San Michele?'

'Maybe so. Okay, I've got to go. Have a think about what you might like to cook.' And, with that, she turned and made her way back to the lift, leaving me to plan menus for the following evening, and Jimmy Whale's return to England.

Chapter 25

'Ready?'

Ludovica shivers, despite the heat, and nods. 'Ready.'

'Gabi?'

I hate it when he calls me Gabi. Only my mother calls me that. I sit on the edge of the fondamenta, dangling my legs in the water. I look across the Grand Canal to the coffee shop opposite. It makes me think of Christmas, somehow. The smell of pastries and hot chocolate, Mother leading us both in, bags of presents in our hands that we are being allowed to carry. But today the sun is baking the fondamenta, so that it almost hurts to sit there bare-legged; and the air smells of petrol and cigarettes.

'Gabi? Gabs? Gabriele?' He pokes me in the arm. 'Day-dreaming again?'

I shake my head.

'What's the matter?'

'Nothing.'

Ludovica speaks up. She is starting to sound bored. 'Come on, Gabriele, are we all going to do this?'

Andrea sighs. 'It doesn't matter, Ludii, let's just leave him. We'll do it ourselves. It's not fair on him. He's so much younger, after all.'

'*Not so much younger. And don't call me Ludii. You know I hate that.*'

'*Sorry.*' He grins. '*Ludo, then?*'

'*No, stop it!*' Her voice rises, just a little, and she looks cross. Andrea is still grinning at her. Then he stops, and looks at me. '*Don't worry, Gabi. You don't have to if you don't want to.*'

'*I don't want to. It's a stupid idea.*'

He nods. '*Okay. Don't worry.*' He points at the coffee shop. '*We'll see you over there. Just run across the bridge and down the other side. See if you can race us, eh? Will you be okay with that?*' His voice has changed now, as he tries to sound like a grown-up talking to a little boy.

I shake my head, violently. '*No, it's okay. I'll do it.*'

'*You're sure? Your mum says you're a good swimmer.*'

'*I'm okay.*'

'*Great. And don't worry, we'll look after you.*'

Andrea looks to his right. There are a few gondolas in the distance, but no vaporetti or motor boats to be seen. Then he leans out as far as he can, and looks to his left, under the Rialto Bridge. '*Okay. We're clear. One – Two Three. GO,*' he shouts, and we plunge into the canal.

As soon as I surface I can hear the sounds of adults shouting at us from the canalside. '*Stupid.*' '*Idiots.*' '*Ignoranti.*' I can hear the sound of a boat approaching, a siren sounding from a vaporetto, and a woman screaming. I swim as fast as I can, my lungs are burning, the other two are ahead of me and, for a moment, I think I do not have the strength to get there in time. And then adult arms are around me, pulling me up and on to the fondamenta.

Someone has run out of the coffee shop. I recognise the owner. He looks at me. '*Gabriele? Ludovica? Dio Cane!*' He stops for *a moment, embarrassed at having sworn in front of children. 'What the hell are you doing? You could have been killed. Wait 'til your mamma comes into this shop again! I'll tell her all about this!'*

Andrea is laughing. He has his hands on his hips, and beams at the owner. 'Don't blame them. It was my fault.'

The owner looks down at this bright-eyed lad, joking and grinning in front of him. Then he slaps him around the head, and stalks back inside the bar.

Andrea is still laughing. He puts his arms around me and Ludovica, and hugs us both. Our clothes are soaked through. The sun will soon dry us off, but the stink of the canal water will remain. Mother and Father will be furious.

Andrea ruffles my soaking wet hair, and moves to kiss Ludovica, who steps back out of his reach. He squeezes her shoulder instead, and laughs once more. 'We did it! We did it!'

Chapter 26

I put the telephone down and rubbed my ear.

'His Excellency?' asked Fede.

'The same.'

'How is he?'

'Not so excellent. He's had better weeks. Two dead British citizens but not the right number of bodies. But at least he started today by getting in some really concentrated shouting practice. At me, unfortunately.'

I closed my eyes and rested my head on the desk. Fede ruffled my hair. 'You don't have to do this, you know? You could just tell him where to go?'

'I know,' I sighed. 'And I have thought about it. Instead of people bringing their crappy problems to me I could be doing my proper job. I could be earning more money.'

'Except . . .'

'Except . . . except sometimes these people with crappy problems are nice people. And so it's nice if I can help them. And sometimes, I admit, it's just a little bit exciting.'

'Like now.'

'Is that bad?'

'It's a bit strange.' She smiled. 'Not actually bad, but definitely strange.'

'It's better than translating lawnmower manuals. It's better than working on a rubbish film script that has no chance of being made.' I sighed. 'And more than that. If I didn't do it, somebody else would. And I worry they wouldn't do it as well.'

'I see. So you're feeling proprietorial about a job which is, to all intents and purposes, an unpaid one, and where a man who is not actually your boss feels free to shout at you?'

'Yes. Kind of.'

'An unpaid job which frequently involves having to deal with unhappy visitors or grieving relatives?'

'Yes.'

'The British foreign service would fail to function adequately without you, that sort of thing?'

'Yes. Does that sound weird?'

'Beyond weird.' She pulled on her coat. 'Okay, I'm off to work. Do you think Her Majesty's Secret Service could release you for long enough to go and buy fish?'

'I should think so. They could always send a helicopter in case of an emergency.'

'Good. You'll do something nice for Uncle Giacomo then?'

'I will spare no time or expense.'

'Wonderful.' She pecked me on the cheek. 'See you later, *tesoro*.'

I could have taken the boat, but decided a good walk to the Rialto market would be the perfect way of shaking the shouting out of my head. Up through Campo Manin, into Campo San Luca and on to San Salvador, where I turned off in order to cross over the Rialto Bridge. The skies were grey, but it was mercifully dry. Winter, proper winter, had yet to arrive. Nevertheless, the city was becoming quieter and I could simply walk across the bridge at this hour instead of fighting my way over it.

There were other places in the city to buy fish, of course; among them a fabulous fishmonger on Giudecca where the catch of the day flapped with freshness, and market stalls on the Cannaregio canal, at San Leonardo and in Campo Santa Margherita. The Rialto market, however, was the closest to the Street of the Assassins. More than that, it had taken years to build up a relationship with Marco and Luciano, and I was not going to jeopardise that for the possibility of saving the occasional euro somewhere at the other end of town.

But there was a sadness to shopping there now. It had become impossible to ignore that there were not as many stalls as there once had been. Even the vegetable stands were now forced to offer overpackaged 'artisan' dried pasta, and packets of spices at three for a tenner, in the hope that some of the tourist hordes would take a break from merely photographing them and actually put a hand in their pocket.

The market, like the city, was dying.

How much longer would Marco and Luciano manage to keep going, I wondered, in a town that was running out of people?

I had been in Venice for just a decade, yet even I had seen its decline. Every year, it seemed, yet another stallholder would be forced to call it a day in the face of rising rents and declining sales. For those that remained, it must have felt as if they now only existed as a museum exhibit to be photographed by visitors.

'*Ciao*, Marco.'

'*Ciao*, Nathan.' Marco grinned his broken-toothed grin and made to shake hands. Then he realised his hand was still black with squid ink, and wiped it on his apron before proffering it again. It would have been rude to refuse, and so I shook it.

'How're things?'

He spread his arms wide, indicating the half-empty market. 'Quiet,' he said, 'as you can see.'

'I don't see Luciano here.'

'Ah, he's taking the morning off. With me and the boy here,' he jabbed his thumb over his shoulder to indicate a bored-looking youth washing the surfaces down, 'we don't need three of us.'

I shook my head. 'Oh Marco, what are we all going to do, eh?'

'I don't know. But eating more fish would be a good start.'

I smiled to myself. I was, I knew, going to leave with more fish than I needed. But I could hardly begrudge him it.

I returned home with three enormous sea bass, bright-eyed and practically flapping. I'd also acquired a dozen butterflied sardines, but they could go in the freezer for another night. I checked my recipe again. It was, perhaps, a little unusual and somewhat out of my comfort zone, but, nevertheless, this was going to be Event Cooking. I was going to cook *zio* Giacomo the dinner of his life.

I put them in the fridge, and went through to the office, where I turned my attention to Jimmy Whale.

I completed the paperwork recording his death, and was about to scan and mail it to the FCO when I realised I had no record of his passport number. The *Questura*, hopefully, might be able to tell me. I picked up the phone.

'Nathan?'

'Hi, Vanni. Jimmy Whale. Do you have his passport? There's some info I need to send to the Foreign and Commonwealth Office.'

'I do. One minute.' I heard him scrabbling around on the other end of the line. 'Here we are, have you got a pen?'

I scribbled the details down. 'Thanks, Vanni. It was at his B&B, then?'

'No. We have the number, of course. Hotels have to record this sort of thing, as you know.'

'I do. But it wasn't found among his possessions?'

'No.'

I paused. 'Any money?'

'No.'

'Bank card?'

'What are you trying to say, Nathan?' said Vanni, in a voice that suggested he knew exactly what I was trying to say.

'You tell me, Vanni. We have a person who's been pulled out of a canal, but no money, no passport, no bank cards to be found anywhere. Is this still being treated as an accidental death?'

Vanni sighed. 'It's "under investigation", Nathan. That's all I can say for now. It's possible everything else you mentioned was in one of his other pockets and got washed away.'

'You don't believe that, do you?'

'No. Not really.'

'What about the Polaroid?'

'One moment.' I heard him riffling papers. 'That was found in his rear trouser pocket.'

'Right. Okay.'

He sighed, again. 'I'll be in touch as soon as I have anything more to give you, Nathan.'

'I'll look forward to it. Thanks, Vanni.'

I put the phone down, and yawned. Coffee. Coffee would be good. Gramsci followed me through to the kitchen, and hopped up on to the worktop, waiting for a watched pot to boil. I scratched the back of his head.

'So, Fat Cat,' I said. 'Mr Whale has been pulled, lifeless, from a canal. There is no money to be found on his person or in his room.'

He snapped, half-heartedly, at my fingers.

'And, as you so rightly point out, there is also no bank card.'

I heard the Moka starting to bubble away.

'More than that, there was no passport and,' I waved my finger in the air, just to give him something to aim at, 'as we know, there is a market in stolen passports.'

He purred. Only Gramsci could make a purr sound like a threat.

'I see you agree. So either Mr Whale was a very unlucky man or,' we looked at each other, 'there is a little more to this than meets the eye.'

He continued to purr.

'Because – again, as we know – a driving licence could also be valuable to sell on, as proof of a fake identity. So – if the unfortunate Mr Whale did indeed meet a bad end – why not take that as well? Unless you actually wanted to speed up identification of the body? To send a message to someone? As a message? Or, more likely, as a warning?'

He stopped purring and stared at me.

'I think you've earned some bonus biscuits.' I reached into the cupboard for his box, and topped up his bowl. He leaped down from the worktop and started to munch away. I weighed the box in my hands. How the hell was he getting through them so quickly? What was going on? Was there genuinely something not right with him? I shook the thought from my head.

I realised, too late, that the Moka was bubbling away and the so-called 'Stromboli effect' was causing hot, burnt coffee to spew out over the stove. I swore and reached for a kitchen towel to mop up the mess, and then cursed some more as I singed my fingers on the hob. I filled the sink with an inch of water, and placed the coffee pot in it, where it hissed away.

A wasted coffee then, but perhaps not so much of a wasted afternoon. There was much to think about.

Chapter 27

'My boy, it's good to see you again.' Giacomo Maturi smiled, and kissed me on both cheeks, which I returned as best I could.

'*Zio* Giacomo, lovely to see you.'

'A pleasure. A pleasure.'

We stood and smiled and nodded at each other, the unspoken matter of his precious *tabarro* – which I had accidentally set fire to six months previously – hanging in the air between us.

'Sit down. Please. I'll fetch us some drinks.' I looked over at Fede. 'Spritz Nathan?'

'Lovely.'

'And you, *zio* Giacomo?'

He raised his eyebrows. 'What, if I might ask, is a Spritz Nathan?'

'It's a spritz with the boring bits removed. That is, the water.'

His eyes crinkled. 'Oh yes. I like that. One of those please.'

I rustled us up three spritzes, took the sea bass out of the fridge, and cast my eyes over the recipe again. Complicated. Perhaps a bit too complicated. But it would be the dish of all dishes. Maturi, I was sure, would be impressed.

I took the drinks through, and we clinked glasses. 'So,' I said, 'how are things at the bank.'

He frowned, ever so slightly. 'I've retired,' he said.

'Oh that's marvellous. Congratulations.' Fede dug me in the ribs.

'A year ago.'

I slapped my forehead. 'Of course. I remember now. Is it that long ago?'

'Since we last met. Yes. More or less.' He took Federica's hand and patted it. 'Now, lovely Federica tries to have lunch with her old *zio* once a month. But . . . well, it's been some time since we last met hasn't it?'

'It has. I'm sorry, *zio* Giacomo.'

'Stop calling me *zio* Giacomo. It makes me think you want something from me.'

This was, of course, true. I waved my hands in apology.

'And stop waving. What are you English like? You go around the world apologising to people? Is that how you built an empire? You went around the world and apologised to it?'

'Sorry, I—'

'Stop it!'

I took a deep breath. 'Okay. Would *Signor* Maturi be better?'

'How long have we known each other, my boy?'

'About three years.'

'Too long to be *Signor* Maturi, then. And only Federica gets to call me *zio* Giacomo. So, just Giacomo will be fine.'

'Okay. Giacomo it is. You know, you could always call me "Nathan", instead of "my boy"?'

He smiled. 'No. "My boy", I like.'

'Well that's fine then. It makes me feel younger at any rate.' I clapped my hands together. 'Well, I'll start on dinner, so I'm afraid I'll have to leave you for a while.'

'Oh, that's a shame.' His brow furrowed. 'Why so?'

'It's a rather complicated dinner I'm afraid. So it's going to take some precision cooking.'

'"Precision cooking"?' He lingered on the words, with suspicion evidently on his mind.

'Yes. It'll take a little bit of work, but I'm sure it'll be worth it.'

'Hmm. Let's have a look, shall we?'

'Er, yes. Sure.'

We went through to the kitchen. I caught sight of Federica staring after us in despair, at the thought of what might be about to happen.

I took out the sea bass, and he looked at them approvingly, with genuine pleasure in his eyes. '*Rialto mercato*?'

'Of course.'

He sighed. 'Ah, you say "of course". Everyone says "of course we buy our fish at *Rialto mercato*". But how many of us really do, eh? Which stall do you use?'

'Marco and Luciano.'

'I know them. Good people.' He shook his head. 'Fewer though. Every year. Hard to remember now, what it was like when I was a young man.'

'Sad, isn't it?' I said. The words seemed trite, but Maturi patted me on the back.

'Yes, you're right. Sad is the word. Every day, something – no matter how small – is taken out of our city. Every day, we decline just a little bit more.' He rubbed his eyes. '*Allora,* enough of this. Tell me about this "precision cooking" of yours.'

'Ah, well now.' I smiled at him. 'I thought to poach them in red wine, and serve them with a vanilla-infused mash.'

Maturi fell silent for a few seconds. Then, 'Are you completely mad?', he said.

'I'm sorry?'

'You should be.' He picked up one of the bass and waved it at me. 'This beautiful animal has died in order to feed us. The least you can do is treat it with respect. If I want something to taste of red wine I will drink a red wine. If I want something to taste of vanilla, I will have an ice cream, not a potato. And most importantly, if I have guests I will cook something that allows me to talk to them instead of having to hide myself away in the kitchen.'

'I'm sorry, I was only trying—'

'And what did I say about apologising?'

'I'm sorr— Look,' I threw my hands up, 'could you at least stop waving fish at me?'

He froze, and then nodded, and – to my great relief – put down the sea bass. He took a deep breath. '*Allora*. What can we do, eh? You have some potatoes, of course?'

'I have.'

'Okay. Wash them please, and bring them here.' He turned the oven on, as I rinsed the potatoes under the tap, praying that I wouldn't somehow be washing them in a displeasing or incorrect manner. He gave them a quick glance, and nodded as if to say that my potato-cleaning skills were satisfactory.

'Roasting tin.'

I rooted around in the cupboard under the oven until I

found one and passed it to him. He quartered the spuds, and dropped them into the tin.

'Olive oil.'

I passed him a bottle of the second-least-expensive super-market brand. He looked at the label and nodded approvingly. 'Good. No point in wasting money on expensive oil for roasting.' He poured a healthy glug over the potatoes, shook an unhealthy amount of salt over the top, and tossed them with his hands. He placed the dish in the oven. 'What are you like at cleaning fish?'

'Pretty good.'

'Okay. Probably better than me. Just take the fins off, none of this filleting nonsense. If I eat a fish, I want it to look like a fish.'

I snipped away with my heftiest pair of scissors, the sharp fins occasionally drawing an 'ow' from me when they punc-tured my thumb. I passed them over to Maturi, who made three sharp parallel slits on both sides of each fish.

'Lemon.'

I passed one over. I wondered if perhaps we ought to be wearing surgical masks.

'Garlic.'

I gave him an entire head, which he smashed open with his fist. He sliced a single clove into thin slivers, pushing each one into the fish with the point of the knife. Then he repeated the operation with a segment of lemon.

'I think we're done.' He checked his watch. 'Seven thirty-two.' He opened the oven, and laid the fish on top of the potatoes. 'Eight o'clock should do. That gives us twenty-eight minutes for another one of your Spritz Nathans and to tell me about your problem.'

'Are you having fun, boys?' Federica's voice came from the living room.

'Absolutely, *cara mia,*' I called back.

Maturi must have seen the expression on my face. 'Oh, my boy, don't feel too bad. It's not so often I get asked out to dinner these days. And when I do, well, I would rather talk than have my host imprisoned in the kitchen.'

I smiled. 'I understand. Really, I do.'

'Especially if he is about to do something terrible to a potato.'

His eyes might just have twinkled a bit, but I was less than one hundred per cent sure. I kept the smile on my face just in case.

He checked his watch. 'Seven thirty-four. Come on then, time for another of these famous spritzes of yours. And we must go and talk to lovely Federica.'

Three fish skeletons sat in the detritus plate in the middle of the table. It had been a very good dinner. I did, however, think rather bitterly of what might have been with my fillets poached in red wine but *zio* Giacomo had enjoyed himself, and it had at least allowed us more time to chat.

Gramsci hauled himself up on to the table, sniffed curiously at the fish bones, then turned away and plopped himself down on the floor again.

'Strange cat,' said Maturi.

'Yes. You could say that.'

'No interest in fish?'

'Not in fresh fish. If somebody opened a tin of tuna two

streets away he'd go berserk. But if I brought home an entire turbot from the market he'd turn his nose up at it.'

Maturi patted his belly and gave a contented little sigh. Then his expression changed. 'Well now. I suppose we'd better get on to discussing the main reason I'm here.'

I was about to protest, and probably ineptly. Federica, thankfully, got in before me. 'The main reason you're here, *zio* Giacomo, is to cook us a marvellous dinner and show us how clever you are.'

He smiled, and reached across the table to squeeze her fingers. 'Well of course it is, dear Federica. So where shall we start?'

I took my phone out and fiddled with it, bringing up the image of the chapel. I passed it over to Maturi.

Federica put her head in her hands.

Maturi held the device as if he were holding a grenade from which the pin had just been removed.

'What on earth?'

'Er, I was just wondering if you could tell us something about the photograph – where it is perhaps? Neither Federica nor myself can identify it.'

'I see. Well I'm very flattered by your opinion of my abilities. But do you really think I might be able to do so from a one-inch image on a mobile phone?'

'Ah. Would it be better if I printed it out?' He nodded. 'I'll be one moment.'

I rushed through to the office. Please, please let the wi-fi be working. Please, please let there be enough toner left. The printer whirred away slowly, as I drummed my fingers in frustration. Then, mercifully, the page dropped from the printer, heavy with ink, and into my hand.

I took it back to the dining table and cleared some space in front of Maturi who made a great show of cleaning his glasses before peering at it.

'Interesting,' he said, tapping his glasses on the table. 'Now, would you mind telling me how you got this. Or is this secret diplomatic business?'

'I suppose it's a bit secret. But no reason why you shouldn't know. It was found in the pocket of a British citizen who was found dead yesterday morning. He'd fallen into the lagoon from the pontoon at Celestia.'

'My goodness. Poor man.' He put his glasses back on, and took another look.

'So. Any ideas?'

'I believe so. Nowhere near Celestia, of course. And not anywhere our unfortunate tourist was likely to be able to visit.'

We both knew he was milking the moment for maximum effect. Federica broke first. 'Come on, *zio* Giacomo. Put us out of our misery.'

'Well, I could be wrong. Difficult to be absolutely sure. But I suspect it's Sant'Ariano. The Bone Island.' He smiled. 'The Isle of the Dead, if you prefer.'

Chapter 28

Giacomo Maturi was not a man to whom one said 'Are you sure?'

My glass of wine was halfway to my lips. I paused, set it down again, and nodded as thoughtfully as I could.

'You think so?' I said.

Maturi waggld his eyebrows. 'You think I'm mistaken?'

I decided it was best to be honest. 'I have no idea. But what makes you think it's Sant'Ariano?'

'As I said, it's difficult to be certain. I've never even seen a photograph of the chapel before. But I've seen drawings. This looks similar enough.'

I drained my glass. 'Okay. This sounds serious. Can I top you up?'

'Thank you.'

'Fede?'

'Oh, I think so.'

'I'll go and open another one.' I went through to the kitchen and decanted some *vino sfuso* into a carafe. Channing had mentioned the Isle of the Dead. I'd assumed he'd meant the cemetery island of San Michele. But now Maturi had used the same words to describe Sant'Ariano.

The most desolate island of the lagoon. The abandoned ossuary of Venice. In years gone by, when there was no more room in the city graveyards, when you had passed more than ten years on San Michele, your remains would be disinterred and taken to the island of bones, in the area known as the Dead Lagoon, and deposited within its surrounding walls. Far from the city, far from Murano and Burano, isolated even from remote Torcello, this is where generations upon generations of Venetians had ultimately found their final resting place. The Isle of the Dead, indeed.

I took our drinks back through. Maturi raised his glass and clinked it with me.

'Okay, Giacomo. Tell me about Sant'Ariano and this photograph.'

'It is, I suppose, a process of elimination. I think I can say with some confidence that I would recognise every chapel in the *centro storico*. This, I do not. Also, the image is not from Murano or Burano. This I can say with some certainty. The portrayal of Christ would seem to be from the sixteenth century. This, again, would fit with the construction of the walls around the island.'

I coughed. 'I'm sorry, Giacomo, but this is beyond me. I don't know much about this stuff.'

Fede put her hand on his arm. '*Zio* Giacomo, I've spent all my life in Venice and even I don't know much about Sant'Ariano. How many people do?'

Maturi harrumphed, yet looked quite pleased at the same time.

'We need to go back many years. Back to when Torcello was the most important island in the lagoon. On the island of Sant'Ariano – we may imagine it was originally called Sant'Adriano, following the name of the martyr – a convent was established. Not just for those poor unfortunates who had little choice other than to become a Bride of Christ. No, this was a place where the most prestigious families of the Republic sent their daughters.'

Federica swirled her wine. 'Lucky daughters,' she said, before draining her glass and holding it out to me to refill.

'It declined over time, as Torcello itself declined. There were many reasons. There were stories about infestations of rats and serpents. But disease is more likely. That part of the lagoon was malarial. The very air was foul. That, as much as anything else, is what drove them away.

'The island remained abandoned for years. Then, in the sixteenth century, the Senate decided it could still serve a purpose. Remember, this is long before Napoleon. There was, at that time, no cemetery island of San Michele. The dead were buried in the city itself.' He chuckled. 'Even where you live now, my boy – only five hundred metres from the Campiello dei Morti. The Field of the Dead. Have you ever wondered why that square is so much higher than the surrounding area? A cemetery that flooded during *acqua alta* would be – *unpleasant* – would it not?

'They surrounded the island with a wall, and built a tiny chapel as an entrance. One hundred years later, all that remained of the monastery and church of Sant'Adriano had been stripped bare. Taken away to provide materials for the church of the Redentore.' He chuckled again. 'You see, so many people talk of Sant'Ariano and think they have never been there. Whereas the chances are they have actually walked across its stones without realising.

'The centuries passed. Every week, the bones in the centre of the island would grow higher and higher. They reached, it is said, a height of three metres. And then, in 1933, it stopped. The boats bearing their sad cargo came no more. No one would land there. The island was left to whatever still lived there.'

'So, what, it's just been left to fall into ruin?' I said.

'Not quite. There was some work done, I think, back in the 1980s.' He grinned. He was, I thought, enjoying telling his story just a little too much. 'It is said – although, I admit, I never saw this myself – that until the 1970s one could clearly see a layer of bones above the height of the wall. Not, perhaps, the sort of thing one might wish to see whilst taking a Sunday afternoon picnic on a neighbouring island.'

'God, no. So did they remove the,' I tried and failed to find a suitably neutral word, 'remains?'

'Nothing so complicated. The land and, shall we say, the *contents* were flattened in order to bring them below the level of the surrounding wall. The main entrance was bricked up, and the exit from the chapel barred with a gate.'

'Have you ever been there?'

'Good heavens, no. Why would one want to? There is nothing of great interest to be seen – nothing, that is, that couldn't be seen from a boat.'

'Not even the chapel?'

He tapped his glasses on the table. 'That, I admit, might be of some interest. This,' he indicated the photograph, 'is probably one of the few images we have of it. So, yes, that might have a certain fascination.'

'Do you know anyone who's actually been there?'

He shook his head. 'No. I suspect it would be too danger-ous. The walls, most likely, are crumbling and unsafe. Not to mention what might lie within. If the stories about rats and snakes are true it would be an unpleasant experience, to put it mildly.'

'People do try, though,' said Federica. 'Not often. But sometimes, in the newspapers, you read that someone's been arrested for trying to land there.'

'Oh yes. It attracts a certain type of visitor, I understand. Those with an attraction to the macabre. The same ones who hear stories about vampires on Poveglia and decide they have to go there.'

Federica smiled at me. 'Those who watch too many horror films, perhaps?'

'Perhaps,' said Maturi. 'I don't understand it myself. I can imagine there being little, if anything, to see and nothing more than a general feeling of melancholy. I can get that from a disappointing *tramezzino*. No, I can think of better ways to spend an afternoon.' He harrumphed. 'Now then, are you going to tell me you've prepared a ridiculously over-complicated dessert?'

I smiled. 'On the contrary, all we have is some cheese.'

He laughed. 'My boy, you're beginning to make progress.'

Maturi made his way home post-cheese and a couple of glasses of disappointing grappa.

Fede put her arms around me. 'Well done, *tesoro*.'

'Was I all right?'

'You were marvellous.'

'Marvellous? I didn't do anything. I invited your uncle over for dinner in order to have him cook for us.'

'He loves cooking, and he loves being the host. So it was just the thing to do.'

'I feel like I've been in a fight.'

'Well, don't. You know what he's like. And he likes you, really.'

'I like him too, you know. In spite of, well, everything. It has to be said, he's never dull and it's been an informative evening.'

'Mmm. So what are you going to do now?'

'I don't know. I was starting to think all this Black Magic nonsense was just, well, nonsense. And now I'm not so sure. I'll have a chat with Rayner again. Perhaps his clerical buddies know something. But other than that,' I shook my head, 'it's been interesting, but I'm not sure it's moved anything further on.'

'Come to bed then. It'll all seem clearer in the morning.'

'Washing-up?'

'Leave that for the morning. Come on.'

She took my hand, and led me through to the bedroom, leaving the fishbones to the mercy of a cat that didn't like fish.

Chapter 29

I stood in the kitchen, shaking my head as I watched Gramsci tapping away at his empty bowl. I took my coffee into the bedroom and sat down on the edge of the bed next to Fede.

'This is going to sound daft,' I began.

She yawned and stretched. 'Okay. Is it going to be important?'

'I don't know. I think so. It's Gramsci . . .'

'Oh.' She rolled over, and pulled a pillow over her head. I counted to five and then whipped it away.

'Hey!'

'Seriously. I'm worried about him. He used to be the apex predator in the flat, and now, well, he just waddles everywhere. I don't understand it.'

'Is that all? Okay, I'll just give him less food in the morning.' She rolled over again.

'Thanks. I hope that's all it is.' Then I realised what she'd just said. 'Hang on a minute.' I whipped the pillow away once more.

'Stop doing that!'

'You said you'll give him less food? *You're* feeding him?'

She yawned. 'Sure. First thing in the morning. I make

a tea or coffee, feed the cat, and come back to bed for a bit.'

'Before I get up?'

'Of course. Not all of us have the luxury of working from home.'

'But I feed him when I get up!'

'You do?'

'Yes! That's it! His diabolical little brain has worked out that he can get two breakfasts if he finishes all the food you've given him by the time I get up! That's why he's become a Very Fat Cat. Hell, that's why he's being nice to you!'

'Is it? How disappointing.'

I ran my hands through my hair. 'Do you realise what this means?'

'We just feed him a little less?'

'You don't understand. It's not a question of giving him fewer biscuits. I've had to do this before. It's like Gene Hackman going cold turkey in *French Connection 2*.'

Fede rolled over and pulled the pillow over her head, gripping the edges tightly. From the kitchen, I could hear Gramsci starting to yowl. I got to my feet and sighed. This was not going to be easy.

It was a long morning. Searching for further information on Sant'Ariano came as light relief after dealing with a cat who considered himself to be on the edge of starvation.

I remembered, as Federica had said, that there had been occasional arrests following attempts to land there. There were a few news stories to be found online, as well as personal accounts from people who had tried, and failed, to find someone who would take them. There were also a number of long-distance photographs of the island. It did not look as dramatic as one might have hoped. Small, flat and overgrown, with few distinguishing features apart from the surrounding wall and tiny chapel, it inevitably disappointed in comparison with the nightmarish visions the name conjured up.

One image showed a sign affixed to the crumbling red brickwork, too small to make out on the webpage. I saved it as a photograph and zoomed in as much as I could. I could read the words 'Ossario di S. Ariano' but little more. I put on my glasses and peered closer. 'Ossario di S. Ariano . . . Arciconfraternità di San Cristoforo e della Misericordia di Venezia.' Nearby, a wooden sign was fixed to the rotting wooden jetty. It said, simply, *divieto di ormeggiare*. Landing prohibited.

Frustratingly, there were no close-up images of the chapel. I searched through the available photographs and videos; most of which promised more than they delivered, being little more than long-distance shots of the island.

There was one exception. A YouTube video, with jerky video quality and seemingly shot on a head cam. There was little or no narration beyond a few muttered words in an English accent.

I watched the slow approach to the island, and the camera lingered on the 'Landing prohibited' sign. Then the unseen cameraman made his way around the outside of the wall. No path to speak of, but it looked feasible, if heavily overgrown underfoot.

The unknown visitor entered the chapel. I paused the video in order to bring up the photograph of the Polaroid on my phone. There was no doubt it was the same location. The statue of Christ was badly faded and water-stained, whilst the walls were almost completely bare of plaster, the result of centuries of damp and neglect. The whole space was, surely, beyond any meaningful restoration.

There appeared to be a space, another room, behind the altar, cordoned off by barred metal gates on either side of the chapel. The cameraman moved to the gate on the right. He reached out a hand and tested it. It didn't move. He shook it again, with greater force this time but, again, it refused to shift. The video blurred as he shook his head in frustration, swearing under his breath.

He moved to the other side of the altar and repeated the procedure. This time the gate shifted, just a little. Again, the image blurred as he applied his shoulder to it and, after a little grunting, it scraped open.

The space behind was a small, featureless room, with fragments of discoloured white plaster clinging to the red brick. A short flight of steps led up to what must have been the interior of the island, the entrance to which was blocked by another barred gate. I don't know what I'd expected to see. Perhaps something out of a Lovecraft-inspired nightmare, a Bosch-like image of hell where vermin chewed on the remains of the long dead. Instead, all that could be seen was a thick forest of vegetation, trees and brambles. The cameraman's hand reached out to the gate and shook it. It didn't move. He tried again, and then the image panned down to show a large, heavy and extremely rusty padlock and chain. The image blurred again as he shook his head. 'Impossible' was the only word I could make out as he muttered under his breath.

The image spun around as he made his way, carefully, back into the chapel. He dropped to his knees, and ran his fingertips across the floor. He stood up again, brushing the dirt from his hands. He bent, slightly, the better to give a clear image of the ground. Then he walked backwards, and raised both his hands to his face as he held up a camera.

A Polaroid camera.

Jimmy Whale.

He spoke again. 'Okay, the light isn't brilliant, but we'll see how it goes.' He moved back a few more steps, and pressed the exposure button. It whirred and clicked through the familiar sounds of an instant camera. He folded it away and held up the photograph.

'Not perfect. Not enough light. I'm going to need to come back some time. There's not as much to see as I thought. It's still been worthwhile though.' He paused. 'Okay, I hope you've enjoyed our visit together to the Isle of the Dead. I'm going to try and get a few more things posted up on the site in the next couple of days. In the meantime I'm heading back to Venice for a hot shower and a spritz. Thanks for watching.'

He turned and left the chapel, and walked along the dirt path on the edge of the island. A boat could be seen at the end of the jetty. The single occupant threw his hand across his face. 'Idiot,' he shouted. 'I told you, don't film me. You want me to leave you here?'

'Sorry man,' the narrator apologised. 'I'll switch it off, okay.' There was a click on the soundtrack, and then the picture cut out.

I rewound it by thirty seconds, and forwarded it in slow

motion. Again, I saw the boatman cover his face. I paused the video, and expanded the screen, zooming in. I could make out the name on the side of the boat. Marcuccio. Not a common name in the Veneto. Good. That meant it wouldn't be too hard to track him down. And *Signor* Marcuccio, it seemed, was a man who could be persuaded to take tourists to visit forbidden islands of the lagoon.

I looked more closely at the YouTube user icon. Long-haired, hippy-ish. It was definitely him. Jimmy Whale. I brought up the 'About' page.

James Whale (not the director). Ghost hunter. Island hopper. Stay tuned to my channel for exclusive shots of some of Europe's most hidden haunts.

I scrolled downwards in case the comments were of use. There weren't very many of them; nevertheless I swiftly became bored with the overuse of the word 'awesome'. Take away the island's historic reputation and what was left? A crumbling wall, a derelict chapel and an interior choked with trees. 'Awesome' seemed to be going a little far.

I scrolled further. There were two dissenting comments amidst the *awesomes*. Someone had posted under the name of 'Anonimo Veneziano'.

'Can I just say these are some of the most idiotic comments I have read on this site? Sant'Ariano is not a place for stupid tourists to go to get their 'kicks'. Nearly all Venetians have the remains of relatives lying there. Show it some respect! Moreover, the place is dangerous. Those walls are crumbling. What happens if you have an accident? You think that guy in the boat is going to wait for you?

Three children went off to Sant'Ariano in August 1980. Only one came back. Remember them. And don't be a damn fool. Stay away from the Isle of the Dead.'

The other, from 'Unknown User', was straight to the point.

'Stay away from Sant'Ariano. It is dangerous.'

Three children? Not just two? And Gabriele was supposed to have drowned near Torcello. The same part of the lagoon, to be sure, but not close enough for the two islands to be confused. Had there been more than one accident in the same year? In the same month?

'Fede?' I called. She stuck her head around the door. 'You heard about the Loredan boy, didn't you? When you were a kid, I mean?'

She nodded. 'I told you. Everyone at school had heard about it. He'd been somewhere near Torcello with his sister, and something had happened. He'd fallen overboard and drowned.'

'But was there anyone else with them?'

She frowned, and then shook her head. 'I think the reports just mentioned the two of them. Gabriele and Ludovica.'

I turned my laptop around to face her. 'Come over here a minute. Take a look at this.'

She read through the comments, until she came to Anonimo Veneziano's.

'What do you think?'

'Difficult to know. But, to be honest, I'd say they've just made a mistake. We're talking about forty years, after all.'

I turned the laptop back to face me, and drummed my fingers on the table. 'I'm not convinced, you know?'

'I'm sure you're not, Mr Holmes. I'll leave you to investigate further.'

'No, wait a minute. Wait a minute. There was something that came up the other day. When I was looking for information on Channing. There was a photo of him with his business partner. The same year, maybe the same month as the accident. Can't remember the name now.' I tapped away at the keyboard. 'Here we go. Darko Kastellic.'

She shook her head. 'I don't know the name.'

'He had a son called Andrea. There's a photograph of them on Channing's boat, not long before the accident.'

She laughed. 'I don't know him either. I'm sorry, *caro*, but I'm being very bad at being *Dottoressa* Watson today.'

'I'm just wondering – what if there really were two kids drowned that day? As *Anonimo* says.'

'I still think it's more likely he's simply made a mistake. Surely we'd all have heard about the other boy?'

'I guess so.' I went back to my computer and searched for 'Andrea Kastellic'. There was nothing to be found. Online newspaper records rarely stretched back that far, yet I knew the photograph of the Channings bringing home Gabriele's body was out there. It was at least possible that other records, other photographs might be as well.

I tried again. 'Andrea Kastellic. Gabriele Loredan.' Nothing. No connection at all between the two boys, and yet the photograph on Channing's boat showed that there had been.

Once more. 'Andrea Kastellic. Gabriele Loredan. Hugo Channing. Cosima Loredan.' Throwing names at the search engine in the hope that something would link up.

It did. Pinterest this time. Photographs of a celebrity magazine from the late 1960s. 'Hugo Channing and Darko

Kastellic share a Martini together at the legendary Harry's Bar.' I clicked on it. *'Business partners by day, best friends by night, Hugo Channing and Darko Kastellic celebrate the conclusion of another deal with a drink at Venice's most famous celebrity hang-out.'*

There were other articles and photographs along the same lines. In an ideal world I would not have had to piece together the history of their business relationship via the medium of Spanish celebrity magazines, but it was all I had.

Slovenian by birth, Kastellic had lived in Trieste for much of his life where he'd made his money in shipping. He'd worked with Channing throughout the 1960s, at the end of which their partnership had come to an abrupt end. Yet the other photograph I had found showed them in each other's company in 1980. Whatever had caused the split between them seemed to have been repaired.

The 1970s had been difficult years for Kastellic. Following his break with Channing, a series of bad business decisions and a certain degree of forgetfulness when it came to dealing with the taxman had led to him being declared bankrupt by the end of the decade. He retired as a result of 'difficult family circumstances' in the early 1980s.

How old would he be now? Was he even still alive? I brought up the online telephone directory for Trieste.

Kastellic, D Via Margherita Hack 85

It could be a different Kastellic, I told myself. Or even a relative. Nevertheless, it was something to check out. I dialled the number. I let it ring and ring, and was on the point of giving up when the line crackled and a voice answered. *'Pronto!'*

'Am I speaking to Mr Darko Kastellic?' There was silence on the line. I tried again. 'Could I speak with *Signor* Darko Kastellic please?'

'Who's calling?'

'My name is Nathan Sutherland. I'm the British Honorary Consul in Venice.'

'Yes?' He lingered over the word, his voice thick with suspicion.

'I'd like to speak to you if I may. If I could perhaps have just five minutes of your time?'

'What about?'

I took a deep breath. 'I'm afraid it's rather a sensitive matter. I don't want to upset you in any way at all but I wonder if—'

He cut me off. 'You're a journalist, aren't you?'

'I'm not a journalist, I assure you, I told you I'm—'

'I've told you before. I don't speak to journalists. Now this time you listen to me.' His voice trembled. 'Don't you call me again. Next time I'll call the police.'

He hung up. A journalist had already called him, then. One in particular, I imagined. I toyed with my phone and wondered if I should call him again. No. Better not to. He was, after all, an old man who had good reason not to wish to be reminded of the events of forty years past. But maybe, just maybe, he would talk to me in person.

I took out Guy's business card and tapped it on the desk. Another conversation with him would be worthwhile. I checked the address he'd scribbled on the back. Hotel Da Ponte, San Zulian. Not too far away.

There was one more thing to investigate. It was entirely possible, of course, that *Anonimo Veneziano* had made a simple mistake. Nevertheless, it was worth trying to speak to him. I clicked on his profile, but no email address was listed. If I was going to get in touch I would have to leave my contact details on a public forum. I didn't like the idea but Jimmy Whale's channel didn't seem to be over-subscribed. The worst that could happen would seem to be my post being deemed insufficiently awesome. I left a message asking him to contact me with my personal email address instead of the consular one, crossed my fingers, and hit submit.

I checked my watch. There was no time now, but I had another project for the future.

'Fede?'

'Yes, *tesoro*?'

'I'm going to call on our journalist friend. In the meantime, how do you feel about a trip to Trieste?'

Chapter 30

The Hotel Da Ponte was modern by Venetian standards, and had recently been refurbished in a way that suggested that the lobby area was likely to be rather more impressive than any of the actual rooms. A young man in chef's whites was hanging around outside the front door, talking on the phone and smoking. Two visitors were waiting to check in. I caught sight of the rack rate. Not cheap, by any stretch of the imagination, but reasonable for this part of town. A porter arrived to take their cases upstairs, and the man behind the reception desk turned to me with a smile.

'Good morning, sir, how can I help you?'

'Good morning. Are you the manager here?'

He smiled and tapped his name tag, with the words 'General Manager' embossed.

'Ah, I see. Good. Excellent. I believe you have a guest staying here, name of Guy Flemyng.' I spelled his surname out for him.

'Oh yes, sir. The English gentleman.' That probably narrowed it down to about fifty per cent of the guests. The English part, anyway. He reached for the telephone. 'Who shall I say is calling, sir?'

'My name's Nathan Sutherland. He called on me the other day. We have an appointment. Well, sort of.'

He dialled the number. We stood there and smiled and nodded at each other, until he gave a sad little shrug of the shoulders and hung up. 'I'm sorry, sir, he doesn't appear to be in his room.'

Damn. 'Ah. That's a shame. Any chance he might be having an early lunch?'

'I'll call the restaurant for you, sir.' Again, we stood, smiled and nodded at each other, as he spoke on the phone. He hung up. 'I'm afraid not.'

I drummed my fingers on the desk. I could just leave it there, of course. The odds were he was just out and around the town, asking questions of anyone who'd listen. Yet he might have a connection with a man who'd been found dead three days previously. I needed to speak to him.

The manager, I could see, was looking over my shoulder at two people who'd just arrived.

'Look,' I said, 'I'm really sorry to put you to this trouble, but could you tell me if at least his room has been cleaned this morning?'

He sighed, a little theatrically, and ran his finger down a list of rooms and names. He shook his head. 'Mr Flemyng, it seems, is having what you would call a "lie-in".'

Flemyng, I remembered, had the appearance of someone who might enjoy the occasional drink. Nevertheless – I checked my watch – it was now one o'clock. 'Could we go up and give him a knock?' I said. 'It might be important.'

He was visibly irritated now. 'I'm sorry, sir, but can I ask what this is about?'

I took out my business card. 'I'm the British Honorary Consul in Venice. It's my duty to assist any of Her Majesty's subjects who might be in need of help in this city. Mr Flemyng contacted me the other day for that very reason.' Maximum portentousness. That usually worked.

He was struggling to ask me questions without seeming impolite. 'And what help did the gentleman require, sir?'

'I can't tell you that.' I paused. 'Confidential information, I'm afraid. Diplomatic reasons.'

He stared down in silence at my card for a few seconds, and then looked towards the entrance, and the young chef who was still smoking away. 'Alvise,' he called. 'Come here for a moment.'

Alvise gave a start, dropped his cigarette and ground it underfoot.

'*Sissignore?*'

'Alvise, what have I told you about smoking outside? You want to smoke, you go out the back. Doesn't look good having a chef smoking outside.'

'Sorry, boss.'

'Filthy habit anyway.'

He grinned. 'All the great chefs smoke, *capo*.'

'And when you are one of these legendary great chefs then I'll allow you to smoke out the front. In the meantime, I'd like you to take this gentleman up to room 301. Just let him give the guest in there a knock on the door, just to see if he's awake.'

'Sure, boss. Any reason?'

'Diplomatic reasons, Alvise. I can't tell you.' He turned to look at Flemyng's pigeonhole, but there was nothing there.

He rummaged in a drawer under the desk, and brought out a key. 'You'll need this.'

He tossed it to Alvise, who caught it, and gave me a thumbs-up. 'Let's go.'

He led me up three flights of stairs, taking them two at a time and making me grateful that my chest was now less tight than it used to be. Flemyng's room lay at the end of the corridor, a 'Do Not Disturb' sign dangling from the handle. We stopped outside. Alvise looked at me.

'So, what do we do now?'

'You've got a master key?'

'Yes, but I thought you would just break the door down.'

'Break the door down? I'm the Honorary Consul, not James Bond.' I knocked on the door. Then I hammered on it. I nodded at Alvise. 'Come on, let's have a look.'

He opened the door, and gave a little bow. 'After you, Mr Bond.'

The room was small, well furnished and had been very professionally trashed. All the drawers had been pulled out with the contents laid systematically on the bed. Pictures had been removed from the walls. The mini-bar had been emptied. The wardrobe doors stood open, and the guest safe was, inevitably, empty.

I went through into the bathroom. The cabinet door was open and the contents had been swept into the sink. The cistern cover had been removed from the toilet.

Alvise whistled. 'Boss isn't going to like this.'

'I imagine not.'

'Son of a bitch, who's done this?' He turned, and made for the door.

'Where are you going?'

'I'm going to tell my boss, as nicely as possible, that some pig of a guest has smashed his room up.'

'Wait a moment.'

'Someone's going to get landed with cleaning this up. He'd better not ask me.'

'Wait. Take a look around. Nothing's been smashed, nothing's been broken. Everything's been taken very carefully apart, piece by piece. Are all the rooms taken?'

'Think so. We're nearly always busy. Even at this time of the year.'

'There you go. Whoever did this must have been absolutely meticulous in avoiding any noise. This isn't a guest getting drunk and trashing a room. Do you know Mr Flemyng?'

'Not really. My girlfriend works in the bar here. When she got home last night, she said he'd been in for a drink at about seven o'clock. Joking about how nobody can pronounce his name properly. Left her twenty euros as a tip.'

I whistled. 'Very generous fellow, Mr Flemyng.'

'Now normally, you know, I'd be jealous. But I figured, well, it's just some old guy trying to be nice.' He looked at me. 'No offence.'

'You know, Alvise, I think I liked you better when you thought I was some kind of super-spy. Come on.' I offered him my elbow. 'You can help me get down the stairs.'

He grinned, and linked his arm in mine. 'So, what, we're just going to leave it like this?'

'We certainly are. That's something for the police to sort. Now let's go and try and explain things to your boss.'

***

Vanni and I sat outside the Hotel Da Ponte, wrapped up against the cold, in order for him to smoke.

'So,' I said. 'I've got a British citizen with an empty grave, another one who's dead, and a third one who's disappeared. You know what this means?'

Vanni shrugged. 'The British are naturally unlucky?'

'It means I'm facing another very difficult conversation with the Ambassador. More than that, something very strange is going on. Guy Flemyng makes it his business to go around town asking questions of anybody who'll listen about an empty grave on San Michele.'

'You said he was a reporter, Nathan. Asking questions goes with the job.'

'Fair enough. We also have a link between him and Jimmy Whale.'

'How so?'

'I found a video on YouTube. Jimmy had gone out to Sant'Ariano. One of the guys who left a comment – he calls himself *Anonimo Veneziano* – suggests that two children drowned off the island in August 1980. He must be referring to the Loredan case. It's too much of a coincidence otherwise.'

Vanni puffed on his cigar, and then turned away from me in order to exhale.

'You don't have to do that, you know?'

'I'm just trying to be considerate.'

'You don't have to be.'

He smiled. 'Whatever. But whoever our anonymous gentleman is, he does seem to be mistaken. There is no record of a second child being involved. And our records show that

Gabriele Loredan drowned in the canal between Mazzorbo and Torcello. Not Sant'Ariano.'

I shook my head, and sipped at my coffee. 'Except that makes no sense. It was the middle of summer. The schools were still on holiday. There are two *vaporetto* stops nearby. If it had happened there, people would have seen it. People would have been able to help.'

Vanni nodded. 'I know, Nathan. But,' he shrugged, 'that is what the records say.'

'Vanni,' I paused, as I searched for the right words, 'is it possible that those records could have been – *corrected*, shall we say?'

'By *corrected*, do you mean *changed*, Nathan?'

I paused. 'Yes. I think that's what I'm saying.'

Vanni puffed furiously at his cigar, and rubbed his eyes. 'Today, it would be extremely difficult.'

'Forty years ago?'

He sighed. 'Less so. What do you want me to say, Nathan?'

'Nothing. But I understand. Thanks, Vanni.'

We sat in silence for a few moments, sipping at the remains of our coffees. I thought it might be diplomatic to change the subject. 'Did the manager tell you anything?'

'He was helpful without actually being helpful. Mr Flemyng had seemed like a nice guest, he had caused no trouble. No, nobody had come to call for him. Everything had always seemed perfectly normal until this morning.'

'So what do you think?'

'I think it's possible that Mr Flemyng might be waking up right now, nursing a stinking hangover and wondering where he is and what the hell he did last night.'

'Possibly. Do you believe that?'

Vanni shook his head. 'No.'

'So what now?'

'We'll have forensics check the place over. Not sure what we're expecting to find, though. At the end of the day, what have we got? A trashed hotel room.'

'And a British citizen has disappeared.'

Vanni waved his finger. '*Possibly* disappeared.' He sighed. 'Okay. I don't think there's anything more we can do here.'

'So what do we do now?'

'We wait. These people usually turn up. In the meantime we'll fill out a missing person's report. If he hasn't turned up by the end of the day, well, we can start liaising with Interpol. That's about all we can do'. He stubbed out the remains of his cigar. 'What are you going to do?'

'Me? I don't *have* to do anything. Not unless any relatives contact me. It's not my job to investigate.'

'So, as I said, what are you going to do?'

'Investigate, of course.'

Vanni smiled, and clapped me on the back.

Chapter 31

Father Michael Rayner telephoned me the following morning. Nothing, he told me, had come of raising the question of Satanic circles in Venice with the members of the ecumenical council. Indeed, an unspoken suggestion had hung in the air that perhaps their venerable friend from England was not quite right in the head. I could tell he wasn't best pleased and so, by way of compensation I committed to reading a lesson at the carol service. It didn't seem like the right moment to introduce Sant'Ariano.

I looked back through my diary. It had been a week since I had spoken to Victor. That meant, almost certainly, that he had found nothing.

I scribbled down Guy Flemyng's name in the middle of a piece of paper and drew a circle around it. What else did I have? I wrote down the words 'San Michele', 'Isle of the Dead' and 'the Circle' around his name. I added the name 'Lucarelli' and scrawled several question marks next to it. Then I added 'Jimmy Whale'. Then I linked them with arrows, just for completeness' sake.

Gramsci miaowed but I shook my head. 'You're not having this one, Fat Cat. It might be useful.' I scrunched up a spare

'Brexit Survival Guide' and tossed it to him. He batted it out of the air and across the room, and scampered to retrieve it.

It had seemed as if everything centred around Flemyng. A man who had spent a week making his way around the city asking questions of the great, the good and even myself about an empty grave on San Michele. A man who seemed to positively relish being seen doing so by Ludovica Loredan. And a man who had now disappeared.

But now poor Jimmy Whale had come along and complicated matters. Poor Jimmy Whale, with his obsession for unexplored places and abandoned islands; and his photograph of Sant'Ariano. The Isle of the Dead mentioned by Hugo Channing only days before.

What to do? Leave everything alone and hope that things would sort themselves out? I shook my head. I was prepared to have Ambassador Maxwell shout at me. But now there was also the case of a deceased British subject. I had a duty to at least provide as much information on that as I could.

Sant'Ariano. It seemed as if Channing had some sort of connection with the place. A fear of it, even? Jimmy had gone out there to make a short film for his YouTube channel. Guy, on the other hand, had never even mentioned it.

Lucarelli? I shook my head. I knew nothing about him. I couldn't even be sure that it was his bell that Ludovica had rung. And Dario – or Dario's mate – would be able to tell me more about him at some point.

That just left the Circle. What had Channing said? Gabriele shouldn't be there. But he'd mentioned Victor. Whatever or wherever this Circle was, Victor Rutherford had been present.

I leaned back in my chair, and linked my fingers behind

my head. I closed my eyes. I had, it seemed, just about man-aged to mend my friendship with my predecessor. I really, really didn't want to risk breaking it again. Breaking it, almost surely, forever. But it seemed he might be the only person who could help me.

It wasn't really a choice. I opened my eyes, leaned forward to pick up the phone, and dialled Rutherford's number before I had time to change my mind.

He answered almost immediately. 'Nathan?' That was a good sign. He must have entered my number into his list of contacts, and the fact that he'd answered so quickly at least meant that he wasn't cutting me off.

'Good morning, Victor. How are things?'

'I'm well, Nathan. Now, might I be correct in thinking that you're wondering if I've discovered anything about that unfortunate business on San Michele?'

'I was.' I paused. 'Have you?'

He chuckled. 'I'm so sorry. I'm afraid not. I really did check through what records I had, but there was nothing to be found. And as to my distant predecessor: well, as I thought, there's no trace of him at all.'

I sighed. 'Well, we kind of thought as much. But I think I might have discovered something.'

'Oh yes?' His voice was curious, but still warm. Not defen-sive. Good.

'I met Channing the other night. Well, I met his daughter, but he was there as well.'

'My goodness. How is he?'

'He's in a terrible state, poor man. His memory seems to have gone almost completely. He doesn't know where he is, and seems to have no memory of ever having been in Italy at all. And yet there was a moment – I was trying to calm him down – when I told him I was the Honorary Consul and that I would help him. But, as I said, he's confused. He seemed to think that I was you. And then he became distressed. He thought he was with you at somewhere called the Circle. He started to shout that Gabriele shouldn't be there. That he shouldn't be at the Circle. He should be on the Isle of the Dead. Do you know what any of that means?'

'The Isle of the Dead. San Michele, I suppose.' He chuckled. 'It sounds rather melodramatic, doesn't it, but then Hugo always did have a theatrical side to him.'

'Victor, it's just a thought, but could he have meant Sant'Ariano?'

'Hmm. Unlikely, I'd have thought. I suppose that's not very far from where his son was drowned, but it's not a place he'd ever have gone.'

'And the Circle?'

'I can't think what on earth that might be.' He paused. 'Oh, hang on a minute. Unless he just means the *Circolo*?'

'The what?'

'The *Circolo Italo-Britannico*. You've never been there?'

'No. Tell me about it.'

'It's a group for British expats and Italian anglophiles. They meet once a week to listen to a lecture on a suitably worthy subject, and then have a prosecco and a chat.'

I laughed, almost in relief. 'Of course. That makes sense. Ludovica told me he no longer remembers any Italian. So that's it. I'd been imagining all sorts of terrible Satanic cults. Witchcraft. That sort of thing.'

Victor laughed as well. 'My goodness me. No, I don't think they're a terribly Satanic bunch. I don't think anything more wicked goes on than snaffling an extra glass of prosecco. And even that's probably only at the Christmas party.'

'I never seem to get invited to those sorts of events.'

'Oh, I'm sure you do, Nathan. Anyway, you should get in touch with them. You could give them a talk. Consular life, etcetera. They love that sort of thing.'

'Free prosecco? Maybe I will. Nibbles as well?'

'There most certainly are.'

'That's settled then. You used to go there with Hugo?'

'Well, I used to see him there pretty regularly. He was something of a mainstay. I was with him when it happened, you know? When he had that massive stroke.'

'I don't know much about that, to be honest.'

'Terrible thing. The evening was supposed to be in his honour as well. A few of us were lining up for photographs, all the grandees and,' he laughed, gently, at the memory, 'me, for some reason. God knows why. And then the poor fellow just dropped like a stone. Never the same again.' A note of concern entered his voice. 'From what you were saying, he's no better.'

'No. Worse if anything. It's pretty distressing to see.' I paused. 'Thanks, Victor. It's been good to talk, you know?'

'For me too, Nathan. Thank you.'

'Any chance of seeing you over in Venice any time?'

'Oh, Nathan, I'd love to. But I'm not sure my knees are really up to it any more. Perhaps I'll see you over here sometime though.'

'Perhaps.' But probably not. 'I hope so.'

'That'd be lovely. Goodbye, Nathan.'

'Goodbye, Victor.'

I hung up. Then I went back to my computer and searched for the *Circolo Italo-Britannico*.

Chapter 32

'Mr Sutherland?' The speaker was a well-dressed man in, I guessed, his late sixties, who spoke with the lightest of Venetian accents.

'That's me.' We shook hands. '*Signor* Trevisan, I presume?' He smiled and nodded. 'We spoke on the phone. It's very kind of you to come out.'

'No problem at all. Could I just ask, before we start, if we might speak in English?'

'Of course.'

'It's for my accent.'

'Well, it's as near to perfect as I've heard, but by all means . . .'

He gave a little bow. 'You are too kind. It is not quite perfect. The chance to practise is one of the reasons why I adore our little *Circolo* here.' He spread his arms, the better to illustrate the splendour of the room.

I had never been to the Palazzo Pesaro Papafava before, possibly because it had one of those names that was almost impossible not to stammer over. The ground floor had been given over to a museum dedicated to Casanova, a well-intentioned exhibition that – as far as I could make out

– suffered somewhat from the lack of anything that had ever belonged to the man himself.

'You wanted to talk about Mr Channing?'

'That's right. He was a member here, I understand?'

'He still is. He isn't able to come any more of course, but it would have seemed inappropriate to withdraw his membership.'

'And his wife and daughter?'

'I don't think they ever came quite so often. It was far more Mr Channing's passion than theirs.'

'I've been told this is where he was taken ill?'

'Indeed.' His expression changed. 'Can I ask you how you know this, Mr Sutherland?'

'My predecessor told me. A man called Victor Rutherford.'

'Oh, I remember him. A delightful man. How is he?'

'He's very well. It's been good to speak to him again.'

'Well, do please pass on my best wishes.'

'I will. I promise.' I tried to move the conversation on to the matter at hand. 'I, erm, don't imagine you keep an archive of events by any chance?'

He smiled. 'Well now, you'd be surprised, Mr Sutherland. We do have one. Of sorts. Come with me.' He led me out of the *sala grande* and into a side room, piled high with stacks of chairs. He patted the side of a wooden filing cabinet. 'This is it. It's incomplete, sadly, but it's a reasonable record of the activities of the *Circolo* over the past half-century. We might only be a social club, but we're not entirely without interest. We had Luigi Nono here, shortly before he died. Emilio Vedova, once. Princess Margaret joined us for a meeting back in 1973, I'm told.'

'Wow. Bet you needed some extra prosecco that night, eh?' He looked confused. 'Sorry. Little joke. Very little. I don't know if you've got any material relating to the night Mr Channing was taken ill?'

There was a flicker of suspicion in *Signor* Trevisan's eyes, but he was obviously far too polite to ask me what my interest was.

'Look, I'll be honest with you. I've got an empty grave on San Michele, and a dead man to repatriate. In short, things are more than a little complicated. But they might just be linked with something that happened at the *Circolo* in the past. When Hugo Channing was taken ill. Can you help me out here? Please.'

The look of suspicion was replaced by one of confusion, but then he nodded, and opened a drawer in the cabinet. He leafed through the cardboard document wallets within.

'Here we are. From the 2011–2012 season.'

'What was the event?'

'It wasn't one. Not properly. More a sort of end-of-season party. So many people go their own way in the summer, you know? Lots of our English friends go back home for the season. And many of our Italian members have second homes in the mountains. And for the rest of us,' he chuckled, 'we go to the Lido, or lock ourselves indoors, turn the air conditioning on, and pray for rain.'

I listened to the *pioggerella* pattering on the windows. 'Seems hard to imagine now.'

'It does, doesn't it? Now let's take a look.' He flicked through the contents of the wallet. 'Here we are. Now, over here, I think.' He beckoned me over to a table, and spread out the contents.

Photographs. Some in black and white, most of them in colour. Happy, smiling people, most of them in near-identical poses of raising glasses of prosecco to the camera. Trevisan sighed. 'It's getting more and more difficult to keep a proper archive these days. Fewer and fewer people use actual cameras.'

I ran my eyes over the photographs, and then stopped and smiled. Victor Rutherford, his hand resting on Trevisan's shoulder, laughing as if sharing a joke. Next to them, leaning on a stick with a glass in his other hand, was a white-haired old man. He was bent over with age, but still recognisable. Hugo Channing. He, too, was laughing.

'That's a nice photograph,' I said.

Trevisan smiled. 'It is, isn't it? Do you know, that was the last time I met Hugo. Well, I went to see him in hospital a few times, but this was certainly the last time I saw him as he was.'

'What happened?' I asked, as gently as I could.

'It was very sudden. It can't have been more than a few minutes after this photograph was taken. We were laughing and joking, as you can see. Facing out towards that window at the end of the *sala grande*, the one that looks over to the Misericordia. One minute he was as you see him here. And then he stopped. He just stopped moving. He said nothing at all. And then he dropped to the floor, before any of us could do anything.'

'Terrible.'

'It was. Poor man.'

'Do you ever see his family?'

'I'm afraid I don't. I used to know Cosima – his wife, you know – quite well, but I haven't seen her for years. Ludovica, I never really knew.'

'She does seem as if she'd be rather difficult to get to know.'

'Perhaps. None of us knows how grief affects people until it affects ourselves, of course. They seemed to retreat in on themselves. Life, as I understand it, seems to revolve around Hugo.'

'I had the impression it always did.' He looked displeased, so I changed the subject. 'You were looking towards the window, you said?' He nodded. I looked over the snapshots once more. Again, all I could see were people in seemingly identical poses. All parties, I supposed, were basically the same.

Then I stopped. I placed my finger on one of the photos, in black and white, and drew it towards the edge of the table, the better to see it clearly.

Trevisan smiled. 'That'll be by Mr Gormley. He's semi-professional, you know. Always says that black and white gives the more perfect image.'

One man stood apart from the crowd, looking directly towards the camera. Curly-haired, round of face. He had a beard, but that didn't stop me from recognising him.

'Guy Flemyng,' I murmured.

'I'm sorry, I don't know the name.'

'He's a journalist who's been in touch with me – and, for that matter, Ludovica Loredan – over the past week. You've never met him?'

Trevisan shook his head.

'He wouldn't have been a member here, then?'

'Oh no. But that's not unusual. We often get visitors. It's quite possible that he was a guest of one of our regulars.'

'Would it be possible to find out who?'

He laughed. 'Dear Mr Sutherland, I think that might be rather tricky. A number of our members are, shall we say, somewhat advanced in age and it's entirely possible they've moved on to a better place in the intervening years.'

I sighed. It had been a bit of a long shot. 'Okay, not to worry. Would you mind if I took a photograph of this?'

'Go ahead, please.'

I took my phone out and switched to the camera. Guy's eyes looked out of the photograph and into mine, as if I were taking a mugshot.

I tucked the phone away inside my jacket. 'Okay, I think that's everything. Thank you. You've been very helpful.'

'My pleasure. So, you're Mr Rutherford's replacement? You should come and visit us.' He smiled. 'Better than that, we'd be delighted if you were to give us a talk. We'd love to hear from someone in the diplomatic service.'

'Well, that's kind of you, but I'm not sure I'm really a diplomat. And I'm sure I wouldn't have anything terribly interesting to relate.'

He chuckled, and patted me on the arm. 'If what I hear is correct, I'm not so sure about that, Mr Sutherland.' I smiled, awkwardly.

We shook hands, and I made my way downstairs, past two visitors who were trying to decide if it was worth the entrance fee to look at things that had, in all likelihood, never belonged to Giacomo Casanova.

I walked back through Cannaregio. Strada Nova was almost empty now of the hordes of tourists that would cram along it in the height of summer, but it still never lost the smell of cheap cosmetics shops and fast food. I hadn't even thought as far ahead as dinner, but it seemed a shame not to stop and grab a meatball at *Alla Vedova*.

'Buongiorno.' The young man behind the bar smiled, his eyes narrowing in faint recognition of a man who came into his *bacaro* perhaps twice a year.

'A small red wine and a meatball please.'

'Of course.' He reached into the cabinet to take out the last remaining *polpetta*.

'Hang on. Wait a moment. That's the last one?'

He nodded.

'In that case I'll have two.' He looked confused. 'Look, that one – splendid as it undoubtedly is – is not going to be quite as good as one that's come fresh out of the fryer. So if I have two, you'll have to get me a freshly made one.'

'Hmm. That's clever.'

'It is, isn't it?'

'I've got a better idea. Why don't you order three?'

'Erm, I'm not sure that even I can manage three.'

'I think you could.'

'Oh.'

'But that's not the point. I'm really hungry. If you order three, I'll take that one,' he indicated the one in the cabinet, 'and I'll give you the wine for free.'

'Right. Are you allowed to do that?'

He shook his head. 'Absolutely not. But I'm only here part-time. Filling in for my brother. So we're going to, aren't we?'

I smiled. 'Well, of course we are.'

He grinned, and picked up the remaining meatball before making his way through to the kitchen. He returned, five minutes later, with a tray of *polpette* steaming away. He laid two paper napkins on a saucer, and placed two fresh meatballs on top of them. I picked one up, and almost dropped it, the heat singeing my fingers even through the paper.

He raised his meatball in salute, as I raised mine in return. We drew the line at clinking them. I bit into mine, through the crispy-crunchy crust into the steaming savoury goodness within. I always forgot just how good they were. Why did I only come twice a year? Perhaps if I became a member of the *Circolo* I'd be able to stop by here every Monday night?

My telephone rang and interrupted my daydreaming.

'Fede?'

'*Ciao, caro.* Are you at home?'

'No. Just checking out a couple of things on the,' I grasped for the right words, 'San Michele business.'

'Okay. Just to let you know I'm going to be late home tonight.'

'Tough day?'

She sighed. 'Not as much progress as I hoped. So I need to stay for a few hours yet.'

'I could meet you there, if you want? We could grab an early dinner nearby.'

'It's a nice idea. But I won't feel like going back to work after dinner and a spritz.'

'You could just not have a spritz?'

'Don't be ridiculous.'

I laughed. 'Okay. Don't worry about it. I'll have something ready for when you get back. See you whenever.'

'Whenever it is. *Ciao, caro.*'

I hung up. I raised my glass of wine, only to find that the contents had evaporated.

'You know what. Perhaps I could manage a third meatball after all?'

He grinned. 'Tell you what, why don't you make that two?'

Chapter 33

I shivered as I shook the rain from my coat, and turned the thermostat up to maximum. It was going to be a cold evening. I checked my watch. Six o'clock and it had already been dark for an hour. Federica would be some time yet, and so I had plenty of time to cook. I had my butterflied sardines in the freezer, but stuffing a dozen small fish didn't appeal to me. I needed something suitably warming for a winter's night.

Ribollita. The classic Tuscan soup for using up stale bread and neglected vegetables. Not, perhaps, the most Venetian thing in the world, but perfect for the weather.

Cannellini beans. A tin of tomatoes. Both in the cupboard, waiting for an occasion like this. Black cabbage, celery and carrots were all to be found in the 'Neglected Vegetables' drawer of the fridge. Onions and garlic were in the 'Useful Vegetables' section.

I went back to the living room, where Gramsci lay curled up on the sofa, the better to conserve his limited reserves of energy on what he surely considered to be his new and unjust starvation diet. He mewed, gazing up at me as imploringly as he could manage, but the effect only succeeded in looking threatening.

'Well now, Fat Cat.' He mewed again. 'Ah, you're right, that's body shaming isn't it? I'm sorry. Anyway, I was going to ask you what we should play? Good music for cooking to on a cold night?' He raised himself, and hopped up on to the arm of the sofa. 'Now, secondary caregiver is not going to be back for an hour or two. So we could, if we wished, play something really distressing.'

I ran my finger along the rows of CDs. '*The Final Cut*, perhaps?' I shook my head. 'No. Too downbeat, even for us, on a night like this. Early Tull, then, or early Hawkwind? Some 1970s Italian prog?' He flopped back down on to the sofa, and curled himself into a ball. 'No strong opinions, then? Truth to tell, I'm not sure myself.'

I scratched my head as I surveyed the rows and rows of recordings. Nothing seemed quite right. Perhaps it was a classical night?

If P is for Pink Floyd then R is for Lou Reed. And Ramones. And Rachmaninov.

Of course. *The Isle of the Dead*.

I put the disc in the player, and turned the music up. An ostinato bass figure swelled from the speakers, growing, wave-like, in intensity. I put my glasses on, the better to look at the CD. The cover art was Arnold Böcklin's painting of the same name; in which an oarsman rows a small boat to a rocky island, dominated by a grove of cypress trees, his only passenger a cowled figure in white. I thought back to the actual photographs I'd seen of Sant'Ariano: flat, overgrown, and devoid of any particularly interesting architectural features. The reality paled in contrast with Böcklin's Gothic vision.

I was pretty sure that, somewhere in my collection, a copy lay buried of an old Boris Karloff film inspired by the same painting. Perhaps there'd be time to watch it before Fede got home? I wasn't sure it would be of much direct use, but I was prepared to give it a go.

I stopped the music in order to listen to it properly from the beginning, and went back to the kitchen. Federica would not be impressed if she returned to find me slumped in front of the television. Dinner needed to be prepared first. I put a pan on the hob, added a healthy glug of olive oil, and made a *soffritto* of onions, carrot, celery and garlic.

I took a look at the black cabbage. Still good. I'd rescued it just in time. I might even get two meals out of it. I tore the bunch in two, and put one half back in the fridge. I opened the 'Neglected Vegetables' drawer and then thought better of it. This surely deserved to be upgraded to the 'Useful Vegetables' side.

I tore the leaves from the stalks and ran them under a tap to remove any dirt. My *soffritto,* in the meantime, was just about done. I chucked in the tomatoes and the beans and gave it all a good stir before letting it come to a simmer.

I ripped the cabbage into smaller pieces and added them to the pan one handful at a time, giving them just enough time to wilt before adding more. I had half a stale ciabatta left from the previous day which I tore it into chunks, setting them aside to add later.

'I think my work is done, puss,' I called through to the living room. Gramsci, now mid-sleep, gave no answer. 'Just one more thing to do.' I took a chunk of parmesan from the fridge, and grated a healthy amount on to a plate, ready to scatter over the soup once it was finished. I cut off the rind and chucked it into the pot to add flavour. Then I munched away on the remains of the cheese as I poured myself a glass of red wine.

I covered the pan and turned down the heat. It could cook away now until Federica came home. Having finished with Rachmaninov and Böcklin, it was time for Val Lewton's and Boris Karloff's version of *The Isle of the Dead*. Fede would be back shortly, but the film – being from a period when films were of a sensible length – was little more than an hour. There might be time.

The doorbell rang. Nobody ever called early on Friday evening. I picked up the door phone, hoping that somebody had simply rung the bell in error, or that it was Fede who'd forgotten her keys. Too early though, surely?

'*Signor* Sutherland.' An Italian voice. Presumably it wasn't consular business, then.

'Yes. Can I help you?'

'I'd like to speak to you for a few moments.'

'Is it important? If not, I wonder if we might make an appointment and—'

He cut me off. 'It is important, yes. Urgent even.'

I cursed under my breath. 'Come on up,' I said, brightly, and pressed the buzzer.

I recognised him at once. The last time we'd met, he'd been in evening dress. Tonight, he was wearing a cheap suit, with his collar unbuttoned despite the presence of a ragged tie. It suited him better. There was a smell of stale, damp cigarette smoke about him, which I found unpleasant. He hung his coat up without asking.

'Can we sit down?'

I nodded. 'Sure.'

I took him through to the office, and he sat down. He took out a packet of cigarettes, and laid a lighter on top of them.

'I'd rather you didn't smoke,' I said.

'I'm not smoking,' he replied.

I forced a smile on to my face. 'I've just given up.'

'Congratulations.'

My guest seemed to be a man of few words, and didn't seem keen on volunteering information. I got to the point. 'So, what can I do for you, *signor* —?'

'Nothing.'

'I don't understand.'

'That's what I want you to do for me. Nothing.'

My scalp prickled. Federica would be back shortly. How shortly? I tried to sneak a look at my watch.

'Seven thirty. I imagine your partner will be home soon.'

'You seem to know a lot about me, *signor*—?'

He waved his hand to shush me. 'Nathan Sutherland, professional translator, English Honorary Consul in Venice. Am I right?'

'You are.'

'Two jobs. They must keep you busy.'

'They do.'

'Then take a break. Step back a bit.'

'From what?'

'From an empty grave on San Michele. You're a busy man. Spend your time elsewhere.'

'I'm afraid I can't do that.'

'No?'

'No. The body of a British national was supposed to be

buried there. It's my duty to at least try and find out what happened.'

'Happened a long time ago, Mr Sutherland. You won't find anything now.'

'Won't I?'

'No.'

'You seem very sure of that.'

'I am.'

'Well, maybe you're right. I've got other things to be getting on with.'

He smiled. 'Good man. I'm sure you have.'

I leaned forward, ever so slightly. 'Oh I have. Such as repatriating the body of a British citizen who drowned the other day. Near Celestia.'

He shook his head. 'I saw the newspapers. Terrible.'

'It is. Strange thing is, he was found with a photograph of an abandoned chapel on the island of Sant'Ariano in his pocket. And I wonder why that was. So, as you can imagine, that's going to take up some time.' I paused. 'A lot of my time, I imagine.'

My guest closed his eyes and nodded. 'I understand. Time that could be better spent elsewhere, perhaps.'

'You think so?'

It was his turn to lean forward. 'Oh yes. I think so. I don't think you should put yourself to too much trouble.'

'Well now,' I said, 'I don't mind a modest amount of trouble.'

Gramsci jumped up on the table, the better to protect me, or, more likely, just to observe what was going on, his paws skidding across the paper I'd been scribbling on earlier.

My guest cast his eyes over it. 'You really do seem to be

working hard on this, Mr Sutherland.' He reached out and touched Gramsci, ever so gently, upon his back. His tail stiffened, ever so slightly.

'Lovely cat,' he said. 'What's his name? Or her name?'

'Gramsci,' I said.

'Communist, are you?'

'Don't know. Still working that one out.'

'I don't like that.' He leaned back in his chair. 'I don't like people without the courage of their convictions.'

Gramsci turned his face to me, and his eyes narrowed as he purred.

'Smart cat. You should listen to him.' His hand whipped out and caught him around the neck. He held Gramsci out in front of him, his little legs flailing to no avail.

I jumped to my feet. 'Son of a bitch. Bastard. Let him go or I'll—'

'What'll you do, Mr Sutherland? One move and I'll snap his neck.'

'And then I'll kill you, you bastard.'

'Will you? Or will I just wait for your girlfriend to return?'

'You—'

'Bastard. Yes. Don't bore me.'

I lunged across the desk, reaching for Gramsci, but he whipped him out of the way.

'Stop it. Okay, just stop it. What do you want?'

'All I want, Mr Sutherland, is for you to drop it. And then you, and your lovely partner, and your lovely cat need never hear from me again.' He held Gramsci out towards me.

'I'll—'

He put his hands to his lips in a shushing motion. 'You'll

do nothing, Mr Sutherland. Now sit down.' Gramsci's claws continued to flail, a dreadful, strangulated wheezing sound emerging from his throat.

I sat down.

'Better. Are we calm now?'

'I'm calm. Just put him down.'

'Say "please".'

'Please. Please, just put him down.'

'Okay.' He never stopped looking at me, but, in one swift move, hurled Gramsci across the room. I heard a thud, and a yowl that at least told me he was alive. I made to leap across the desk, but before I could move my guest had upturned it and pushed it back on top of me. I fell backwards, cracking my head against the radiator. My head spun, and pain scythed through my legs as the heavy desk landed on my shins. I forced myself to keep my eyes open.

My assailant stood looking down at me. My head was ringing, yet I could still hear Gramsci howling away in the corner.

'Now, it would be nice to stay and wait for your girlfriend, but I've got things to do. Just think about what I said, Mr Sutherland.' He paused. 'I'm not hearing anything.'

I did my best to speak. 'I'll think about it,' I gasped.

'Good man. Well, in that case, I don't think there's anything more to say.' He turned to go, and I tried to shift the desk off me, but then he turned once more, leaned down, and punched me in the face.

At which point the lights went out.

Someone was holding me. Stroking my hair. Slowly the room swam back into view.

'It's all right, my love. It's all right.'

Federica.

Her face was bending over mine, her hair just brushing my face. Her eyes were red.

'Fede?'

'Shh. It's okay. Can you move?'

'I think so.'

'Okay. I'm going to try to move the desk off you. Can you help me?'

I nodded, and wished I hadn't. 'Ow.' I raised myself to a sitting position and then, with Fede's help, managed to shift the desk off my legs.

'Can you stand?'

'I think so.' I stumbled to my feet. 'Ow,' I repeated.

'Come on. Come and sit down.'

I limped across the room, and slumped onto the sofa.

'How's your head?'

I rubbed it. 'Painful.' I took my hand away. 'No blood. I guess that's a good sign.' Then I rubbed my shins. 'How do I look?'

'Not brilliant. Might be best not to receive any clients for a few days. So tell me, which bits of you don't hurt?'

'I think my shoulders are okay.'

'Good.' She gave them a rub. 'So come on, then. Tell me all about it.'

'I had an unusual client.' I told her what had happened. 'What's the time?'

'Quarter to eight.'

'Is that all? Thank God, you just missed him.' I sighed. 'Bloody hell, a smoke would be good.'

'I know. But you're not going to.'

I shook my head. 'Ow. No, I'm not. A drink would be even better.'

'Not yet. We're going to get that head looked at first. And then you're going to call Vanni.'

'You're right.' I got to my feet and stretched. My head and legs ached, but everything seemed to be in working order. Still, it would be sensible to go up to *pronto soccorso* just in case.

'Good. I'll ring for an ambulance.'

I shook my head again, and regretted it. 'I don't need an ambulance.'

'Nathan, you've banged your head and been punched in the face. There is no way we are going to walk up to the hospital.' She reached for her phone. 'I'll call them now.' She jabbed a finger at the sofa. 'Go on. Sit down. Lie down. Whatever helps.'

I lay back down on the sofa and closed my eyes. Then there was a thud on my chest and the scrabbling of claws. I opened my eyes again. Gramsci's face was a few inches away, his eyes boring into mine.

'That didn't go so well, did it, puss?' He, of course, said nothing. 'I think we could both have done better there, couldn't we? Didn't really give a good account of ourselves.'

He lay there on my chest, flexing his claws and digging them into my shirt.

'But I tell you what, though. We're going to get the bastard next time. Aren't we?'

His chest rumbled as he purred, softly and menacingly, as his tail swished around. Despite my aching head, I couldn't stop myself from smiling.

Chapter 34

Ed heard the door of the Brazilians closing. 'Morning, Nat.'

'Morning, Ed.'

Then he stood up from where he'd been working behind the bar and saw my face. 'Bloody hell. What have you been doing?'

'Unsatisfied client.'

'You're not kidding.' His expression changed. 'Seriously, man, have you been to the police?'

'Yes.'

'And?'

'I gave them a description. And a name. Or at least an educated guess.'

'You want to see a doctor as well.'

'Done that. Fede made sure I went to *pronto soccorso* last night.'

'Everything okay?'

'Yeah. Going to hurt for a couple of days, mind.' I plonked a big paper bag of drugs down on the counter. 'Just been to pick these up from the *farmacia*. Everything needed to keep me going for the next couple of days. The doctor says I should avoid caffeine for a bit. So, any chance of a coffee?'

'Decaf?'

'Certainly not.'

'Is that wise, Nat?'

'It's very wise. Federica will shout at me if I make one at home.'

He laughed. 'Okay. But don't say a word. And come round later, eh? I'll have a couple of drinks behind the bar for you.'

'I will. I'm meeting Dario later.' I smiled. 'I'm supposed to avoid alcohol as well.'

'See you both, then. You're sure you're all right, Nat?'

'Yeah. I'm fine. A few bruises but I'll be okay.' He slid my coffee across the bar, and I patted him on the shoulder. 'Listen, I was just wondering. The guy who gave me a working-over last night. Late forties, maybe, shaven head. Stubble. Smelled of cheap fags. Have you seen anyone like that around here in the last few days? You know, in a *lurking* kind of way?'

Ed paused for a moment, then scratched his head. 'To be honest, Nathan, with the exception of the hair, that could kind of have described you for most of the past five years.'

'Oh thanks. Thanks for that.' I downed my coffee in one and immediately felt better.

He smiled at me. 'See you later, eh? I was serious about the drinks.'

'How are you feeling now?' asked Federica, as I stepped through the door.

'Not too bad. Ed has promised me a free drink. A savage beating in exchange for a Negroni doesn't seem like such a bad exchange. And then there are these.' I emptied the contents of my bag on to the table. 'Paracetamol. Ibuprofen. The mighty but humble aspirin. All my painkilling needs.'

'You've been to the Brazilians?' she asked, her eyes narrowing.

'Only for decaf.'

She tried to look stern, failed, and gave me a hug. 'You're such a terrible liar. Don't ever change.'

My mobile rang. I looked at it, and sat down heavily on the sofa. A UK number. One I didn't recognise. I thought I knew what that meant.

'Are you all right?'

I shook my head. 'No. But I need to take this.' I pressed the receive button and put on my most serious voice. 'Nathan Sutherland, Honorary Consul.'

It was thirty minutes before I was able to hang up. Federica sat down next to me and leaned her head on my shoulder. We sat in silence for a few minutes, as I rested my head on hers, my eyes closed.

She rubbed my back. 'Are you okay?'

I tried, and failed, to keep my voice steady. 'Not really.'

She waited a few moments, until she realised that I wasn't going to speak again. 'Who was it?'

'His mum. Jimmy's mum.'

Again, we sat in silence. 'Want to talk?'

'Yes.'

'Come on then.'

I took a deep breath. 'It was most of the cycle, really. Shock, of course. Moving swiftly on to denial. *Are you sure? Could you be mistaken? Is this a joke?* Anger. *When will I be able to have my son's body? Why must I wait so long? Is there anyone else to speak to? Who's your superior?* And then depression. Except it's not depression. It's just a woman sobbing uncontrollably on the other end of the telephone. We never made it as far as acceptance.

'Do you know what was worst? I think it was her voice. She sounded broken. It was like hearing somebody age in front of you.

'She was proud of him, you know? He still lived at home. Worked in an off-licence, and saved all his money for holidays and photographic equipment. He wrote books, she told me. You can find them on Amazon. Disused railway stations in London and Paris. Abandoned churches in Venice. And now he was working on one on the ghostly islands of the lagoon.' I took a deep breath. 'She was so proud of him.' My voice cracked.

'Oh, *caro*, I'm sorry.'

'Not as sorry as that bastard is going to be.'

'Nathan, you don't know that Jimmy Whale was murdered. Not for sure.'

'Maybe not yet. But I'm bloody well going to find out.' I touched my face, my fingertips tracing gently over the cuts and bruises, and we sat in silence as I took a few deep breaths.

'So, tell me. What's going to make you feel better?'

I managed to crack a half-smile. 'I suppose "a cigarette" is the wrong answer?'

'It is.'

'Okay then. Answer B is "solving the mystery".'

'There we go. That's what we'll do. After lunch.' She got to her feet, went to the door, and pulled on her coat. 'Come on.'

'Where are we going?'

'Don't know. Don't care. Let's just walk. Let's just get you out of here and blow the cobwebs away. Then we'll have lunch somewhere other than the Brazilians, and, if you're good, I might even let you have a prosecco with that.'

'I thought I was supposed to avoid alcohol for a bit? Isn't there something about it impairing cognitive function?'

Fede looked at me for a few seconds, and smiled ever so slightly. 'I think we can risk that. Come on.'

Chapter 35

Dario shook his head. 'Nat, man, you don't look good.'

'Thanks, Dario. You know, quite a few people have been saying that to me today.' I looked around the Brazilians. Some of the regulars hurriedly turned away and started chatting amongst themselves. I stood up and waved at them. 'I'm still here, you know? Yes, I've been in a fight. Yes, I've been beaten up. I'm totally fine talking about it.'

There was an awkward silence. I sat down again.

'You're not fine, are you?'

'*Be*'. I've been better.'

'I'm sorry. I should have had this guy checked out sooner. My buddy Franco got in touch yesterday. I thought it would just wait until we next had a beer. If I'd let you know . . .' His words were tripping over themselves now, and I gave him a gentle punch on the shoulder.

'It's okay, Dario. Don't worry about it. Go on then, what have you found?'

He took out a folded sheet of paper, and spread it on the table in front of us. It was a photocopied article from *Il Gazzettino,* from five years ago. Nevertheless, I recognised the face at once.

'The guy's name is Lucarelli, as you said.'

'I knew it. Son of a bitch, I knew it.'

'He'd been a cop. Not a good one.'

I read through the article. Giorgio Lucarelli of Mestre. Suspended from the police pending investigation. Bribery and corruption. Also implicated in the sale of stolen passports and identity cards.

'He was sacked maybe six months after this,' Dario continued. 'And then Franco tells me he set up as a private investigator.'

'Don't you need a licence for that sort of thing?'

'Technically, yes. But all you really need is a sign or a business card with some sort of nice shield-type logo and the words "Private Investigator", and you're good to go.'

'So, what sort of stuff does he do?'

'Got a problem with late payments? Clients taking too long to pay up? Lucarelli's your man.'

'So not really Private Investigations then?'

'No. More like Money with Menaces. Recently heard of doing security work for hotels. For events and the like, you know?'

'Would one of those be the Ca' Sagredo?'

'I don't know. I'll see if I can find out.'

'Don't worry about it. It might just help to join things up, that's all. Lovely man, anyway, by the sound of it.' I felt the bruise on my head and winced. 'Stolen passports, you say?'

'Yes. Does that mean anything?'

'It might do. Jimmy Whale. The young British guy who drowned off Celestia the other day. His passport was missing.'

'Mmm.' He sipped at his beer. 'So what are we going to do?'

'What do you mean, we?'

'Vally and Emily are away for a few more days. Just until I get the flat properly sorted out. So, I've got time to help.'

I drained my glass. 'Okay. How about this? How about we get the bus over to Mestre, pay a call on this son of a bitch and kick seven shades of shit out of him until he tells us the truth?'

Dario shook his head. 'No.'

'No. Tell me why not?'

'Because we're not the sort of people who do things like that. We're the good guys.'

I closed my eyes, and nodded. 'Ah, you're right. Bloody difficult though, isn't it?'

'So is giving up smoking and motorcycling, *vecio*. And we can manage that.'

In spite of myself, I smiled. 'Blimey, when did you become a wise old man?'

'I'm right though, yes?'

'Yes. You are. Which means I need to go to Trieste.'

'Trieste? Why?'

'Because there's a man there I need to speak to. About San Michele and Sant'Ariano, and something that happened nearly forty years ago.'

'What about work?'

'I've got a surgery tomorrow, but I can cancel it.'

'I could cover it, if you like?'

I paused. 'It's kind of you but—'

'After last time?'

'Exactly. Anyway, with the bruises it might be as well for me to take a couple of days off. Don't want to scare the clients, after all. As for translating the terrible film script – well, a few days away from that might be a bit of a blessing to be honest.'

'Okay. I understand. So, what's Sant'Ariano got to do with this?'

'The English guy who drowned had been there the day before. Then someone left a message on his Youtube channel. They mentioned two kids who drowned near there back in 1980. Two kids, not one. Gabriele Loredan. And somebody who might be called Andrea Kastellic. So, there's a link there, it's just that I've got no idea what it is. Have you ever been out to Sant'Ariano?'

He shook his head. 'No. I had friends who did. Just as a dare, you know, when we were kids. I remember they caught hell off their parents when they found out.'

'You never did, though?'

'No. Seemed too dangerous.' He smiled. 'Even for me. You ever been to Trieste before?'

'First time. Federica's been a few times, though. She's coming along to look after me.'

'Doesn't she have work to do?'

'She's going to take a day off. It's partly that – well, I'd kind of like us both to be together and not in Venice – just in case Lucarelli decides to pay us a call again.'

'Sure, Nat. I understand.' His face brightened. 'Hey, Vally and Emily are still with *Nonno* and *Nonna*. I could give them a call, if you like? I'm sure they'd be happy to put you up for the night, if you wanted to make a proper break of it.'

'Thanks, but it's just,' I rubbed my face, 'I'm kind of worried about making a bad impression. "Hi there, I'm Dario's friend. I'm the Honorary Consul in Venice. Oh yes, and I've just been in a fight.'

Dario laughed. 'I get it. But let me know if there's anything I can do, eh?'

'I will. Thanks.'

'Okay. I think we need another beer.' He held two fingers up to Ed, who nodded. 'You know Nat, you should just go back to the cops. Tell Vanni you know who this guy is for certain now. Let him sort it out.'

'I know. And I will. But I think we're close now and, whoever this guy in Trieste is, he might be more likely to talk to me than to the police. And maybe then the whole San Michele thing can be laid to rest.'

He smiled at the little joke. 'And what about this guy, Flemyng?'

'Disappeared. I don't know where or why, or if he's still asking questions of anyone willing to talk.'

'And Mr Whale?'

'It sounds bad, but I find myself hoping that he really did just fall in and drown. Because the alternative is more complicated than I'd like . . .'

Chapter 36

Fede and I sat in a café in Piazza Unità d'Italia, and tried to stop shivering.

'I did warn you,' she said.

'You said it might be windy and a bit cold. I hadn't expected this.' I tore open a sachet of sugar with my trembling hands, and tipped the contents into my coffee; then stirred it as best I could, my shaking fingers rattling the spoon against the cup. I breathed in its aroma and felt ever-so-slightly better. I sipped at it, and felt its warmth spreading from my tongue to my throat and throughout my whole body. I leaned back in my chair and sighed.

'Good coffee.'

'It should be. I always felt it was something they did particularly well in Trieste. Probably the Austrian influence. Obviously, that's an opinion I keep to myself in Venice.'

'I can imagine.' I cleared the condensation from the window with the sleeve of my coat, and looked out at the piazza. The sky was dark with clouds, and the city appeared as if in a blue half-light. The journey, by train, had taken little more than two hours. I had snoozed most of the early part of the journey, as the train made its way through the featureless plains of the Veneto. Federica had advised me to set my alarm for the latter part of the journey, as we climbed into the region of Friuli-Venezia Giulia, and the train took us around the Gulf of Trieste.

In the end, I was woken up by my mobile phone informing me that we had passed from Italy to Slovenia. Two minutes later it told me that we had passed back again. And again. And yet again. It made me smile. The status of the city had always been fluid, passing from the French to the Austrians to the Italians to the Yugoslavs and finally, following seven post-war years as a city state, back to the Italians. It was no wonder my humble telephone had got confused. I had to admit, though, that the view across the gulf, even on such a foul day as this, had been one worth waking up for.

We had been about to leave the station, when Fede laid a hand on my arm to hold me back. She pulled a woolly hat on to her head, and wrapped a scarf around the lower part of her face so that only her eyes were visible.

I pushed at the door to the exit but, again, she held me back.

'Mmmph!'

'Sorry?'

She pulled her scarf down. 'Are you going out like that?'

'Er, yes.'

'No hat, no scarf? I told you to bring a hat and scarf.'

'I've got a scarf. Somewhere. I couldn't find it this morning. And I've never liked woolly hats.' She narrowed her eyes. 'Not that they don't look good on you of course. I've got an umbrella, though.' I took a tiny folding one from my pocket.

She shook her head in despair and pulled the scarf back

up before gesturing towards the exit. I pushed the door open and went outside.

The blast hit me square in the chest and pushed me back into Fede. She must, I think, have been prepared for this as she was there to catch me and push me through the door and out into the piazza. Through streaming eyes, I could see pedestrians, wrapped up in layer upon layer of Gore-Tex, bent double against the wind, making their way along the street as best they could. My coat flapped and whipped around me as I struggled to button it. I managed to force my umbrella open and held it against the gale for a couple of seconds until it was whipped from my hands and bounced along the road, causing a car to swerve and honk furiously at me, before taking flight and disappearing over the Gulf of Trieste.

Federica slid her arm under mine and half steered, half dragged me along the front as we fought our way against the wind for what seemed an interminable amount of time, until we reached the Piazza Unità d'Italia, where – realising that I was turning blue – she pulled me into the nearest café.

I became aware that she was speaking to me. 'Shame about your umbrella,' she said.

'Probably halfway to Slovenia by now.' My breath had fogged the window, and I wiped it clear with my sleeve once more. Grandiose Austrian architecture, in a city on the very fringes of Italy, on the border of the old Eastern bloc. A city neither here nor there.

'So what do you think?' said Fede.

'I think it's cold.'

'And?'

'Wet.'

'And?'

'Windy.'

'Otherwise okay?'

I shrugged. 'I think it's probably quite . . . nice?'

She laughed, and sipped at her coffee. 'You're not seeing it at its best. It's lovely in the sunshine.'

'Dario wanted me to come last year, you know? Iron Maiden were playing here.'

'You didn't want to?'

'Never been that into them, to be honest. I felt a bit bad about it at first. Thinking I should have gone to keep him company. But now,' I smiled, 'I feel as if I got away with it.'

'It's a lovely city. Seriously. We must come back in the spring.'

'We must?'

'Yes. I don't want you to get the wrong impression. You just need to be prepared for the wind in the winter months. Oh, and the fact that wherever you want to go is probably going to be uphill.'

I smiled. 'Ah, well now, I'm used to that. I once lived in Edinburgh, remember?' I looked down at my left hand. I could still, just about, see where the ring had been on my third finger.

She noticed the gesture, and smiled, reaching over to rub my finger with hers. 'So, have you thought about what to say to Mr Kastellic?'

'No idea. It might not be so easy.' I'd attempted to telephone him once more, the previous day, and he'd hung up on me almost immediately, shouting that he wouldn't speak to journalists. 'There's been nothing about his family in the press, has there? Nothing on the back of Gabriele's grave being empty?'

She shook her head. 'No.'

'Strange, then. Why say he doesn't want to be bothered by journalists if, as it seems, they manifestly aren't bothering him? Or does he mean one in particular? Guy, of course.'

'That makes sense. Perhaps Guy discovered something about the Kastellic boy in the same way you did?'

'Perhaps,' I said.

'Guy,' she paused, 'who is now missing.'

'Yes. I had thought of that.' I tried to change the subject. 'Thanks again for coming.'

'I thought it might help if you needed to speak to someone. Given that you look as if you've been in a fight.'

'I *have* been in a fight!'

She smiled and – gently – touched the side of my face, before unfolding a map of the city and spreading it out on the table. 'Here we are. Via Margherita Hack. It shouldn't be more than ten minutes' walk away.'

'Uphill?'

'Of course.'

I looked outside at the rain-lashed square and shivered. 'Come on then,' I said.

I left a couple of euros on the counter, and we made our way out into the maelstrom.

'This is it?'

Federica nodded.

'Nice.'

Kastellic's home – a modernist bungalow, in contrast to the

grander Hapsburg-period buildings that surrounded it – was more modest in size than I might have expected. Nevertheless, whilst inevitably being uphill it was not, perhaps, quite as uphill as all that, and the presence of nearby shops made me think that Mr Kastellic had chosen wisely for his later years.

'Okay, let's do it.' I looked at Fede. 'Erm, might it be best if you sort of stood in front of me as much as possible? At least until we get him talking.' I moved behind her and she rang the bell.

There was no answer. We waited and waited but no one came.

'Are you sure it rang?' I said.

'Quite sure.'

'Let's just try once more.' I reached over her shoulder in order to press it again, but she must have heard movement from inside, slapping my hand away and fixing her most dazzling smile on to her face.

'Yes?' The speaker was an elderly man, silver-haired and cadaverous, with dark-rimmed eyes that made me think he could use more sleep.

'Mr Kastellic?' said Federica.

He looked us both up and down, and then shook his head. 'I don't speak to journalists,' he said. He made to close the door, but Fede stuck her hand out and held it open.

'You want me to start shouting and screaming? You want to see what my neighbours will think, when they see an old man being threatened in his own house? What the police will think?'

'Please. We're not from the press.'

'Police, then? I don't talk to police either.'

'We're not police. Or journalists. I promise,' I said. 'Look, if it makes any difference, I'm the British Honorary Consul in Venice. I telephoned you the other day.'

'You what?' His voice was still laden with suspicion, but at least he'd stopped trying to slam the door on us.

'My name's Nathan Sutherland. I'm the consul in Venice as I said.' I took my card out and showed it to him.

'I don't understand. What's that to do with me?'

'Maybe nothing. Maybe everything. It's about the death of a British citizen,' I half lied.

'So, do I have to speak to you?'

'No, you don't. But we've come quite a long way to see you. And it's cold, and it's windy and I'm wet through and about to die of exposure. Please.'

He looked from Federica to me and back again. Then he nodded. 'Very well. You'd better come in.'

'Sit down, please.'

I looked around in the hope of finding something that might serve as a seat. There was scarcely an inch of usable space in the room. Books were piled everywhere; great tottering, dusty piles of hardbacks, paperbacks, coffee-table books and art books, yellow-spined columns of Italian *gialli*, airport novels and blockbusters of years gone by, their titles largely forgotten by now and the covers fading with age.

Similarly, the walls themselves were hardly to be seen, concealed behind mazy, chaotic arrangements of photographs. Take everything out and the room would probably be twice the size.

I found something that might once have been a chaise-longue, covered in back issues of the *New York Review of Books*. I made a half-arsed attempt at moving them, before he tutted and knocked my hand away, sweeping them all into a pile before depositing them on top of a stack of leather-bound volumes on the history of Trieste. It swayed alarmingly, but he nodded with satisfaction and motioned that we could be seated.

We sat down. Carefully.

'You're a great reader, I can see,' I said, and immediately felt ridiculous for stating the obvious.

He stared at me. 'You look terrible,' he said.

'I feel terrible.'

'What happened to you?'

'Would you like me to say I walked into a door?'

'The truth would be better.'

'Okay. I was threatened and beaten up by a man who wants me to stop investigating the empty grave of a boy called Gabriele Loredan on the island of San Michele.' I watched him closely, but he gave little reaction at the mention of Gabriele's name.

'And what has that to do with you?'

'Gabriele was a British citizen, despite his name. I'm the British consul. I'm trying to establish exactly what happened.'

'And so what does this have to do with me?'

'I think you know, Mr Kastellic.' He said nothing. 'Gabriele was the son of Hugo Channing. Your business partner of the time.' He remained silent. 'More than that, Gabriele was drowned on the same day.' I paused, trying to reformulate the words into something less cold, 'I mean, there was an accident in which—'

'In which what?'

'In which your son Andrea was drowned.'

He leaned on a table for support, sending a stack of books rocking. 'What are you talking about?'

'I'm sorry, that was clumsy of me. I was trying to find the right words.'

'You are a journalist, aren't you? I told you never to call me again.'

'Mr Kastellic, there's some confusion here—'

'There's no confusion at all. I should call the police. Right now. It was a few days ago, wasn't it? Ringing up an old man. Telling him his son is dead. People can go to prison for this.'

'Mr Kastellic, I swear to you that wasn't me.'

His eyes were still full of suspicion. 'Why should I believe you?'

'You've seen my card. You can telephone the British embassy if you wish. They'll vouch for me,' I lied.

He jabbed his thumb at Federica. 'And her?'

Fede stiffened. 'She's here because her Italian is better,' I said. 'But mainly because she's more diplomatic in situations like this.'

'I don't imagine she could be any worse.'

I ran my hands through my damp hair. 'Mr Kastellic, I'm very sorry about what has happened. But it would really help if you could tell me why you think somebody phoned you up to say – to say the things they did.'

'I don't know. There are some sick people in the world.'

'I'm sorry.'

'So you keep saying.' He shook his head. 'I don't understand where this nonsense has come from. My son is not dead. He lives in Argentina now.'

'What?'

He picked up a photograph in a frame, and ran his fingers over it. 'This is him.' He passed it to me. A black-and-white photograph of a young man, on the verge of adulthood, in a Juventus T-shirt. Curly-haired, with dark eyes and the beginnings of a moustache, he smiled out at the camera.

I smiled at Kastellic. 'Handsome lad,' I said.

'He still is. Not a boy any more, of course.' He took the photo from me, and replaced it on the table. 'Is it too early to offer you tea? Everyone tells me the British always drink tea at five o'clock.'

'That's kind. I prefer coffee if that's—'

'I can't drink coffee any more.'

'Tea will be lovely, thank you.'

'And the *signorina?*' He didn't look at her.

'Tea would be delightful, thank you,' said Fede, her voice all sweetness and light.

'I'll be a few minutes.' He navigated his way to the door, through the stacks of books. 'Don't touch anything while I'm gone.'

Fede waited until he had left the room, and then laughed, drily. '*Signorina.* Not been called that in a few years.' I got to my feet. 'What are you doing?' she whispered.

'I just want to have a quick look around. Don't worry, I'll be careful.' I moved around the stacks to the wall, scanning the photographs. My eyes came to rest on a photo of a young man in military dress, standing in front of a church. 'Where's this?' I asked.

Fede craned her head to look closer. 'St Spiridon, I think.'

'Correct, *Signorina.*' Kastellic had re-entered the room

without us noticing. 'The Serbian Orthodox Church in Trieste. That was my older brother, Ivan. He was with the partisans. He was shot one week after that photograph was taken.'

'I'm sorry.' My eyes continued to scan the pictures on the wall. I was, I knew, being more than a little rude, but I didn't know how much time he was going to grant us. Then I saw a photograph, taken, I assumed on Channing's boat. Cosima, in white swimsuit, impossibly beautiful with her dark Louise Brooks bob. Channing, bare-chested (had he spent the entire 1960s without a shirt?) and in dark glasses. And next to them, a tall man in a white polo shirt and slacks, his black hair swept back, grinning at the camera.

'Handsome devil, wasn't I?' said Kastellic.

'You were,' I murmured. 'You all were.'

'I assume you've spoken to them. Given what has happened. How are they?'

'Cosima is well. Still a very lovely woman. But Hugo is dreadfully ill.'

'Is he?' He bowed his head. 'Tell me more.'

'He has dementia. He no longer knows where he is. He has some memories of who he is, or who he was. I think he just about recognises his daughter. But that's all.'

Kastellic closed his eyes and nodded. Then his eyes flicked open, and he looked at me. He smiled.

'Good,' he said.

Chapter 37

I felt my skin crawl, and shook my head. 'Mr Kastellic, I don't think you understand.'

'Oh I do. I understand perfectly.'

'If you could see him, it would be impossible not to have pity for him.'

'I don't have pity for him. I am happy for him.' He shook his head. 'You don't understand, of course. How could you? You're too young. We're the sum of our memories, they say. What if there are things we wished we could forget?

'I remember the day of the accident. Ludovica was a young woman by then, but terror had made a child of her. Cosima, trying to be brave, trying to hold herself together for her daughter. And then the two of them, Hugo and Cosima, setting out in their boat. Bringing their son home for the last time.' He drew in a deep breath and closed his eyes. 'So, yes, I am happy for him, if he no longer remembers that he once had a son. Do you understand now?'

'I think so,' I said.

'That was the last summer I saw him. We met back in the 1960s, you know? I was just a businessman. A good one, yes, a successful one, but just a businessman. He was different.

With his racing team and his glamorous wife and his palazzo in Venice.

'But we got on. That was the strange thing. We started off as partners. Shipping. Import and export. That was always my line. Then we became friends. Always used to holiday together. Skiing in the winter. Yachting in the summer. Good days.'

He paused. I waited what seemed an appropriate amount of time before I spoke. 'So what happened?' I said.

Kastellic took another photo down from the wall, running his fingers over it again. Cosima, glowing, with a baby in her arms; and, next to her, Kastellic.

'It's a cliché, of course, but I never understood quite what she saw in him. Oh, yes, he was a millionaire, but she was beautiful and came from a noble family. I think she deserved better.' He gestured around him. 'I don't think Hugo ever read a book in his life. She always seemed so much more intelligent than him.

'My marriage broke up – to Andrea's mother – in the late 1960s. Cosima and I, well, we had been close for a while. I had hoped she would leave Hugo. I didn't care about the partnership any more. I had sufficient money. But, in my heart of hearts, I knew she never would. She was very traditional in that respect. And so our holidays together became few and far between. My boy had always been friends with Ludovica. And I think in some ways he saw Cosima as being like a second mother to him. We went to spend the summer of 1980 with them. To see them, perhaps, for one last time. All friends together again. And then, one day, Gabriele went out on a boat with his sister. And never came back.

'Andrea and I had spent the day together. Father and son things, you know? I think they blamed us. Thinking that if Andrea had been there, Gabriele might have been saved. We left, just after the funeral, for the last time.' His voice broke, just a little, and he dabbed at his eyes. 'I am alone now, Mr Sutherland. I have been since Andrea left for Argentina. I'm not just happy for Hugo. I think perhaps I envy him.'

I waited until the silence was too heavy not to be broken. 'Mr Kastellic, the journalist who spoke to you the other day. Was his name Guy Flemyng?'

He shook his head, looking old and tired now. 'He didn't give me a name. Or if he did, I don't remember it.'

'Do you remember what you talked about? It might be important.'

'We didn't talk about anything. I told him to go to hell. Except less politely.'

'What did he ask you?'

'He told me he was writing a book about Channing. Salacious nonsense, it sounded like. Sun, sex and scandal. That sort of thing.' He stretched and yawned. 'I need to rest, now. I'd like you to go.'

'I understand. Thank you, Mr Kastellic.' I looked over at Fede, feeling a twinge of guilt as I realised I'd cut her out of the conversation completely. 'Federica?'

She was standing, with Andrea's picture in her hands, seemingly captivated by the profusion of photographs on the walls.

'Fede?' I repeated. 'I think we ought to be going.'

She turned around, her brightest smile on her face. 'Of course. I'm sorry, I'm miles away. Head completely in the clouds.' She looked down at Andrea's face again. 'Such a handsome young man.' She put it back in place. 'Lovely photographs. It's been so kind of you, Mr Kastellic.'

He adjusted the picture, moving it a centimetre to the right. 'Thank you, *Signorina.*' He showed us to the door. He didn't offer to shake hands, and we made our way outside into the horizontal rain.

'Wasn't there anything at room temperature?' I grumbled, as Fede returned from the buffet car with two small bottles of chilled prosecco and two plastic cups.

'Best I could do, *caro.* It'll have to do.'

I took one of the bottles from her, rolling it around in my hand. 'You know, this is still warmer than I feel.' I leaned back in my seat, unscrewed the pretend plastic cork and poured half the contents into my cup. We clinked glasses as best we could.

The Gulf of Trieste was receding in the distance, as the train began its descent to the northern plains of the Veneto. 'So, what was all that about?' I asked.

'What was what?'

'All that "Oh what a handsome boy, what lovely photos" stuff.'

'Oh. You mean when he was telling you a pack of lies?'

'You don't believe him?'

'Of course not. You don't, do you?'

I shrugged. 'I don't know. I thought he seemed genuinely upset.'

Fede rolled her eyes. 'I despair at times.'

'Oh, very well. Tell me why, *Dottoressa.*'

'There are no other photographs of Andrea.'

'What? There must be?'

'No. Not one. Unless you count baby photographs. I admit I can't be sure about those. They all look the same to me.'

'Are you sure?'

Fede glared at me over the rim of her plastic cup. 'Nathan, one of us has a job that involves staring at visual images in great detail, all day, every day. And one of us doesn't. There isn't a single other photograph of him. Andrea isn't in Argentina. He's at the bottom of the lagoon.'

'Wow.' I drank the last of my prosecco.

'I'm right, aren't I?'

'You are.'

'Am I a brilliant girlfriend?' I made to kiss her but she pushed me away, waving a finger. 'Uh-uh. Am I?'

'Always,' I smiled. And then I kissed her. 'So why is he lying?'

'He's an old man now. Maybe, in his own strange way, he's trying to protect Cosima from something. Find out what, exactly, and we've solved it. What do you think about Mr Flemyng?'

'That's a bit strange. Ringing Kastellic to tell him he knows his son was killed wouldn't seem to be the way to encourage him to talk further.'

'Maybe he was trying to provoke him? Just trying to get a reaction.'

'Yes, but why?'

'That goes on the "to be discovered" list, Mr Holmes.'

'Uh-huh. It all links up, though. Some way or other. Something happened on the lagoon forty years ago. Ludovica knows about it. Kastellic knows about it. Flemyng knows about it. And Sant'Ariano is the key.'

'So now what?'

I turned my miniature prosecco upside down, and watched the sad remains of the contents dribble into my plastic cup. 'Well, right now, I'm going to go to the bar and get another brace of these. And then tomorrow I need to go and speak to a man about a boat.'

Chapter 38

Mother and Father are angry, of course, when they hear about Rialto. For the next few days, Mother takes us out to the Lido to play on the beach. Father needs to have time to talk with Andrea's father, she says. We have to be very good, and not distract him. Besides, it is good for us to have Andrea here, she says, good for me and Ludovica to have a friend.

We have spent the whole summer with Andrea. I am bored now. Bored and tired. I want to stay at home, to lie in my room and read, but Mother and Father say I must go out.

I am starting to hate Andrea. I hate the way he looks at Ludovica and then at me, smiling as if I was just a stupid little boy.

But tomorrow he will go home. There will be still be a few weeks before school begins again. Precious weeks to lie in my room and read fumetti.

We are lying in the cortile of our palazzo, resting against the vera da pozzo, *the pink marble cool against our shoulders. Through the water-gate, we can see the waters of the canal rippling, casting green-blue reflections on the walls.*

We should take the boat out, says Andrea. We should all have one last adventure together.

I tell him no, we are not allowed. Father will be angry with us.

He laughs and says I am such a little boy. Afraid of Daddy.

He touches Ludovica's bare shoulder, just for a moment. And then he looks from her, to me, then back again. And he laughs once more.

Ludovica joins in and, for a moment, I hate them both.

He stops, and tries to look serious, to look grown-up. I'm sorry, he says. It's not your fault. It's just that you're so young.

Andrea, I know, is five years older than me. Just five years, yet, for a child, that seems a lifetime. I clench my fists, digging my nails into my palms. He wants to make me feel like a little boy.

I'm not too young, I tell him. I have taken the boat out many times.

Ludovica looks at me, but says nothing. I look right back at her. Many times, I tell her. And on my own. Without you. She says nothing. I think, perhaps, she smiles for a moment.

Good, says Andrea. It's settled. You, brave captain, can take us out in the boat.

Our last great adventure.

Chapter 39

Bar al Canton, in the northern part of Castello, was unknown to me. A painting of comic-strip hero Corto Maltese, cigarette dangling from his lips, dominated the area behind the bar, whilst the walls were decorated with anti-fascist stickers and posters of demonstrations against the widely-hated giant cruise ships. A big screen TV played an adventurous, and quirky, programme of Venetian ska.

I checked the time, and rechecked the message on my telephone. He should be here by now. The woman behind the bar returned my smile.

'*Ciao.*'

'*Ciao.*'

'Can I help you?' she asked, in English.

'I hope so. I'm waiting for someone. I'm told he's a regular here.'

'Oh. What's his name?'

'Heh. I'm afraid I don't actually know.' *Mr Anonymous*, I thought, would just lead to unnecessary confusion.

'No worries, *caro*. Something to drink, something to eat?'

'I think I will, thanks.' I cast my eyes over the pastries in the cabinet, then a blast of cold air hit me as the door opened.

'*Ciao, Gianni!*' She beamed. 'Is he your new friend?'

I looked over at the giant, grizzled figure in the waterproof jacket. 'I hope so.' I extended my hand. 'Can I call you Gianni? Or would you prefer *Signor Anonimo*?'

He grinned and crunched my hand in what I hoped was meant to be a friendly way. 'Gianni is good, thanks. Mr Sutherland, yes?'

'Nathan is fine. Can I get you a drink?'

'Sure.' He ruffled his hair and turned to the barista. '*Un'ombra, cara.*'

Red wine. I looked outside. Kids were still making their way to school. But I'd been in Venice long enough not to be surprised by Strong Drink being taken at this hour. I couldn't – quite – face one myself and settled for a *caffè corretto*. After all, what could be more natural than a shot of grappa in a breakfast coffee?

'You know this place?' he said.

I shook my head. 'First time.'

'I've been coming here for over thirty years. Good place. Anti-fascist, you know?'

I took another glance around the stickers and posters. 'I'd never have guessed,' I smiled. 'So. How did you come across that video?'

'I've got a boat hire business up here. A young English guy walked into the yard just a few days ago. Asked me if I could take him out to Sant'Ariano.' He shook his head again. 'Stupid kid. I've had a few of them over the years. Anyway, there'd been stories in the papers about the grave of the Loredan boy. That got me thinking about what happened that day.'

'Sorry, just one moment. I don't understand how Sant'Ariano is coming into this?'

'Because that's where it happened, my friend.'

'But the reports said Torcello-Mazzorbo?'

He laughed, a great, rumbling smoker's laugh. 'Yeah. That's what the story was. Bullshit. Anyway, I started thinking that maybe this guy was a journalist or something. So I did a quick search and I found the same as you. I thought I should leave him a warning.'

'It's actually dangerous, then?'

He shrugged. 'Maybe. Why risk it? Anyway, I'm Venetian. I'll have family in there, somewhere. I don't like the idea of *stranieri* – no offence – trampling over them.'

'I understand.' I took a pause to sip at my coffee. 'The official story is that there were two children in the boat. Just two?'

'Yeah.' He took a tin of tobacco from his pocket and started to roll a cigarette. 'Also bullshit, my friend.'

'I don't understand.'

'Look. I used to go fishing in those days, in that part of the lagoon. And that afternoon, I'm telling you, I saw three young people in a boat heading towards Sant'Ariano. Three of them, you understand?'

I opened my mouth to speak.

'Are you going to say "are you sure?"' I nodded. 'Well don't. The boat was a Riva. Smart boat. Not something you wouldn't recognise. And there were three kids in it. Three. And I'm not the only one who saw them.'

'No? But why wasn't it reported?'

He rubbed the fingers and thumb of his left hand together,

as he continued rolling his smoke with his right. 'Money, you know? There were others out in that part of the lagoon that day. And one minute they're talking to the cops, *yes officer, there were three kids in the boat*. And then later, it's *yeah but the sun was in my eyes, I think maybe there were only two. And thinking about it, it was definitely nearer Torcello*.' He laughed again. 'Sons of bitches, nobody ever offered me any money.'

'But you kept quiet?'

He shrugged. 'Hey, if somebody asks me, I say I saw three kids.' His face broke into a grin. 'But nobody asks me.'

I finished my coffee and drummed my fingers on the bar, thinking. He had, I noticed, finished his wine. 'Can I get you another?'

He shook his head. 'Still got to go to work, you know. Anything else?'

'Maybe. Do you know a *Signor* Marcuccio?'

'Kind of. He's got a place not far from here. Near Celestia.'

'Would he be the sort of person who might take a boat out to Sant'Ariano?'

He looked at me for a moment, then grinned again. 'I wouldn't know, my friend.' He patted me on the back. 'Thanks for the drink.' He walked to the door, and then turned around, rubbing thumb and forefinger together again. 'I wouldn't know,' he repeated.

I smiled and gave him a wave, then reached for my wallet. Corto Maltese stared down at me, the speech bubble coming from his mouth reading '*Venezia sarà la mia fine*.' *Venice will be my end*. Or *Venice will be the death of me*. No kidding, Corto, I thought, as I slid a banknote across the bar.

***

Signor Marcuccio had a small boatyard, not far from the Celestia stop. A boat stood on chocks on a slipway, whilst the garage behind held various outboard motors and engines on benches. He appeared to have no employees. Greying of hair and moustache, he lay on his back sizing up the hull from beneath. I coughed to attract his attention.

'Can I help you?' A non-Venetian accent, as I'd expected.

'I hope so.'

He got to his feet, and lit up a damp cigarette. Since I'd given up, it was starting to seem as if every stranger I encountered smoked constantly.

'What do you need? It's a busy time of year. Or as busy as I ever get, anyway.'

'Really? I wouldn't have thought that.'

'You'd be surprised.' He jabbed a thumb in the direction of the boat. 'Nobody with a boat wants to go out on the lagoon at this time of year. Not if they've got a choice. So everybody brings them in for work. If you want the hull cleaned,' he tapped the side of the boat, 'I can fit you in tomorrow. Any work on the engine, you'll have to wait a couple of days.'

'Thanks, but it's not that. I'm more interested in hiring a boat?'

He looked at me. 'You're moving house? Okay, that might take a few more days. I'd need to come round, take a look, make an estimate. Then I'd need to hire a couple of *ragazzi.*'

'No, I'm just interested in hiring a boat.'

He shook his head. 'Mister, I think you've got the wrong place. I don't do that sort of work.' He dragged on the cigarette, then ground the butt out underneath his heel, smearing a trail of damp tobacco across the wet slipway. 'Your Italian's good. But you're not from round here, are you?'

I smiled at him. 'Neither are you.'

'Puglia. Moved here ten years ago.' He shook his head. 'Not one of my smarter decisions.'

'Sorry to hear that.'

'Don't know what I was thinking. A *Pugliese* running a boat repair yard for Venetians? Maybe in my next life I'll try something easier, like selling refrigerators to eskimos.' He laughed.

'I see. I guess it must be difficult.' I paused. 'You sure I can't hire a boat from you?'

'I'm sure.' He pointed at a boat moored nearby. 'I've only got the one boat. Can't risk anything happening to it. What if someone damages it, or doesn't bring it back?'

'That can happen?'

'It can do. Kids messing around mostly. I don't need the aggravation. I tell you what, though: if I did have a spare for hire I could have been coining it in this week.'

I tried to keep my voice as neutral as possible. 'You could?'

'Sure. I've been asked twice. What's going on? I keep telling people no, I don't do boat hire. You want a tourist boat, you go somewhere else.' He looked up at the grey skies. 'Ideally in about five months' time.'

Two other people. 'Do you remember their names?'

'No idea. I don't imagine I asked for them.'

'Would you recognise them?' I took an envelope out of my pocket, and slipped out the printouts that I'd made. One of Jimmy Whale that I'd taken from his website, and one of Flemyng at the *Circolo*.

He turned his head away. 'Can't be sure.'

I sighed inwardly. I'd thought it might come to this, so I'd come prepared.

'Could you be sure for twenty euros?'

He grinned at me. 'I'm not asking for money, my friend. I just need my glasses, that's all.'

I could feel myself blushing. 'I'm sorry.'

He patted me on the shoulder. 'You've been in Italy too long, Englishman.' He reached into the top pocket of his overall, took out a pair of spectacles and wiped them on his sleeve. 'Let's have a proper look, then.' I passed the photographs to him. He moved them back and forth in front of his face, as if playing the trombone. 'Need to get my eyes checked again,' he said. 'But this guy I recognize,' he pointed at Flemyng, 'although he didn't have a beard. The other one, not so sure. It's not much of a photo.'

It was true. The photograph, or selfie, showed Jimmy grinning at the camera with his face half-covered by his precious Polaroid SX70. 'I know. Best I could find. But it could be?'

'Yeah. It could be.'

'They both asked you if you'd take them to Sant'Ariano, didn't they?'

His eyes widened. '*Cazzo,*' he swore, before fumbling for another cigarette.

'I'm right, aren't I?'

He fumbled with his lighter, trying and failing to get his roll-up to light. I searched in my pockets, through force of habit, and realised that I was unable to help him. Finally, he succeeded, and puffed away.

'Yes,' he said.

I said nothing, and we stood there in silence until he threw the remains of the cigarette on to the slipway.

'They offered me money, you know. Money I could do with.'

'And so?' I had the feeling he wanted me to ask.

He shook his head. 'No. Not worth it. This business is hanging on by a thread. If my boat gets impounded,' he drew a finger across his throat, 'that's it. Game over.'

'I understand.' This next step was going to require some top diplomacy. I wished Federica was there. I took another print from the envelope. A freeze-frame from the YouTube video. '*Signor* Marcuccio. There's something I think you should see.'

He held it up to his face, and then lowered it, slowly, as he stared into my eyes.

'The name "Marcuccio" is on the side of the boat,' I said. 'That's not a Venetian name. There's no other boat-hire or maintenance company of that name in the *Pagine Gialle*.'

He rubbed his forehead, and screwed his eyes closed as if in the hope that the image would have disappeared when he opened them again. 'That's not my boat,' he said, after a long silence.

'I don't understand.'

'I used to have two. I sold one a year ago. Just to make ends meet, you know. That one out there is all I've got left now. Son of a bitch didn't paint my name out. He could be doing anything with it.'

'It rather looks like he is. Look, you must have a name for the new owner, surely?'

He shook his head. 'Guy called Boscolo, over in Chioggia.

But it's not just me that's having a hard time. He went bust six months ago. Anyone could have that damn boat now.'

'And they're running some sort of illegal business taking tourists out to Sant'Ariano. In a boat with your name on the side.'

'*Cazzo.*' He swore, again. 'Where did you get this?'

'It's on the internet.'

'How many people have seen it?'

'Not many. Perhaps a few dozen. But the man who hired that boat was found dead just a few days ago. It might not be long before the police start taking an interest.'

He leaned against the upturned boat and rhythmically thumped his head against the hull. 'Look,' he said, and his voice was tired, 'this is all I've got now. This boat, this yard. If the police come round, if they impound the boat even for a couple of weeks, then I'm ruined.' He ran his hands through his hair. 'I'm too old to start again. Not now. What am I going to do, Englishman?'

'I don't know. Not for sure. But,' I took a deep breath, 'you might be able to help me. Maybe we can sort this out together.'

'How?'

'You can take me out to Sant'Ariano.'

He shook his head. 'Forget it.'

'You've got nothing to lose. Sooner or later the police are going to look at that video and come calling.'

He breathed deeply. 'Okay. I'm not saying I will. But suppose you tell me what your interest in this is?'

'I'm the British Honorary Consul. The dead man was a UK citizen. I'm trying to find out what happened to him.'

'And you need to go to Sant'Ariano to find out?'

'I don't know. But maybe.'

Marcuccio shook his head. 'This is a stupid idea.'

'I know. But it's the only one I've got. What do you think?'

'I think I'm as crazy as you are. But okay, I'll do it. Not now, though.' He looked around. 'Still way too early. Too many boats out there, too many *vaporetti*. We'd be seen. Give me your number, I'll give you a call later.'

I gave him a business card, and we shook hands.

Chapter 40

'You look happy,' said Federica.

'I should be. I've just been talking to the unluckiest businessman in Venice about hiring a boat.'

'Did it go well?'

'I think it did. I'm expecting a call at,' my telephone rang, and I smiled at the number, 'any moment now.' I tapped the keypad. '*Signor* Marcuccio?'

'Mr Sutherland?'

'Speaking.'

'I was thinking about tonight. Are you sure you still want to do this?'

'I certainly am.'

He gave a hollow laugh. 'I was hoping you might have changed your mind.'

'I can't do that. This is something I need to sort out. And just maybe it'll sort out your problems as well.'

'That's the only reason I'll do it.' He took a deep breath. 'Look, I'm not allowed to land on Sant'Ariano. You know that, I know that.'

'Of course.'

'But I can give you maybe twenty minutes there. Maximum. Is that going to be enough for you?'

'I guess it'll have to be. What time should I come round?'

'Ten o'clock tonight. When it's properly dark. When there's less traffic on the lagoon. That's as early as I dare.'

'I'll see you then. And thanks. Really.'

I hung up, and tucked the phone back in my pocket. Then I saw the expression on Federica's face and my smile froze.

'Have I done something wrong?' I asked, as innocently as I could.

Her expression didn't change. 'Are you crazy? Are you completely and utterly crazy?' I opened my mouth to speak. 'No. No, don't say anything. All I want to hear from you is a Yes or a No. Ideally a No. Are you genuinely thinking of going out to Sant'Ariano tonight?'

'Yes.'

'And when were you planning on telling me about this?'

'Er, round about now.'

'Okay.' She rubbed her nose. 'Firstly, you are not allowed to land there. And by the sounds of it, *Signor*—'

'Marcuccio.'

'*Signor* Marcuccio is also very aware of that.'

'He doesn't have to be involved. Not properly. He just needs to give me a bit of time there.'

'Okay. Let's assume he does that. What are you expecting to find?'

'I have no idea. Some evidence that might link back to what happened out on the lagoon forty years ago. It sounded like Jimmy had found something on the video. He said he needed to go back.'

'Jimmy – Mr Whale – might have been murdered, Nathan.' I couldn't really think of anything to say to that.

She sighed, and looked at her watch. 'Okay. Time for a prosecco. I'd suggest a Negroni but, under the circumstances, that might be unwise. Then you can cook dinner. That should give us plenty of time to be there by ten.'

'Sure.' I did a double-take. 'Hang on. "Us"?'

'Yes.' She folded her arms. 'Either I come with you, or I sit at home watching the shadows lengthening and wondering if my idiot boyfriend is lying in a shallow grave on an abandoned island. Amazing as it may seem, that's not much of a choice. Are you going to argue?'

'No.'

'Good. Prosecco please. Then dinner. And it had better be good.'

'You didn't tell me there'd be two of you,' said Marcuccio.

'Is that important?'

He shook his head. 'No. No problem. Plenty of space for us all.' Then he looked from me to Federica and back again, and grinned. 'Your boyfriend's taking you on a strange date, *Signora.*'

'It's not a date. And, at the moment, the word "boyfriend" is hanging by a thread.'

He turned to me. 'You ever had a boat?'

'Nope. Never even driven one. I don't even know if that's the right verb.'

'How about you, *Signora?*'

'My uncle does. A 1960s Riva.'

'Lovely boat. I restored one of them once, you know? Years ago, when I was a young guy. Always loved being on the water.' He stared out over the lagoon, and shook his head. 'Then it became my job and, well, it just became work.'

'Wait a minute,' I said. 'Zio Giacomo has a boat?'

'Sure. It's his pride and joy. He keeps saying he'll take us out one day. Probably better if we wait until spring, though.'

I looked outside. The skies had cleared and the rain had ceased. Out in the dark of the Dead Lagoon, the only light would be that of the moon. 'But you know how to pilot – is that the right word – a boat?'

'Of course.'

'So, erm, any reason why we couldn't have borrowed zio Giacomo's boat?'

'Like I said, it's his pride and joy. Besides, I assumed you wanted something inconspicuous. Have you ever seen a Riva? They couldn't be more conspicuous if you had Sophia Loren sprawled over the front.'

Marcuccio coughed and looked at his watch. 'Come on, let's get this over with.'

We made our way outside, and he jumped down into the back of the boat, before settling himself into the pilot's seat. Federica followed, and then I let myself down from the *fondamenta* with slightly less elegance.

Marcuccio opened up the throttle and we moved away from the *fondamenta* and into the lagoon. 'We'd better take it slowly,' he said. 'Don't want to attract attention. Wouldn't be a time to get stopped for speeding.'

The moon was bright and high in the sky, and it was fearfully cold, and colder still as we moved into the open lagoon. Yet, as I turned to Federica I could see the broad smile on her face. I remembered a conversation with *zio* Giacomo – *Venice is not just the city, my boy. Venice is the lagoon.* And, despite everything, I felt myself smiling too.

Even on a cold November night the area around Murano would be more likely to have water traffic. Marcuccio took the route that passed by Vignole, then up past Sant'Erasmo and San Francesco del Deserto. Around Burano, its brightly coloured houses glowing in the street lights. Then past Torcello, and into the Dead Lagoon proper. He throttled back to keep the noise to a minimum, as we moved past a cluster of tiny islands, one home to a single ruined building; one with a faded and chipped sign that read 'No Hunting'. And then it lay ahead of us. The low, flat island of Sant'Ariano.

'We need to be careful here,' said Marcuccio. 'The lagoon is shallow. Sandbanks. Go off the marked channel, run aground at this time of night and you're in trouble. Big trouble. Imagine being trapped here, on your own. No one coming. At this time of year.' He shivered, and throttled back further. Beyond Sant'Ariano I could see the bulk of the larger island of La Cura, and, beyond that, lights from the villa of Santa Cristina, now the property of the Swarovski family.

The engine was barely ticking over now, as we bobbed in the lagoon directly in front of the Isle of the Dead.

'Okay. Twenty minutes. That's what you've got.' He opened out the throttle, and gently guided us to the end of the jetty. He cut the engine and threw a rope around one of the mooring posts, tying us up.

'I'll go first,' said Fede.

'Wait a moment. Why you?'

'That jetty doesn't look in great condition. I'm lighter than you. If it's sound, I can tell you. If it isn't, better the two of you trying to pull me out than the other way around.'

I couldn't really argue with that. She reached out and gave the mooring post an experimental shake. 'Sound enough.' She hauled herself on to the jetty, and took a few steps. 'Okay, it's in a bit of a state, but if you stick to the sides it should be fine.'

'I like the sound of that word "should".'

I followed her up, and we made our way to the shore. The path underfoot was grassy and slippery. At least, I thought, if you slid into the lagoon here, the waters would be shallow.

We could see the lights of Torcello shining in the distance to the west. The occasional cloud would pass across the moon, but with the aid of torches, there was sufficient light.

'Twenty minutes, okay? Not one more,' said Marcuccio.

I nodded. 'Twenty minutes.'

He cut the engine, and turned his attention to rolling another cigarette, leaving Fede and myself alone on the island of bone.

Chapter 41

We walked along the path outside the walls, until I thought we'd gone a sufficient distance not to be overheard.

'So,' said Federica, 'what are we going to do?'

'I just want to have a look around. Nothing more. Just to see if there's anything that doesn't seem right. If there's anything at all that I can take back to Vanni, which will give him enough ammunition to bring people out here and properly look around.'

'And what are you expecting to find? I think I know, but tell me anyway.'

'The body of Andrea Kastellic in an unmarked grave.'

'Based on that online video by Mr Whale?'

'More than that. We know young Andrea was with Ludovica and Gabriele during the summer. We have one witness – Mr Anonimo – who swears that there were three kids on the boat and that money changed hands – with witnesses, perhaps with the press, maybe even with the police. The lagoon is shallow around here. Another body would have been washed ashore quickly.'

'And so, what, we start digging?'

'I don't want to do that. But maybe.'

'Do you even think we're capable of doing that? Dig down God knows how far?'

'It won't be like that. We're not looking for a coffin that's six feet down. If there's anything there, it'll be a shallow grave. And, given the amount of time that's passed, the body will be a skeleton by now.' I grimaced. 'I had to look that up.'

'So what happens if anybody happens to motor past?'

'Unlikely at this hour. It's not going to be the police at any rate. And if it's just a member of the public, well, would you stop to see who's landed on Sant'Ariano at night?'

'No. But I might call the police and ask them to have a look.'

'Fair point. We'll just have to step it out as quickly as we can.' I paused. 'This place is supposed to be crawling with rats and snakes, isn't it?'

'Yes. Why?'

'Oh. No reason. Come on.'

We made our way further along the path, walking in silence now, the only sound the lapping of the waves against the shore, until we reached the crumbling chapel.

Federica stopped. 'I think you should go first.'

'Me? Why?'

'Well, this was your idea. Besides, you like this sort of thing.'

'Only in films, as I said.' I paused. 'Why are we whispering?'

'We're showing respect.' She gave me a nudge. 'Go on.'

The temperature was cooler inside, and the air smelled of damp leaves. I shone my torch around. The emaciated Christ gazed down with sightless eyes. I looked right, and then left.

'Okay. Let's check over here.' I led the way through to the

rear chamber, and made my way up the steps to the entrance to the ossuary itself. I put my hand upon the rusting iron gate, and tested it. Then I yanked it harder, pulled it towards me and it scraped across the floor.

'There's something down here, Nathan. Just shine your torch over here.' Fede bent down to pick something up. A padlock.

'Rusted through?'

She shook her head. 'No. Someone's taken a bolt-cutter to it.'

'That must have been in the last couple of days. It was still fastened in Jimmy's video.'

I pulled on the gate once again, and managed to drag it open far enough for us to make our way through into the ossuary itself.

The beam of the torch picked out thick, thick under-growth and spiny bushes. Something moved at the limit of my beam, and I jumped back. Fede was there to catch me.

'You okay?'

'I am. Sorry. Something just freaked me out for a moment.'

I took a step further into the undergrowth, checking all the time as to what was beneath my feet. Something crunched beneath my shoe. 'God,' I whispered. Fede placed her hand on my shoulder. I took another step, when something scratched across my forehead.

'Ow!' The shock was enough to make me jump again, and I was unable to keep my voice down.

'What is it?'

I drew my hand across my forehead, and my fingers came away moist with blood. 'It's nothing serious. Just brambles.'

I took another step, and then stopped. 'It's impossible. It's just too thick.' I flashed the torchlight around. 'But you know what? I think someone's been here before us. You can see where someone's had a go at hacking their way through.'

'Jimmy Whale?' said Federica.

'Perhaps. Although his video shows that he didn't get this far. It's possible he came back but didn't have time to post the video up. Whoever it was, they didn't get far. It's a jungle in here.'

I shone the beam around my ankles. Again, I heard something move in the distance. A scuttling or slithering sound? I tried not to think about it. I took another step forward, and, again, something crunched beneath my foot. I looked down.

Bone.

Bone everywhere. Arms, legs, fingers, ribcages, skulls. I shone the torch further into the dark, then swung it left and then right. Wherever I looked, the ground was carpeted with human remains.

'God,' I breathed.

Federica gripped my arm. 'Nathan. There's nothing to be seen here. Nothing except all this.'

'You're right. This is crazy. We shouldn't be here. Come on, let's go. Turn around carefully and I'll follow you out. Just mind where you put your feet.'

We inched our way back to the rear chamber. I closed my eyes and breathed deeply, bending over and resting my hands on my knees.

Federica rubbed my back. 'Are you all right, *caro*?'

I shook my head. 'Not really.' I straightened up and took a few more deep breaths. 'There's something about this place.

It's not right being here. But I want one more look at the chapel on the way out.'

'There's nothing to see, Nathan,' she repeated.

'I don't know. I'm thinking about Jimmy's video. Let's take a look at the altar area.'

I made my way back into the chapel, and dropped to my knees in front of it. For a moment, I wondered what Father Rayner might have thought if he'd seen me in that position, and almost smiled. I shone my torch on the ground, and trailed my fingers across the earth.

I looked up at Federica. 'There's been digging here, hasn't there?'

She nodded. 'What do you want to do, Nathan?'

I looked up at the gaunt face of Christ, and shuddered. 'Nothing.'

'Are you sure?'

'Absolutely. I don't think there's anything to be found. I think whatever – whoever – was buried here has been moved.' I got to my feet. 'I think it's been moved in there.' I pointed towards the rear chamber and the ossuary. I took my phone out and took a few photographs. The lighting was less than perfect but it would have to do. 'I don't know if this will be enough for Vanni, but it's worth a go.'

Federica patted my arm. 'Okay. Let's go.' Then her grip tightened. 'Shit. What's that?'

I opened my mouth to speak, but then I heard it too. The sound of an engine starting, and of a boat moving across the lagoon.

I took a quick look at my watch. We'd been, at most, fifteen minutes. 'I don't believe it. I just don't believe it.' I ran outside, and tore along the path, slipping in the mud. For a moment, I felt as if I was going to topple into the lagoon as my feet slithered, but Fede was there to steady me.

Up ahead of us, I could see Marcuccio's boat pulling away from the jetty.

'Hey, you bastard!' I ran out along the jetty, feeling it shudder beneath my feet. 'Come back here, you son of a bitch!'

Marcuccio turned his head, but I couldn't see the expression on his face. Then he turned back, and the boat continued along its way.

'Bastard!' I shouted after him. I made my way back along the jetty, to where Federica was waiting.

She patted me on the shoulder. 'Maybe swearing at him wasn't the smartest thing to do, Nathan?'

'Possibly not. Sorry. But why the hell would he have left us here?'

'Maybe he saw or heard something coming. Another good reason not to be shouting.' She sighed. 'So, what do we do now?'

'I guess we try and ring someone with a boat. Do you think *zio* Giacomo would come and pick us up?'

'He would. Is that a conversation you want to have?'

'Can't think of a better one.' I took out my phone. 'Except, of course, there's no signal here.' I held it up, and waved it around, in the hope of getting a solitary bar.

'Okay. Let's try mine.' She patted her jacket. 'It's in my handbag. I left it on the altar.' She walked back along the path, and then turned around to see me still waving my phone in the air. 'Will you be okay here on your own?'

'I should think so.' I stretched up as high as I could and craned my head backwards. 'I think I've almost got something.'

She shook her head and made her way back to the chapel.

I felt something crick in my back, and so I lowered my arm and tucked my phone away. Then I rubbed my neck, turning it painfully this way and that. Brilliant. Welcome to middle age, Nathan.

I was about to make my way after Federica, when I heard the sound of a boat approaching. Marcuccio. I sighed with relief. Whatever he'd seen must have passed, and so he'd turned back. I walked out to the end of the jetty and waved my hands in the air.

'Ahoy there!' Did people still say that?

I could see the boat more clearly now and realised, with a sinking feeling in my heart, that it wasn't Marcuccio's. Still, it was at least a boat. Whether it was the police or a private one, we'd just have to plead stupidity. I thought of Federica's likely response to that idea. Okay, *I'd* just have to plead stupidity.

It drew closer, the light from the prow shining in my face. I raised my hand to shield my eyes. It wasn't a police boat. Good, that made things slightly easier.

I waved again. 'I'm sorry,' I shouted. 'I've done something really stupid.'

The pilot switched off the light on the prow, and throttled back, coasting in until he was close enough to tie up. He hauled himself on to the jetty, and walked towards me. I could see his face now. My eyes strained to adjust to the light, but I could make out his features. Shaven-headed, and dressed in a cheap raincoat to match his cheap jacket.

Lucarelli stepped towards me, and pulled a gun from his pocket.

'You certainly have, Mr Sutherland,' he said.

Chapter 42

'Good evening, *Signor* Lucarelli,' I said. 'I didn't expect to see you here.'

'I don't imagine you did.'

'Would you like me to put my hands up?'

'That would be good.'

I raised my hands, and gave an 'Ow' as my neck cricked again.

'Still working too hard?'

'It never stops, I'm afraid. I guess you could call this overtime.'

I risked a glance to my right, doing my best to conceal it as a wince of pain. There was no sign of Federica. 'How did you know I was here?'

'Marcuccio hires boats out, and doesn't care where they're taken. I made it worth his while to call me in the event of anyone enquiring about Sant'Ariano.'

Marcuccio hadn't been expecting two of us. We'd been with him nearly all the time. It was just possible that he hadn't mentioned Federica to Lucarelli.

'Damn.' I shook my head. 'He seemed like a nice guy, you know? I even felt sorry for him.'

'You're a terrible judge of character, Mr Sutherland.'

'Not always. And my cat never is.' I could see that his hands were terribly scratched, and thought back to the interior of the ossuary. 'I see you've been working hard as well.'

He smiled at me. 'Why don't you tell me what I've been up to?'

'It's not a lovely thought. But I think you've exhumed the body of a young man called Andrea Kastellic from a shallow grave, and moved the remains somewhere inside the ossuary.'

'Very good.'

'A dirty job.'

'Not as bad as you might think. The body was reduced to a skeleton years ago. Making my way through the interior was the most difficult part.' He held his hands, briefly, in front of his face and shook his head as he looked at them.

'You want to put something on those.'

'I will. As soon as I get home.'

I paused, just for a moment. 'I don't imagine Ludovica is one for getting her hands dirty.'

He shook his head. 'I don't understand,' he said. Then he looked at me. We both smiled at each other.

'You're a good employee, aren't you? She first came across you at the presentation at Ca' Sagredo, didn't she? She must have thought you seemed like someone who could do a job for her. I wasn't sure at first, you know? For all I knew, she really did have a friend in a tower block on Via Piave. So tell me, why does she need to call on you in person? I'm prepared to believe it could be your good looks and charm – or is it more likely that you think the police might have an *intercettazione* on your line?'

He shook his head. The smile never left his face. 'I have no idea what you're talking about, Mr Sutherland. You believe whatever you want to believe. Now we're wasting time. Why don't you come with me?' He motioned with the gun. 'Come on,' he repeated.

I moved my hands slowly, rubbing the back of my neck. 'I don't suppose I could put my hands down?' I said.

Lucarelli shook his head. 'Don't be silly. Oh, one more thing.' He turned his head slightly, in order to face the chapel, cupped a hand to the side of his mouth and called out. 'Come out, come out, *bella signora*.'

Ah, shit.

There was no response, and no sign of Federica.

'Five seconds, please, or I'll shoot your boyfriend in the head. Five, four, three, two . . . '

Federica emerged from the chapel. Lucarelli gave an exaggerated little bow. '*Signora*. Sorry to miss you the other night.' He motioned with the gun. 'Over here please. Just so we're all in the same place.'

'I can't believe you waited until two!' I hissed.

'Sorry. I thought he was bluffing.'

'I don't suppose you managed to get through?'

'Yes, I did actually.' She beamed at Lucarelli. 'The police will be here shortly.'

He smiled back at her, equally brightly. 'I don't think so. There's a *carabinieri* station on Burano. If they were coming, they'd be here by now.' He put a finger to his lips. 'Shush a moment.' Then he put a hand to his ear, pretending to listen. 'No, I don't hear anything.' He waved the gun at the two of us. 'Come on then. Let's get going.'

Fede and I exchanged a glance. I shook my head.

'Very sensible. You could rush me, of course. I admit I'm not very good with a gun. But I could hit at least one of you. Do you want to risk that? No?' He glanced at his watch. 'Time is getting on. You first, please, *Signora.*' Again, he gave a little bow. I admit I knew very little about Lucarelli, save his propensity for casual violence, but he seemed to be entirely too proud of his own little jokes. 'I'll need you to pilot, *Signora.* I understand you can do that? I'll sit behind with Mr Sutherland.'

Fede fired up the engine, and Lucarelli followed me into the back of the boat. 'Let's just keep going in the same direction, shall we? Nice and slowly. Just a group of friends, having a boat trip on a moonlit night, and not wanting to disturb anyone who might be asleep.'

We passed by La Cura and then Santa Cristina, where the lights of the villa were lit and the sound of music drifted across the water.

'It seems the Swarovskis are entertaining. Don't suppose there's any chance we could just drop by? Late-night spritz, that sort of thing?'

Lucarelli moved away from me, and put his head to one side. 'Do you ever stop joking?'

'Dunno. Do you ever stop hitting people?'

He lashed out with the gun, whipping the barrel across my forehead. I cried out, bent double, and waited for my vision to clear. I wiped my hand across my face to stop the blood from dripping into my eyes. I slipped my hand into my pocket to pull out a handkerchief and my fingers curled around the horseshoe-shaped brass name plate for Dario's flat. I drew it out, as carefully as I could, concealing it within the handkerchief as I dabbed at the blood.

Lucarelli grabbed me and pulled me closer to him, at the same time pressing the gun into my forehead. 'You listen here, you piece of shit. No one is coming. Do you understand that? No one is coming. No one is ever going to find you.'

We passed by Santa Cristina and into a wider stretch of water in the north of the lagoon. The deepest part. Ahead of us we could see the lights of *terraferma* and hear the sounds of traffic on the distant autostrada.

'Okay. That's far enough. Stop here.'

Federica throttled back and we sat there in the near-silence, listening to the distant sounds of the cars on the mainland and the gentle rumble of the boat's motor.

'Cut the engine.'

Federica didn't move.

Lucarelli sighed, and got to his feet, levelling the gun at me. 'I'm tired. I want to be at home in front of the television, not freezing my balls off in the middle of the lagoon. I'll give you five seconds again. Five, four, three, two . . .'

I heard the click of Lucarelli's revolver, but it was drowned out by the roar of the engine as Federica yanked the throttle fully open and wrenched the steering wheel to the left. There was no great burst of acceleration, but it was enough to throw us back in our seats. I heard a shot explode in the air and turned to see Lucarelli steadying the gun for another. Fede wrenched the wheel first one way and then the other as the engine screamed, and Lucarelli dropped the weapon as he tried to steady himself. I stretched for it and, with my fingertips, managed to tip it over the side. He stamped on my hand and I screamed with the pain, just as Fede heaved the boat in another direction, unbalancing him. I curled the nameplate around my fingers, and punched him as hard as I could. Once. Twice. Three times, and I heard a satisfying crack from his jaw before he tumbled over the side and into the freezing lagoon.

Federica cut the engine. My ears were still ringing from its roar, but I heard Lucarelli cry out. And then there was nothing but the silence of the Dead Lagoon and the distant rumble of traffic.

'Can you see him? Nathan, can you see him?'

I looked over the side. He was floating, face down, just metres away. 'I can see him.'

'We can't leave him there.'

'I think we can.'

She punched my arm. 'No, we can't. We're not those sorts of people, remember. Come on.'

We hauled him on board, where he vomited up water and then lay still. I looked around for something to tie him up with, but then decided he didn't look in any shape to cause trouble.

I pulled Federica to me and tried to approximate one of Dario's bone-crushing hugs.

'Are you all right?'

She nodded. 'You're a bit of a mess though.'

I wiped my forehead and looked at my bloodied fingers. My knuckles were also starting to smart. 'Back to *pronto soccorso*?'

'I guess so. You're going to start getting a bit of a reputation.'

I laughed, only semi-hysterically, and hugged her again. 'You are an absolute bloody star, you know?'

'I know. Why do you go anywhere without me?'

'Two! I can't believe you waited until bloody two again.'

'Sorry, *caro*. It took me the first three seconds to think of something to do. We're going to be in trouble for this, aren't we?'

'Probably.' I looked down at Lucarelli. 'But not as much as he is.' My phone plinged. 'Hey. How about that? I've got a signal.'

We slumped down together in the boat, still laughing, and I dialled Vanni's mobile number.

Chapter 43

Vanni puffed away on one of his cheap cigars that – to my tired and nicotine-starved brain – could have been a vintage Cuban from the collection of Fidel Castro or Winston Churchill.

'So, Nathan,' he said, 'when you told me you were going to do some investigating I naively assumed you meant going through consular records. That sort of thing. Instead of which you meant "having a life-or-death struggle on a forbidden island". I wonder how I could possibly have misinterpreted that?'

I couldn't really think of anything to say beyond 'Sorry.'

'And to top it off, you then called me late at night to say you were somewhere in the middle of the lagoon with an unconscious ex-policeman in the boat.'

'That's about it. I couldn't think who else to call.' He cut me off before I could squeeze in another 'sorry'.

'So, how's Lucarelli?' I said.

'Hmph. He's well enough, considering.' He chuckled. 'Do you know, Nathan, you managed to break his jaw?'

I rubbed my knuckles, raw and bruised. I dredged up a laugh. 'Did I now? Has he got anything to say for himself?'

'Nothing at all. Won't say anything until he sees a lawyer.'

'Figures. We could have left the bastard to drown, you know? Don't think I didn't consider it.'

Vanni screwed up his eyes as if in pain. 'No, no. That wouldn't have done at all. That would just have complicated things.'

'What, you mean I'd be sitting here facing a murder charge?'

'Let's just say we'd be having an awkward conversation. And awkward conversations are things I'm always in favour of avoiding.'

'What now, then?'

'Go home. Have a good sleep. Rest those knuckles.'

'Don't worry. I wasn't planning on giving them another workout. Is that it?'

'What do you mean?'

'Regarding the two of us having been out to Sant'Ariano.'

'Oh yes. Well, try not to do that again. I'll have to shout at you for that. Perhaps I can do that over lunch one day. You'll be paying, of course.'

'Of course.' I cleared my throat. 'And, I suppose, we kind of have committed an assault. Although I'm not quite sure why I'm reminding you.'

'Ah, well now, that could have been awkward. But with a little bit of creative filing I might be able to work around that. Do you know, we've found a number of interesting things in Mr Lucarelli's possession?'

'Such as?'

'A passport.'

'Jimmy Whale's?'

'The very same.'

'So, what happens to him now?'

'Leave that with us. We've had an *intercettazione* on his line for some time. Mainly with regard to the trade in stolen passports. There are any number of charges we can bring against him. Some of them might even stick. Whatever, I don't think he'll be going anywhere for some time.'

'What about Marcuccio? Lucarelli said he knew he took money to run visitors out to Sant'Ariano.'

Vanni shrugged. 'I don't know if we can prove anything there. But it might be worth me making a call to the *Guardia di Finanza*. It sounds like they might want to have a double check of *Signor* Marcuccio's books.' He chuckled. '"I sold my boat to a man called Boscolo in Chioggia." Boscolo. My goodness me. Most common surname in Chioggia. Really, Nathan?'

'Okay, okay. I'm a terrible judge of character. I can't always have Gramsci with me to give me his opinion.' I changed the subject. 'Anyway, what about the connection with the Loredans? With Ludovica?'

He shook his head. 'Nathan, I know you've got some kind of obsession with this but let's be clear. There is no evidence of any connection at all between them. And none whatsoever of her having done anything illegal.' He sighed. 'I'll be honest with you, there's very little chance of us investigating this.'

'What if Lucarelli turns *pentito*?'

'A different matter. We'll see what happens if he does.'

I closed my eyes, and rubbed my knuckles. 'There's an empty grave on San Michele. A shallow grave on Sant'Ariano. And a British tourist who might have been murdered because his unusual hobby led him to be in the wrong place at the wrong time. I won't let this rest, Vanni.'

'We won't either, Nathan.'

'But you don't think you're going to get anywhere, do you?'

He didn't answer.

I stood outside the *Questura* feeling in desperate need of a sandwich, a drink and a cigarette. Two of which, I knew, wouldn't do me any good. I'd head back to the Street of the Assassins, tell Federica that – apart from having to book an appointment to be shouted at by Vanni – we appeared to have got away with it, and then perhaps we could celebrate with lunch out. Following which, I was going to have a very, very long sleep.

I felt my telephone buzzing from inside my jacket. The temptation had been to switch it off altogether, but I couldn't risk missing anything that might relate to Jimmy Whale's repatriation.

'*Pronto.*'

'Hello, Nathan.'

'Guy?'

'The very same. How are you?'

'Not too good. Because of you. Where have you been?'

'Long story. I see you've been busy. Checking up on me.'

I felt a twitch of anger. 'I wouldn't like to think you've been following me, Guy.'

'Not at all. But if you will leave your email address on a public site like Youtube, or if you will click on someone's LinkedIn profile . . . Didn't you know that gets recorded?'

'I do now.'

'I'm leaving soon, Nathan. I don't know how much more I can do here. But I would like to meet up, just one last time.'

'Oh, I'd very much like that, Guy. I think we've got lots to talk about. So, tell me where.'

With the exception of the bar at the *Ospedale*, Fondamente Nove was not an area of town that I was familiar with for the purposes of eating and drinking. I felt cold and tired, and my bones ached, but the message had been absolutely clear. He'd meet me here, meet me once, and then no more. It was one last throw of the dice.

Bar Tintoretto had, apparently, once been a favourite hang-out of the great painter; a fact that was only spoiled by the original building having burned down three hundred years previously. Its replacement had served as a launderette for the past thirty years before being turned into what could only be described as an early Baroque theme bar. *Bar Tintoretto* with its amplified electric classical music and cheap reproductions of *The Abduction of the Body of St Mark* was never going to be the sort of bar worthy of dragging me across town on a wet afternoon.

Still, I was grateful to get out of the cold, and took a look around as I swept the rain from my hair. Not many punters at this hour. I supposed it might start getting busier later, but wouldn't have bet on it. This part of town was far away from the student areas, and nor was it somewhere where tourists would hang around after dark. Neither did it seem like the sort of place designed to appeal to locals. Whatever the market was, it was a niche one.

'*Signore?*'

I smiled at the barman. '*Spritz bitter.*'

He threw a couple of ice cubes in a glass, and went to mix

my drink. I took another look around, and shook my head. I wondered how long it would be before the owner started regretting ever having given up on the launderette.

The barista slid my drink over to me. It was a bright, almost fluorescent, orange in colour.

'I'm sorry, I asked for Campari.'

He frowned. 'You said Spritz *bitte*.'

'I said Spritz *bitter*. Not *bitte*. I'm not German.'

'You don't like Aperol?'

'Too sweet for me. Sorry.'

He snatched the glass back, and tipped the contents away, muttering something about my accent under his breath. He half-filled the glass with white wine and chucked in the bare minimum of Campari, before squirting in a distressingly large amount of sparkling water and pushing the glass back across the bar. I took a sip. The sickly-sweet taste of Aperol still clung to the sides. He looked at me as if challenging me to say something. I was in no mood for any sort of confrontation and dredged up a smile.

'Mr Sutherland? Nathan?'

'Hello, Guy. I'm very glad to see you're still alive. Even if you have been stalking me.'

'Well, you may say that, but it seems to me that it's you who've been doing the stalking.' He smiled. 'I'm in need of a drink.' He looked at my glass. 'Do you want another?'

'Not of these, no.' I waved to the barman. 'I'd like a bottle of your second-least expensive prosecco please. And two glasses.' The barman gave me a withering look. 'I'm not really supposed to be drinking. And prosecco isn't really drinking.'

Guy looked me up and down. 'You've been in the wars.'

'Yes. As I said, because of you.'

'I'm sorry. Come on, let's sit down.' He took me to a table in the corner, looking out upon the lagoon and San Michele.

'*Cin cin.*' We clinked glasses. 'We've wasted a lot of time on you. The police and myself. Missing persons reports, that sort of thing.'

'I thought it might be best to disappear. For a few days at least, after I found that my hotel room had been trashed. I just went out and found myself another hotel where I slipped them some money not to ask for my *documento*.'

'So your details were never passed on to the police. That's why nobody could find you. Any chance you might tell me what sort of hotels do this sort of thing?' He shook his head. 'Your room, then. Would this be the work of a certain *Signor* Lucarelli, by any chance?'

'I imagine so. We met briefly at Ca' Sagredo, as you know. I wasn't desperate to spend more time in his company.'

'What was he looking for?'

Guy reached into his coat and took out a thick white envelope. 'My book. Or the basis for it. It would have been pointless, anyway. It's not as if it's not backed up.'

'Unless he'd killed you as well, of course. From what I understand, Google would have kept your secrets safe forever.' I took a sip of my spritz, winced, slid the glass away and turned my attention to the prosecco. 'You saw Jimmy Whale's video on Sant'Ariano, obviously. I assume the second comment was yours?'

'I wanted to scare him off. I knew there would be others taking an interest.'

'Except, of course, it was too late. Jimmy hired a boat to go out there again, late at night this time. But he never got that far. He was met at Celestia by Lucarelli . . .'

'I was sorry about that. I didn't want anybody else to get hurt.'

I nodded. 'I believe you.' I looked out at the lagoon, and pointed towards the sculpture that seemed to float in the water in front of San Michele. Two figures in a boat, one of them gesturing towards the island. 'I don't have much occasion to come up this way,' I said. 'It's not a part of town I really know. But I've always liked that.'

Guy shook his head. 'I don't know it.'

'*Dante's Barge*. By an artist called Georgy Fragulyan. Armenian, I think. It was already in place by the time I moved to Venice. Thing is, it took me years to work out what it actually was. I thought it was Christ leading St Mark to his final resting place. *"Pax tibi Marce, evangelista meus, hic requiescet corpus tuum".'* I rolled the words around my tongue. 'And then I found out it was Virgil showing Dante the way to the underworld. I think I liked my interpretation better.' I paused for a moment. 'It wasn't here, of course, when you left Venice. Was it?'

'Long after my time, I'm afraid.' He spoke without thinking, and then his eyes filled with suspicion. We sat there without speaking, listening to the electric remix of Vivaldi. Eventually, he broke the silence. 'What are you trying to say, Nathan?'

I ignored his question. 'Lovely out there isn't it? Even in this weather. So peaceful, for the moment.' I refilled our glasses. 'And we have plenty to talk about. So, let's talk, Gabriele.'

Chapter 44

He closed his eyes for a moment, and nodded to himself. Then he smiled.

'How did you know?'

'It took me a while. I think the first clue was the whole "pretending not to speak Italian" thing. Calling the cemetery "San Michelle". That was trying just a little bit too hard with the Englishman abroad act, especially when I found out you'd helped Father Michael with a piece of translation. And then I remembered you'd said you read the Italian press.'

'I see.'

'But the main thing was seeing your photograph in the archives of the *Circolo*. Then everything Hugo had said to me began to make sense. "Gabriele – he shouldn't be here at the Circle." I suppose you could say it was your father who told me.'

'Hugo Channing is not my father, Nathan, as I expect you know by now.'

'I understand. At least, I'm trying to understand.' I refilled his glass. 'So, as I said, let's talk.'

He nodded, slowly. 'Where to begin, Mr Sutherland. I

suppose you could say it starts with a dream. Always the same dream . . .'

Andrea said he wanted to see the Bone Island. The Isle of the Dead.

I told him he was crazy.

He laughed at me, and said I was scared. Scared of the snakes and the rats and the crawling things.

And the ghosts.

I am scared but he is laughing at me and now Ludovica is laughing as well. Again, he looks at us both. And falls silent.

For a moment, I hate him so much I want to cry. I screw my eyes shut, and breathe deeply and, when I open them again, we set out for Sant'Ariano.

I take the boat past Torcello, and into the Dead Lagoon.

The walls of the island are of crumbling red brick. The jetty is wooden, and rotten, but I tie the boat up and we walk to the shore. We lie there, our backs pressed against the wall.

I close my eyes. The smell of the lagoon is in my nostrils, the lapping of the water in my ears. Father, I know, will be angry if he ever finds out. And yet, for that moment, I am happy.

I open my eyes. Andrea's hand is resting on Ludovica's shoulder. His face drops towards hers, for a kiss. She moves away, slaps his hand and says 'No.' Then she laughs, out of embarrassment, trying to break the awkwardness.

Andrea nods. He stares down at his feet for a moment, running a hand through his curls. Then he looks up once more, from me to Ludovica and back again.

I ask him why he keeps looking at us like that.

His smile widens.

It is because you do not look alike, he says.

I know this is true. When they think I am not listening, people whisper how beautiful Ludovica, with her dark eyes and high cheekbones, is. No one has ever stopped Mother or Father in the street to tell them what a handsome son they have. Only Andrea's father has ever said anything like that to me. Ludovica's hair is dark, and rich, and straight. Mine is curly. Like Andrea's.

Like Andrea's.

He is still staring at us. Still smiling.

Ludovica spits on the baked earth. 'You are an idiot, Andrea.'

'And your mother is a whore.'

The words hit me like a blow.

Ludovica flails at him, slapping him. He grabs her arm, and twists it behind her, making her shriek with pain. I jump to my feet, but he pushes me back down, and my head cracks against the wall. I want to cry, but I will not let him see me break down. I throw my arm across my face. Ludovica is still crying out.

'You know when you are grown-up, Ludovica? When your mother and father have died? You will have to share everything with me. So you'd better be nice to me.'

Ludovica twists and turns in his arms. He pulls her towards him, and kisses her full on the mouth. I can see blood on her lips, as she pulls herself away. She is screaming now.

'Better be nice to me,' he laughs.

Someone will hear her, I think. Someone will come. I screw up my eyes, and look across the waters, shining in the midday sun. There is no one. No one, at this hour, is here in this part of the Dead Lagoon.

'Half of everything is going to be mine.' He turns and looks at me, laughing. 'The bastard will get nothing.'

Both of us are crying now. I try to punch him. He releases Ludovica, and grabs me. This time, it is I who twists in his arms, trying to free myself. 'Silly boy. Stupid child. Little bastard son of a whore. Puttana troia.'

My mother.

Impossible.

And yet, when I look into his face, into his dark eyes, I can see only my own.

He throws me to the ground. The hate is knotting up my insides, making it hard to breathe, hard to see. All I want to do is to hit him, to hurt him, to kill him. He makes an obscene gesture with his hands. I scrabble around on the ground, looking for something to hit him with. A stone?

Blood is roaring in my ears, drowning the sound of Ludovica's shrieks. And then there is silence. Andrea stares down at me, but his eyes are empty now. His face is split from forehead to chin.

He topples to the bare earth. And Ludovica and I are alone on the island of bone.

'I saw the bloodied stone in Ludovica's hand. I was crying. That was the only sound. She had been hysterical, but then she realised she had to be the grown-up. She turned and threw the stone into the lagoon, and then looked down at Andrea. We couldn't do the same with him, she told me. The waters were shallow. The body would be found within hours. We would hide him in the chapel. No one ever looked there. Then we would go home, and tell Mother and Father what had happened, and they would make everything all right. You believe that, don't you, when you're a kid? You always think your parents can put everything right.'

I shook my head, but said nothing.

'She told me she would go home and bring them back, but I would need to stay and watch. Just in case anyone came. If anybody did I would have to do something – anything – to hide Andrea's body. Anything to distract them.

'I begged her to let me go instead but she said she was too frightened. She knew I could do it. Her brave little brother. So, I settled down in the chapel to watch over Andrea as she took the boat back.

'I don't know to this day if she knew what she was going to do when she set out. But when she reached the part of the lagoon between Mazzorbo and Torcello, she started to scream. She was picked up by the police and taken home. Her little brother, showing off, had fallen into the lagoon, she said.

'I sat there for hours. Completely alone, except for Andrea. I kept talking to him, hoping he'd wake up. The shadows lengthened and it grew dark. I could hear the sounds of the rats from within. Rats and worse things. I clamped my eyes shut and said my prayers. I said that I was sorry for Andrea, that it had been an accident and prayed and prayed that Ludovica would be safe and that someone would come soon.

'I was frightened at first, when I heard the sounds of the boats over the water, but then I heard my name being called. It was Mother. She'd come to help me, to save me and to make everything all right again. There were two boats. I didn't understand why. Mother and Father were in one, and there were two men in the other, men who I knew worked for Father. They came into the chapel, and Father looked down at Andrea and nodded. He turned to the two of them and told them that they knew what to do. Then Mother picked me up and carried me to the boat. Sleep now, Gabi, she said. Everything will be different tomorrow.

'I heard the sounds of the boat and the water and I felt safe. And happy. I slept for the whole of the journey back, and remember being taken upstairs and tucked into bed.'

'Wait a moment,' I said. 'That was when the photograph was taken. "The Channings bring their son home for the last time." The photograph that was in every Italian newspaper the following day.'

Gabriele nodded. 'I lay there in bed until the shouting started. I pulled the bedclothes over my head, but it wasn't enough. I had to know what was going on. I opened my bedroom door and crept out. Down the corridor to the door that opens into the living room. It was open, just a crack. You've seen where they lived, I imagine?' I nodded. 'That image on the ceiling? Lucifer falling from heaven? I remember how it used to terrify me as a little boy. And I remember Darko Kastellic, on his feet, looking down at Mother and Father, and telling them exactly what he wanted and exactly what they were going to give him as the price for his silence. I remember looking from his face to that of Satan, and thinking that I could no longer tell the difference.

'I heard Hugo and mother arguing, late into the night. Of how he could hardly bear to look at me. How he had lost half of everything because of her bastard child, because of my mother and Darko. How I would be a burden around his neck until one of us died.

'The next morning Mother told me I had to be very brave. I was doing a good thing, she said. I would have to go away, just for a little while. Father, she told me, knew people in

England with whom I could stay. And schools where I could go.

'I went to school. Studied. Went to university. Got a regular job. But over the years, the letters and money from home dried up. I think I was, perhaps, eighteen years old when I realised what they'd done. That they'd disappeared me. That I would never be brought back to Venice, and that I would never see my mother again.'

'But how could she possibly have agreed to this?'

'Hugo told her that if she didn't, he would divorce her and she would never see either of her two children again. The law would have been on his side. He was the wronged party. He didn't want his inheritance to go to anyone other than his precious Ludovica.

'It would have been easiest to have an empty coffin, and pretend my body had been washed out into the Adriatic. But everyone had now seen a photograph of Cosima Loredan carrying what they assumed to be the body of her dead son. Money had to change hands for the right people to look the other way. The coroner, perhaps even your predecessor. And the people that *Anonimo Veneziano* mentioned. They would have needed paying off as well. *It was a bright day, I couldn't be sure what I was seeing.* That sort of thing. And so, Mother and Father played the part of grieving parents at a sham funeral.

'I understood then, just why Darko Kastellic came to visit us so often. He was asking Hugo for money. Their relationship had broken down years ago. His business was failing. But he knew his bastard son was growing up as a Loredan. That gave him power, and the accident gave him absolute power. Half of everything, to keep silent.'

'You spoke to him. On the telephone.'

'I wanted to hear his voice.'

'You told him you were writing a book. That you were investigating the events of forty years ago. Was that just to frighten him?'

'I honestly don't know. I suppose I wanted to provoke a reaction, any reaction, from him.'

'I've met him. He's old now, of course, but his mind is sharp. You could meet him.'

Gabriele shook his head. 'Why would I want to do that?'

'He's your father.'

He laughed, as if the idea was genuinely amusing. 'He was never a father to me. I was just something he could use. He weaponised his own children in order to extort money from Hugo.'

I shook my head. 'My God.'

He laughed again. 'Oh, Nathan. I'm afraid the Almighty's not been very present in my life. We're not on speaking terms any more.'

'Why did you come back? Why now?'

'I left it as late as I dared. The old man, I knew, was in poor health. I wanted to be sure I was going to get my share of his money.' He patted the envelope. 'I have the whole story here, Nathan. I'm going to provide proof. My DNA can be checked. It can be proved that I am the son of Darko Kastellic and Cosima Loredan.'

'Gabriele, that won't make any difference. The law doesn't work that way here. If you're not Hugo's son, you won't inherit anything. It'll all go to Cosima and Ludovica.'

'Ludovica will buy my silence. For the sake of her parents.'

He smiled at me. 'That's why I made a great play of being seen asking questions of everyone. Every time she saw me speaking with you or with the priest, I thought it would scare her just that little bit more. Until she broke.' He shook his head. 'Evidently my sister is not so easily frightened. But I am going to get my money, Nathan. Or else I am going to bring it all crashing down. The whole rotten, filthy thing.' He looked at my glass. 'You've hardly touched your prosecco.'

'I never thought I'd say this, but I don't really feel like it.'

'You know the truth now, Nathan. Everything. I've been honest with you. Now I want you to do something for me.'

'Do you now? I've already collected a few bruises on your behalf, Gabriele.' I touched the side of my face and winced. 'But go on then. Tell me what it is.'

'Just be there. When I meet Ludovica. For the last time.'

'She agreed to that?'

'I promised she would never see or hear from me again.'

'Where are we going? Your home?'

He shook his head. 'No. She doesn't want to risk my mother seeing me. It had to be somewhere altogether more neutral.' He chuckled but, again, there was no humour in his eyes. 'My final resting place.'

Chapter 45

I saw the man I still thought of as my father on just one more occasion.

I had not been back to Venice for many years. It hurt me when shopkeepers and baristas would fail to recognise my accent and treat me as a tourist. It was not the city I had left. I no longer felt part of it.

I felt afraid, at first. How would the old man react? I had arrived with the idea of confronting him in the company of all his important friends, in the middle of Venetian high society. That, I knew, would be his greatest nightmare. Childish, perhaps, but I had replayed the scene so often in my mind. In the end my courage failed me and I simply stood there, as the party moved around me, and drank prosecco. I have never been a particularly brave man. Hugo Channing was correct in that, at least.

No, I could not confront him there. Perhaps later. Perhaps we would go to his palazzo – my home – together.

And then we saw each other, across the room. He looked at me, and I looked back at him. Into his eyes, back through the decades.

The boy is no good . . .

He is weak . . .

I can no longer bear to look at him . . .

He must go. You must understand that? No one need know. I have lost half of everything. It is the only way to save us . . .

He stared into my eyes, and said nothing. And then he fell to the ground.

Immediately, of course, people ran to him. I slipped outside, in the midst of the confusion, down the stairs and out into the streets.

You may wonder how I felt? It would be easy to say that I felt hatred, rage. Or perhaps even love. The urge to hug him, to roll back the years and make everything all right again. But the truth is simply that I felt nothing. Nothing at all.

Perhaps I am more like Ludovica than anyone thought?

There are just the three of us now.

Our footsteps echo more. The rooms are darker, the shadows longer.

The house is quieter, of course, in the absence of Gabriele. In the absence of . . . my brother?

Mother and Father tell me this is the way that things must be. Nothing is spoken of Sant'Ariano. Occasionally, when they think I am not listening, I hear them whispering. Then, when they notice, they stop and look at me. In the first weeks, the first months, I would hear Mother crying at night.

She does not cry any more.

There are just the three of us now. Everything is in its right place. Andrea's father has left. Gabriele has left. I know we will not see them again.

They still talk to me as if I were a child. Gabriele has had to go away for a short while, they say, but I know we will not see

*him again. I see it in their eyes. I know that they know what
happened that day. I am, I suppose, a fortunate young woman.
Always Daddy's little girl. So I will be here for them, always. For
Mother. For Father. I will let nothing hurt them, ever again.
Ever.*

And I have not cried since Sant'Ariano.

Chapter 46

Gabriele and I were the only ones to disembark at *Cimitero*. I checked my watch. The gates would be closing soon and there were few people to be seen. At this hour, everybody had left or, at least, was preparing to leave.

We walked through the gate that separated the Catholic section from the *Reparto Evangelico*. There was no one to be seen beyond the figure of a woman in black, near the supposed grave of Gabriele Loredan.

'Good evening, Mr Sutherland.' If she was surprised, she hid it well.

'*Signora* Loredan.'

She turned to my companion. 'Welcome, Gabriele.'

'Ludovica.'

'Why is Mr Sutherland here?'

Gabriele made to speak, but I shushed him. 'Just for company, Ludovica.' I looked around at the lengthening shadows. 'Time is getting on. Time for you to have a conversation you should have had decades ago.' I stepped back into the shelter of the Trentinaglia chapel. 'I'll just stand back here. Give you time to talk properly.' I rested my hand on the scaffolding, felt it move, and stepped away hurriedly.

Ludovica looked at Guy – or Gabriele – and smiled. 'You want money, of course. Will a cheque do?'

He shook his head. 'No. That won't do at all. I want it all. My proper share. When the old man dies.'

'That isn't going to happen, Gabriele. You have no proper share. You are not part of this family.'

'Then I will go to the papers. And I will go to the police. And I will tell them everything.'

She raised an eyebrow. 'Tell them *what*, Gabriele?'

'About you, and Andrea, and Mother and Father. And about what happened on Sant'Ariano.'

'Oh, Gabriele.' She moved forward and made to touch his cheek, but he shrank back. 'You're tired. You need to rest. Go back to your hotel. We will talk tomorrow. Or, if you prefer, I can give you some money now. A few hundred, for the hotel and your flight home.'

'That won't do, Ludovica. Half of everything. The same as Darko Kastellic.'

'Gabriele, it wasn't me who sent you away. Mother and Father – *my* father – did. It was the only thing they could do.'

'They sent me away to protect you, and punish me. For something I didn't do. Of course, Hugo was going to look after you and not me. Not the bastard son of a whore. I grew up in a land full of strangers. And now I am back, and I want my money and I want my life back.'

'I can't do that, Gabi. Nobody can. I am sorry.'

Gabriele took a deep breath. 'Then you'll know what I'll do.'

She smiled at him. 'I understand. You must do what you have to do.' She took out her mobile phone, unlocked it, and offered it to him. 'Take it. Go on.' He looked uncertain, and his hands shook as he took it from her. 'Good. Well done, Gabi. There are a number of journalists in the contacts list. From *La Nuova*. *Il Gazzettino*. *La Repubblica*. Possibly the *Corriere*, I can't quite remember. It'll save you time. Go on. Call someone.'

Gabriele looked at the screen, breathing heavily.

'This is what you want, Gabi. Isn't it?'

His hands continued to shake.

'Make the call, little brother. Bring the truth to light after forty years.' She paused. 'Break Mother's heart.' She lingered on every word. 'I hear her every night, you know? When she says her prayers. She always prays that you are living a good life, and that you are happy.'

Gabriele shook his head. He was crying.

'Make that call and everything will be known. No more lies. Everyone will know about us and about what happened. Everyone. Journalists will be camped outside our palazzo. The telephone will ring, constantly. Everyone will, of course, want to talk to Mother. The filthiest, darkest moment in our history will be there for everyone to see. And Mother will know that you – you, Gabriele – did this for money. Just like your father. And I wonder if she will pray for you any more?'

'No.' He choked out the word, and dropped to his knees.

Ludovica walked over to him and gently took the phone. from his hands. 'You are not part of this family, Gabi. You never were. Not really.' She nodded at the tombstone. 'This is why I wanted to meet you here. This is where you belong. You are nothing but a shadow now.'

She let her hand rest on his shoulder for a moment, and

then turned to me. 'Mr Sutherland, could you take Gabriele back to his hotel. Please make sure he's looked after.'

I didn't move.

'You may go now, Gabriele. Mr Sutherland will go with you.'

I shook my head. 'I don't think so, Ludovica.'

She smiled at me. 'You don't think so? What do you think, then, Mr Sutherland?'

'Oh, right now I'm thinking that as soon as I leave here I'm going to go straight to the police and tell them absolutely everything. You see, unlike Gabriele, I've got no skin in this game. I think honesty is probably the best policy.'

Her eyes sparkled. 'And what will you tell them, Mr Sutherland? What will you tell them?'

'I'll tell them about a death that occurred nearly forty years ago, and a shallow grave on Sant'Ariano. Forensics will identify the body as Andrea. His father is still alive, they'll be able to check the DNA. And they'll be able to show that he died a violent death.'

She continued to smile at me. 'And now I know you're bluffing.'

'You do? The police are investigating. We'll see what they'll have to say.'

'They'll have nothing to say. Because there will be nothing to find.' She turned to Gabriele. 'Andrea now lies somewhere in the interior of Sant'Ariano. There are tens of thousands, perhaps hundreds of thousands of skeletons there. How will they identify a single one on an island made of bone?'

I shrugged. 'I don't know. But what I do know is this: I am going to make sure that every newspaper in the land covers this story. If Gabriele can't do it, I will. Your mother will go to her grave knowing that every grubby little secret in your family history is going to be brought to light. All of it.'

'And I will pursue you through every court in the land and ruin you.'

I laughed. 'This is Italy. You'll have to wait a long time.'

She lowered her voice. 'I could simply have you – *stopped*. If I were to wish it.'

'Another shallow grave on Sant'Ariano?'

'If you like. Other locations, I understand, are available.'

'Except that isn't going to happen. Your friend Lucarelli is currently trying to explain just how he happens to have the passport of a British citizen who was found drowned in the lagoon a week ago. You told him to look out for any British person trying to get to Sant'Ariano, didn't you? And poor Jimmy Whale, with his unusual hobby, just happened to be in the wrong place at the wrong time.'

'But, as you know, there is no connection to be proved between myself and this *Signor* Lucarelli. No connection at all.'

'Think back, Ludovica. Did you ever telephone him? Even once? Did you know the police were tapping his phone? And when you were there – did you leave anything – anything that could possibly be traced back to you? Because the police will be swarming over his apartment even as we speak.'

'They will find nothing. Because there is nothing to find.' But doubt had entered her voice. 'I am sorry, but Gabriele – Guy – has wasted your time.'

'Perhaps I have.' Gabriele got slowly to his feet. 'I wanted my money, yes. Truth be told, it'd still be useful. But most of all I wanted my life back. I wanted my family back. And now,' he turned to her and shook his head, 'now I'm wondering why the hell I ever wanted to be part of this family again.'

He moved to her and laid his hand against her cheek. 'My big sister. Daddy's special girl. I was so jealous of you. But perhaps I was the lucky one. I've lived a life. It may not have been the one I wanted, but I've lived a life. And you – you spent your days here, waiting patiently on Mother and doting on Father. Look what it's done to you. Cold. Frigid. An emotional cripple. It's eaten you away. There's almost nothing left of you now.'

'Bastard.' Her voice was shaking.

'Yes, I am. We know that. Keep the money, Ludovica. Keep your secrets.' He paused. 'But how old are Mother and Father now? How long before you're completely alone? When the only sound you'll ever hear is that of your own footsteps.' A terrible smile passed across his face, and for one fleeting moment I could see a resemblance to his sister. 'Except you'll always have to listen for mine. One morning, when you're on your own, when Mother and Father have died, you'll wake up and see your face on the front of the newspapers. Every night, before you go to sleep, you'll wonder if that will be the last night when your secret will be safe. You're right. I won't hurt Mother. But I will be a shadow following you until the day you die. You will never be rid of me, Ludovica.'

'Bastard,' she repeated. She slapped him, dragging her nails down his cheek and drawing blood.

'I won't hit you. Ludovica. You know that.'

'You'll have to, you bastard. Or else I'm going to kill you.'

She bent to pick up a fragment of tombstone from the ground, and swung it at him. Gabriele took a step back, slipping and falling on the wet grass. Ludovica stood over him, poised to bring the stone crashing down.

I threw myself at her, throwing one arm around her and grabbing her hand with the other. She stepped back, raking her shoe down my shin. The pain made me loosen my grip for a moment. It was enough. She freed her arm, and elbowed me in the face, sending me sprawling backwards.

Gabriele was on his feet now, and stumbled back as she swung at him again. I grabbed her once more, and tried to pin her arms.

'Ludovica. Don't do this. Please. We can fix this.'

'We can't.' Her voice was choked. 'The only way to fix this is for Gabriele to go back where he belongs.'

'I can't do that, Ludii. You know I can't.'

'Then I'm going to have to kill you. Both of you.' She broke my grip, and was on Gabriele once more. She struck him across the face, and he stumbled backwards, into the scaffolding supporting the roof of the Trentinaglia chapel. She grabbed him and threw him against it. Slamming his head against the upright. Again. And again.

'Ludii . . .'

And again . . .

I saw the whole structure shiver. Then there was a deafening roar as it collapsed around them. And then a moment of utter silence. I ran over to them and tried to shift the beams. Ludovica's eyes were wide open, and staring. Gabriele tried to speak, but then his eyes rolled back and he lay still, blood trickling from his mouth and nose.

'Ludovica,' I said. 'Oh my God, Ludovica, what have you done?'

I heard voices from behind me and turned to the main gate. A group of people, attracted by the noise, had come to investigate.

'Call an ambulance. Quickly. Please,' I cried out. The hospital was just minutes away across the lagoon. But I knew it was too late.

Chapter 47

Vanni riffled through the pile of papers in front of him, then jogged them together and slid them inside a manila envelope. He gave a nod and a little harrumph of satisfaction, before reaching for a cigar. He clicked his lighter and then paused.

'Do you mind?' he asked.

I shook my head. 'I think Chandler had a line about enjoying one's vices by proxy. Go ahead.'

He lit up, and leaned back in his chair, his eyes sparkling. 'Wise man, Mr Chandler.' He closed his eyes, and smoked in silence for a few seconds, before leaning forward again. He reached across the desk, and drummed his fingers on the envelope.

'We'll be able to file this away soon. Nicely done, Nathan, nicely done.'

'It doesn't feel like it, Vanni. There's no happy ending here.'

He sighed. 'You're not a cop, Nathan. Endings is what we do. Happy ones are a bonus.'

'As you said, I'm not a cop. I'm—'

' —the Honorary Consul. I know. But even you can't fix everything.'

'Lost passports. Stolen wallets. It's not like this. Three people have died.'

'I know. If it helps, it isn't always easy for us.'

I sat and watched him smoke, trying not to inhale too deeply. There was, I knew, a *tabaccheria* along the *fondamenta* that would be open and . . . I shook my head.

'You all right, Nathan?' said Vanni.

'Oh yes. Just wrestling with my personal demons.'

'Everything under control, I trust.'

'Just about.' I paused. 'What's going to happen to Cosima?'

He shrugged. 'I don't know. We could make a case against her. She was complicit in breaking a number of laws. A number of police officers must have been bribed. And the examining magistrate, I imagine. Certifying that the body was in the coffin when it was screwed down.'

'So, will you?'

'Not my choice. As long as it looks as if we're at least trying to apply the law, that'll do for me.' He paused. 'Some of those officers are still alive and enjoying retirement. They have friends, you know. There might not be much will to investigate further.'

I shook my head. Vanni was a good cop. A good man. But sometimes his cynicism was too much for me.

'Besides,' he continued. 'Would there be any point? She's an old woman who's lived with knowledge of this for half her life. She lost her son decades ago. She's lost her daughter. She has a husband who no longer knows who she is. We could apply the law, but would it be justice?'

I shrugged. 'Big question. I expect Father Rayner would have something to say about "Vengeance is Mine."'

'Another very wise man, Father Rayner. I was wondering, Nathan. What's going to happen to that hole in the ground on San Michele?'

'I spoke to the *padre* about that. He thinks it would be appropriate if Gabriele were laid to rest there. Properly, this time.'

Vanni nodded. 'I understand.'

'But,' I continued, 'that's not likely to happen for some time. Not until the investigation is over and the body is released. And presumably Cosima would need to give her consent. There are all sorts of hoops to jump through. He is, technically, a British citizen. That means I'll be pulled into it as well.'

'You'll sort it out, Nathan. You and Father Rayner. And then there'll be an ending to it.'

'But not a happy one.'

'No.' He gave a sad smile. 'But as I said, sometimes endings are the best we can hope for.'

We shook hands and I walked out of the *Questura* and along the *fondamenta*. I stopped outside the *tabaccheria* for a moment, then shook my head and walked on, turning the collar of my coat up against the early-morning drizzle.

Chapter 48

'You wanted to see me?' I said.

Cosima nodded. She looked her age for the first time since I had met her. 'I thought perhaps you owed me that.'

'I think I do. This shouldn't be happening of course. I'm a witness to everything that happened.'

'I know. The Commissario has been most helpful.' I raised an eyebrow, and she shook her head. 'Not like that. No money changing hands. Not this time. I think, perhaps, he just wanted to show some sympathy towards an old woman.'

'You won't go to jail, you understand?'

I wasn't sure if she'd heard me, but then she nodded, slowly. She glanced over at Hugo, asleep as ever in his chair.

'Cosima, you shouldn't have to look after him. Not by yourself.'

'I won't. I'll get *badanti* in. We should have done it long before now. But Ludovica . . .' She let the sentence trail off.

'What will you do now?' I said.

She sat in silence for a while. 'I'll make sure Hugo is taken care of, of course.' Her voice broke. 'There are just the two of us now.' She looked over at the dining table, where two candles were burning. 'But not for long, perhaps.'

'Why did you ask me to come here?' I said.

'I thought you'd want to know the truth, Mr Sutherland. To speak face-to-face. No lies this time. Just the answers.'

'I'm not sure they interest me. Not that much. How you dealt with the witnesses who said they saw three children in the boat, and not two. Burying Andrea in the chapel. Dealing with the police, with the coroner.'

'Hugo always said that if you threw enough money at a problem, you could make it go away. And that's what he did. All of a sudden, it seemed that witnesses were mistaken. There had only ever been two children in the boat. More money changed hands with the right people, and then an empty coffin was buried on San Michele, and my son flew out of Italy to start a new life in England.' She paused. 'Do you think I'm a monster, Mr Sutherland?'

I shook my head. 'No. I don't think any of you were.' I looked over at Hugo. 'Your husband was the only one who told me the truth, you know? Everyone else – you, Ludovica, Kastellic, even Gabriele – just lied and lied and lied. How can you do that year upon year? Did it start to seem like the truth?'

She said nothing.

'I am so sorry this has happened. I hope you understand that.'

'There's no need for apologies, Mr Sutherland. Not now.'

'Will you be okay?'

She smiled again and, for a moment, I could see Ludovica's face. 'I will be. Like my daughter, I have not cried for a very long time.'

The old man stirred in his chair. 'Ludovica?'

Cosima moved to his side and knelt down, stroking his hair. 'It's all right, darling. I'm here now.' Hugo Channing smiled, and patted her hand. Cosima turned to me. 'You may go now.'

I nodded, and pulled on my coat. I stopped at the door to look back at them, Hugo smiling in his chair and stroking the hand of his long-forgotten wife. I walked slowly down the stairs, then through the *cortile*, thick with moss and smelling of damp.

I closed the main door, and stepped back to look up at that thin sliver of Venetian Gothic, illuminated by a green-tinted glow from inside. I turned and walked away. A ten-minute walk home, and there would be Federica, and Gramsci, and dinner to cook and silly arguments to be had about what music to play. And tomorrow, I would go over to Giudecca, drink too much wine and lose money in a long-overdue game of *scopa*.

Chapter 49

We ran out of prosecco mid-evening, so Valentina sent me and Dario out to go to the wine shop. We walked back to campo San Giacomo dell'Orio with plastic bags containing *vino sfuso* straining in our arms.

'You don't think we've bought a little too much, do you?'

He shrugged. 'If it is, you can always come back tomorrow.'

'Dario, I'm not sure Valentina had us moving in together in mind when you suggested moving back to Venice.'

He laughed. 'I guess not.' He turned through a full circle, taking in the church, the shops and bars, and the few bare trees in the square. 'Look at all this, eh? Imagine, just a few years and Emily will be playing out here with the rest of the kids.'

I shivered. 'Perhaps not on a cold November evening.'

He smiled, and then grabbed my arm with his free hand as something caught his eye. 'That bar on the corner there. You ever been?' I shook my head. 'We'll have to. I remember going there years ago as a young guy. Great *cichèti.*'

'I suppose it might have changed a bit?'

'We'll still need to check it out. We're going to need a new bar. We won't be able to spend so much time at Toni's.'

I stopped in my tracks. 'Dario, are you actually saying we'll keep going back to Toni's?'

'Sure. Why not?'

'You live in Venice now. There are hundreds, maybe thousands of bars here. We could sit outside and watch the sun going down over San Giacomo dell'Orio. Why would we want to go back to Mestre and sit outside on a busy road?'

He smiled. 'Stay long enough, and sometimes they bring you snacks.'

I laughed. 'I give up. I really do. And anyway, if we need a bar, we have the Brazilians.'

'No. That won't do. That's your bar. We need our bar.'

We walked through the square, and passed a restaurant. The air was heavy with the smell of fried fish. 'This place is good,' I said.

'Smells like it.'

'We'll have to come here. All five of us. When the spring comes.'

'We will.' He took a deep breath. 'This is strange for me, you know? Coming home again. And you English are lucky, having a word like "home".' He turned and looked back over his shoulder, at the darkening square. 'This will be where Emily grows up.'

'Not bad, eh?'

'Not bad at all.' He reached into his jacket for his keys. 'Come on. The girls will be wondering where we are. They'll think we've stopped for a drink on the way.'

'Like that thought never crossed your mind?'

He laughed again, and stopped to admire the shiny brass

horseshoe affixed to the door with the names 'Costa-Visintin' on it.

Later, much later, Dario decided he was in the mood for a little Genesis and *The Lamb Lies Down on Broadway*. At which point we decided it was probably time to leave.

'We should wake Emily up. Just to ask her to say goodbye.'

Vally – I was finally thinking of her as Vally, instead of Valentina – rolled her eyes. 'No. We shouldn't.'

'Yes, we definitely should. This is our first night back in Venice. I want her to remember it.'

'Okay. Do you promise to get up and look after her when she wakes up at three in the morning?'

'Of course I do.' There was a moment of silence, as we all looked at him. 'I promise, okay?' He went through into the bedroom and returned with Emily, tiny, pyjama-ed and more than half asleep.

'Say goodnight, Emily.'

Emily waved her little hand in our general direction, like a bored actress on Oscar night saluting her fans. Dario held her out to Federica, who shook her head. 'You take her, Nathan.'

'Me?'

'Yes.' She smiled. 'I think you ought to.'

Dario passed her over to me, and she snuggled, uncomplainingly, into my arms. She smelled of soap and talcum powder. I had no idea what on earth I was supposed to do. And then I remembered the little boy, in the palazzo on the Zattere, whose parents had never, ever smiled at him the way that Dario and Vally were smiling at Emily. I kissed the top of her head.

'Oh, Emily,' I said. 'You are a lucky, lucky little girl.' I passed her back to Dario. 'Is it me, or is rather dusty in here?'

'I'll see you tomorrow, *vecio*, eh? We've got that bar to find.'

Vally prodded him gently in the chest. 'Not tomorrow. You've got proper work to do tomorrow. There's still plenty to sort out in this apartment. And besides, I think you're going to need to sleep in tomorrow morning. You can go out and play with Nathan the day after.'

We hugged each other, and said goodnight.

'Families, eh?' said Federica, once we were on our own.

'I know. Tolstoy would have had something to say about it.'

'Are you happy, *caro*?'

I nodded, but said nothing.

'I think you needed tonight, didn't you?'

'Well, I wasn't in the mood to cook,' I breezed.

She saw through me, of course. 'That's not what I meant and you know it.'

'Of course it isn't.' I stopped, and turned through a full circle, my arms spread wide. 'Look at all this, eh? Venice is going to sleep. And there's one more family in the city tonight.'

She smiled at me. 'You're a bit pissed, aren't you?'

'I am. Are you cross?'

She leaned her head on my shoulder. 'No. I'm glad you're happy. And yes, there's one more family in Venice, *grazie al cielo*. We need more of them.'

'Families, eh?' I repeated. 'So what are we, then?'

'How do you mean?'

'Well, I mean, are we a family?'

'I don't know. What would you call us?'

'Difficult to say. A collective, maybe.'

'The Ravagnan–Sutherland collective?'

'I like that. It has a nice ring to it.' I paused, and then the words tumbled out. 'But what if we stopped being a collective and became a family? Or what if we decided to stop calling ourselves a collective and decided to start calling ourselves a family? Or what if—'

Federica stopped me in my tracks, and placed her finger on my lips. 'And now I know you really are drunk.'

I kissed the tip of her finger. 'Oh. Are you cross?'

It was dark, but I like to think her eyes were sparkling. 'No. I'm not cross. But I don't think this is a conversation for drunk boyfriends to be having.'

'Oh.' My shoulders slumped. 'Tomorrow then?'

'Tomorrow you'll be hungover.'

'Monday, then?'

'Monday, I think, you have pencilled in with Dario. "Finding a new bar", I think it was.'

'Right.' I paused. 'But we will have this conversation?'

She pulled me towards her, and kissed me on the lips. 'Oh I think we will, *caro.*'

And with that, Federica linked her arm in mine, and we made our way through the darkened square and into the night.

Glossary

ACTV the public transport operator in Venice

allora well now

Argento, Dario Italian director of horror and *giallo* cinema, including *Suspiria*, *Deep Red* and *The Bird with the Crystal Plumage*

bacaro a typical Venetian bar, usually offering a variety of *cichèti*

badante a caregiver, or in-home nurse

Bava, Mario Italian director of horror and *giallo* cinema, including *Black Sunday*, *Blood and Black Lace* and *Danger: Diabolik*

brioche asking for a brioche in Venice will typically get you a croissant

carabinieri the military wing of the police force

cazzo expletive (relatively strong!)

cellulare mobile phone

caro/cara/tesoro/tesora/vecio terms of endearment

cichèti (cichetti in Italian) traditional Venetian bar snacks

compagno comrade

commissario police commissioner

Conad a chain of Italian supermarkets

cortile courtyard

crepi the appropriate response to *in bocce al lupo*

denuncia a complaint to the police

Dio Cane! an expression of disappointment, anger or surprise. Be careful about using this in company as it's blasphemous

divisa uniform

defunti (plural) dead, deceased

FCO Foreign and Commonwealth Office

fondamenta typically the street parallel to a canal

fumetti comic books

frutti di bosco fruits of the forest

Il Gazzettino a daily newspaper of Venice and the Veneto

grandi signore fine ladies, *grandes dames*

in bocca al lupo good luck

incunabulo an incunable or incunabulum is defined as a document printed (not handwritten) in Europe before year 1501

Intercettazione telephone tapping

macchiatone a coffee that is somewhere between a regular espresso and a cappuccino. Literally 'a big *macchiato*'. I have come to the conclusion that it's a Venetian invention as my attempts to order it down south have been met with incomprehension

mammone a mummy's boy

marinaio the 'conductor' on board a *vaporetto*

messa in scena the elements that comprise a single shot in a film, the *mise-en-scene*

Montgomery, Elizabeth American actress, most famous for the television series *Bewitched*.

I morti All Souls' Day

Nonno/Nonna Grandad/Grandma

La Nuova a newspaper of Venice and the Veneto

Ognissanti All Saints' Day

Pagine Gialle the Italian equivalent of the Yellow Pages

piano nobile the principal floor of a *palazzo*, typically the second storey in Venice

porta door

portego a salon or reception room on the *piano nobile*

poverino 'poor little thing'

Pronto? a typical response upon answering the phone, roughly equivalent to saying 'Ready.'

pronto soccorso the accident and emergency department of a hospital

puttana troia unpleasant and misogynist insult, roughly equivalent to *filthy whore*

Questura police station

ragazzi/ragazze lads/girls

Reparto Evangelico the Protestant section on the cemetery island of San Michele

San Pietro the fish known as John Dory in English, so called because the distinctive dark spot on the flesh is said to be the thumbprint of the Apostle Peter

signorina the diminutive of *signora*, previously used to denote a young girl or unmarried woman. Its use today can be seen as being pejorative or patronising

soffritto finely chopped and gently fried vegetables which form the basis of a soup or sauce

Soprintendenza a local authority of the Ministry of National Heritage, with authority for overseeing the protection of cultural heritage

Steele, Barbara English actress, an iconic presence in 1960s Italian horror cinema

tabarro the traditional Venetian-style cloak, made of a single piece of material

tessera sanitaria health insurance card

terrazzo typical Venetian flooring, made of marble or granite chips set in concrete and polished until smooth

torrefazione a coffee shop, in the sense of a shop that sells beans or ground coffee

tramezzino the traditional Italian-style sandwich; triangles of white bread with the filling typically heaped up in the middle

vaporetto the style of boat used in the public transport system in Venice

Vietato Fumare no smoking

Notes and Acknowledgements

Italian women do not take their husbands' surnames upon marrying, although children will normally inherit their fathers' names. Therefore, name plates above doorbells will typically have the surnames of both husband and wife engraved on them. Hence 'Costa-Visintin' for Dario and Valentina.

I have seen the island of Sant'Ariano from a distance, but I have never set foot on it. Our neighbour, keen to take us out on the lagoon in his boat, whistled and shook his head when I mentioned it. It would seem best not to go there.

Locations in the book are as described, with the exception of the non-existent Palazzo Loredan on the Zattere, and the Hotel Da Ponte. The Bar Tintoretto is also my invention, given that there is nowhere to eat or drink that close to the *Ospedale*.

Whilst researching this book, I found *Isole abbandonate della laguna veneziana / The abandoned islands of the Venetian Lagoon* (St Mark's Press) by Giorgio and Maurizio Crovato to be of great use.

My gratitude to all those of you who have written to tell me how much they enjoy Nathan's adventures. Thank you. It really does make a difference.

I finish, as ever, with my thanks to my agent John Beaton; Colin Murray, my editor; Krystyna, Rebecca, Jess, Andy and everyone at Constable; and, of course, to my dear wife Caroline whose limits of patience are really far greater than I deserve.